ALL THE PRETTY HORSES

John Grady Cole is the last bewildered survivor of long generations of Texas ranchers . . .

As his grandfather dies, and his parents succumb to their own worries and desires, John is cut off from the only life he has ever wanted.

He runs off to Mexico with his friend Lacey Rawlins. Befriending a third boy on the way, they enter a country beyond their imagining: barren and beautiful, rugged yet cruelly civilized. But a place where dreams are paid for in blood . . .

In their search for a life that no longer exists, the boys' story is a classic adventure from the lost heart of the wild American West: an adventure that within months will leave one of them dead – the other two aged beyond any normal reckoning . . .

Yet throughout it all John Grady Cole will survive. The last American cowboy: steeped in the sort of wisdom that comes only from love and loss and excruciating pain.

All the Pretty Horses – the first book in *The Border Trilogy* – is a grand love story: a novel about childhood passing, along with innocence and a lost American age. Magnificent in the variety of its achievement, it is a living parable of responsibility and revenge and survival.

Praise for *All the Pretty Horses*

'The novel's hero, as in the five that came before, is the English language – or perhaps I should say the American language. In either case, the book itself is truly heroic and an unabating pleasure to read.'
Shelby Foote

'Cormac McCarthy's supple and stunning language, the breadth in his characters, his sense of the physicality of landscape, an evocation of biblical themes to which he is equal, and a pure gift for conveyance distinguish him as a contemporary writer almost without equal. In *All the Pretty Horses* he enters new country. The ride is exhilarating, the journey fetching, haunting, and draining, like any great step worth taking.'
Barry Lopez

'Among a small fraternity of writers and academics, McCarthy has a standing second to none, far out of proportion to his name recognition or sales. A cult figure with a reputation as a writer's writer, especially in the South and in England, McCarthy has sometimes been compared with Joyce and Faulkner. There isn't anyone remotely like him in contemporary American literature.' NEW YORK TIMES

'This is a novel so exuberant in its prose, so offbeat in its setting and so mordant and profound in its deliberations that one searches in vain for comparisons in American literature. None of McCarthy's previous works, not even the award-winning *The Orchard Keeper* (1965) or the much-admired *Blood Meridian* (1985) quite prepares the reader for the singular achievement of this first installment of the projected *Border Trilogy*.' PUBLISHERS WEEKLY

'About as tone-perfect and emotionally resonant a novel as has ever been written about the American West.' ENTERTAINMENT WEEKLY

'A book of remarkable beauty and strength, the work of a master in perfect command of his medium.' WASHINGTON POST

'He is a singular voice in American fiction and with his novels he has cut a lofty benchmark for his contemporaries.' NEWSDAY

Cormac McCarthy lives in El Paso, Texas. *All the Pretty Horses* is his sixth novel, and the first book in *The Border Trilogy*. *Blood Meridian*, *Child of God* and *Suttree* are also published in Picador.

ALL THE PRETTY HORSES

Cormac McCarthy

Volume One
The Border Trilogy

PICADOR

First published in Great Britain 1993 by Pan Books Limited

This paperback Picador edition published 1993 by Pan Books Limited
a division of Pan Macmillan Publishers Limited
Cavaye Place London SW10 9PG
and Basingstoke

Associated companies throughout the world

ISBN 0 330 32532 9

3 5 7 9 8 6 4 2

A CIP catalogue record for this book is available from
the British Library

Printed by Cox & Wyman Ltd, Reading, Berkshire

ALL THE PRETTY HORSES

I

THE CANDLEFLAME and the image of the candleflame caught in the pierglass twisted and righted when he entered the hall and again when he shut the door. He took off his hat and came slowly forward. The floorboards creaked under his boots. In his black suit he stood in the dark glass where the lilies leaned so palely from their waisted cutglass vase. Along the cold hallway behind him hung the portraits of forebears only dimly known to him all framed in glass and dimly lit above the narrow wainscotting. He looked down at the guttered candlestub. He pressed his thumbprint in the warm wax pooled on the oak veneer. Lastly he looked at the face so caved and drawn among the folds of funeral cloth, the yellowed moustache, the eyelids paper thin. That was not sleeping. That was not sleeping.

It was dark outside and cold and no wind. In the distance a calf bawled. He stood with his hat in his hand. You never combed your hair that way in your life, he said.

Inside the house there was no sound save the ticking of the mantel clock in the front room. He went out and shut the door.

Dark and cold and no wind and a thin gray reef beginning along the eastern rim of the world. He walked out on the prairie and stood holding his hat like some supplicant to the darkness over them all and he stood there for a long time.

As he turned to go he heard the train. He stopped and waited for it. He could feel it under his feet. It came boring out of the east like some ribald satellite of the coming sun howling and bellowing in the distance and the long light of the headlamp running through the tangled mesquite brakes and creating out of the night the endless fenceline down the dead straight right of way and sucking it back again wire and post mile on mile into the darkness after where the boilersmoke disbanded slowly along the faint new horizon and the sound came lagging and he stood still holding his hat in his hands in the passing ground-shudder watching it till it was gone. Then he turned and went back to the house.

She looked up from the stove when he came in and looked him up and down in his suit. Buenos días, guapo, she said.

He hung the hat on a peg by the door among slickers and blanketcoats and odd pieces of tack and came to the stove and got his coffee and took it to the table. She opened the oven and drew out a pan of sweetrolls she'd made and put one on a plate and brought it over and set it in front of him together with a knife for the butter and she touched the back of his head with her hand before she returned to the stove.

I appreciate you lightin the candle, he said.

Cómo?

La candela. La vela.

No fui yo, she said.

La señora?

Claro.

Ya se levantó?

Antes que yo.

He drank the coffee. It was just grainy light outside and Arturo was coming up toward the house.

HE SAW his father at the funeral. Standing by himself across the little gravel path near the fence. Once he went out to the street to his car. Then he came back. A norther had blown in about midmorning and there were spits of snow in the air with blowing dust and the women sat holding on to their hats. They'd put an awning up over the gravesite but the weather was all sideways and it did no good. The canvas rattled and flapped and the preacher's words were lost in the wind. When it was over and the mourners rose to go the canvas chairs they'd been sitting on raced away tumbling among the tombstones.

In the evening he saddled his horse and rode out west from the house. The wind was much abated and it was very cold and the sun sat blood red and elliptic under the reefs of bloodred cloud before him. He rode where he would always choose to ride, out where the western fork of the old Comanche road coming down out of the Kiowa country to the north passed through the westernmost section of the ranch and you could see the faint trace of it bearing south over the low prairie that lay between the north and middle forks of the Concho River. At the hour he'd always choose when the shadows were long and the ancient road was shaped before him in the rose and canted light like a dream of the past where the painted ponies and the riders of that lost nation came down out of the north with their faces chalked and their long hair plaited and each armed for war which was their life and the women and children and women with children at their breasts all of them pledged in blood and redeemable in blood only. When the wind was in the north you could hear them, the horses and the breath of the horses and the horses' hooves that were shod in rawhide and the rattle of lances and the constant drag of the travois poles in the sand like the passing of some enormous serpent and the young boys naked on wild horses jaunty as circus riders and hazing wild horses before them and the dogs trotting with their tongues aloll and foot-slaves following half naked and sorely burdened and above all the low chant of their traveling song which the riders sang as they rode, nation and ghost of nation passing in a soft chorale across that mineral waste to darkness bearing lost to all history and all remembrance like a grail the sum of their secular and transitory and violent lives.

He rode with the sun coppering his face and the red wind blowing out of the west. He turned south along the old war trail and he rode out to the crest of a low rise and dismounted and dropped the reins and walked out and stood like a man come to the end of something.

There was an old horseskull in the brush and he squatted and picked it up and turned it in his hands. Frail and brittle. Bleached paper white. He squatted in the long light holding it, the comicbook teeth loose in their sockets. The joints in the cranium like a ragged welding of the bone plates. The muted run of sand in the brainbox when he turned it.

What he loved in horses was what he loved in men, the blood and the heat of the blood that ran them. All his reverence and all his fondness and all the leanings of his life were for the ardenthearted and they would always be so and never be otherwise.

He rode back in the dark. The horse quickened its step. The last of the day's light fanned slowly upon the plain behind him and withdrew again down the edges of the world in a cooling blue of shadow and dusk and chill and a few last chitterings of birds sequestered in the dark and wiry brush. He crossed the old trace again and he must turn the pony up onto the plain and homeward but the warriors would ride on in that darkness they'd become, rattling past with their stone-age tools of war in default of all substance and singing softly in blood and longing south across the plains to Mexico.

THE HOUSE was built in eighteen seventy-two. Seventy-seven years later his grandfather was still the first man to die in it. What others had lain in state in that hallway had been carried there on a gate or wrapped in a wagonsheet or delivered crated up in a raw pineboard box with a teamster standing at the door with a bill of lading. The ones that came at all. For the most part they were dead by rumor. A yellowed scrap of newsprint. A letter. A telegram. The original ranch was twenty-three hundred acres out of the old Meusebach survey of the Fisher-Miller grant, the original house a oneroom hovel of sticks and wattle. That was in eighteen sixty-six. In that same year the first cattle were driven through what was still Bexar County and across the north end of the ranch and on to Fort Sumner and Denver. Five years later his great-grandfather sent six hundred steers over that same trail and with the money he built the house and by then the ranch was already eighteen thousand acres. In eighteen eighty-three they ran the first barbed wire. By eighty-six the buffalo were gone. That same winter a bad die-up. In eighty-nine Fort Concho was disbanded.

His grandfather was the oldest of eight boys and the only one to live past the age of twenty-five. They were drowned, shot, kicked by horses. They perished in fires. They seemed to fear only dying in bed. The last two were killed in Puerto Rico in eighteen ninety-eight and in that year he married and brought his bride home to the ranch and he must have walked out and stood looking at his holdings and reflected long upon the ways of God and the laws of primogeniture. Twelve years later when his wife was carried off in the influenza epidemic they still had no children. A year later he married his dead wife's older sister and a year after this the boy's mother was born and that was all the borning that there was. The Grady name was buried with that old man the day the norther blew the lawnchairs over the dead cemetery grass. The boy's name was Cole. John Grady Cole.

HE MET his father in the lobby of the St Angelus and they walked up Chadbourne Street to the Eagle Cafe and sat in a booth at the back. Some at the tables stopped talking when they came in. A few men nodded to his father and one said his name.

The waitress called everybody doll. She took their order and flirted with him. His father took out his cigarettes and lit one and put the pack on the table and put his Third Infantry Zippo lighter on top of it and leaned back and smoked and looked at him. He told him his uncle Ed Alison had gone up to the preacher after the funeral was said and shook his hand, the two of them standing there holding onto their hats and leaning thirty degrees into the wind like vaudeville comics while the canvas flapped and raged about them and the funeral attendants raced over the grounds after the lawnchairs, and he'd leaned into the preacher's face and screamed at him that it was a good thing they'd held the burial that morning because the way it was making up this thing could turn off into a real blow before the day was out.

His father laughed silently. Then he fell to coughing. He took a drink of water and sat smoking and shaking his head.

Buddy when he come back from up in the panhandle told me one time it quit blowin up there and all the chickens fell over.

The waitress brought their coffee. Here you go, doll, she said. I'll have your all's orders up in just a minute.

She's gone to San Antonio, the boy said.

Dont call her she.

Mama.

I know it.

They drank their coffee.

What do you aim to do?

About what?

About anything.

She can go where she wants to.

The boy watched him. You aint got no business smokin them things, he said.

His father pursed his lips and drummed his fingers on the table and looked up. When I come around askin you what I'm supposed to do you'll know you're big enough to tell me, he said.

Yessir.

You need any money?

No.

He watched the boy. You'll be all right, he said.

The waitress brought their dinner, thick china lunchplates with steak and gravy and potatoes and beans.

I'll get your all's bread.

His father tucked his napkin into his shirt.

It aint me I was worried about, the boy said. Can I say that?

His father took up his knife and cut into the steak. Yeah, he said. You can say that.

The waitress brought the basket of rolls and set it on the table and went away. They ate. His father didn't eat much. After a while he pushed the plate back with his thumb and reached and got another cigarette and tapped it against the lighter and put it in his mouth and lit it.

You can say whatever's on your mind. Hell. You can bitch at me about smokin if you want.

The boy didnt answer.

You know it aint what I wanted dont you?

Yeah. I know that.

You lookin after Rosco good?

He aint been rode.

Why dont we go Saturday.

All right.

You dont have to if you got somethin else to do.

I aint got nothin else to do.

His father smoked, he watched him.

You dont have to if you dont want to, he said.

I want to.

Can you and Arturo load and pick me up in town?

Yeah.

What time?

What time'll you be up?

I'll get up.

We'll be there at eight.

I'll be up.

The boy nodded. He ate. His father looked around. I wonder who you need to see in this place to get some coffee, he said.

HE AND RAWLINS had unsaddled the horses and turned them out in the dark and they were lying on the saddleblankets and using the saddles for pillows. The night was cold and clear and the sparks rising from the fire raced hot and red among the stars. They could hear the trucks out on the highway and they could see the lights of the town reflected off the desert fifteen miles to the north.

What do you aim to do? Rawlins said.

I dont know. Nothin.

I dont know what you expect. Him two years oldern you. Got his own car and everthing.

There aint nothin to him. Never was.

What did she say?

She didnt say nothin. What would she say? There aint nothin to say.

Well I dont know what you expect.

I dont expect nothin.

Are you goin on Saturday?

No.

Rawlins took a cigarette out of his shirtpocket and sat up and took a coal from the fire and lit the cigarette. He sat smoking. I wouldnt let her get the best of me, he said.

He tipped the ash from the end of the cigarette against the heel of his boot.

She aint worth it. None of em are.

He didnt answer for a while. Then he said: Yes they are.

When he got back he rubbed down the horse and put him up and walked up to the house to the kitchen. Luisa had gone to bed and the house was quiet. He put his hand on the coffeepot to test it and he took down a cup and poured it and walked out and up the hallway.

He entered his grandfather's office and went to the desk and turned on the lamp and sat down in the old oak swivelchair. On the desk was a small brass calendar mounted on swivels that changed dates when you tipped it over in its stand. It still said September 13th. An ashtray. A glass paperweight. A blotter that said Palmer Feed and Supply. His mother's highschool graduation picture in a small silver frame.

The room smelled of old cigarsmoke. He leaned and turned

off the little brass lamp and sat in the dark. Through the front window he could see the starlit prairie falling away to the north. The black crosses of the old telegraph poles yoked across the constellations passing east to west. His grandfather said the Comanche would cut the wires and splice them back with horse-hair. He leaned back and crossed his boots on the desktop. Dry lightning to the north, forty miles distant. The clock struck eleven in the front room across the hall.

She came down the stairs and stood in the office doorway and turned on the wall switch light. She was in her robe and she stood with her arms cradled against her, her elbows in her palms. He looked at her and looked out the window again.

What are you doing? she said.

Settin.

She stood there in her robe for a long time. Then she turned and went back down the hall and up the stairs again. When he heard her door close he got up and turned off the light.

There were a few last warm days yet and in the afternoon sometimes he and his father would sit in the hotel room in the white wicker furniture with the window open and the thin crocheted curtains blowing into the room and they'd drink coffee and his father would pour a little whiskey in his own cup and sit sipping it and smoking and looking down at the street. There were oilfield scouts' cars parked along the street that looked like they'd been in a warzone.

If you had the money would you buy it? the boy said.

I had the money and I didnt.

You mean your backpay from the army?

No. Since then.

What's the most you ever won?

You dont need to know. Learn bad habits.

Why dont I bring the chessboard up some afternoon?

I aint got the patience to play.

You got the patience to play poker.

That's different.

What's different about it?

Money is what's different about it.

They sat.

There's still a lot of money in the ground out there, his father said. Number one I C Clark that come in last year was a big well.

He sipped his coffee. He reached and got his cigarettes off the table and lit one and looked at the boy and looked down at the street again. After a while he said:

I won twenty-six thousand dollars in twenty-two hours of play. There was four thousand dollars in the last pot, three of us in. Two boys from Houston. I won the hand with three natural queens.

He turned and looked at the boy. The boy sat with the cup in front of him halfway to his mouth. He turned and looked back out the window. I dont have a dime of it, he said.

What do you think I should do?

I dont think there's much you can do.

Will you talk to her?

I caint talk to her.

You could talk to her.

Last conversation we had was in San Diego California in nineteen forty-two. It aint her fault. I aint the same as I was. I'd like to think I am. But I aint.

You are inside. Inside you are.

His father coughed. He drank from his cup. Inside, he said.

They sat for a long time.

She's in a play or somethin over there.

Yeah. I know.

The boy reached and got his hat off the floor and put it on his knee. I better get back, he said.

You know I thought the world of that old man, dont you?

The boy looked out the window. Yeah, he said.

Dont go to cryin on me now.

I aint.

Well dont.

He never give up, the boy said. He was the one told me not

to. He said let's not have a funeral till we got somethin to bury, if it aint nothin but his dogtags. They were fixin to give your clothes away.

His father smiled. They might as well of, he said. Only thing fit me was the boots.

He always thought you all would get back together.

Yeah, I know he did.

The boy stood and put on his hat. I better get on back, he said.

He used to get in fights over her. Even as a old man. Anybody said anything about her. If he heard about it. It wasnt even dignified.

I better get on.

Well.

He unpropped his feet from the windowsill. I'll walk down with you. I need to get the paper.

They stood in the tiled lobby while his father scanned the headlines.

How can Shirley Temple be getting divorced? he said.

He looked up. Early winter twilight in the streets. I might just get a haircut, he said.

He looked at the boy.

I know how you feel. I felt the same way.

The boy nodded. His father looked at the paper again and folded it.

The Good Book says that the meek shall inherit the earth and I expect that's probably the truth. I aint no freethinker, but I'll tell you what. I'm a long way from bein convinced that it's all that good a thing.

He looked at the boy. He took his key out of his coatpocket and handed it to him.

Go on back up there. There's somethin belongs to you in the closet.

The boy took the key. What is it? he said.

Just somethin I got for you. I was goin to give it to you at Christmas but I'm tired of walkin over it.

Yessir.

Anyway you look like you could use some cheerin up. Just leave the key at the desk when you come down.

Yessir.

I'll see you.

All right.

He rode back up in the elevator and walked down the hall and put the key in the door and walked in and went to the closet and opened it. Standing on the floor along with two pairs of boots and a pile of dirty shirts was a brand new Hamley Formfitter saddle. He picked it up by the horn and shut the closet door and carried it to the bed and swung it up and stood looking at it.

Hell fire and damnation, he said.

He left the key at the desk and swung out through the doors into the street with the saddle over his shoulder.

He walked down to South Concho Street and swung the saddle down and stood it in front of him. It was just dark and the streetlights had come on. The first vehicle along was a Model A Ford truck and it came skidding quarterwise to a halt on its mechanical brakes and the driver leaned across and rolled down the window part way and boomed at him in a whiskey voice: Throw that hull up in the bed, cowboy, and get in here.

Yessir, he said.

IT RAINED all the following week and cleared. Then it rained again. It beat down without mercy on the hard flat plains. The water was over the highway bridge at Christoval and the road was closed. Floods in San Antonio. In his grandfather's slicker he rode the Alicia pasture where the south fence was standing in water to the top wire. The cattle stood islanded, staring bleakly at the rider. Redbo stood staring bleakly at the cattle. He pressed the horse's flanks between his bootheels. Come on, he said. I dont like it no bettern you do.

He and Luisa and Arturo ate in the kitchen while she was gone. Sometimes at night after supper he'd walk out to the road and catch a ride into town and walk the streets or he'd stand outside the hotel on Beauregard Street and look up at the room on the fourth floor where his father's shape or father's shadow would pass behind the gauzy window curtains and then turn and pass back again like a sheetiron bear in a shooting-gallery only slower, thinner, more agonized.

When she came back they ate in the diningroom again, the two of them at opposite ends of the long walnut table while Luisa made the service. She carried out the last of the dishes and turned at the door.

Algo más, señora?

No, Luisa. Gracias.

Buenas noches, señora.

Buenas noches.

The door closed. The clock ticked. He looked up.

Why couldnt you lease me the ranch?

Lease you the ranch.

Yes.

I thought I said I didnt want to discuss it.

This is a new subject.

No it's not.

I'd give you all the money. You could do whatever you wanted.

All the money. You dont know what you're talking about. There's not any money. This place has barely paid expenses for twenty years. There hasnt been a white person worked here since before the war. Anyway you're sixteen years old, you cant run a ranch.

Yes I can.

You're being ridiculous. You have to go to school.

She put the napkin on the table and pushed back her chair and rose and went out. He pushed away the coffeecup in front of him. He leaned back in the chair. On the wall opposite above the sideboard was an oilpainting of horses. There were half a dozen of them breaking through a pole corral and their manes were long and blowing and their eyes wild. They'd been copied out of a book. They had the long Andalusian nose and the bones of their faces showed Barb blood. You could see the hindquarters of the foremost few, good hindquarters and heavy enough to make a cuttinghorse. As if maybe they had Steeldust in their blood. But nothing else matched and no such horse ever was that he had seen and he'd once asked his grandfather what kind of horses they were and his grandfather looked up from his plate at the painting as if he'd never seen it before and he said those are picturebook horses and went on eating.

HE WENT UP the stairs to the mezzanine and found Franklin's name lettered in an arc across the pebbled glass of the door and took off his hat and turned the knob and went in. The girl looked up from her desk.

I'm here to see Mr Franklin, he said.

Did you have an appointment?

No mam. He knows me.

What's your name?

John Grady Cole.

Just a minute.

She went into the other room. Then she came out and nodded.

He rose and crossed the room.

Come in son, said Franklin.

He walked in.

Set down.

He sat.

When he'd said what he had to say Franklin leaned back and looked out the window. He shook his head. He turned back and folded his hands on the desk in front of him. In the first place, he said, I'm not really at liberty to advise you. It's called conflict of interest. But I think I can tell you that it is her property and she can do whatever she wants with it.

I dont have any sayso.

You're a minor.

What about my father.

Franklin leaned back again. That's a sticky issue, he said.

They aint divorced.

Yes they are.

The boy looked up.

It's a matter of public record so I dont guess it's out of confidence. It was in the paper.

When?

It was made final three weeks ago.

He looked down. Franklin watched him.

It was final before the old man died.

The boy nodded. I see what you're sayin, he said.

It's a sorry piece of business, son. But I think the way it is is the way it's goin to be.

Couldnt you talk to her?

I did talk to her.

What did she say?

It dont matter what she said. She aint goin to change her mind.

He nodded. He sat looking down into his hat.

Son, not everbody thinks that life on a cattle ranch in west Texas is the second best thing to dyin and goin to heaven. She dont want to live out there, that's all. If it was a payin proposition that'd be one thing. But it aint.

It could be.

Well, I dont aim to get in a discussion about that. Anyway, she's a young woman and my guess is she'd like to have a little more social life than what she's had to get used to.

She's thirty-six years old.

The lawyer leaned back. He swiveled slightly in the chair, he tapped his lower lip with his forefinger. It's his own damned fault. He signed ever paper they put in front of him. Never lifted a hand to save himself. Hell, I couldnt tell him. I told him to get a lawyer. Told? I begged him.

Yeah, I know.

Wayne tells me he's quit goin to the doctor.

He nodded. Yeah. Well, I thank you for your time.

I'm sorry not to have better news for you. You damn sure welcome to talk to somebody else.

That's all right.

What are you doin out of school today?

I laid out.

The lawyer nodded. Well, he said. That would explain it.

The boy rose and put on his hat. Thanks, he said.

The lawyer stood.

Some things in this world cant be helped, he said. And I believe this is probably one of em.

Yeah, the boy said.

AFTER CHRISTMAS she was gone all the time. He and Luisa and Arturo sat in the kitchen. Luisa couldnt talk about it without crying so they didnt talk about it. No one had even told her mother, who'd been on the ranch since before the turn of the century. Finally Arturo had to tell her. She listened and nodded and turned away and that was all.

In the morning he was standing by the side of the road at daybreak with a clean shirt and a pair of socks in a leather satchel together with his toothbrush and razor and shavingbrush. The satchel had belonged to his grandfather and the blanketlined duckingcoat he wore had been his father's. The first car that passed stopped for him. He got in and set the satchel on the floor and rubbed his hands together between his knees. The driver leaned across him and tried the door and then pulled the tall gear-lever down into first and they set out.

That door dont shut good. Where are you goin?

San Antonio.

Well I'm goin as far as Brady Texas.

I appreciate it.

You a cattlebuyer?

Sir?

The man nodded at the satchel with its straps and brass catches. I said are you a cattlebuyer.

No sir. That's just my suitcase.

I allowed maybe you was a cattlebuyer. How long you been standin out there?

Just a few minutes.

The man pointed to a plastic knob on the dash that glowed a dull orange color. This thing's got a heater in it but it dont put out much. Can you feel it?

Yessir. Feels pretty good to me.

The man nodded at the gray and malignant dawn. He moved his leveled hand slowly before him. You see that? he said.

Yessir.

He shook his head. I despise the wintertime. I never did see what was the use in there even bein one.

He looked at John Grady.

You dont talk much, do you? he said.

Not a whole lot.

That's a good trait to have.

It was about a two hour drive to Brady.

They drove through the town and the man let him out on the other side.

You stay on Eighty-seven when you get to Fredericksburg. Dont get off on Two-ninety you'll wind up in Austin. You hear?

Yessir. I appreciate it.

He shut the door and the man nodded and lifted one hand and the car turned around in the road and went back. The next car by stopped and he climbed in.

How far you goin? the man said.

Snow was falling in the San Saba when they crossed it and snow was falling on the Edwards Plateau and in the Balcones the limestone was white with snow and he sat watching out while the gray flakes flared over the windshield glass in the sweep of the wipers. A translucent slush had begun to form along the edge of the blacktop and there was ice on the bridge over the Pedernales. The green water sliding slowly away past the dark bankside trees. The mesquites by the road so thick with mistletoe they looked like liveoaks. The driver sat hunched up over the wheel whistling silently to himself. They got into San Antonio at three oclock in the afternoon in a driving snowstorm and he climbed out and thanked the man and walked up the street and into the first cafe he came to and sat at the counter and put the satchel on the stool beside him. He took the little paper menu out of the holder and opened it and looked at it and looked at the clock on the back wall. The waitress set a glass of water in front of him.

Is it the same time here as it is in San Angelo? he said.

I knew you was goin to ask me somethin like that, she said. You had that look.

Do you not know?

I never been in San Angelo Texas in my life.

I'd like a cheeseburger and a chocolate milk.

Are you here for the rodeo?

No.

It's the same time, said a man down the counter.

He thanked him.

Same time, the man said. Same time.

She finished writing on her pad and looked up. I wouldnt go by nothin he said.

He walked around town in the snow. It grew dark early. He stood on the Commerce Street bridge and watched the snow vanish in the river. There was snow on the parked cars and the traffic in the street by dark had slowed to nothing, a few cabs or trucks, headlights making slowly through the falling snow and passing in a soft rumble of tires. He checked into the YMCA on Martin Street and paid two dollars for his room and went upstairs. He took off his boots and stood them on the radiator and took off his socks and draped them over the radiator beside the boots and hung up his coat and stretched out on the bed with his hat over his eyes.

At ten till eight he was standing in front of the boxoffice in his clean shirt with his money in his hand. He bought a seat in the balcony third row and paid a dollar twenty-five for it.

I never been here before, he said.

It's a good seat, the girl said.

He thanked her and went in and tendered his ticket to an usher who led him over to the red carpeted stairs and handed him the ticket back. He went up and found his seat and sat waiting with his hat in his lap. The theatre was half empty. When the lights dimmed some of the people in the balcony about him got up and moved forward to seats in front. Then the curtain rose and his mother came through a door onstage and began talking to a woman in a chair.

At the intermission he rose and put on his hat and went down to the lobby and stood in a gilded alcove and rolled a cigarette and stood smoking it with one boot jacked back against the wall behind him. He was not unaware of the glances that drifted his way from the theatregoers. He'd turned up one leg of his jeans into a small cuff and from time to time he leaned and tipped into this receptacle the soft white ash of his cigarette. He saw a few men in boots and hats and he nodded gravely to them, they to him. After a while the lights in the lobby dimmed again.

He sat leaning forward in the seat with his elbows on the empty seatback in front of him and his chin on his forearms and he watched the play with great intensity. He'd the notion that there would be something in the story itself to tell him about the way the world was or was becoming but there was not. There was nothing in it at all. When the lights came up there was applause and his mother came forward several times and all the cast assembled across the stage and held hands and bowed and then the curtain closed for good and the audience rose and made their way up the aisles. He sat for a long time in the empty theatre and then he stood and put on his hat and went out into the cold.

When he set out in the morning to get his breakfast it was still dark and the temperature stood at zero. There was half a foot of snow on the ground in Travis Park. The only cafe open was a Mexican one and he ordered huevos rancheros and coffee and sat looking through the paper. He thought there'd be something in the paper about his mother but there wasnt. He was the only customer in the cafe. The waitress was a young girl and she watched him. When she set the platter down he put the paper aside and pushed his cup forward.

Más cafe? she said.

Sí por favor.

She brought the coffee. Hace mucho frío, she said.

Bastante.

He walked up Broadway with his hands in his coatpockets and his collar turned up against the wind. He walked into the lobby of the Menger Hotel and sat in one of the lounge chairs and crossed one boot over the other and opened the paper.

She came through the lobby about nine oclock. She was on the arm of a man in a suit and a topcoat and they went out the door and got into a cab.

He sat there for a long time. After a while he got up and folded the paper and went to the desk. The clerk looked up at him.

Have you got a Mrs Cole registered? he said.

Cole?

Yes.

Just a minute.

The clerk turned away and checked the registrations. He shook his head. No, he said. No Cole.

Thanks, he said.

THEY RODE TOGETHER a last time on a day in early March when the weather had already warmed and yellow mexicanhat bloomed by the roadside. They unloaded the horses at McCullough's and rode up through the middle pasture along Grape Creek and into the low hills. The creek was clear and green with trailing moss braided over the gravel bars. They rode slowly up through the open country among scrub mesquite and nopal. They crossed from Tom Green County into Coke County. They crossed the old Schoonover road and they rode up through broken hills dotted with cedar where the ground was cobbled with traprock and they could see snow on the thin blue ranges a hundred miles to the north. They scarcely spoke all day. His father rode sitting forward slightly in the saddle, holding the reins in one hand about two inches above the saddlehorn. So thin and frail, lost in his clothes. Looking over the country with those sunken eyes as if the world out there had been altered or made suspect by what he'd seen of it elsewhere. As if he might never see it right again. Or worse did see it right at last. See it as it had always been, would forever be. The boy who rode on slightly before him sat a horse not only as if he'd been born to it which he was but as if were he begot by malice or mischance into some queer land where horses never were he would have found them anyway. Would have known that there was something missing for the world to be right or he right in it and would have set forth to wander wherever it was needed for as long as it took until he came upon one and he would have known that that was what he sought and it would have been.

In the afternoon they passed through the ruins of an old ranch on that stony mesa where there were crippled fenceposts propped among the rocks that carried remnants of a wire not seen in that country for years. An ancient pickethouse. The wreckage of an old wooden windmill fallen among the rocks. They rode on. They walked ducks up out of potholes and in the evening they descended through low rolling hills and across the red clay floodplain into the town of Robert Lee.

They waited until the road was clear before they walked the horses over the board bridge. The river was red with mud. They rode up Commerce Street and turned up Seventh and rode up Austin Street past the bank and dismounted and tied their horses in front of the cafe and went in.

The proprietor came over to take their order. He called them by name. His father looked up from the menu.

Go ahead and order, he said. He wont be here for a hour.

What are you havin?

I think I'll just have some pie and coffee.

What kind of pie you got? the boy said.

The proprietor looked toward the counter.

Go on and get somethin to eat, his father said. I know you're hungry.

They ordered and the proprietor brought their coffee and went back to the counter. His father took a cigarette out of his shirtpocket.

You thought any more about boardin your horse?

Yeah, the boy said. Thought about it.

Wallace might let you feed and swamp out stalls and such as that. Trade it out thataway.

He aint goin to like it.

Who, Wallace?

No. Redbo.

His father smoked. He watched him.

You still seein that Barnett girl?

He shook his head.

She quit you or did you quit her?

I dont know.

That means she quit you.

Yeah.

His father nodded. He smoked. Two horsemen passed outside in the road and they studied them and the animals they rode. His father stirred his coffee a long time. There was nothing to stir because he drank it black. He took the spoon and laid it smoking on the paper napkin and raised the cup and looked at it and drank. He was still looking out the window although there was nothing there to see.

Your mother and me never agreed on a whole lot. She liked horses. I thought that was enough. That's how dumb I was. She was young and I thought she'd outgrow some of the notions she had but she didnt. Maybe they were just notions to me. It wasnt just the war. We were married ten years before the war come along. She left out of here. She was gone from the time you were six months old till you were about three. I know you know somethin about that and it was a mistake not to of told you. We separated. She was in California. Luisa looked after you. Her and Abuela.

He looked at the boy and he looked out the window again.

She wanted me to go out there, he said.

Why didnt you?

I did. I didnt last long at it.

The boy nodded.

She come back because of you, not me. I guess that's what I wanted to say.

Yessir.

The proprietor brought the boy's dinner and the pie. The boy reached for the salt and pepper. He didn't look up. The proprietor brought the coffeepot and filled their cups and went away. His father stubbed out his cigarette and picked up his fork and stabbed at the pie with it.

She's goin to be around a long longerm me. I'd like to see you all make up your differences.

The boy didnt answer.

I wouldnt be here if it wasnt for her. When I was in Goshee I'd talk to her by the hour. I made her out to be like somebody who could do anything. I'd tell her about some of the other old boys that I didnt think was goin to make it and I'd ask her to look after them and to pray for them. Some of them did make it too. I guess I was a little crazy. Part of the time anyway. But if it hadnt of been for her I wouldnt of made it. No way in this world. I never told that to nobody. She dont even know it.

The boy ate. Outside it was growing dark. His father drank coffee. They waited for Arturo to come with the truck. The last thing his father said was that the country would never be the same.

People dont feel safe no more, he said. We're like the Comanches was two hundred years ago. We dont know what's goin to show up here come daylight. We dont even know what color they'll be.

THE NIGHT was almost warm. He and Rawlins lay in the road where they could feel the heat coming off the blacktop against their backs and they watched stars falling down the long black slope of the firmament. In the distance they heard a door slam. A voice called. A coyote that had been yammering somewhere in the hills to the south stopped. Then it began again.

Is that somebody hollerin for you? he said.

Probably, said Rawlins.

They lay spreadeagled on the blacktop like captives waiting some trial at dawn.

You told your old man? said Rawlins.

No.

You goin to?

What would be the point in it?

When do you all have to be out?

Closing's the first of June.

You could wait till then.

What for?

Rawlins propped the heel of one boot atop the toe of the other. As if to pace off the heavens. My daddy run off from home when he was fifteen. Otherwise I'd of been born in Alabama.

You wouldnt of been born at all.

What makes you say that?

Cause your mama's from San Angelo and he never would of met her.

He'd of met somebody.

So would she.

So?

So you wouldnt of been born.

I dont see why you say that. I'd of been born somewheres.

How?

Well why not?

If your mama had a baby with her other husband and your daddy had one with his other wife which one would you be?

I wouldnt be neither of em.

That's right.

Rawlins lay watching the stars. After a while he said: I could still be born. I might look different or somethin. If God wanted me to be born I'd be born.

And if He didnt you wouldnt.

You're makin my goddamn head hurt.

I know it. I'm makin my own.

They lay watching the stars.

So what do you think? he said.

I dont know, said Rawlins.

Well.

I could understand if you was from Alabama you'd have ever reason in the world to run off to Texas. But if you're already in Texas. I don't know. You got a lot more reason for leavin than me.

What the hell reason you got for stayin? You think somebody's goin to die and leave you somethin?

Shit no.

That's good. Cause they aint.

The door slammed. The voice called again.

I better get back, Rawlins said.

He rose and swiped at the seat of his jeans with one hand and put his hat on.

If I dont go will you go anyways?

John Grady sat up and put his hat on. I'm already gone, he said.

HE SAW HER one last time in town. He'd been to Cullen Cole's shop on North Chadbourne to get a broken bridlebit welded and he was coming up Twohig Street when she came out of the

Cactus Drug. He crossed the street but she called to him and he stopped and waited while she came over.

Were you avoiding me? she said.

He looked at her. I guess I didnt have any thoughts about it one way or the other.

She watched him. A person cant help the way they feel, she said.

That's good all the way around, aint it?

I thought we could be friends.

He nodded. It's all right. I aint goin to be around here all that much longer.

Where are you going?

I aint at liberty to say.

Whyever not?

I just aint.

He looked at her. She was studying his face.

What do you think he'd say if he seen you standin here talkin to me?

He's not jealous.

That's good. That's a good trait to have. Save him a lot of aggravation.

What does that mean.

I dont mean nothin. I got to go.

Do you hate me?

No.

You dont like me.

He looked at her. You're wearin me out, girl, he said. What difference does it make? If you got a bad conscience just tell me what you want me to say and I'll say it.

It wouldnt be you saying it. Anyway I dont have a bad conscience. I just thought we could be friends.

He shook his head. It's just talk, Mary Catherine. I got to get on.

What if it is just talk? Everything's talk isnt it?

Not everything.

Are you really leaving San Angelo?

Yeah.

You'll be back.

Maybe.

I dont have any bad feelings against you.

You got no reason to.

She looked off up the street where he was looking but there wasnt much to look at. She turned back and he looked at her eyes but if they were wet it was just the wind. She held out her hand. At first he didnt know what she was doing.

I dont wish you anything but the best, she said.

He took her hand, small in his, familiar. He'd never shaken hands with a woman before. Take care of yourself, she said.

Thank you. I will.

He stood back and touched the brim of his hat and turned and went on up the street. He didnt look back but he could see her in the windows of the Federal Building across the street standing there and she was still standing there when he reached the corner and stepped out of the glass forever.

HE DISMOUNTED and opened the gate and walked the horse through and closed the gate and walked the horse along the fence. He dropped down to see if he could skylight Rawlins but Rawlins wasnt there. He dropped the reins at the fence corner and watched the house. The horse sniffed the air and pushed its nose against his elbow.

That you, bud? Rawlins whispered.

You better hope so.

Rawlins walked the horse down and stood and looked back at the house.

You ready? said John Grady.

Yeah.

They suspect anything?

Naw.

Well let's go.

Hang on a minute. I just piled everthing on top of the horse and walked him out here.

John Grady picked up the reins and swung up into the saddle. Yonder goes a light, he said.

Damn.

You'll be late for your own funeral.

It aint even four yet. You're early.

Well let's go. There goes the barn.

Rawlins was trying to get his soogan tied on behind the saddle. There's a switch in the kitchen, he said. He aint to the barn yet. He might not even be goin out there. He might just be gettin him a glass of milk or somethin.

He might just be loadin a shotgun or somethin.

Rawlins mounted up. You ready? he said.

I been ready.

They rode out along the fenceline and across the open pastureland. The leather creaked in the morning cold. They pushed the horses into a lope. The lights fell away behind them. They rode out on the high prairie where they slowed the horses to a walk and the stars swarmed around them out of the blackness. They heard somewhere in that tenantless night a bell that tolled and ceased where no bell was and they rode out on the round dais of the earth which alone was dark and no light to it and which carried their figures and bore them up into the swarming stars so that they rode not under but among them and they rode at once jaunty and circumspect, like thieves newly loosed in that dark electric, like young thieves in a glowing orchard, loosely jacketed against the cold and ten thousand worlds for the choosing.

BY NOON the day following they'd made some forty miles. Still in country they knew. Crossing the old Mark Fury ranch in the night where they'd dismounted at the crossfences for John Grady to pull the staples with a catspaw and stand on the wires while Rawlins led the horses through and then raise the wires back and beat the staples into the posts and put the catspaw back in his saddlebag and mount up to ride on.

How the hell do they expect a man to ride a horse in this country? said Rawlins.

They dont, said John Grady.

They rode the sun up and ate the sandwiches John Grady had brought from the house and at noon they watered the horses at an old stone stocktank and walked them down a dry creekbed among the tracks of cattle and javelina to a stand of cotton-woods. There were cattle bedded under the trees that rose at their approach and stood looking at them and then moved off.

They lay in the dry chaff under the trees with their coats rolled up under their heads and their hats over their eyes while the horses grazed in the grass along the creekbed.

What did you bring to shoot? said Rawlins.

Just Grandad's old thumb-buster.

Can you hit anything with it?

No.

Rawlins grinned. We done it, didnt we?

Yeah.

You think they'll be huntin us?

What for?

I dont know. Just seems too damn easy in a way.

They could hear the wind and they could hear the sound of the horses cropping.

I'll tell you what, said Rawlins.

Tell me.

I dont give a damn.

John Grady sat up and took his tobacco from his shirtpocket and began making a cigarette. About what? he said.

He wet the cigarette and put it in his mouth and took out his matches and lit the cigarette and blew the match out with the smoke. He turned and looked at Rawlins but Rawlins was asleep.

They rode on again in the late afternoon. By sunset they

could hear trucks on a highway in the distance and in the long cool evening they rode west along a rise from which they could see the headlights on the highway going out and coming back random and periodic in their slow exchange. They came to a ranch road and followed it out to the highway where there was a gate. They sat the horses. They could see no gate on the far side of the highway. They watched the lights of the trucks along the fence both east and west but there was no gate there.

What do you want to do? said Rawlins.

I dont know. I'd like to of got across this thing tonight.

I aint leadin my horse down that highway in the dark.

John Grady leaned and spat. I aint either, he said.

It was growing colder. The wind rattled the gate and the horses stepped uneasily.

What's them lights? said Rawlins.

I'd make it Eldorado.

How far is that do you reckon?

Ten, fifteen miles.

What do you want to do?

They spread their bedrolls in a wash and unsaddled and tied the horses and slept till daybreak. When Rawlins sat up John Grady had already saddled his horse and was strapping on his bedroll. There's a cafe up the road here, he said. Could you eat some breakfast?

Rawlins put on his hat and reached for his boots. You're talkin my language, son.

They led the horses up through a midden of old truckdoors and transmissions and castoff motorparts behind the cafe and they watered them at a metal tank used for locating leaks in innertubes. A Mexican was changing a tire on a truck and John Grady walked over and asked him where the men's room was. He nodded down the side of the building.

He got his shaving things out of his saddlebag and went into the washroom and shaved and washed and brushed his teeth and combed his hair. When he came out the horses were tied to a picnic table under some trees and Rawlins was in the cafe drinking coffee.

He slid into the booth. You ordered? he said.

Waitin on you.

The proprietor came over with another cup of coffee. What'll you boys have? he said.

Go ahead, said Rawlins.

He ordered three eggs with ham and beans and biscuits and Rawlins ordered the same with a sideorder of hotcakes and syrup.

You better load up good.

You watch me, said Rawlins.

They sat with their elbows propped on the table and looked out the window south across the plains to the distant mountains lying folded in their shadows under the morning sun.

That's where we're headed, said Rawlins.

He nodded. They drank their coffee. The man brought their breakfasts on heavy white crockery platters and came back with the coffeepot. Rawlins had peppered his eggs till they were black. He spread butter over the hotcakes.

There's a man likes eggs with his pepper, said the proprietor.

He poured their cups and went back to the kitchen.

You pay attention to your old dad now, Rawlins said. I'll show you how to deal with a unruly breakfast.

Do it, said John Grady.

Might just order the whole thing again.

The store had nothing in the way of feed. They bought a box of dried oatmeal and paid their bill and went out. John Grady cut the paper drum in two with his knife and they poured the oatmeal into a couple of hubcaps and sat on the picnic table and smoked while the horses ate. The Mexican came over to look at the horses. He was not much older than Rawlins.

Where you headed? he said.

Mexico.

What for?

Rawlins looked at John Grady. You think he can be trusted?

Yeah. He looks all right.

We're runnin from the law, Rawlins said.

The Mexican looked them over.

We robbed a bank.

He stood looking at the horses. You aint robbed no bank, he said.

You know that country down there? said Rawlins.

The Mexican shook his head and spat. I never been to Mexico in my life.

When the animals had eaten they saddled them again and led them around to the front of the cafe and down the drive and across the highway. They walked them along the bar ditch to the gate and led them through the gate and closed it. Then they mounted up and rode out the dirt ranch road. They rode it for a mile or so until it veered away to the east and they left it and set out south across the rolling cedar plains.

They reached the Devil's River by midmorning and watered the horses and stretched out in the shade of a stand of black-willow and looked at the map. It was an oilcompany roadmap that Rawlins had picked up at the cafe and he looked at it and he looked south toward the gap in the low hills. There were roads and rivers and towns on the American side of the map as far south as the Rio Grande and beyond that all was white.

It dont show nothin down there, does it? said Rawlins.

No.

You reckon it aint never been mapped?

There's maps. That just aint one of em. I got one in my saddlebag.

Rawlins came back with the map and sat on the ground and traced their route with his finger. He looked up.

What? said John Grady.

There aint shit down there.

They left the river and followed the dry valley to the west. The country was rolling and grassy and the day was cool under the sun.

You'd think there'd be more cattle in this country, Rawlins said.

You'd think so.

They walked doves and quail up out of the grass along the ridges. Now and then a rabbit. Rawlins stepped down and slid his little 25-20 carbine out of the bootleg scabbard he carried it in and walked out along the ridge. John Grady heard him shoot. In a little while he came back with a rabbit and he reholstered the carbine and took out his knife and walked off a ways and squatted and gutted the rabbit. Then he rose and wiped the blade on his trouserleg and folded shut the knife and came over and took his horse and tied the rabbit by its hind legs to his bedroll strap and mounted up again and they went on.

Late afternoon they crossed a road that ran to the south and in the evening they reached Johnson's Run and camped at a pool in the otherwise dry gravel bed of the watercourse and watered the horses and hobbled them and turned them out to graze. They built a fire and skinned out the rabbit and skewered it on a green limb and set it to broil at the edge of the fire. John Grady opened his blackened canvas campbag and took out a small enameled tin coffeepot and went to the creek and filled it. They sat and watched the fire and they watched the thin crescent moon above the black hills to the west.

Rawlins rolled a cigarette and lit it with a coal and lay back against his saddle. I'm goin to tell you somethin.

Tell it.

I could get used to this life.

He drew on the cigarette and held it out to one side and tapped the ash with a delicate motion of his forefinger. It wouldnt take me no time at all.

They rode all day the day following through rolling hill country, the low caprock mesas dotted with cedar, the yuccas in white bloom along the eastfacing slopes. They struck the Pandale road in the evening and turned south and followed the road into town.

Nine buildings including a store and filling station. They

tied their horses in front of the store and went in. They were dusty and Rawlins was unshaven and they smelled of horses and sweat and woodsmoke. Some men sitting in chairs at the back of the store looked up when they entered and then went on talking.

They stood at the meatcase. The woman came from the counter and walked behind the case and took down an apron and pulled a chain that turned on the overhead lightbulb.

You do look like some kind of desperado, John Grady said.

You dont look like no choir director, said Rawlins.

The woman tied the apron behind her and turned to regard them above the white enameled top of the meatcase. What'll you boys have? she said.

They bought baloney and cheese and a loaf of bread and a jar of mayonnaise. They bought a box of crackers and a dozen tins of vienna sausage. They bought a dozen packets of koolaid and a slab end of bacon and some tins of beans and they bought a five pound bag of cornmeal and a bottle of hotsauce. The woman wrapped the meat and cheese separate and she wet a pencil with her tongue and totted up the purchases and then put everything together in a number four grocery bag.

Where you boys from? she said.

From up around San Angelo.

You all ride them horses down here?

Yes mam.

Well I'll declare, she said.

When they woke in the morning they were in plain view of a small adobe house. A woman had come out of the house and slung a pan of dishwater into the yard. She looked at them and went back in again. They'd hung their saddles over a fence to dry and while they were getting them a man came out and stood watching them. They saddled the horses and led them out to the road and mounted up and turned south.

Wonder what all they're doin back home? Rawlins said.

John Grady leaned and spat. Well, he said, probably they're havin the biggest time in the world. Probably struck oil. I'd say they're in town about now pickin out their new cars and all.

Shit, said Rawlins.

They rode.

You ever get ill at ease? said Rawlins.

About what?

I dont know. About anything. Just ill at ease.

Sometimes. If you're someplace you aint supposed to be I guess you'd be ill at ease. Should be anyways.

Well suppose you were ill at ease and didnt know why. Would that mean that you might be someplace you wasnt supposed to be and didnt know it?

What the hell's wrong with you?

I dont know. Nothin. I believe I'll sing.

He did. He sang: Will you miss me, will you miss me. Will you miss me when I'm gone.

You know that Del Rio radio station? he said.

Yeah, I know it.

I've heard it told that at night you can take a fencewire in your teeth and pick it up. Dont even need a radio.

You believe that?

I dont know.

You ever tried it?

Yeah. One time.

They rode on. Rawlins sang. What the hell is a flowery boundary tree? he said.

You got me, cousin.

They passed under a high limestone bluff where a creek ran down and they crossed a broad gravel wash. Upstream were potholes from the recent rains where a pair of herons stood footed to their long shadows. One rose and flew, one stood. An hour later they crossed the Pecos River, putting the horses into the ford, the water swift and clear and partly salt running over the limestone bedrock and the horses studying the water before them and placing their feet with great care on the broad traprock plates and eyeing the shapes of trailing moss in the rips below the ford where they flared and twisted electric green in the morning light. Rawlins leaned from the saddle and wet his hand in the river and tasted it. It's gypwater, he said.

They dismounted among the willows on the far side and made sandwiches with the lunchmeat and cheese and ate and sat smoking and watching the river pass. There's been somebody followin us, John Grady said.

Did you see em?

Not yet.

Somebody horseback?

Yeah.

Rawlins studied the road across the river. Why aint it just somebody ridin?

Cause they'd of showed up at the river by now.

Maybe they turned off.

Where to?

Rawlins smoked. What do you reckon they want?

I dont know.

What do you want to do?

Let's just ride. They'll either show or they wont.

They came up out of the river breaks riding slowly side by side along the dusty road and onto a high plateau where they could see out over the country to the south, rolling country covered with grass and wild daisies. To the west a mile away ran a wire fence strung from pole to pole like a bad suture across the gray grasslands and beyond that a small band of antelope all of whom were watching them. John Grady turned his horse sideways and sat looking back down the road. Rawlins waited.

Is he back there? he said.

Yeah. Somewheres.

They rode till they came to a broad swale or bajada in the plateau. A little off to the right was a stand of closegrown cedar and Rawlins nodded at the cedars and slowed his horse.

Why dont we lay up yonder and wait on him?

John Grady looked back down the road. All right, he said. Let's ride on a ways and then double back. He sees our tracks quit the road here he'll know where we're at.

All right.

They rode on another half mile and then left the road and cut back toward the cedars and dismounted and tied their horses and sat on the ground.

You reckon we got time for a smoke? said Rawlins.

Smoke em if you got em, said John Grady.

They sat smoking and watching the backroad. They waited a long time but nobody came. Rawlins lay back and put his hat over his eyes. I aint sleepin, he said. I'm just restin.

He hadnt been asleep long before John Grady kicked his boot. He sat up and put on his hat and looked. A rider was coming along the road. Even at that distance they both remarked on the horse.

He came along till he was not more than a hundred yards down the road. He had on a broadbrim hat and bib overalls. He slowed the horse and looked down the bajada directly at them. Then he came on again.

It's some kid, Rawlins said.

That's a hell of a horse, said John Grady.

Aint it though.

You think he saw us?

No.

What do you want to do?

Give him a minute and then we'll just ride into the road behind him.

They waited till he was all but out of sight and then they untied the horses and mounted and rode up out of the trees and into the road.

When he heard them he stopped and looked back. He pushed his hat back on his head and sat the horse in the road and watched them. They rode up one at either side.

You huntin us? said Rawlins.

He was a kid about thirteen years old.

No, he said. I aint huntin you.

How come you followin us?

I aint followin you.

Rawlins looked at John Grady. John Grady was watching the kid. He looked off toward the distant mountains and then back at the kid and finally at Rawlins. Rawlins sat with his hands composed upon the pommel of his saddle. You aint been followin us? he said.

I'm goin to Langtry, the kid said. I dont know who you all are.

Rawlins looked at John Grady. John Grady was rolling a smoke and studying the kid and his outfit and his horse.

Where'd you get the horse? he said.

It's my horse.

He put the cigarette in his mouth and took a wooden match from his shirtpocket and popped it with his thumbnail and lit the cigarette. Is that your hat? he said.

The boy looked up at the hatbrim over his eyes. He looked at Rawlins.

How old are you? said John Grady.

Sixteen.

Rawlins spat. You're a lyin sack of green shit.

You dont know everthing.

I know you aint no goddamn sixteen. Where are you comin from?

Pandale.

You seen us in Pandale last night, didnt you?

Yeah.

What'd you do, run off?

He looked from one of them to the other. What if I did?

Rawlins looked at John Grady. What do you want to do?

I dont know.

We could sell that horse in Mexico.

Yeah.

I aint diggin no grave like we done that last one.

Hell, said John Grady, that was your idea. I was the one said just leave him for the buzzards.

You want to flip to see who gets to shoot him?

Yeah. Go ahead.

Call it, said Rawlins.

Heads.

The coin spun in the air. Rawlins caught it and slapped it down on top of his wrist and held his wrist where they could see it and lifted his hand away.

Heads, he said.

Let me have your rifle.

It aint fair, said Rawlins. You shot the last three.

Well go on then. You can owe me.

Well hold his horse. He might not be gunbroke.

You all are just funnin, said the boy.

What makes you so sure?

You aint shot nobody.

What makes you think you wouldnt be somebody good to start with?

You all are just funnin. I knowed you was all along.

Sure you did, said Rawlins.

Who's huntin you? John Grady said.

Nobody.

They're huntin that horse though, aint they?

He didnt answer.

You really headed for Langtry?

Yeah.

You aint ridin with us, said Rawlins. You'll get us thowed in the jailhouse.

It belongs to me, the boy said.

Son, said Rawlins, I dont give a shit who it belongs to. But it damn sure dont belong to you. Let's go bud.

They turned their horses and chucked them up and trotted out along the road south again. They didnt look back.

I thought he'd put up more of a argument, said Rawlins.

John Grady flipped the stub of the cigarette into the road before them. We aint seen the last of his skinny ass.

By noon they'd left the road and were riding southwest through the open grassland. They watered their horses at a steel stocktank under an old F W Axtell windmill that creaked slowly in the wind. To the south there were cattle shaded up in a stand of emory oak. They meant to lay clear of Langtry and they talked about crossing the river at night. The day was warm and they washed out their shirts and put them on wet and mounted up and rode on. They could see the road behind them for several miles back to the northeast but they saw no rider.

That evening they crossed the Southern Pacific tracks just east of Pumpville Texas and made camp a half mile on the far side of the right of way. By the time they had the horses brushed and staked and a fire built it was dark. John Grady stood his saddle upright to the fire and walked out on the prairie and stood listening. He could see the Pumpville watertank against the purple sky. Beside it the horned moon. He could hear the horses cropping grass a hundred yards away. The prairie otherwise lay blue and silent all about.

They crossed highway 90 midmorning of the following day and rode out onto a pastureland dotted with grazing cattle. Far to the south the mountains of Mexico drifted in and out of the uncertain light of a moving cloud-cover like ghosts of mountains. Two hours later they were at the river. They sat on a low bluff and took off their hats and watched it. The water was the color of clay and roily and they could hear it in the rips downstream. The sandbar below them was thickly grown with willow and carrizo cane and the bluffs on the far side were stained and cavepocked and traversed by a constant myriad of swallows. Beyond that the desert rolled as before. They turned and looked at each other and put on their hats.

They rode upriver to where a creek cut in and they rode down the creek and out onto a gravel bar and sat the horses and studied the water and the country about. Rawlins rolled a cigarette and crossed one leg over the pommel of the saddle and sat smoking.

Who is it we're hidin from? he said.

Who aint we?

I dont see where anybody could be hidin over there.

They might say the same thing lookin at this side.

Rawlins sat smoking. He didnt answer.

We can cross right down yonder off of that shoal, John Grady said.

Why dont we do it now?

John Grady leaned and spat into the river. I'll do whatever you want, he said. I thought we agreed to play it safe.

I'd sure like to get it behind me if we're goin to.

I would too pardner. He turned and looked at Rawlins.

Rawlins nodded. All right, he said.

They rode back up the creek and dismounted and unsaddled the horses on the gravel bar and staked them out in the creekside grass. They sat under the shade of the willows and ate vienna sausages and crackers and drank koolaid made from creekwater. You think they got vienna sausages in Mexico? Rawlins said.

Late in the afternoon he walked up the creek and stood on the level prairie with his hat in his hand and looked out across the blowing grass to the northeast. A rider was crossing the plain a mile away. He watched him.

When he got back to the camp he woke up Rawlins.

What is it? said Rawlins.

There's somebody comin. I think it's that gunsel.

Rawlins adjusted his hat and climbed up the bank and stood looking.

Can you make him out? called John Grady.

Rawlins nodded. He leaned and spat.

If I cant make him out I can damn sure make out that horse.

Did he see you?

I dont know.

He's headed this way.

He probably seen me.

I think we ought to run him off.

He looked back at John Grady again. I got a uneasy feelin about that little son of a bitch.

I do too.

He aint as green as he looks, neither.

What's he doin? said John Grady.

Ridin.

Well come on back down. He might not of seen us.

He's stopped, said Rawlins.

What's he doin?

Ridin again.

They waited for him to arrive if he would. It wasnt long before the horses raised their heads and stood staring downstream. They heard the rider come down into the creek bed, a rattling of gravel and a faint chink of metal.

Rawlins got his rifle and they walked out down the creek to the river. The kid was sitting the big bay horse in the shallow water off the gravel bar and looking across the river. When he turned and saw them he pushed his hat back with his thumb.

I knowed you all hadnt crossed, he said. There's two deer feedin along the edge of them mesquite yon side.

Rawlins squatted on the gravel bar and stood the rifle in front of him and held it and rested his chin on the back of his arm. What the hell are we goin to do with you? he said.

The kid looked at him and he looked at John Grady. There wont be nobody huntin me in Mexico.

That all depends on what you done, said Rawlins.

I aint done nothin.

What's your name? said John Grady.

Jimmy Blevins.

Bullshit, said Rawlins. Jimmy Blevins is on the radio.

That's another Jimmy Blevins.

Who's followin you?

Nobody.

How do you know?

Cause there aint.

Rawlins looked at John Grady and he looked at the kid again. You got any grub? he said.

No.

You got any money?

No.

You're just a deadhead.

The kid shrugged. The horse took a step in the water and stopped again.

Rawlins shook his head and spat and looked out across the river. Tell me just one thing.

All right.

What the hell would we want you with us for?

He didnt answer. He sat looking at the sandy water running past them and at the thin wicker shadows of the willows running out over the sandbar in the evening light. He looked out to the blue sierras to the south and he hitched up the shoulder strap of his overalls and sat with his thumb hooked in the bib and turned and looked at them.

Cause I'm an American, he said.

Rawlins turned away and shook his head.

They crossed the river under a white quartermoon naked and pale and thin atop their horses. They'd stuffed their boots upside down into their jeans and stuffed their shirts and jackets after along with their warbags of shaving gear and ammunition and they belted the jeans shut at the waist and tied the legs loosely about their necks and dressed only in their hats they led the horses out onto the gravel spit and loosed the girthstraps and mounted and put the horses into the water with their naked heels.

Midriver the horses were swimming, snorting and stretching their necks out of the water, their tails afloat behind. They quartered downstream with the current, the naked riders leaning forward and talking to the horses, Rawlins holding the rifle aloft in one hand, lined out behind one another and making for the alien shore like a party of marauders.

They rode up out of the river among the willows and rode singlefile upstream through the shallows onto a long gravel beach where they took off their hats and turned and looked back at the country they'd left. No one spoke. Then suddenly they put their horses to a gallop up the beach and turned and came back, fanning with their hats and laughing and pulling up and patting the horses on the shoulder.

Goddamn, said Rawlins. You know where we're at?

They sat the smoking horses in the moonlight and looked at one another. Then quietly they dismounted and unslung their clothes from about their necks and dressed and led the horses up out of the willow breaks and gravel benches and out upon the plain where they mounted and rode south onto the dry scrublands of Coahuila.

They camped at the edge of a mesquite plain and in the morning they cooked bacon and beans and cornbread made from meal and water and they sat eating and looking out at the country.

When'd you eat last? Rawlins said.

The other day, said the Blevins boy.

The other day.

Yeah.

Rawlins studied him. Your name aint Blivet is it?

It's Blevins.

You know what a blivet is?

What.

A blivet is ten pounds of shit in a five pound sack.

Blevins stopped chewing. He was looking out at the country to the west where cattle had come out of the breaks and were standing on the plain in the morning sun. Then he went on chewing again.

You aint said what your all's names was, he said.

You aint never asked.

That aint how I was raised, said Blevins.

Rawlins stared at him bleakly and turned away.

John Grady Cole, said John Grady. This here is Lacey Rawlins.

The kid nodded. He went on chewing.

We're from up around San Angelo, said John Grady.

I aint never been up there.

They waited for him to say where he was from but he didnt say.

Rawlins swabbed out his plate with a crumbly handful of the

cornbread and ate it. Suppose, he said, that we wanted to trade that horse off for one less likely to get us shot.

The kid looked at John Grady and looked back out to where the cattle were standing. I aint tradin horses, he said.

You dont care for us to have to look out for you though, do you?

I can look out for myself.

Sure you can. I guess you got a gun and all.

He didnt answer for a minute. Then he said: I got a gun.

Rawlins looked up. Then he went on spooning up the cornbread. What kind of a gun? he said.

Thirty-two twenty Colt.

Bullshit, said Rawlins. That's a rifle cartridge.

The kid had finished eating and sat swabbing out his plate with a twist of grass.

Let's see it, said Rawlins.

He set the plate down. He looked at Rawlins and then he looked at John Grady. Then he reached into the bib of his overalls and came out with the pistol. He rolled it in his hand with a forward flip and handed it toward Rawlins butt-first upside down.

Rawlins looked at him and looked at the pistol. He set his plate down in the grass and took the gun and turned it in his hand. It was an old Colt Bisley with guttapercha grips worn smooth of their checkering. The metal was a dull gray. He turned it so as to read the script on top of the barrel. It said 32-20. He looked at the kid and flipped open the gate with his thumb and put the hammer at halfcock and turned the cylinder and ran one of the shells into his palm with the ejector rod and looked at it. Then he put it back and closed the gate and let the hammer back down.

Where'd you get a gun like this? he said.

At the gittin place.

You ever shot it?

Yeah, I shot it.

Can you hit anything with it?

The kid held out his hand for the pistol. Rawlins hefted it in his palm and turned it and passed it to him.

You want to throw somethin up I'll hit it, the kid said.

Bullshit.

The kid shrugged and put the pistol back in the bib of his overalls.

Throw what up? said Rawlins.

Anything you want.

Anything I throw you can hit.

Yeah.

Bullshit.

The kid stood up. He wiped the plate back and forth across the leg of his overalls and looked at Rawlins.

You throw your pocketbook up in the air and I'll put a hole in it, he said.

Rawlins stood. He reached in his hip pocket and took out his billfold. The kid leaned and set the plate in the grass and took out the pistol again. John Grady put his spoon in his plate and set the plate on the ground. The three of them walked out onto the plain in the long morning light like duelists.

He stood with his back to the sun and the pistol hanging alongside his leg. Rawlins turned and grinned at John Grady. He held the billfold between his thumb and finger.

You ready, Annie Oakley? he said.

Waitin on you.

He pitched it up underhanded. It rose spinning in the air, very small against the blue. They watched it, waiting for him to shoot. Then he shot. The billfold jerked sideways off across the landscape and opened out and fell twisting to the ground like a broken bird.

The sound of the pistolshot vanished almost instantly in that immense silence. Rawlins walked out across the grass and bent and picked up his billfold and put it in his pocket and came back.

We better get goin, he said.

Let's see it, said John Grady.

Let's go. We need to get away from this river.

They caught their horses and saddled them and the kid kicked out the fire and they mounted up and rode out. They rode side by side spaced out apart upon the broad gravel plain curving away along the edge of the brushland upriver. They rode without speaking and they took in the look of the new country. A hawk in the top of a mesquite dropped down and flew low along the vega and rose again up into a tree a half mile to the east. When they had passed it flew back again.

You had that pistol in your shirt back on the Pecos, didnt you? said Rawlins.

The kid looked at him from under his immense hat. Yeah, he said.

They rode. Rawlins leaned and spat. You'd of shot me with it I guess.

The kid spat also. I didnt aim to get shot, he said.

They rode up through low hills covered with nopal and creosote. Midmorning they struck a trail with horsetracks in it and turned south and at noon they rode into the town of Reforma.

They rode singlefile down the cart track that served as a street. Half a dozen low houses with walls of mud brick slumping into ruin. A few jacales of brush and mud with brush roofs and a pole corral where five scrubby horses with big heads stood looking solemnly at the horses passing in the road.

They dismounted and tied their horses at a little mud tienda and entered. A girl was sitting in a straightback chair by a sheetiron stove in the center of the room reading a comicbook by the light from the doorway and she looked up at them and looked at the comicbook and then looked up again. She got up and glanced toward the back of the store where a green curtain hung across a doorway and she put the book down in the chair and crossed the packed clay floor to the counter and turned and stood. On top of the counter were three clay jars or ollas. Two of them were empty but the third was covered with the tin lid from a lardpail and the lid was notched to accommodate the handle of an enameled tin dipper. Along the wall behind her were three or four board shelves that held canned goods and cloth and thread and candy. Against the far wall was a hand-made pineboard mealbox. Above it a calendar nailed to the mud wall with a stick. Other than the stove and the chair that was all there was in the building.

Rawlins took off his hat and pressed his forearm against his forehead and put the hat back on. He looked at John Grady. She got anything to drink?

Tiene algo que tomar? said John Grady.

Sí, said the girl. She moved to take up her station behind the jars and lifted away the lid. The three riders stood at the counter and looked.

What is that? said Rawlins.

Sidrón, said the girl.

John Grady looked at her. Habla inglés? he said.

Oh no, she said.

What is it? said Rawlins.

Cider.

He looked into the jar. Let's have em, he said. Give us three. Mande?

Three, said Rawlins. Tres. He held up three fingers.

He got out his billfold. She reached to the shelves behind and got down three tumblers and stood them on the board and took up the dipper and dredged up a thin brown liquid and filled the glasses and Rawlins laid a dollar bill on the counter. It had a hole in it at each end. They reached for the glasses and John Grady nodded at the bill.

He about deadcentered your pocketbook didnt he?

Yeah, said Rawlins.

He lifted up his glass and they drank. Rawlins stood thoughtfully.

I dont know what that shit is, he said. But it tastes pretty good to a cowboy. Let us have three more here.

They set their glasses down and she refilled them. What do we owe? said Rawlins.

She looked at John Grady.

Cuánto, said John Grady.

Para todo?

Sí.

Uno cincuenta.

How much is that? said Rawlins.

It's about three cents a glass.

Rawlins pushed the bill across the counter. You let your old dad buy, he said.

She made change out of a cigar box under the counter and laid the Mexican coins out on the counter and looked up. Rawlins set his empty glass down and gestured at it and paid for three more glasses and took his change and they took their glasses and walked outside.

They sat in the shade of the pole and brush ramada in front of the place and sipped their drinks and looked out at the desolate stillness of the little crossroads at noon. The mud huts. The dusty agave and the barren gravel hills beyond. A thin blue rivulet of drainwater ran down the clay gully in front of the store and a goat stood in the rutted road looking at the horses.

There aint no electricity here, said Rawlins.

He sipped his drink. He looked out down the road.

I doubt there's ever even been a car in here.

I dont know where it would come from, said John Grady.

Rawlins nodded. He held the glass to the light and rolled the cider around and looked at it. You think this here is some sort of cactus juice or what?

I dont know, said John Grady. It's got a little kick to it, dont it?

I think it does.

Better not let that youngn have no more.

I've drunk whiskey, said Blevins. This aint nothin.

Rawlins shook his head. Drinkin cactus juice in old Mexico, he said. What do you reckon they're sayin at home about now?

I reckon they're sayin we're gone, said John Grady.

Rawlins sat with his legs stretched out before him and his boots crossed and his hat over one knee and looked out at the alien land and nodded. We are, aint we? he said.

They watered the horses and loosed the cinches to let them blow and then took the road south such road as it was, riding single file through the dust. In the road were the tracks of cows, javelinas, deer, coyotes. Late afternoon they passed another collection of huts but they rode on. The road was deeply gullied and it was washed out in the draws and in the draws were cattle dead from an old drought, just the bones of them cloven about with the hard dry blackened hide.

How does this country suit you? said John Grady.

Rawlins leaned and spat but he didnt answer.

In the evening they came to a small estancia and sat the horses at the fence. There were several buildings scattered out behind the house and a pole corral with two horses standing in it. Two little girls in white dresses stood in the yard. They looked at the riders and then turned and ran into the house. A man came out.

Buenas tardes, he said.

He walked out the fence to the gate and motioned them through and showed them where to water their horses. Pásale, he said. Pásale.

They ate by oillight at a small painted pine table. The mud walls about them were hung with old calendars and magazine pictures. On one wall was a framed tin retablo of the Virgin. Under it was a board supported by two wedges driven into the wall and on the board was a small green glass with a blackened candlestub in it. The Americans sat shoulder to shoulder along one side of the table and the two little girls sat on the other side and watched them in a state of breathlessness. The woman ate with her head down and the man joked with them and passed the plates. They ate beans and tortillas and a chile of goatmeat ladled up out of a clay pot. They drank coffee from enameled tin cups and the man pushed the bowls toward them and gestured elaborately. Deben comer, he said.

He wanted to know about America, thirty miles to the north. He'd seen it once as a boy, across the river at Acuña. He had brothers who worked there. He had an uncle who'd lived some years in Uvalde Texas but he thought he was dead.

Rawlins finished his plate and thanked the woman and John Grady told her what he'd said and she smiled and nodded demurely. Rawlins was showing the two little girls how he could pull his finger off and put it back on again when Blevins crossed his utensils in the plate before him and wiped his mouth on his sleeve and leaned back from the table. There was no back to the bench and Blevins flailed wildly for a moment and then crashed to the floor behind him, kicking the table underneath and rattling the dishes and almost pulling over the bench with Rawlins and John Grady. The two girls stood instantly and clapped their hands and shrieked with delight. Rawlins had gripped the table to save himself and he looked down at the boy lying in the floor. I'll be goddamned, he said. Excuse me mam.

Blevins struggled up, only the man offering to help him.

Está bien? he said.

He's all right, said Rawlins. You caint hurt a fool.

The woman had leaned forward to right a cup, to quiet the children. She could not laugh for the impropriety of it but the brightness in her eyes did not escape even Blevins. He climbed over the bench and sat down again.

Are you all ready to go? he whispered.

We aint done eatin, said Rawlins.

He looked around uneasily. I caint set here, he said.

He was sitting with his head lowered and was whispering hoarsely.

Why caint you set there? said Rawlins.

I dont like to be laughed at.

Rawlins looked at the girls. They were sitting again and their eyes were wide and serious again. Hell, he said. It's just kids.

I dont like to be laughed at, whispered Blevins.

Both the man and the woman were looking at them with concern.

If you dont like to be laughed at dont fall on your ass, said Rawlins.

You all excuse me, said Blevins.

He climbed out over the bench and picked up his hat and put it on and went out. The man of the house looked worried and he leaned to John Grady and made a whispered inquiry. The two girls sat looking down at their plates.

You think he'll ride on? said Rawlins.

John Grady shrugged. I doubt it.

The householders seemed to be waiting for one of them to get up and go out after him but they did not. They drank their coffee and after a while the woman rose and cleared away the plates.

John Grady found him sitting on the ground like a figure in meditation.

What are you doin? he said.

Nothin.

Why dont you come back inside.

I'm all right.

They've offered us to spend the night.

Go ahead.

What do you aim to do?

I'm all right.

John Grady stood watching him. Well, he said. Suit yourself.

Blevins didnt answer and he left him sitting there.

The room they slept in was at the back of the house and it smelled of hay or straw. It was small and there was no window to it and on the floor were two pallets of straw and sacking with serapes over them. They took the lamp the host handed them and thanked him and he bowed out the low doorway and bid them goodnight. He didnt ask about Blevins.

John Grady set the lamp on the floor and they sat in the straw ticks and took off their boots.

I'm give out, said Rawlins.

I hear you.

What all did the old man say about work in this part of the country?

He says there's some big ranches yon side of the Sierra del Carmen. About three hundred kilometers.

How far's that?

Hundred and sixty, hundred and seventy miles.

You reckon he thinks we're desperados?

I dont know. Pretty nice about it if he does.

I'd say so.

He made that country sound like the Big Rock Candy Mountains. Said there was lakes and runnin water and grass to the stirrups. I cant picture country like that down here from what I've seen so far, can you?

He's probably just tryin to get us to move on.

Could be, said John Grady. He took off his hat and lay back and pulled the serape over him.

What the hell's he goin to do, said Rawlins. Sleep out in the yard?

I reckon.

Maybe he'll be gone in the mornin.

Maybe.

He closed his eyes. Dont let that lamp burn out, he said. It'll black the whole house.

I'll blow it out here in a minute.

He lay listening. There was no sound anywhere. What are you doin? he said.

Nothin.

He opened his eyes. He looked over at Rawlins. Rawlins had his billfold spread out across the blanket.

What are you doin?

I want you to look at my goddamned drivers license.

You wont need em down here.

There's my poolhall card. Got it too.

Go to sleep.

Look at this shit. He shot Betty Ward right between the eyes.

What was she doin in there? I didnt know you liked her.

She give me that picture. That was her schooldays picture.

In the morning they ate a huge breakfast of eggs and beans and tortillas at the same table. No one went out to get Blevins and no one asked about him. The woman packed them a lunch in a cloth and they thanked her and shook hands with the man and walked out in the cool morning. Blevins' horse was not in the corral.

You think we're this lucky? said Rawlins.

John Grady shook his head doubtfully.

They saddled the horses and they offered to pay the man for their feed but he frowned and waved them away and they shook hands again and he wished them a good voyage and they mounted up and rode out down the rutted track south. A dog followed them out a ways and then stood watching after them.

The morning was fresh and cool and there was woodsmoke in the air. When they topped the first rise in the road Rawlins spat in disgust. Look yonder, he said.

Blevins was sitting the big bay horse sideways in the road.

They slowed the horses. What the hell do you reckon is wrong with him? said Rawlins.

He's just a kid.

Shit, said Rawlins.

When they rode up Blevins smiled at them. He was chewing tobacco and he leaned and spat and wiped his mouth with the underside of his wrist.

What are you grinnin at?

Mornin, said Blevins.

Where'd you get the tobacco at? said Rawlins.

Man give it to me.

Man give it to you?

Yeah. Where you all been?

They rode their horses past him either side and he fell in behind.

You all got anything to eat? he said.

Got some lunch she put up for us, said Rawlins.

What have you got?

Dont know. Aint looked.

Well why dont we take a look?

Does it look like lunchtime to you?

Joe, tell him to let me have somethin to eat.

His name aint Joe, said Rawlins. And even if it was Evelyn he aint goin to give you no lunch at no seven oclock in the mornin.

Shit, said Blevins.

They rode till noon and past noon. There was nothing along the road save the country it traversed and there was nothing in the country at all. The only sound was the steady clop of the horses along the road and the periodic spat of Blevins' tobacco juice behind them. Rawlins rode with one leg crossed in front of him, leaning on his knee and smoking pensively as he studied the country.

I believe I see cottonwoods yonder, he said.

I believe I do too, said John Grady.

They ate lunch under the trees at the edge of a small ciénaga. The horses stood in the marshy grass and sucked quietly at the water. She'd tied the food up in a square of muslin and they spread the cloth on the ground and selected from among the quesadillas and tacos and bizcochos like picnickers, leaning back on their elbows in the shade with their boots crossed before them, chewing idly and observing the horses.

Back in the old days, said Blevins, this'd be just the place where Comanches'd lay for you and bushwhack you.

I hope they had some cards or a checkerboard with em while they was waitin, said Rawlins. It dont look to me like there's been nobody down this road in a year.

Back in the old days you had a lot more travelers, said Blevins.

Rawlins eyed balefully that cauterized terrain. What in the putrefied dogshit would you know about the old days? he said.

You all want any more of this? said John Grady.

I'm full as a tick.

He tied up the cloth and stood and began to strip out of his clothes and he walked out naked through the grass past the horses and waded out into the water and sat in it to his waist. He spread his arms and lay backward into the water and disappeared. The horses watched him. He sat up out of the water and pushed his hair back and wiped his eyes. Then he just sat.

They camped that night in the floor of a wash just off the road and built a fire and sat in the sand and stared into the embers.

Blevins are you a cowboy? said Rawlins.

I like it.

Everybody likes it.

I dont claim to be no top hand. I can ride.

Yeah? said Rawlins.

That man yonder can ride, said Blevins. He nodded across the fire toward John Grady.

What makes you say that?

He just can, that's all.

Suppose I was to tell you he just took it up. Suppose I was to tell you he's never been on a horse a girl couldnt ride.

I'd have to say you was pullin my leg.

Suppose I was to tell you he's the best I ever saw.

Blevins spat into the fire.

You doubt that?

No, I dont doubt it. Depends on who you seen ride.

I seen Booger Red ride, said Rawlins.

Yeah? said Blevins.

Yeah.

You think he can outride him?

I know for a fact he can.

Maybe he can and maybe he caint.

You dont know shit from applebutter, said Rawlins. Booger Red's been dead forever.

Dont pay no attention to him, said John Grady.

Rawlins recrossed his boots and nodded toward John Grady. He cant take my part of it without braggin on hisself, can he?

He's full of shit, said John Grady.

You hear that? said Rawlins.

Blevins leaned his chin toward the fire and spat. I dont see how you can say somebody is just flat out the best.

You cant, said John Grady. He's just ignorant, that's all.

There's a lot of good riders, said Blevins.

That's right, said Rawlins. There's a lot of good riders. But there's just one that's the best. And he happens to be settin right yonder.

Leave him alone, said John Grady.

I aint botherin him, said Rawlins. Am I botherin you?

No.

Tell Joe yonder I aint botherin you.

I said you wasnt.

Leave him alone, said John Grady.

DAYS TO COME they rode through the mountains and they crossed at a barren windgap and sat the horses among the rocks and looked out over the country to the south where the last shadows were running over the land before the wind and the sun to the west lay blood red among the shelving clouds and the distant cordilleras ranged down the terminals of the sky to fade from pale to pale of blue and then to nothing at all.

Where do you reckon that paradise is at? said Rawlins.

John Grady had taken off his hat to let the wind cool his head. You cant tell what's in a country like that till you're down there in it, he said.

There's damn sure a bunch of it, aint there.

John Grady nodded. That's what I'm here for.

I hear you, cousin.

They rode down through the cooling blue shadowland of the north slope. Evergreen ash growing in the rocky draws. Persimmon, mountain gum. A hawk set forth below them and circled in the deepening haze and dropped and they kicked their feet out of the stirrups and put the horses forward with care down the shaly rock switchbacks. At just dark they benched out on a gravel shelf and made their camp and that night they heard what they'd none heard before, three long howls to the south-west and all afterwards a silence.

You hear that? said Rawlins.

Yeah.

It's a wolf, aint it?

Yeah.

He lay on his back in his blankets and looked out where the quartermoon lay cocked over the heel of the mountains. In that false blue dawn the Pleiades seemed to be rising up into the darkness above the world and dragging all the stars away, the great diamond of Orion and Cepella and the signature of Cassiopeia all rising up through the phosphorous dark like a sea-net. He lay a long time listening to the others breathing in their sleep while he contemplated the wildness about him, the wildness within.

It was cold in the night and in the dawn before daylight when they woke Blevins was already up and had a fire going on the ground and was huddled over it in his thin clothes. John Grady crawled out and got his boots and jacket on and walked out to study the new country as it shaped itself out of the darkness below them.

They drank the last of the coffee and ate cold tortillas with a thin stripe of bottled hotsauce down the middle.

How far down the road you think this'll get us? said Rawlins.

I aint worried, said John Grady.

Your pardner yonder looks a little misgive.

He aint got a lot of bacon to spare.

You aint neither.

They watched the sun rise below them. The horses standing out on the bench grazing raised their heads and watched it. Rawlins drank the last of his coffee and shook out his cup and reached in his shirtpocket for his tobacco.

You think there'll be a day when the sun wont rise?

Yeah, said John Grady. Judgment day.

When you think that'll be?

Whenever He decides to hold it.

Judgment day, said Rawlins. You believe in all that?

I dont know. Yeah, I reckon. You?

Rawlins put the cigarette in the corner of his mouth and lit it and flipped away the match. I dont know. Maybe.

I knowed you was a infidel, said Blevins.

You dont know a goddamned thing, said Rawlins. Just be quiet and dont make no bigger ass of yourself than what you already are.

John Grady got up and walked over and picked up his saddle by the horn and threw his blanket over his shoulder and turned and looked at them. Let's go, he said.

They were down out of the mountains by midmorning and riding on a great plain grown with sideoats grama and basket-grass and dotted with lechugilla. Here they encountered the first riders they'd seen and they halted and watched while they approached on the plain a mile away, three men on horses leading a train of packanimals carrying empty kiacks.

What do you reckon they are? said Rawlins.

We ought not to be stopped like this, said Blevins. If we can see them they can see us.

What the hell is that supposed to mean? said Rawlins.

What would you think if you seen them stop?

He's right, said John Grady. Let's keep ridin.

They were zacateros headed into the mountains to gather chino grass. If they were surprised to see Americans horseback in that country they gave no sign. They asked them if they'd seen a brother to one of them who was in the mountains with his wife and two grown girls but they'd seen no one. The Mexicans sat their horses and took in their outfits with slow movements of their dark eyes. They themselves were a rough lot, dressed half in rags, their hats marbled with grease and sweat, their boots mended with raw cowhide. They rode old squareskirted sad-dles with the wood worn through the leather and they rolled cigarettes in strips of cornhusks and lit them with esclarajos of flint and steel and bits of fluff in an empty cartridge case. One of them carried an old worn Colt stuck in his belt with the gate flipped open to keep it from sliding through and they smelled of smoke and tallow and sweat and they looked as wild and strange as the country they were in.

Son de Tejas? they said.

Sí, said John Grady.

They nodded.

John Grady smoked and watched them. For all their shabbiness they were well mounted and he watched those black eyes to see could he tell what they thought but he could tell nothing. They spoke of the country and of the weather in the country and they said that it was yet cold in the mountains. No one offered to dismount. They looked out over the terrain as if it were a problem to them. Something they'd not quite decided about. The little mules entrained behind them had dropped asleep standing almost as soon as they'd halted.

The leader finished his cigarette and let fall the stub of it into the track. Bueno, he said. Vámonos.

He nodded at the Americans. Buena suerte, he said. He put the long rowels of his spurs to the horse and they moved on. The mules passed on behind them eyeing the horses in the road and switching their tails although there seemed to be no flies in that country at all.

In the afternoon they watered the horses at a clear stream running out of the southwest. They walked the creek and drank and filled and stoppered their canteens. There were antelope out on the plain perhaps two miles distant, all standing with their heads up.

They rode on. There was good grass in the level floor of the valley and cattle the color of housecats to tortoiseshell and calico moved off constantly before them up through the buckthorn or stood along the low rise of ancient ground running down to the east to watch them as they passed along the road. That night they camped in the low hills and they cooked a jackrabbit that Blevins had shot with his pistol. He fielddressed it with his pocketknife and buried it in the sandy ground with the skin on and built the fire over it. He said it was the way the indians did.

You ever eat a jackrabbit? said Rawlins.

He shook his head. Not yet, he said.

You better rustle some more wood if you aim to eat thisn. It'll cook.

What's the strangest thing you ever ate?

Strangest thing I ever ate, said Blevins. I guess I'd have to say that would be a oyster.

A mountain oyster or a real oyster?

A real oyster.

How were they cooked?

They wasnt cooked. They just laid there in their shells. You put hotsauce on em.

You ate that?

I did.

How'd it taste?

About like you'd expect.

They sat watching the fire.

Where you from, Blevins? said Rawlins.

Blevins looked at Rawlins and looked back into the fire. Uvalde County, he said. Up on the Sabinal River.

What'd you run off for?

What'd you?

I'm seventeen years old. I can go wherever I want.

So can I.

John Grady was sitting with his legs crossed in front of him leaning against his saddle and smoking a cigarette. You've run off before, ain't you? he said.

Yeah.

What'd they do, catch you?

Yeah. I was settin pins in a bowlin alley in Ardmore Oklahoma and I got dogbit by a bulldog took a chunk out of my leg the size of a Sunday roast and it got infected and the man I worked for carried me down to the doctor and they thought I had rabies or somethin and all hell busted loose and I got shipped back to Uvalde County.

What were you doin in Ardmore Oklahoma?

Settin pins in a bowlin alley.

How come you wound up there?

There was a show was supposed to come through Uvalde, town of Uvalde, and I'd saved up to go see it but they never showed up because the man that run the show got thowed in jail in Tyler Texas for havin a dirty show. Had this striptease that was part of the deal. I got down there and it said on the poster they was goin to be in Ardmore Oklahoma in two weeks and that's how come me to be in Ardmore Oklahoma.

You went all the way to Oklahoma to see a show?

That's what I'd saved up to do and I meant to do it.

Did you see the show in Ardmore?

No. They never showed up there neither.

Blevins hauled up one leg of his overalls and turned his leg to the firelight.

Yonder's where that son of a bitch bit me, he said. I'd as soon been bit by a alligator.

What made you set out for Mexico? said Rawlins.

Same reason as you.

What reason is that?

Cause you knowed they'd play hell sowed in oats findin your ass down here.

There aint nobody huntin me.

Blevins rolled down the leg of his overalls and poked at the fire with a stick. I told that son of a bitch I wouldnt take a whippin off of him and I didnt.

Your daddy?

My daddy never come back from the war.

Your stepdaddy?

Yeah.

Rawlins leaned forward and spat into the fire. You didnt shoot him did you?

I would of. He knowed it too.

What was a bulldog doin in a bowlin alley?

I didnt get bit in the bowlin alley. I was workin in the bowlin alley, that's all.

What were you doin that you got dogbit?

Nothin. I wasnt doin nothin.

Rawlins leaned and spat into the fire. Where were you at at the time?

You got a awful lot of goddamned questions. And dont be spittin in the fire where I got supper cookin.

What? said Rawlins.

I said dont be spittin in the fire where I got supper cookin.

Rawlins looked at John Grady. John Grady had started to laugh. He looked at Blevins. Supper? he said. You'll think supper when you try and eat that stringy son of a bitch.

Blevins nodded. You let me know if you dont want your share, he said.

What they dredged smoking out of the ground looked like some desiccated effigy from a tomb. Blevins put it on a flat rock and peeled away the hide and scraped the meat off the bones into their plates and they soaked it down with hotsauce and rolled it in the last of the tortillas. They chewed and watched one another.

Well, said Rawlins. It aint all that bad.

No it aint, said Blevins. Truth is, I didnt know you could eat one at all.

John Grady stopped chewing and looked at them. Then he went on chewing again. You all been out here longer than me, he said. I thought we all started together.

The following day on the track south they began to encounter small ragged caravans of migrant traders headed toward the northern border. Brown and weathered men with burros three or four in tandem atotter with loads of candelilla or furs or goathides or coils of handmade rope fashioned out of lechugilla or the fermented drink called sotol decanted into drums and cans and strapped onto packframes made from treelimbs. They carried water in the skins of hogs or in canvas bags made waterproof with candelilla wax and fitted with cowhorn spigots and some had women and children with them and they would shoulder the packanimals off into the brush and relinquish the road to the caballeros and the riders would wish them a good day and they would smile and nod until they passed.

They tried to buy water from the caravans but they had no coin among them small enough with which to do so. When Rawlins offered a man fifty centavos for the half pennysworth of water it would take to fill their canteens the man would have no part of it. By evening they'd bought a canteenful of sotol and were passing it back and forth among themselves as they rode and soon they were quite drunk. Rawlins drank and swung up the cap by its thong and screwed it down and took the canteen by its strap and turned to swing it to Blevins. Then he caught it back. Blevins' horse was plodding along behind with an empty saddle. Rawlins eyed the animal stupidly and pulled his horse up and called to John Grady riding ahead.

John Grady turned and sat looking.

Where's he at?

Who knows? Layin back yonder somewheres I reckon.

They rode back, Rawlins leading the riderless horse by the bridlereins. Blevins was sitting in the middle of the road. He still had his hat on. Whoo, he said when he saw them. I'm drunkern shit.

They sat their horses and looked down at him.

Can you ride or not? said Rawlins.

Does a bear shit in the woods? Hell yes I can ride. I was ridin when I fell off.

He stood uncertainly and peered about. He reeled past them and felt his way among the horses. Flank and flew, Rawlins' knee. Thought you all had done rode off and left me, he said.

Next time we will leave your skinny ass.

John Grady reached and took the reins and held the horse while Blevins lurched aboard. Let me have them reins, said Blevins. I'm a goddamned buckaroo is what I am.

John Grady shook his head. Blevins dropped the reins and reached to get them and almost slid off down the horse's shoulder. He saved himself and sat up with the reins and pulled the horse around sharply. Certified goddamn broncpeeler, what I mean, he said.

He dug his heels in under the horse and it squatted and went forward and Blevins fell backwards into the road. Rawlins spat in disgust. Just leave the son of a bitch lay there, he said.

Get on the goddamned horse, said John Grady, and quit assin around.

By early evening all the sky to the north had darkened and the spare terrain they trod had turned a neuter gray as far as eye could see. They grouped in the road at the top of a rise and looked back. The storm front towered above them and the wind was cool on their sweating faces. They slumped bleary-eyed in their saddles and looked at one another. Shrouded in the black thunderheads the distant lightning glowed mutely like welding seen through foundry smoke. As if repairs were under way at some flawed place in the iron dark of the world.

It's fixin to come a goodn, said Rawlins.

I caint be out in this, said Blevins.

Rawlins laughed and shook his head. Listen at this, he said.

Where do you think you're goin to go? said John Grady.

I dont know. But I got to get somewheres.

Why cant you be out in it?

On account of the lightnin.

Lightnin?

Yeah.

Damn if you dont look about halfway sober all of a sudden, said Rawlins.

You afraid of lightnin? said John Grady.

I'll be struck sure as the world.

Rawlins nodded at the canteen hung by its strap from the pommel of John Grady's saddle. Dont give him no more of that shit. He's comin down with the DT's.

It runs in the family, said Blevins. My grandaddy was killed in a minebucket in West Virginia it run down in the hole a hunnerd and eighty feet to get him it couldnt even wait for him to get to the top. They had to wet down the bucket to cool it fore they could get him out of it, him and two other men. It fried em like bacon. My daddy's older brother was blowed out of a derrick in the Batson Field in the year nineteen and four, cable rig with a wood derrick but the lightnin got him anyways and him not nineteen year old. Great uncle on my mother's side—mother's side, I said—got killed on a horse and it never singed a hair on that horse and it killed him graveyard dead they had to cut his belt off him where it welded the buckle shut and I got a cousin aint but four years oldern me was struck down in his own yard comin from the barn and it paralyzed him all down one side and melted the fillins in his teeth and soldered his jaw shut.

I told you, said Rawlins. He's gone completely dipshit.

They didnt know what was wrong with him. He'd just twitch and mumble and point at his mouth like.

That's a out and out lie or I never heard one, said Rawlins.

Blevins didnt hear. Beads of sweat stood on his forehead. Another cousin on my daddy's side it got him it set his hair on fire. The change in his pocket burned through and fell out on the ground and set the grass alight. I done been struck twice how come me to be deaf in this one ear. I'm double bred for death by fire. You got to get away from anything metal at all. You dont know what'll get you. Brads in your overalls. Nails in your boots.

Well what do you intend to do?

He looked wildly toward the north. Try and outride it, he said. Only chance I got.

Rawlins looked at John Grady. He leaned and spat. Well, he said. If there was any doubt before I guess that ought to clear it up.

You cant outride a thunderstorm, said John Grady. What the hell is wrong with you?

It's the only chance I got.

He'd no sooner said it than the first thin crack of thunder reached them no louder than a dry stick trod on. Blevins took off his hat and passed the sleeve of his shirt across his forehead and doubled the reins in his fist and took one last desperate look behind him and whacked the horse across the rump with the hat.

They watched him go. He tried to get his hat on and then lost it. It rolled in the road. He went on with his elbows flapping and he grew small on the plain before them and more ludicrous yet.

I aint takin no responsibility for him, said Rawlins. He reached and unhooked the canteen from John Grady's saddle-horn and put his horse forward. He'll be a layin in the road down here and where do you reckon that horse'll be?

He rode on, drinking and talking to himself. I'll tell you where that horse'll be, he called back.

John Grady followed. Dust blew from under the tread of the horses and twisted away down the road before them.

Run plumb out of the country, called Rawlins. That's where. Gone to hell come Friday. That's where the goddamn horse'll be.

They rode on. There were spits of rain in the wind. Blevins' hat lay in the road and Rawlins tried to ride his horse over it but the horse stepped around it. John Grady slid one boot out of the stirrup and leaned down and picked up the hat without dismounting. They could hear the rain coming down the road behind them like some phantom migration.

Blevins' horse was standing saddled by the side of the road tied to a clump of willows. Rawlins turned and sat his horse in the rain and looked at John Grady. John Grady rode through the willows and down the arroyo following the occasional bare footprint in the rainspotted loam until he came upon Blevins crouched under the roots of a dead cottonwood in a caveout where the arroyo turned and fanned out onto the plain. He was naked save for an outsized pair of stained undershorts.

What the hell are you doin? said John Grady.

Blevins sat gripping his thin white shoulders in either hand. Just settin here, he said.

John Grady looked out over the plain where the last remnants of sunlight were being driven toward the low hills to the south. He leaned and dropped Blevins' hat at his feet.

Where's your clothes at?

I took em off.

I know that. Where are they?

I left em up yonder. Shirt had brass snaps too.

If this rain hits hard there'll be a river come down through here like a train. You thought about that?

You aint never been struck by lightnin, said Blevins. You dont know what it's like.

You'll get drowned settin there.

That's all right. I aint never been drowned before.

You aim to just set there?

That's what I aim to do.

John Grady put his hands on his knees. Well, he said. I'll say no more.

A long rolling crack of thunder went pealing down the sky to the north. The ground shuddered. Blevins put his arms over his head and John Grady turned the horse and rode back up the arroyo. Great pellets of rain were cratering the wet sand underfoot. He looked back once at Blevins. Blevins sat as before. A thing all but inexplicable in that landscape.

Where's he at? said Rawlins.

He's just settin out there. You better get your slicker.

I knowed when I first seen him the son of a bitch had a loose wingnut, said Rawlins. It was writ all over him.

The rain was coming down in sheets. Blevins' horse stood in the downpour like the ghost of a horse. They left the road and followed the wash up toward a stand of trees and took shelter under the barest overhang of rock, sitting with their knees stuck out into the rain and holding the standing horses by the bridlereins. The horses stepped and shook their heads and the lightning cracked and the wind tore through the acacia and paloverde and the rain went slashing down the country. They heard a horse running somewhere out in the rain and then they just heard the rain.

You know what that was dont you? said Rawlins.

Yeah.

You want a drink of this?

I dont think so. I think it's beginnin to make me feel bad.

Rawlins nodded and drank. I think it is me too, he said.

By dark the storm had slacked and the rain had almost ceased. They pulled the wet saddles off the horses and hobbled them and walked off in separate directions through the chaparral to stand spraddlelegged clutching their knees and vomiting. The browsing horses jerked their heads up. It was no sound they'd ever heard before. In the gray twilight those retchings seemed to echo like the calls of some rude provisional species loosed upon that waste. Something imperfect and malformed lodged in the heart of being. A thing smirking deep in the eyes of grace itself like a gorgon in an autumn pool.

In the morning they caught up the horses and saddled them and tied on the damp bedrolls and led the horses out to the road.

What do you want to do? said Rawlins.

I reckon we better go find his skinny ass.

What if we just went on.

John Grady mounted up and looked down at Rawlins. I dont believe I can leave him out here afoot, he said.

Rawlins nodded. Yeah, he said. I guess not.

He rode down the arroyo and encountered Blevins coming up in the same condition in which he'd left him. He sat the horse. Blevins was picking his way barefoot along the wash, carrying one boot. He looked up at John Grady.

Where's your clothes at? said John Grady.

Washed away.

Your horse is gone.

I know it. I done been out to the road once.

What do you aim to do?

I dont know.

You dont look like the demon rum's dealt kindly with you.

My head feels like a fat lady's sat on it.

John Grady looked out at the morning desert shining in the new sun. He looked at the boy.

You've wore Rawlins completely out. I reckon you know that.

You never know when you'll be in need of them you've despised, said Blevins.

Where the hell'd you hear that at?

I dont know. I just decided to say it.

John Grady shook his head. He reached and unbuckled his saddlebag and took out his spare shirt and pitched it down to Blevins.

Put that on before you get parboiled out here. I'll ride down and see if I can see your clothes anywheres.

I appreciate it, said Blevins.

He rode down the wash and he rode back. Blevins was sitting in the sand in the shirt.

How much water was in this wash last night?

A bunch.

Where'd you find the one boot at?

In a tree.

He rode down the wash and out over the gravel fan and sat looking. He didnt see any boot. When he came back Blevins was sitting as he'd left him.

That boot's gone, he said.

I figured as much.

John Grady reached down a hand. Let's go.

He swung Blevins in his underwear up onto the horse behind him. Rawlins will pitch a pure hissy when he sees you, he said.

Rawlins when he saw him seemed too dismayed to speak.

He's lost his clothes, said John Grady.

Rawlins turned his horse and set off slowly down the road. They followed. No one spoke. After a while John Grady heard something drop into the road and he looked back and saw Blevins' boot lying there. He turned and looked at Blevins but

Blevins was peering steadily ahead from under the brim of his hat and they rode on. The horses stepped archly among the shadows that fell over the road, the bracken steamed. Bye and bye they passed a stand of roadside cholla against which small birds had been driven by the storm and there impaled. Gray nameless birds espaliered in attitudes of stillborn flight or hanging loosely in their feathers. Some of them were still alive and they twisted on their spines as the horses passed and raised their heads and cried out but the horsemen rode on. The sun rose up in the sky and the country took on new color, green fire in the acacia and paloverde and green in the roadside run-off grass and fire in the ocotillo. As if the rain were electric, had grounded circuits that the electric might be.

So mounted they rode at noon into a waxcamp pitched in the broken footlands beneath the low stone mesa running east and west before them. There was a small clearwater branch here and the Mexicans had dug an open firebox and lined it with rock and scotched their boiler into the bank over it. The boiler was made from the lower half of a galvanized watertank and to bring it to this location they'd run a wooden axleshaft through the bottom and made a wooden spider whereby to bed the axle in the open end and with a team of horses rolled the tank across the desert from Zaragoza eighty miles to the east. The track of flattened chaparral was still visible bending away over the floor of the desert. When the Americans rode into their camp there were several burros standing there that had just been brought down from the mesa loaded with the candelilla plant they boiled for wax and the Mexicans had left the animals to stand while they ate their dinner. A dozen men dressed most of them in what looked to be pajamas and all of them in rags squatting under the shade of some willows and eating with tin spoons off of clay plates. They looked up but they did not stop eating.

Buenos días, said John Grady. They responded in a quick dull chorus. He dismounted and they looked at the spot where he stood and looked at each other and then went on eating.

Tienen algo que comer?

One or two of them gestured toward the fire with their spoons. When Blevins slid from the horse they looked at each other again.

The riders got their plates and utensils out of the saddlebags and John Grady got the little enameled pot out of the blackened cookbag and handed it to Blevins together with his old wooden-handled kitchen fork. They went to the fire and filled their plates with beans and chile and took each a couple of blackened corn tortillas from a piece of sheetiron laid over the fire and walked over and sat under the willows a little apart from the workers. Blevins sat with his bare legs stretched out before him but they looked so white and exposed lying there on the ground that he seemed ashamed and he tried to tuck them up under him and to cover his knees with the tails of the borrowed shirt he wore. They ate. The workers had for the most part finished their meal and they were leaning back smoking cigarettes and belching quietly.

You goin to ask em about my horse? said Blevins.

John Grady chewed thoughtfully. Well, he said. If it's here they ought to be able to figure out it belongs to us.

You think they'd steal it?

You aint never goin to get that horse back, said Rawlins. We hit a town down here somewheres you better see if you can trade that pistol for some clothes and a bus ticket back to wherever it is you come from. If there are buses. Your buddy yonder might be willin to haul your ass all over Mexico but I damn sure aint.

I aint got the pistol, said Blevins. It's with the horse.

Shit, said Rawlins.

Blevins ate. After a while he looked up. What'd I ever do to you? he said.

You aint done nothin to me. And you aint goin to. That's the point.

Leave him be, Lacey. It aint goin to hurt us to try and help the boy get his horse back.

I'm just tellin him the facts, said Rawlins.

He knows the facts.

He dont act like it.

John Grady wiped his plate with the last of the tortilla and ate the tortilla and set the plate on the ground and commenced to roll a cigarette.

I'm goddamned starved, said Rawlins. You reckon they'd care if we went back for seconds?

They wont care, said Blevins. Go ahead.

Who asked you? said Rawlins.

John Grady started to reach in his pocket for a match and then he rose and walked over to the workers and squatted and asked for a light. Two of them produced esclarajos from their clothes and one struck him a light and he leaned and lit the cigarette and nodded. He asked about the boiler and the loads of candelilla still tied on the burros and the workers told them about the wax and one of them rose and walked off and came back with a small gray cake of it and handed it to him. It looked like a bar of laundrysoap. He scraped it with his fingernail and sniffed it. He held it up and looked at it.

Qué vale? he said.

They shrugged.

Es mucho trabajo, he said.

Bastante.

A thin man in a stained leather vest with embroidery on the front was watching John Grady with narrowed and speculative eyes. John Grady handed back the wax and this man hissed at him and jerked his head.

John Grady turned.

Es su hermano, el rubio?

He meant Blevins. John Grady shook his head. No, he said.

Quíen es? said the man.

He looked across the clearing. The cook had given Blevins some lard and he sat rubbing it into his sunburned legs.

Un muchacho, no más, he said.

Algún parentesco?

No.

Un amigo.

John Grady drew on the cigarette and tapped the ash against the heel of his boot. Nada, he said.

No one spoke. The man in the vest studied John Grady and he looked across the clearing at Blevins. Then he asked John Grady if he wished to sell the boy.

He didnt answer for a moment. The man may have thought he was weighing the matter. They waited. He looked up. No, he said.

Qué vale? said the man.

John Grady stubbed out the cigarette against the sole of his boot and rose.

Gracias por su hospitalidad, he said.

The man offered that he would trade for him in wax. The others had turned to listen to him. Now they turned and looked at John Grady.

John Grady studied them. They did not look evil but it was no comfort to him. He turned and crossed the clearing toward the standing horses. Blevins and Rawlins rose.

What did they say? said Blevins.

Nothing.

Did you ask them about my horse?

No.

Why not?

They dont have your horse.

What was that guy talkin about?

Nothing. Get the plates. Let's go.

Rawlins looked across the clearing at the seated men. He took up the trailing reins and swung up into the saddle.

What's happened, bud? he said.

John Grady mounted and turned the horse. He looked back at the men and he looked at Blevins. Blevins stood with the plates.

What was he lookin at me for? he said.

Put them in the bag and get your ass up here.

They aint washed.

Do like I told you.

Some of the men had risen. Blevins stuffed the plates into the bag and John Grady reached down and swung him up onto the horse behind him.

He pulled the horse around and they rode out of the camp and into the road south. Rawlins looked back and put his horse into a trot and John Grady came up and they rode side by side down the narrow rutted track. No one spoke. When they were clear of the camp a mile or so Blevins asked what it was that the man in the vest had wanted but John Grady didnt answer. When Blevins asked again Rawlins looked back at him.

He wanted to buy you, he said. That's what he wanted.

John Grady didnt look at Blevins.

They rode on in silence.

What did you go and tell him that for? said John Grady. There wasnt no call to do that.

They camped that night in the low range of hills under the Sierra de la Encantada and the three of them sat about the fire in silence. The boy's bony legs were pale in the firelight and coated with road dust and bits of chaff that had stuck to the lard. The drawers he wore were baggy and dirty and he did indeed look like some sad and ill used serf or worse. John Grady parceled out to him the bottom blanket from his bedroll and he wrapped himself in it and lay by the fire and was soon asleep. Rawlins shook his head and spat.

Goddamn pitiful, he said. You thought any more about what I said?

Yeah, said John Grady. I thought about it.

Rawlins stared long into the red heart of the fire. I'll tell you somethin, he said.

Tell me.

Somethin bad is goin to happen.

John Grady smoked slowly, his arms around his updrawn knees.

This is just a jackpot, said Rawlins. What this is.

At noon the next day they rode into the pueblo of Encantada at the foot of the low range of pollarded mountains they'd been skirting and the first thing they saw was Blevins' pistol sticking out of the back pocket of a man bent over into the engine compartment of a Dodge car. John Grady saw it first and he could have named things he'd rather have seen.

Yonder's my goddamn pistol, sang out Blevins.

John Grady reached behind and grabbed him by the shirt or he'd have slid down from the horse.

Hold on, idjit, he said.

Hold on hell, said Blevins.

What do you think you're goin to do?

Rawlins had put his horse alongside of them. Keep ridin, he hissed. Good God almighty.

Some children were watching from a doorway and Blevins was looking back over his shoulder.

If that horse is here, said Rawlins, they wont have to send for Dick Tracy to figure out who it belongs to.

What do you want to do?

I dont know. Get off the damn street. May be too late anyways. I say we stash him in a safe place somewheres till we can look around.

Does that suit you, Blevins?

It dont make a damn if it suits him or not, said Rawlins. He dont have a say in it. Not if he wants my help he dont.

He rode past them and they turned off down a clay gully that passed for a street. Quit lookin back, damn it, said John Grady.

They left him with a canteen of water in the shade of some cottonwoods and told him to stay out of sight and then they rode slowly back through the town. They were picking their way along one of those rutted gullies of which the town was composed when they saw the horse looking out of the sashless window of an abandoned mud house.

Keep ridin, said Rawlins.

John Grady nodded.

When they got back to the cottonwoods Blevins was gone. Rawlins sat looking over the barren dusty countryside. He reached in his pocket for his tobacco.

I'm goin to tell you somethin, cousin.

John Grady leaned and spat. All right.

Ever dumb thing I ever done in my life there was a decision I made before that got me into it. It was never the dumb thing. It was always some choice I'd made before it. You understand what I'm sayin?

Yeah. I think so. Meanin what?

Meanin this is it. This is our last chance. Right now. This is the time and there wont be another time and I guarantee it.

Meanin just leave him?

Yessir.

What if it was you?

It aint me.

What if it was?

Rawlins twisted the cigarette into the corner of his mouth and plucked a match from his pocket and popped it alight with his thumbnail. He looked at John Grady.

I wouldnt leave you and you wouldnt leave me. That aint no argument.

You realize the fix he's in?

Yeah. I realize it. It's the one he's put hisself in.

They sat. Rawlins smoked. John Grady crossed his hands on the pommel of his saddle and sat looking at them. After a while he raised his head.

I cant do it, he said.

Okay.

What does that mean?

It means okay. If you cant you cant. I think I knew what you'd say anyways.

Yeah, well. I didnt.

They unsaddled and staked out the horses and lay in the dry

leaves under the cottonwoods and after a while they slept. When they woke it was almost dark. The boy was squatting there watching them.

It's a good thing I aint a rogue, he said. I could of slipped up on you all and carried off everthing you own.

Rawlins turned and looked at him from under his hat and turned back. John Grady sat up.

What did you all find out? said Blevins.

Your horse is here.

Did you see him?

Yeah.

What about the saddle?

We didnt see no saddle.

I aint leavin here till I get all my stuff.

There you go, said Rawlins. Listen at that.

What's he say? said Blevins.

Never mind, said John Grady.

If it was his stuff it'd be different I bet. Then he'd be for gettin it back, wouldnt he?

Dont egg it on.

Listen, shit-for-brains, said Rawlins. If it wasnt for this man I wouldnt be here at all. I'd of left your ass back up in that arroyo. No, I take that back. I'd of left you up on the Pecos.

We'll try and get your horse back, said John Grady. If that wont satisfy you then you let me know right now.

Blevins stared at the ground.

He dont give a shit, said Rawlins. I could of wrote it down. Get shot dead for horsestealin it dont mean a damn thing to him. He expects it.

It aint stealin, said Blevins. It's my horse.

A lot of ice that'll cut. You tell this man what you intend to do cause I guarantee you I dont give a big rat's ass.

All right, said Blevins.

John Grady studied him. We get you your horse you'll be ready to ride.

Yeah.

We got your word on that?

Word's ass, said Rawlins.

Yeah, said Blevins.

John Grady looked at Rawlins. Rawlins lay under his hat. He turned back to Blevins. All right, he said.

He got up and got his bedroll and came back and handed Blevins a blanket.

We goin to sleep now? said Blevins.

I am.

Did you all eat?

Yeah, said Rawlins. Sure we ate. Wouldnt you of? We eat a big steak apiece and split a third one.

Damn, said Blevins.

They slept until the moon was down and they sat in the dark and smoked. John Grady watched the stars.

What time you make it to be, bud? said Rawlins.

First quarter moon sets at midnight where I come from.

Rawlins smoked. Hell. I believe I'll go back to bed.

Go ahead. I'll wake you.

All right.

Blevins went to sleep as well. He sat watching the firmament unscroll up from behind the blackened palisades of the mountains to the east. Toward the village all was darkness. Not even a dog barked. He looked at Rawlins rolled asleep in his soogan and he knew that he was right in all he'd said and there was no help for it and the dipper standing at the northern edge of the world turned and the night was a long time passing.

When he called them out it was not much more than an hour till daylight.

You ready? said Rawlins.

Ready as I'm liable to get.

They saddled the horses and John Grady handed his stake-rope to Blevins. You can make a hackamore out of that, he said.

All right.

Keep it under your shirt, said Rawlins. Dont let nobody see it.

There aint nobody to see it, said Blevins.

Dont bet on it. I see a light up yonder already.

Let's go, said John Grady.

There were no houselamps lit in the street where they'd seen the horse. They rode along slowly. A dog that had been sleeping in the dirt rose up and commenced barking and Rawlins made a throwing motion at it and it slunk off. When they got to the house where the horse was stabled John Grady got down and walked over and looked in the window and came back.

He aint here, he said.

It was dead quiet in the little mud street. Rawlins leaned and spat. Well, shit, he said.

You all sure this is the place? said Blevins.

It's the place.

The boy slid from the horse and picked his way gingerly with his bare feet across the road to the house and looked in. Then he climbed through the window.

What the hell's he doin? said Rawlins.

You got me.

They waited. He didnt come back.

Yonder comes somebody.

Some dogs started up. John Grady mounted up and turned the horse and went back up the road and sat the horse in the dark. Rawlins followed. Dogs were beginning to bark all back through the town. A light came on.

This is by God it, aint it? said Rawlins.

John Grady looked at him. He was sitting with the carbine upright on his thigh. From beyond the buildings and the din of dogs there came a shout.

You know what these sons of bitches'll do to us? said Rawlins. You thought about that?

John Grady leaned forward and spoke to the horse and put his hand on the horse's shoulder. The horse had begun to step nervously and it was not a nervous horse. He looked toward the houses where they'd seen the light. A horse whinnied in the dark.

That crazy son of a bitch, said Rawlins. That crazy son of a bitch.

All out bedlam had broken across the lot. Rawlins pulled his horse around and the horse stamped and trotted and he whacked it across the rump with the barrel of the gun. The horse squatted and dug in with its hind hooves and Blevins in his underwear atop the big bay horse and attended by a close retinue of howling dogs exploded into the road in a shower of debris from the rotted ocotillo fence he'd put the horse through.

The horse skittered past Rawlins sideways, Blevins clinging to the animal's mane and snatching at his hat. The dogs swarmed wildly over the road and Rawlins' horse stood and twisted and shook its head and the big bay turned a complete circle and there were three pistol shots from somewhere in the dark all evenly spaced that went pop pop pop. John Grady put the heels of his boots to his horse and leaned low in the saddle and he and Rawlins went pounding up the road. Blevins passed them both, his pale knees clutching the horse and his shirttail flying.

Before they reached the turn at the top of the hill there were three more shots from the road behind them. They turned onto the main track south and went pounding through the town. Already there were lamps lit in a few small windows. They passed through at a hard gallop and rode up into the low hills. First light was shaping out the country to the east. A mile south of the town they caught up with Blevins. He'd turned his horse in the road and he was watching them and watching the road behind them.

Hold up, he said. Let's listen.

They tried to quiet the gasping animals. You son of a bitch, said Rawlins.

Blevins didnt answer. He slid from his horse and lay in the road listening. Then he got up and pulled himself back up onto the horse.

Boys, he said, they're a comin.

Horses?

Yeah. I'll tell you right now straight out there aint no way you all can keep up with me. Let me take the road since it's me they're huntin. They'll follow the dust and you all can slip off into the country. I'll see you down the road.

Before they could agree or disagree he'd hauled the horse around by the hackamore and was pounding off up the track.

He's right, said John Grady. We better get off this damned road.

All right.

They rode out through the brush in the dark, taking the lowest country they could keep to, lying along the necks of their mounts that they not be skylighted.

We're fixin to get the horses snakebit sure as the world, said Rawlins.

It'll be daylight soon.

Then we can get shot.

In a little while they heard horses on the road. Then they heard more horses. Then all was quiet.

We better get somewheres, said Rawlins. It's fixin to get daylight sure enough.

Yeah, I know it.

You think when they come back they'll see where we quit the road?

Not if enough of em has rode over it.

What if they catch him?

John Grady didnt answer.

He wouldnt have no qualms about showin em which way we'd headed.

Probably not.

You know not. All they'd have to do would be look at him crossways.

Then we better keep ridin.

Well I dont know about you but I'm about to run out of horse.

Well tell me what you want to do.

Shit, said Rawlins. We aint got no choice. We'll see what daylight brings. Maybe one of these days we might find some grain somewheres in this country.

Maybe.

They slowed the horses and rode to the crest of the ridge. Nothing moved in all that gray landscape. They dismounted and walked out along the ridge. Small birds were beginning to call from the chaparral.

You know how long it's been since we eat? said Rawlins.

I aint even thought about it.

I aint either till just now. Bein shot at will sure enough cause you to lose your appetite, wont it?

Hold up a minute.

What is it?

Hold up.

They stood listening.

I dont hear nothin.

There's riders out there.

On the road?

I dont know.

Can you see anything?

No.

Let's keep movin.

John Grady spat and stood listening. Then they moved on.

At daylight they left the horses standing in a gravel wash and climbed to the top of a rise and sat among the ocotillos and watched the country back to the northeast. Some deer moved out feeding along the ridge opposite. Other than that they saw nothing.

Can you see the road? said Rawlins.

No.

They sat. Rawlins stood the rifle against his knee and took his tobacco from his pocket. I believe I'll smoke, he said.

A long fan of light ran out from the east and the rising sun swelled blood red along the horizon.

Look yonder, said John Grady.

What.

Over yonder.

Two miles away riders had crested a rise. One, two. A third. Then they dropped from sight again.

Which way are they headed?

Well cousin I dont know for sure but I got a pretty good notion.

Rawlins sat holding the cigarette. We're goin to die in this goddamned country, he said.

No we aint.

You think they can track us on this ground?

I dont know. I dont know that they cant.

I'll tell you what, bud. They get us bayed up out here somewheres with the horses give out they're goin to have to come over the barrel of this rifle.

John Grady looked at him and he looked back out where the riders had been. I'd hate to have to shoot my way back to Texas, he said.

Where's your gun at?

In the saddlebag.

Rawlins lit the cigarette. I ever see that little son of a bitch again I'll kill him myself. I'm damned if I wont.

Let's go, said John Grady. They still got a lot of ground to cover. I'd rather to make a good run as a bad stand.

They rode out west with the sun at their back and their shadows horse and rider falling before them tall as trees. The country they found themselves in was old lava country and they kept to the edge of the rolling black gravel plain and kept watch behind them. They saw the riders again, south of where they would have put them. And then once more.

If them horses aint bottomed out I believe they'd be comin harder than that, said Rawlins.

I do too.

Midmorning they rode to the crest of a low volcanic ridge and turned the horses and sat watching.

What do you think? said Rawlins.

Well, they know we aint got the horse. That's for sure. They might not be as anxious to ride this ground as you and me.

You got that right.

They sat for a long time. Nothing moved.

I think they've quit us.

I do too.

Let's keep movin.

By late afternoon the horses were stumbling. They watered them out of their hats and drank the other canteen dry themselves and mounted again and rode on. They saw the riders no more. Toward evening they came upon a band of sheepherders camped on the far side of a deep arroyo that was floored with round white rocks. The sheepherders seemed to have selected the site with an eye to its defense as did the ancients of that country and they watched with great solemnity the riders making their way along the other side.

What do you think? said John Grady.

I think we ought to keep ridin. I'm kindly soured on the citizens in this part of the country.

I think you're right.

They rode on another mile and descended into the arroyo to look for water. They found none. They dismounted and led the horses, the four of them stumbling along into the deepening darkness, Rawlins still carrying the rifle, following the senseless tracks of birds or wild pigs in the sand.

Nightfall found them sitting on their blankets on the ground with the horses staked a few feet away. Just sitting in the dark with no fire, not speaking. After a while Rawlins said: We should of got water from them herders.

We'll find some water in the mornin.

I wish it was mornin.

John Grady didnt answer.

Goddamn Junior is goin to piss and moan and carry on all night. I know how he gets.

They probably think we've gone crazy.

Aint we?

You think they caught him?

I dont know.

I'm goin to turn in.

They lay in their blankets on the ground. The horses shifted uneasily in the dark.

I'll say one thing about him, said Rawlins.

Who?

Blevins.

What's that?

The little son of a bitch wouldnt stand still for nobody high-jackin his horse.

In the morning they left the horses in the arroyo and climbed up to watch the sun rise and see what the country afforded. It had been cold in the night in the sink and when the sun came up they turned and sat with their backs to it. To the north a thin spire of smoke stood in the windless air.

You reckon that's the sheepcamp? said Rawlins.

We better hope it is.

You want to ride back up there and see if they'll give us some water and some grub?

No.

I dont either.

They watched the country.

Rawlins rose and walked off with the rifle. After a while he came back with some nopal fruit in his hat and poured them out on a flat rock and sat peeling them with his knife.

You want some of these? he said.

John Grady walked over and squatted and got out his own knife. The nopal was still cool from the night and it stained their fingers blood red and they sat peeling the fruit and eating it and spitting the small hard seeds and picking the spines out of their fingers. Rawlins gestured at the countryside. There aint much happenin out there, is there?

John Grady nodded. Biggest problem we got is we could run

into them people and not even know it. We never even got a good look at their horses.

Rawlins spat. They got the same problem. They dont know us neither.

They'd know us.

Yeah, said Rawlins. You got a point.

Course we aint got no problem at all next to Blevins. He'd about as well to paint that horse red and go around blowin a horn.

Aint that the truth.

Rawlins wiped the blade of his knife on his trousers and folded it shut. I believe I'm losin ground with these things.

Peculiar thing is, what he says is true. It is his horse.

Well it's somebody's horse.

It damn sure dont belong to them Mexicans.

Yeah. Well he's got no way to prove it.

Rawlins put the knife in his pocket and sat inspecting his hat for nopal stickers. A goodlookin horse is like a good-lookin woman, he said. They're always more trouble than what they're worth. What a man needs is just one that will get the job done.

Where'd you hear that at?

I dont know.

John Grady folded away his knife. Well, he said. There's a lot of country out there.

Yep. Lot of country.

God knows where he's got to.

Rawlins nodded. I'll tell you what you told me.

What's that?

We aint seen the last of his skinny ass.

They rode all day upon the broad plain to the south. It was noon before they found water, a silty residue in the floor of an adobe tank. In the evening passing through a saddle in the low hills they jumped a spikehorn buck out of a stand of juniper and Rawlins shucked the rifle backward out of the bootleg scabbard and raised and cocked it and fired. He'd let go the reins and the horse bowed up and hopped sideways and stood trembling and he stepped down and ran to the spot where he'd seen the little buck and it lay dead in its blood on the ground. John Grady rode up leading Rawlins' horse. The buck was shot through the base of the skull and its eyes were just glazing. Rawlins ejected the spent shell and levered in a fresh round and lowered the hammer with his thumb and looked up.

That was a hell of a shot, said John Grady.

That was blind dumb-ass luck is what that was. I just raised up and shot.

Still a hell of a shot.

Let me have your beltknife. If we dont founder on deermeat I'm a chinaman.

They dressed out the deer and hung it in the junipers to cool and they made a foray on the slope for wood. They built a fire and they cut paloverde poles and cut forked uprights to lay them in and Rawlins skinned the buck out and sliced the meat in strips and draped it over the poles to smoke. When the fire had burned down he skewered the backstraps on two greenwood sticks and propped the sticks with rocks over the coals. Then they sat watching the meat brown and sniffed the smoke where fat dropped hissing in the coals.

John Grady walked out and unsaddled the horses and hobbled them and turned them out and came back with his blanket and saddle.

Here you go, he said.

What's that?

Salt.

I wish we had some bread.

How about some fresh corn and potatoes and apple cobbler?

Dont be a ass.

Aint them things done yet?

No. Set down. They wont never get done with you standin there thataway.

They ate the tenderloins one apiece and turned the strips of meat on the poles and lay back and rolled cigarettes.

I've seen them vaqueros worked for Blair cut a yearling heifer so thin you could see through the meat. They'd bone one out damn near in one long sheet. They'd hang the meat on poles all the way around the fire like laundry and if you come up on it at night you wouldnt know what it was. It was like lookin through somethin and seein its heart. They'd turn the meat and mend the fire in the night and you'd see em movin around inside it. You'd wake up in the night and this thing would be settin out there on the prairie in the wind and it would be glowin like a hot stove. Just red as blood.

This here meat's goin to taste like cedar, said John Grady.

I know it.

Coyotes were yapping along the ridge to the south. Rawlins leaned and tipped the ash from his cigarette into the fire and leaned back.

You ever think about dyin?

Yeah. Some. You?

Yeah. Some. You think there's a heaven?

Yeah. Dont you?

I dont know. Yeah. Maybe. You think you can believe in heaven if you dont believe in hell?

I guess you can believe what you want to.

Rawlins nodded. You think about all the stuff that can happen to you, he said. There aint no end to it.

You fixin to get religion on us?

No. Just sometimes I wonder if I wouldnt be better off if I did.

You aint fixin to quit me are you?

I said I wouldnt.

John Grady nodded.

You think them guts might draw a lion? said Rawlins.

Could.

You ever seen one?

No. You?

Just that one dead that Julius Ramsey killed with the dogs up on Grape Creek. He climbed up in the tree and knocked it out with a stick for the dogs to fight.

You think he really done that?

Yeah. I think probably he did.

John Grady nodded. He might well could of.

The coyotes yammered and ceased and then began again.

You think God looks out for people? said Rawlins.

Yeah. I guess He does. You?

Yeah. I do. Way the world is. Somebody can wake up and sneeze somewhere in Arkansas or some damn place and before you're done there's wars and ruination and all hell. You dont know what's goin to happen. I'd say He's just about got to. I dont believe we'd make it a day otherwise.

John Grady nodded.

You dont think them sons of bitches might of caught him do you?

Blevins?

Yeah.

I dont know. I thought you was glad to get shut of him.

I dont want to see nothin bad happen to him.

I dont either.

You reckon his name is Jimmy Blevins sure enough?

Who knows.

In the night the coyotes woke them and they lay in the dark and listened to them where they convened over the carcass of the deer, fighting and squalling like cats.

I want you to listen to that damned racket, said Rawlins.

He got up and got a stick from the fire and shouted at them and threw the stick. They hushed. He mended the fire and turned the meat on the greenwood racks. By the time he was back in his blankets they were at it again.

They rode all day the day following through the hill country to the west. As they rode they cut strips of the smoked and half dried deermeat and chewed on it and their hands were black and greasy and they wiped them on the withers of the horses and passed the canteen of water back and forth between them and admired the country. There were storms to the south and masses of clouds that moved slowly along the horizon with their long dark tendrils trailing in the rain. That night they camped on a ledge of rock above the plains and watched the lightning all along the horizon provoke from the seamless dark the distant mountain ranges again and again. Crossing the plain the next morning they came upon standing water in the bajadas and they watered the horses and drank rainwater from the rocks and they climbed steadily into the deepening cool of the mountains until in the evening of that day from the crest of the cordilleras they saw below them the country of which they'd been told. The grasslands lay in a deep violet haze and to the west thin flights of waterfowl were moving north before the sunset in the deep red galleries under the cloudbanks like schoolfish in a burning sea and on the foreland plain they saw vaqueros driving cattle before them through a gauze of golden dust.

They made camp on the south slope of the mountain and spread their blankets in the dry dirt under an overhanging ledge of rock. Rawlins took horse and rope and dragged up before their camp an entire dead tree and they built a great bonfire against the cold. Out on the plain in the shoreless night they could see like a reflection of their own fire in a dark lake the fire of the vaqueros five miles away. It rained in the night and the rain hissed in the fire and the horses came in out of the darkness and stood with their red eyes shifting and blinking and in the morning it was cold and gray and the sun a long time coming.

By noon they were on the plain riding through grass of a kind they'd not seen before. The path of the driven cattle lay through the grass like a place where water had run and by midafternoon they could see the herd before them moving west and within an hour they'd caught them up.

The vaqueros knew them by the way they sat their horses and they called them caballero and exchanged smoking material with them and told them about the country. They drove the cattle on to the west fording creeks and a small river and driving pockets of antelope and whitetail deer before them out of the stands of enormous cottonwoods through which they passed and they moved on until late in the day when they came to a fence and began to drift the cattle south. There was a road on the other side of the fence and in the road were the tracks of tires and the tracks of horses from the recent rains and a young girl came riding down the road and passed them and they ceased talking. She wore english riding boots and jodhpurs and a blue twill hacking jacket and she carried a ridingcrop and the horse she rode was a black Arabian saddlehorse. She'd been riding the horse in the river or in the ciénagas because the horse was wet to its belly and the leather fenders of the saddle were dark at their lower edges and her boots as well. She wore a flatcrowned hat of black felt with a wide brim and her black hair was loose under it and fell halfway to her waist and as she rode past she turned and smiled and touched the brim of the hat with her crop and the vaqueros touched their hatbrims one by one down to the last of those who'd pretended not even to see her as she passed. Then she pushed the horse into a gaited rack and disappeared down the road.

Rawlins looked at the caporal of the vaqueros but the caporal put his horse forward and rode up the line. Rawlins fell back among the riders and alongside John Grady.

Did you see that little darlin? he said.

John Grady didnt answer. He was still looking down the road where she'd gone. There was nothing there to see but he was looking anyway.

An hour later in the failing light they were helping the vaqueros drive the cattle into a holdingpen. The gerente had ridden up from the house and he sat his horse and picked his teeth and watched the work without comment. When they were done the caporal and another vaquero took them over and introduced them namelessly and the five of them rode together back down to the gerente's house and there in the kitchen at a metal table under a bare lightbulb the gerente questioned them closely as to their understanding of ranch work while the caporal seconded their every claim and the vaquero nodded and said that it was so and the caporal volunteered testimony on his own concerning the qualifications of the güeros of which they themselves were not even aware, dismissing doubt with a sweep of his hand as if to say that these were things known to everyone. The gerente leaned back in his chair and studied them. In the end they gave their names and spelled them and the gerente put them in his book and then they rose and shook hands and walked out in the early darkness where the moon was rising and the cattle were calling and the yellow squares of windowlight gave warmth and shape to an alien world.

They unsaddled the horses and turned them into the trap and followed the caporal up to the bunkhouse. A long adobe building of two rooms with a tin roof and concrete floors. In one room a dozen bunks of wood or metal. A small sheetiron stove. In the other room a long table with benches for seats and a woodburning cookstove. An old wooden safe that held glasses and tinware. A soapstone sink with a zinc-covered sideboard. The men were already at the table eating when they entered and they went to the sideboard and got cups and plates and stood at the stove and helped themselves to beans and tortillas and a rich stew made from kid and then went to the table where the vaqueros nodded to them and made expansive gestures for them to be seated, eating the while with one hand.

After dinner they sat at the table and smoked and drank coffee and the vaqueros asked them many questions about America and all the questions were about horses and cattle and none about them. Some had friends or relatives who had been there but to most the country to the north was little more than a rumor. A thing for which there seemed no accounting. Someone brought a coal-oil lamp to the table and lit it and shortly thereafter the generator shut down and the lightbulbs hanging by their cords from the ceiling dimmed to a thin orange wire and winked out. They listened with great attention as John Grady answered their questions and they nodded solemnly and they were careful of their demeanor that they not be thought to have opinions on what they heard for like most men skilled at their work they were scornful of any least suggestion of knowing anything not learned at first hand.

They carried their dishes to a galvanized tub full of water and soapcurd and they carried the lamp to their bunks at the farther end of the bunkhouse and unrolled the ticks down over the rusty springs and spread their blankets and undressed and blew out the lamp. Tired as they were they lay a long time in the dark after the vaqueros were asleep. They could hear them breathing deeply in the room that smelled of horses and leather and men and they could hear in the distance the new cattle still not bedded down in the holdingpen.

I believe these are some pretty good old boys, whispered Rawlins.

Yeah, I believe they are too.

You see them old highback centerfire rigs?

Yeah.

You reckon they think we're on the run down here?

Aint we?

Rawlins didnt answer. After a while he said: I like hearin the cattle out there.

Yeah. I do too.

He didnt say much about Rocha, did he?

Not a lot.

You reckon that was his daughter?

I'd say it was.

This is some country, aint it?

Yeah. It is. Go to sleep.

Bud?

Yeah.

This is how it was with the old waddies, aint it?

Yeah.

How long do you think you'd like to stay here?

About a hundred years. Go to sleep.

II

THE HACIENDA de Nuestra Señora de la Purísima Concepción was a ranch of eleven thousand hectares situated along the edge of the Bolsón de Cuatro Ciénagas in the state of Coahuila. The western sections ran into the Sierra de Anteojo to elevations of nine thousand feet but south and east the ranch occupied part of the broad barrial or basin floor of the bolsón and was well watered with natural springs and clear streams and dotted with marshes and shallow lakes or lagunas. In the lakes and in the streams were species of fish not known elsewhere on earth and birds and lizards and other forms of life as well all long relict here for the desert stretched away on every side.

La Purísima was one of very few ranches in that part of Mexico retaining the full complement of six square leagues of land allotted by the colonizing legislation of eighteen twenty-four and the owner Don Héctor Rocha y Villareal was one of the few hacendados who actually lived on the land he claimed, land which had been in his family for one hundred and seventy years. He was forty-seven years old and he was the first male heir in all that new world lineage to attain such an age.

He ran upwards of a thousand head of cattle on this land. He kept a house in Mexico City where his wife lived. He flew his own airplane. He loved horses. When he rode up to the gerente's house that morning he was accompanied by four friends and by a retinue of mozos and two packanimals saddled with hardwood kiacks, one empty, the other carrying their noon provisions. They were attended by a pack of greyhound dogs and the dogs were lean and silver in color and they flowed among the legs of the horses silent and fluid as running mercury and the horses paid them no mind at all. The hacendado halloed the house and the gerente emerged in his shirtsleeves and they spoke briefly and the gerente nodded and the hacendado spoke to his friends and then all rode on. When they passed the bunkhouse and rode through the gate and turned into the road upcountry some of the vaqueros were catching their horses in the trap and leading them out to saddle them for the day's work. John Grady and Rawlins stood in the doorway drinking their coffee.

Yonder he is, said Rawlins.

John Grady nodded and slung the dregs of coffee out into the yard.

Where the hell do you reckon they're goin? said Rawlins.

I'd say they're goin to run coyotes.

They aint got no guns.

They got ropes.

Rawlins looked at him. Are you shittin me?

I dont think so.

Well I'd damn sure like to see it.

I would too. You ready?

They worked two days in the holdingpens branding and earmarking and castrating and dehorning and inoculating. On the third day the vaqueros brought a small herd of wild three year old colts down from the mesa and penned them and in the evening Rawlins and John Grady walked out to look them over. They were bunched against the fence at the far side of the enclosure and they were a mixed lot, roans and duns and bays and a few paints and they were of varied size and conformation. John Grady opened the gate and he and Rawlins walked in and he closed it behind them. The horrified animals began to climb over one another and to break up and move along the fence in both directions.

That's as spooky a bunch of horses as I ever saw, said Rawlins.

They dont know what we are.

Dont know what we are?

I dont think so. I dont think they've ever seen a man afoot.

Rawlins leaned and spat.

You see anything there you'd have?

There's horses there.

Where at?

Look at that dark bay. Right yonder.

I'm lookin.

Look again.

That horse wont weigh eight hundred pounds.

Yeah he will. Look at the hindquarters on him. He'd make a cowhorse. Look at that roan yonder.

That coonfooted son of a bitch?

Well, yeah he is a little. All right. That other roan. That third one to the right.

The one with the white on him?

Yeah.

That's kindly a funny lookin horse to me.

No he aint. He's just colored peculiar.

You dont think that means nothin? He's got white feet.

That's a good horse. Look at his head. Look at the jaw on him. You got to remember their tails are all growed out.

Yeah. Maybe. Rawlins shook his head doubtfully. You used to be awful particular about horses. Maybe you just aint seen any in a long time.

John Grady nodded. Yeah, he said. Well. I aint forgot what they're supposed to look like.

The horses had grouped again at the far end of the pen and stood rolling their eyes and running their heads along each others' necks.

They got one thing goin for em, said Rawlins.

What's that.

They aint had no Mexican to try and break em.

John Grady nodded.

They studied the horses.

How many are there? said John Grady.

Rawlins looked them over. Fifteen. Sixteen.

I make it sixteen.

Sixteen then.

You think you and me could break all of em in four days?

Depends on what you call broke.

Just halfway decent greenbroke horses. Say six saddles. Double and stop and stand still to be saddled.

Rawlins took his tobacco from his pocket and pushed back his hat.

What you got in mind? he said.

Breakin these horses.

Why four days?

You think we could do it?

They intend puttin em in the rough-string? My feelin is that any horse broke in four days is liable to come unbroke in four more.

They're out of horses is how come em to be down here in the first place.

Rawlins dabbed tobacco into the cupped paper. You're tellin me that what we're lookin at here is our own string?

That's my guess.

We're lookin at ridin some coldjawed son of a bitch broke with one of them damned mexican ringbits.

Yeah.

Rawlins nodded. What would you do, sideline em?

Yep.

You think there's that much rope on the place?

I dont know.

You'd be a woreout sumbuck. I'll tell you that.

Think how good you'd sleep.

Rawlins put the cigarette in his mouth and fished about for a match. What else do you know that you aint told me?

Armando says the old man's got horses all over that mountain.

How many horses.

Somethin like four hundred head.

Rawlins looked at him. He popped the match and lit the cigarette and flipped the match away. What in the hell for?

He'd started a breeding program before the war.

What kind of horses?

Media sangres.

What the hell is that.

Quarterhorses, what we'd call em.

Yeah?

That roan yonder, said John Grady, is a flat-out Billy horse if he does have bad feet.

Where do you reckon he come from?

Where they all come from. Out of a horse called José Chiquito.

Little Joe?

Yeah.

The same horse?

The same horse.

Rawlins smoked thoughtfully.

Both of them horses were sold in Mexico, said John Grady. One and Two. What he's got up yonder is a big yeguada of mares out of the old Traveler-Ronda line of horses of Sheeran's.

What else? said Rawlins.

That's it.

Let's go talk to the man.

THEY STOOD in the kitchen with their hats in their hands and the gerente sat at the table and studied them.

Amansadores, he said.

Sí.

Ambos, he said.

Sí. Ambos.

He leaned back. He drummed his fingers on the metal tabletop.

Hay dieciseis caballos en el potrero, said John Grady. Podemos amansarlos en cuatro días.

They walked back across the yard to the bunkhouse to wash up for supper.

What did he say? said Rawlins.

He said we were full of shit. But in a nice way.

Is that a flat-out no do you reckon?

I dont think so. I dont think he can leave it at that.

They went to work on the green colts daybreak Sunday morning, dressing in the half dark in clothes still wet from their washing them the night before and walking out to the potrero before the stars were down, eating a cold tortilla wrapped around a scoop of cold beans and no coffee and carrying their fortyfoot maguey catchropes coiled over their shoulders. They carried saddleblankets and a bosalea or riding hackamore with a metal noseband and John Grady carried a pair of clean gunnysacks he'd slept on and his Hamley saddle with the stirrups already shortened.

They stood looking at the horses. The horses shifted and stood, gray shapes in the gray morning. Stacked on the ground outside the gate were coils of every kind of rope, cotton and manilla and plaited rawhide and maguey and ixtle down to lengths of old woven hair mecates and handplaited piecings of bindertwine. Stacked against the fence were the sixteen rope hackamores they'd spent the evening tying in the bunkhouse.

This bunch has done been culled once up on the mesa, aint it?

I'd say so.

What do they want with the mares?

They ride em down here.

Well, said Rawlins. I can see why they're hard on a horse. Puttin up with them bitches.

He shook his head and stuffed the last of the tortilla in his jaw and wiped his hands on his trousers and undid the wire and opened the gate.

John Grady followed him in and stood the saddle on the ground and went back out and brought in a handful of ropes and hackamores and squatted to sort them. Rawlins stood building his loop.

I take it you dont give a particular damn what order they come in, he said.

You take it correctly, cousin.

You dead set on sackin these varmints out?

Yep.

My old daddy always said that the purpose of breakin a horse was to ride it and if you got one to break you just as well to saddle up and climb aboard and get on with it.

John Grady grinned. Was your old daddy a certified peeler?

I never heard him claim to be. But I damn sure seen him hang and rattle a time or two.

Well you're fixin to see some more of it.

We goin to bust em twice?

What for?

I never saw one that completely believed it the first time or ever doubted it the second.

John Grady smiled. I'll make em believe, he said. You'll see.

I'm goin to tell you right now, cousin. This is a heathenish bunch.

What is it Blair says? No such thing as a mean colt?

No such thing as a mean colt, said Rawlins.

The horses were already moving. He took the first one that broke and rolled his loop and forefooted the colt and it hit the ground with a tremendous thump. The other horses flared and bunched and looked back wildly. Before the colt could struggle up John Grady had squatted on its neck and pulled its head up and to one side and was holding the horse by the muzzle with the long bony head pressed against his chest and the hot sweet breath of it flooding up from the dark wells of its nostrils over his face and neck like news from another world. They did not smell like horses. They smelled like what they were, wild animals. He held the horse's face against his chest and he could feel along his inner thighs the blood pumping through the arteries and he could smell the fear and he cupped his hand over the horse's eyes and stroked them and he did not stop talking to the horse at all, speaking in a low steady voice and telling it all that he intended to do and cupping the animal's eyes and stroking the terror out.

Rawlins took one of the lengths of siderope from around his neck where he'd hung them and made a slipnoose and hitched it around the pastern of the hind leg and drew the leg up and halfhitched it to the horse's forelegs. He freed the catchrope and pitched it away and took the hackamore and they fitted it over the horse's muzzle and ears and John Grady ran this thumb in the animal's mouth and Rawlins fitted the mouthrope and then slipnoosed a second siderope to the other rear leg. Then he tied both sideropes to the hackamore.

You all set? he said.

All set.

He let go the horse's head and rose and stepped away. The horse struggled up and turned and shot out one hind foot and snatched itself around in a half circle and fell over. It got up and kicked again and fell again. When it got up the third time it stood kicking and snatching its head about in a little dance. It stood. It walked away and stood again. Then it shot out a hindleg and fell again.

It lay there for a while thinking things over and when it got up it stood for a minute and then it hopped up and down three times and then it just stood glaring at them. Rawlins had got his catchrope and was building his loop again. The other horses watched with great interest from the far side of the potrero.

These sumbucks are as crazy as a shithouse rat, he said.

You pick out the one you think is craziest, said John Grady, and I'll give you a finished horse this time Sunday week.

Finished for who?

To your satisfaction.

Bullshit, said Rawlins.

By the time they had three of the horses sidelined in the trap blowing and glaring about there were several vaqueros at the gate drinking coffee in a leisurely fashion and watching the proceedings. By midmorning eight of the horses stood tied and the other eight were wilder than deer, scattering along the fence and bunching and running in a rising sea of dust as the day warmed, coming to reckon slowly with the remorselessness of this rendering of their fluid and collective selves into that condition of separate and helpless paralysis which seemed to be among them like a creeping plague. The entire complement of vaqueros had come from the bunkhouse to watch and by noon all sixteen of the mesteños were standing about in the potrero sidehobbled to their own hackamores and faced about in every direction and all communion among them broken. They looked like animals trussed up by children for fun and they stood waiting for they knew not what with the voice of the breaker still running in their brains like the voice of some god come to inhabit them.

When they went down to the bunkhouse for dinner the vaqueros seemed to treat them with a certain deference but whether it was the deference accorded the accomplished or that accorded to mental defectives they were unsure. No one asked them their opinion of the horses or queried them as to their method. When they went back up to the trap in the afternoon there were some twenty people standing about looking at the horses—women, children, young girls and men—and all waiting for them to return.

Where the hell did they come from? said Rawlins.

I dont know.

Word gets around when the circus come to town, dont it?

They passed nodding through the crowd and entered the trap and fastened the gate.

You picked one out? said John Grady.

Yeah. For pure crazy I nominate that bucketheaded son of a bitch standin right yonder.

The grullo?

Grullo-lookin.

The man's a judge of horseflesh.

He's a judge of craziness.

He watched while John Grady walked up to the animal and tied a twelvefoot length of rope to the hackamore. Then he led it through the gate out of the potrero and into the corral where the horses would be ridden. Rawlins thought the horse would shy or try to rear but it didnt. He got the sack and hobbleropes and came up and while John Grady talked to the horse he hobbled the front legs together and then took the mecate rope and handed John Grady the sack and he held the horse while for the next quarter hour John Grady floated the sack over the animal and under it and rubbed its head with the sack and passed it across the horse's face and ran it up and down and between the animal's legs talking to the horse the while and rubbing against it and leaning against it. Then he got the saddle.

What good do you think it does to waller all over a horse thataway? said Rawlins.

I dont know, said John Grady. I aint a horse.

He lifted the blanket and placed it on the animal's back and smoothed it and stood stroking the animal and talking to it and then he bent and picked up the saddle and lifted it with the cinches strapped up and the off stirrup hung over the horn and sat it on the horse's back and rocked it into place. The horse never moved. He bent and reached under and pulled up the strap and cinched it. The horse's ears went back and he talked to it and then pulled up the cinch again and he leaned against the horse and talked to it just as if it were neither crazy nor lethal. Rawlins looked toward the corral gate. There were fifty or more people watching. Folk were picnicking on the ground. Fathers held up babies. John Grady lifted off the stirrup from the saddlehorn and let it drop. Then he hauled up the cinchstrap again and buckled it. All right, he said.

Hold him, said Rawlins.

He held the mecate while Rawlins undid the sideropes from the hackamore and knelt and tied them to the front hobbles. Then they slipped the hackamore off the horse's head and John Grady raised the bosalea and gently fitted it over the horse's nose and fitted the mouthrope and headstall. He gathered the reins and looped them over the horse's head and nodded and Rawlins knelt and undid the hobbles and pulled the slipnooses until the siderope loops fell to the ground at the horse's rear hooves. Then he stepped away.

John Grady put one foot in the stirrup and pressed himself flat against the horse's shoulder talking to it and then swung up into the saddle.

The horse stood stock still. It shot out one hindfoot to test the air and stood again and then it threw itself sideways and twisted and kicked and stood snorting. John Grady touched it up in the ribs with his bootheels and it stepped forward. He reined it and it turned. Rawlins spat in disgust. John Grady turned the horse again and came back by.

What the hell kind of a bronc is that? said Rawlins. You think that's what these people paid good money to see?

By dark he'd ridden eleven of the sixteen horses. Not all of them so tractable. Someone had built a fire on the ground outside the potrero and there were something like a hundred people gathered, some come from the pueblo of La Vega six miles to the south, some from farther. He rode the last five horses by the light of that fire, the horses dancing, turning in the light, their red eyes flashing. When they were done the horses stood in the potrero or stepped about trailing their hackamore ropes over the ground with such circumspection not to tread upon them and snatch down their sore noses that they moved with an air of great elegance and seemliness. The wild and frantic band of mustangs that had circled the potrero that morning like marbles swirled in a jar could hardly be said to exist and the animals whinnied to one another in the dark and answered back as if some one among their number were missing, or some thing.

When they walked down to the bunkhouse in the dark the bonfire was still burning and someone had brought a guitar and someone else a mouth-harp. Three separate strangers offered them a drink from bottles of mescal before they were clear of the crowd.

The kitchen was empty and they got their dinner from the stove and sat at the table. Rawlins watched John Grady. He was chewing woodenly and half tottering on the bench.

You aint tired are you, bud? he said.

No, said John Grady. I was tired five hours ago.

Rawlins grinned. Dont drink no more of that coffee. It'll keep you awake.

When they walked out in the morning at daybreak the fire was still smoldering and there were four or five men lying asleep on the ground, some with blankets and some without. Every horse in the potrero watched them come through the gate.

You remember how they come? said Rawlins.

Yeah. I remember em. I know you remember your buddy yonder.

Yeah, I know the son of a bitch.

When he walked up to the horse with the sack it turned and went trotting. He walked it down against the fence and picked up the rope and pulled it around and it stood quivering and he walked up to it and began to talk to it and then to stroke it with the sack. Rawlins went to fetch the blankets and the saddle and the bosalea.

By ten that night he'd ridden the entire remuda of sixteen horses and Rawlins had ridden them a second time each. They rode them again Tuesday and on Wednesday morning at daybreak with the first horse saddled and the sun not up John Grady rode toward the gate.

Open her up, he said.

Let me saddle a catch-horse.

We aint got time.

If that son of a bitch sets your ass out in the stickers you'll have time.

I guess I'd better stay in the saddle then.

Let me saddle up one of these good horses.

All right.

He rode out of the trap leading Rawlins' horse and waited while Rawlins shut the gate and mounted up beside him. The green horses stepped and sidled nervously.

This is kindly the blind leadin the blind, aint it?

Rawlins nodded. It's sort of like old T-Bone Watts when he

worked for daddy they all fussed about him havin bad breath. He told em it was bettern no breath at all.

John Grady grinned and booted the horse forward into a trot and they set out up the road.

Midafternoon he'd ridden all the horses again and while Rawlins worked with them in the trap he rode the little grullo of Rawlins' choice up into the country. Two miles above the ranch where the road ran by sedge and willow and wild plum along the edge of the laguna she rode past him on the black horse.

He heard the horse behind him and would have turned to look but that he heard it change gaits. He didnt look at her until the Arabian was alongside his horse, stepping with its neck arched and one eye on the mesteño not with wariness but some faint equine disgust. She passed five feet away and turned her fineboned face and looked full at him. She had blue eyes and she nodded or perhaps she only lowered her head slightly to better see what sort of horse he rode, just the slightest tilt of the broad black hat set level on her head, the slightest lifting of the long black hair. She passed and the horse changed gaits again and she sat the horse more than well, riding erect with her broad shoulders and trotting the horse up the road. The mesteño had stopped and sulled in the road with its forefeet spread and he sat looking after her. He'd half meant to speak but those eyes had altered the world forever in the space of a heartbeat. She disappeared beyond the lakeside willows. A flock of small birds rose up and passed back over him with thin calls.

That evening when Antonio and the gerente came up to the trap to inspect the horses he was teaching the grullo to back with Rawlins in the saddle. They watched, the gerente picking his teeth. Antonio rode the two horses that were standing saddled, sawing them back and forth in the corral and pulling them up short. He dismounted and nodded and he and the gerente looked over the horses in the other wing of the corral and then they left. Rawlins and John Grady looked at each other. They unsaddled the horses and turned them in with the remuda and walked back down to the house carrying their saddles and gear and washed up for supper. The vaqueros were at the table and they got their plates and helped themselves at the stove and got their coffee and came to the table and swung a leg over and sat down. There was a clay dish of tortillas in the center of the table with a towel over it and when John Grady pointed and asked that it be passed there came hands from both sides of the table to take up the dish and hand it down in this manner like a ceremonial bowl.

Three days later they were in the mountains. The caporal had sent a mozo with them to cook and see to the horses and he'd sent three young vaqueros not much older than they. The mozo was an old man with a bad leg named Luis who had fought at Torreón and San Pedro and later at Zacatecas and the boys were boys from the country, two of them born on the hacienda. Only one of the three had ever been as far as Monterrey. They rode up into the mountains trailing three horses apiece in their string with packhorses to haul the grub and cooktent and they hunted the wild horses in the upland forests in the pine and madroño and in the arroyos where they'd gone to hide and they drove them pounding over the high mesas and penned them in the stone ravine fitted ten years earlier with fence and gate and there the horses milled and squealed and clambered at the rock slopes and turned upon one another biting and kicking while John Grady walked among them in the sweat and dust and bedlam with his rope as if they were no more than some evil dream of horse. They camped at night on the high headlands where their windtattered fire sawed about in the darkness and Luis told them tales of the country and the people who lived in it and the people who died and how they died. He'd loved horses all his life and he and his father and two brothers had fought in the cavalry and his father and his brothers had died in the cavalry but they'd all despised Victoriano Huerta above all other men and the deeds of Huerta above all other visited evils. He said that compared to Huerta Judas was himself but another Christ and one of the young vaqueros looked away and another blessed himself. He said that war had destroyed the country and that men believe the cure for war is war as the curandero prescribes the serpent's flesh for its bite. He spoke of his campaigns in the deserts of Mexico and he told them of horses killed under him and he said that the souls of horses mirror the souls of men more closely than men suppose and that horses also love war. Men say they only learn this but he said that no creature can learn that which his heart has no shape to hold. His own father said that no man who has not gone to war horseback can ever truly understand the horse and he said that he supposed he wished that this were not so but that it was so.

Lastly he said that he had seen the souls of horses and that it was a terrible thing to see. He said that it could be seen under certain circumstances attending the death of a horse because the horse shares a common soul and its separate life only forms it out of all horses and makes it mortal. He said that if a person understood the soul of the horse then he would understand all horses that ever were.

They sat smoking, watching the deepest embers of the fire where the red coals cracked and broke.

Y de los hombres? said John Grady.

The old man shaped his mouth how to answer. Finally he said that among men there was no such communion as among horses and the notion that men can be understood at all was probably an illusion. Rawlins asked him in his bad spanish if there was a heaven for horses but he shook his head and said that a horse had no need of heaven. Finally John Grady asked him if it were not true that should all horses vanish from the face of the earth the soul of the horse would not also perish for there would be nothing out of which to replenish it but the old man only said that it was pointless to speak of there being no horses in the world for God would not permit such a thing.

They drove the mares down through the draws and arroyos out of the mountains and across the watered grasslands of the bolsón and penned them. They were at this work for three weeks until by the end of April they had over eighty mares in the trap, most of them halterbroke, some already sorted out for saddlehorses. By then the roundup was underway and droves of cattle were moving daily down out of the open country onto the ranch pastures and although some of the vaqueros had no more than two or three horses to their string the new horses stayed in the trap. On the second morning of May the red Cessna plane came in from the south and circled the ranch and banked and dropped and glided from sight beyond the trees.

An hour later John Grady was standing in the ranch house kitchen with his hat in his hands. A woman was washing dishes at the sink and a man was sitting at the table reading a newspaper. The woman wiped her hands on her apron and went off into another part of the house and in a few minutes she returned. Un ratito, she said.

John Grady nodded. Gracias, he said.

The man rose and folded the newspaper and crossed the kitchen and came back with a wooden rack of butcher and boning knives together with an oilstone and set them out on the paper. At the same moment Don Héctor appeared in the doorway and stood looking at John Grady.

He was a spare man with broad shoulders and graying hair and he was tall in the manner of norteños and light of skin. He entered the kitchen and introduced himself and John Grady shifted his hat to his left hand and they shook hands.

María, said the hacendado. Café por favor.

He held out his hand palm upward toward the doorway and John Grady crossed the kitchen and entered the hall. The house was cool and quiet and smelled of wax and flowers. A tallcase clock stood in the hallway to the left. The brass weights stirred behind the casement doors, the pendulum slowly swept. He turned to look back and the hacendado smiled and extended his hand toward the diningroom doorway. Pásale, he said.

They sat at a long table of english walnut. The walls of the room were covered with blue damask and hung with portraits of men and horses. At the end of the room was a walnut sideboard with some chafingdishes and decanters set out upon it and along the windowsill outside taking the sun were four cats. Don Héctor reached behind him and took a china ashtray from the sideboard and placed it before them and took from his shirtpocket a small tin box of english cigarettes and opened them and offered them to John Grady and John Grady took one.

Gracias, he said.

The hacendado placed the tin on the table between them and took a silver lighter from his pocket and lit the boy's cigarette and then his own.

Gracias.

The man blew a thin stream of smoke slowly downtable and smiled.

Bueno, he said. We can speak english.

Como le convenga, said John Grady.

Armando tells me that you understand horses.

I've been around em some.

The hacendado smoked thoughtfully. He seemed to be waiting for more to be said. The man who'd been sitting in the kitchen reading the paper entered the room with a silver tray carrying a coffee service with cups and creampitcher and a sugarbowl together with a plate of bizcochos. He set the tray on the table and stood a moment and the hacendado thanked him and he went out again.

Don Héctor set out the cups himself and poured the coffee and nodded at the tray. Please help yourself, he said.

Thank you. I just take it black.

You are from Texas.

Yessir.

The hacendado nodded again. He sipped his coffee. He was seated sideways to the table with his legs crossed. He flexed his foot in the chocolatecolored veal boot and turned and looked at John Grady and smiled.

Why are you here? he said.

John Grady looked at him. He looked down the table where the shadows of the sunning cats sat in a row like cutout cats all leaning slightly aslant. He looked at the hacendado again.

I just wanted to see the country, I reckon. Or we did.

May I ask how old are you?

Sixteen.

The hacendado raised his eyebrows. Sixteen, he said.

Yessir.

The hacendado smiled again. When I was sixteen I told people I was eighteen.

John Grady sipped his coffee.

Your friend is sixteen also?

Seventeen.

But you are the leader.

We dont have no leaders. We're just buddies.

Of course.

He nudged the plate forward. Please, he said. Help yourself.

Thank you. I just got up from the breakfast table.

The hacendado tipped the ash from his cigarette into the china ashtray and sat back again.

What is your opinion of the mares, he said.

There's some good mares in that bunch.

Yes. Do you know a horse called Three Bars?

That's a thoroughbred horse.

You know the horse?

I know he run in the Brazilian Grand Prix. I think he come out of Kentucky but he's owned by a man named Vail out of Douglas Arizona.

Yes. The horse was foaled at Monterey Farm in Paris Kentucky. The stallion I have bought is a half brother out of the same mare.

Yessir. Where's he at?

He is enroute.

He's where?

Enroute. From Mexico. The hacendado smiled. He has been standing at stud.

You intend to raise racehorses?

No. I intend to raise quarterhorses.

To use here on the ranch?

Yes.

You aim to breed this stallion to your mares.

Yes. What is your opinion?

I dont have a opinion. I've known a few breeders and some with a world of experience but I've noticed they were all pretty short on opinions. I do know there's been some good cowhorses sired out of thoroughbreds.

Yes. How much importance do you give to the mare?

Same as the sire. In my opinion.

Most breeders place more confidence in the horse.

Yessir. They do.

The hacendado smiled. I happen to agree with you.

John Grady leaned and tipped the ash from his cigarette. You dont have to agree with me.

No. Nor you with me.

Yessir.

Tell me about the horses up on the mesa.

There may be a few of them good mares still up there but not many. The rest I'd pretty much call scrubs. Even some of them might make a half decent cowhorse. Just all around using kind of a horse. Spanish ponies, what we used to call em. Chihuahua horses. Old Barb stock. They're small and they're a little on the light side and they dont have the hindquarters you'd want in a cuttinghorse but you can rope off of em . . .

He stopped. He looked at the hat in his lap and ran his fingers along the crease and looked up. I aint tellin you nothin you dont know.

The hacendado took up the coffeepitcher and poured their cups.

Do you know what a criollo is?

Yessir. That's a argentine horse.

Do you know who Sam Jones was?

I do if you're talkin about a horse.

Crawford Sykes?

That's another of Uncle Billy Anson's horses. I heard about that horse all my life.

My father bought horses from Mr Anson.

Uncle Billy and my grandaddy were friends. They were born within three days of each other. He was the seventh son of the Earl of Litchfield. His wife was a actress on the stage.

You are from Christoval?

San Angelo. Or just outside of San Angelo.

The hacendado studied him.

Do you know a book called *The Horse of America*, by Wallace?

Yessir. I've read it front to back.

The hacendado leaned back in his chair. One of the cats rose and stretched.

You rode here from Texas.

Yessir.

You and your friend.

Yessir.

Just the two of you?

John Grady looked at the table. The paper cat stepped thin and slant among the shapes of cats thereon. He looked up again. Yessir, he said. Just me and him.

The hacendado nodded and stubbed out his cigarette and pushed back his chair. Come, he said. I will show you some horses.

THEY SAT opposite on their bunks with their elbows on their knees leaning forward and looking down at their folded hands. After a while Rawlins spoke. He didnt look up.

It's a opportunity for you. Aint no reason for you to turn it down that I can see.

If you dont want me to I wont. I'll stick right here.

It aint like you was goin off someplace.

We'll still be workin together. Bringin in horses and all.

Rawlins nodded. John Grady watched him.

You just say the word and I'll tell him no.

Aint no reason to do that, said Rawlins. Its a opportunity for you.

In the morning they ate breakfast and Rawlins went out to work the pens. When he came in at noon John Grady's tick was rolled up at the head of his bunk and his gear was gone. Rawlins went on to the back to wash up for dinner.

THE BARN was built on the english style and it was sheathed with milled one by fours and painted white and it had a cupola and a weathervane on top of the cupola. His room was at the far end next to the saddleroom. Across the bay was another cubicle where there lived an old groom who'd worked for Rocha's father. When John Grady led his horse through the barn the old man came out and stood and looked at the horse. Then he looked at its feet. Then he looked at John Grady. Then he turned and went back into his room and shut the door.

In the afternoon while he was working one of the new mares in the corral outside the barn the old man came out and watched him. John Grady said him a good afternoon and the old man nodded and said one back. He watched the mare. He said she was stocky. He said rechoncha and John Grady didnt know what it meant and he asked the old man and the old man made a barrel shape with his arms and John Grady thought he meant that she was pregnant and he said no she wasnt and the old man shrugged and went back in.

When he took the mare back to the barn the old man was pulling the cinchstrap on the black Arabian. The girl stood with her back to him. When the shadow of the mare darkened the bay door she turned and looked.

Buenas tardes, he said.

Buenas tardes, she said. She reached and slid her fingers under the strap to check it. He stood at the bay door. She raised up and passed the reins over the horse's head and put her foot in the stirrup and stood up into the saddle and turned the horse and rode down the bay and out the door.

That night as he lay in his cot he could hear music from the house and as he was drifting to sleep his thoughts were of horses and of the open country and of horses. Horses still wild on the mesa who'd never seen a man afoot and who knew nothing of him or his life yet in whose souls he would come to reside forever.

They went up into the mountains a week later with the mozo and two of the vaqueros and after the vaqueros had turned in in their blankets he and Rawlins sat by the fire on the rim of the mesa drinking coffee. Rawlins took out his tobacco and John Grady took out cigarettes and shook the pack at him. Rawlins put his tobacco back.

Where'd you get the readyrolls?

In La Vega.

He nodded. He took a brand from the fire and lit the cigarette and John Grady leaned and lit his own.

You say she goes to school in Mexico City?

Yeah.

How old is she?

Seventeen.

Rawlins nodded. What kind of a school is it she goes to?

I dont know. It's some kind of a prep school or somethin.

Fancy sort of school.

Yeah. Fancy sort of school.

Rawlins smoked. Well, he said. She's a fancy sort of girl.

No she aint.

Rawlins was leaning against his propped saddle, sitting with his legs crossed sideways on to the fire. The sole of his right boot had come loose and he'd fastened it back with hogrings stapled through the welt. He looked at the cigarette.

Well, he said. I've told you before but I dont reckon you'll listen now any more than you done then.

Yeah. I know.

I just figure you must enjoy cryin yourself to sleep at night.

John Grady didnt answer.

This one of course she probably dates guys got their own airplanes let alone cars.

You're probably right.

I'm glad to hear you say it.

It dont help nothin though, does it?

Rawlins sucked on the cigarette. They sat for a long time. Finally he pitched the stub of the cigarette into the fire. I'm goin to bed, he said.

Yeah, said John Grady. I guess that's a good idea.

They spread their soogans and he pulled off his boots and stood them beside him and stretched out in his blankets. The fire had burned to coals and he lay looking up at the stars in their places and the hot belt of matter that ran the chord of the dark vault overhead and he put his hands on the ground at either side of him and pressed them against the earth and in that coldly burning canopy of black he slowly turned dead center to the world, all of it taut and trembling and moving enormous and alive under his hands.

What's her name? said Rawlins in the darkness.

Alejandra. Her name is Alejandra.

Sunday afternoon they rode into the town of La Vega on horses they'd been working out of the new string. They'd had their hair cut with sheepshears by an esquilador at the ranch and the backs of their necks above their collars were white as scars and they wore their hats cocked forward on their heads and they looked from side to side as they jogged along as if to challenge the countryside or anything it might hold. They raced the animals on the road at a fifty-cent bet and John Grady won and they swapped horses and he won on Rawlins' horse. They rode the horses at a gallop and they rode them at a trot and the horses were hot and lathered and squatted and stamped in the road and the campesinos afoot in the road with baskets of garden-stuff or pails covered with cheesecloth would press to the edge of the road or climb through the roadside brush and cactus to watch wide eyed the young horsemen on their horses passing and the horses mouthing froth and champing and the riders calling to one another in their alien tongue and passing in a muted fury that seemed scarcely to be contained in the space allotted them and yet leaving all unchanged where they had been: dust, sunlight, a singing bird.

In the tienda the topmost shirts folded upon the shelves when shaken out retained a square of paler color where dust had settled on the cloth or sun had faded it or both. They sorted through the stacks to find one with sleeves long enough for Rawlins, the woman holding out the sleeve along the out-stretched length of his arm, the pins caught in her mouth like a seamstress where she meant to refold, repin the shirt, shaking her head doubtfully. They carried stiff new canvas pants to the rear of the store and tried them on in a bedroom that had three beds in it and a cold concrete floor that had once been painted green. They sat on one of the beds and counted their money.

How much are these britches if they're fifteen pesos?

Just remember that two pesos is two bits.

You remember it. How much are they?

A dollar and eighty-seven cents.

Hell, said Rawlins. We're in good shape. We get paid in five days.

They bought socks and underwear and they piled everything on the counter while the woman totted up the figures. Then she wrapped the new clothes in two separate parcels and tied them with string.

What have you got left? said John Grady.

Four dollars and somethin.

Get a pair of boots.

I lack some havin enough.

I'll let you have the difference.

You sure?

Yeah.

We got to have some operatin capital for this evenin.

We'll still have a couple of dollars. Go on.

What if you want to buy that sweet thing a soda pop?

It'll set me back about four cents. Go on.

Rawlins handled the boots dubiously. He stood one against the sole of his own raised boot.

These things are awful small.

Try these.

Black?

Sure. Why not.

Rawlins pulled on the new boots and walked up and down the floor. The woman nodded approvingly.

What do you think? said John Grady.

They're all right. These underslung heels take some gettin used to.

Let's see you dance.

Do what?

Dance.

Rawlins looked at the woman and he looked at John Grady. Shit, he said. You're lookin at a dancin fool.

Hit it there a few steps.

Rawlins executed a nimble ninestep stomp on the old board floor and stood grinning in the dust he'd raised.

Qué guapo, said the woman.

John Grady grinned and reached in his pocket for his money.

We've forgot to get gloves, said Rawlins.

Gloves?

Gloves. We get done sportin we're goin to have to go back to work.

You got a point.

Them old hot maggie ropes have eat my hands about up.

John Grady looked at his own hands. He asked the woman where the gloves were and they bought a pair apiece.

They stood at the counter while she wrapped them. Rawlins was looking down at his boots.

The old man's got some good silk manilla ropes in the barn, said John Grady. I'll slip one out to you quick as I get a chance.

Black boots, said Rawlins. Aint that the shits? I always wanted to be a badman.

ALTHOUGH THE NIGHT was cool the double doors of the grange stood open and the man selling the tickets was seated in a chair on a raised wooden platform just within the doors so that he must lean down to each in a gesture akin to benevolence and take their coins and hand them down their tickets or pass upon the ticketstubs of those who were only returning from outside. The old adobe hall was buttressed along its outer walls with piers not all of which had been a part of its design and there were no windows and the walls were swagged and cracked. A string of electric bulbs ran the length of the hall at either side and the bulbs were covered with paper bags that had been painted and the brushstrokes showed through in the light and the reds and greens and blues were all muted and much of a piece. The floor was swept but there were pockets of seeds underfoot and drifts of straw and at the far end of the hall a small orchestra labored on a stage of grainpallets under a bandshell rigged from sheeting. Along the foot of the stage were lights set in fruitcans among colored crepe that smoldered throughout the night. The mouths of the cans were lensed with tinted cellophane and they cast upon the sheeting a shadowplay in the lights and smoke of antic demon players and a pair of goathawks arced chittering through the partial darkness overhead.

John Grady and Rawlins and a boy named Roberto from the ranch stood just beyond the reach of light at the door among the cars and wagons and passed among themselves a pint medicinebottle of mescal. Roberto held the bottle to the light.

A las chicas, he said.

He drank and handed off the bottle. They drank. They poured salt from a paper onto their wrists and licked it off and Roberto pushed the cob stopper into the neck of the bottle and hid the bottle behind the tire of a parked truck and they passed around a pack of chewing gum.

Listos? he said.

Listos.

She was dancing with a tall boy from the San Pablo ranch and she wore a blue dress and her mouth was red. He and Rawlins and Roberto stood with other youths along the wall and watched the dancers and watched beyond the dancers the young girls at the far side of the hall. He moved along past the groups. The air smelled of straw and sweat and a rich spice of colognes. Under the bandshell the accordion player struggled with his instrument and slammed his boot on the boards in countertime and stepped back and the trumpet player came forward. Her eyes above the shoulder of her partner swept across him where he stood. Her black hair done up in a blue ribbon and the nape of her neck pale as porcelain. When she turned again she smiled.

He'd never touched her and her hand was small and her waist so slight and she looked at him with great forthrightness and smiled and put her face against his shoulder. They turned under the lights. A long trumpet note guided the dancers on their separate and collective paths. Moths circled the paper lights aloft and the goathawks passed down the wires and flared and arced upward into the darkness again.

She spoke in an english learned largely from schoolbooks and he tested each phrase for the meanings he wished to hear, repeating them silently to himself and then questioning them anew. She said that she was glad that he'd come.

I told you I would.

Yes.

They turned, the trumpet rapped.

Did you not think I would?

She tossed her head back and looked at him, smiling, her eyes aglint. Al contrario, she said. I knew you would come.

At the band's intermission they made their way to the refreshment stand and he bought two lemonades in paper cones and they went out and walked in the night air. They walked along the road and there were other couples in the road and they passed and wished them a good evening. The air was cool and it smelled of earth and perfume and horses. She took his arm and she laughed and called him a mojado-reverso, so rare a creature and one to be treasured. He told her about his life. How his grandfather was dead and the ranch sold. They sat on a low concrete watertrough and with her shoes in her lap and her naked feet crossed in the dust she drew patterns in the dark water with her finger. She'd been away at school for three years. Her mother lived in Mexico and she went to the house on Sundays for dinner and sometimes she and her mother would dine alone in the city and go to the theatre or the ballet. Her mother thought that life on the hacienda was lonely and yet living in the city she seemed to have few friends.

She becomes angry with me because I always want to come here. She says that I prefer my father to her.

Do you?

She nodded. Yes. But that is not why I come. Anyway, she says I will change my mind.

About coming here?

About everything.

She looked at him and smiled. Shall we go in?

He looked toward the lights. The music had started.

She stood and bent with one hand on his shoulder and slipped on her shoes.

I will introduce you to my friends. I will introduce you to Lucía. She is very pretty. You will see.

I bet she aint as pretty as you.

Oh my. You must be careful what you say. Besides it is not true. She is prettier.

He rode back alone with the smell of her perfume on his shirt. The horses were still tied and standing at the edge of the barn but he could not find Rawlins or Roberto. When he untied his horse the other two tossed their heads and whinnied softly to go. Cars were starting up in the yard and groups of people were moving along the road and he untracted the greenbroke horse out from the lights and into the road before mounting up. A mile from the town a car passed full of young men and they were going fast and he reined the horse to the side of the road and the horse skittered and danced in the glare of the headlights and as they passed they called out at him and someone threw an empty beercan. The horse reared and pitched and kicked out and he held it under him and talked to it as if nothing at all had happened and after a while they went on again. The boil of dust the car had left lay before them down the narrow straight as far as he could see roiling slowly in the starlight like something enormous uncoiling out of the earth. He thought the horse had handled itself well and as he rode he told it so.

THE HACENDADO had bought the horse through an agent sight unseen at the spring sales in Lexington and he'd sent Armando's brother Antonio to get the animal and bring it back. Antonio left the ranch in a 1941 International flatbed truck towing a homemade sheetmetal trailer and he was gone two months. He carried with him letters in both english and spanish signed by Don Héctor stating his business and he carried a brown bank envelope tied with a string in which was a great deal of money in both dollars and pesos together with sight-drafts on banks in Houston and Memphis. He spoke no english and he could neither read nor write. When he got back the envelope was gone together with the spanish letter but he had the english letter and it was separated into three parts along the lines of its folding and it was dogeared and coffeestained and stained with other stains some of which may have been blood. He'd been in jail once in Kentucky, once in Tennessee, and three times in Texas. When he pulled into the yard he got out and walked stiffly to the house and knocked at the kitchen door. María let him in and he stood with his hat in his hand while she went for the hacendado. When the hacendado entered the kitchen they shook hands gravely and the hacendado asked after his health and he said that it was excellent and handed him the pieces of the letter together with a sheaf of bills and receipts from cafes and gas stations and feedstores and jails and he handed him the money he had left including the change in his pockets and he handed him the keys to the truck and lastly he handed him the factura from the Mexican aduana at Piedras Negras together with a long manilla envelope tied with a blue ribbon that contained the papers on the horse and the bill of sale.

Don Héctor piled the money and the receipts and the papers on the sideboard and put the keys in his pocket. He asked if the truck had proved satisfactory.

Sí, said Antonio. Es una troca muy fuerte.

Bueno, said the hacendado. Y el caballo?

Está un poco cansado de su viaje, pero es muy bonito.

So he was. He was a deep chestnut in color and stood sixteen hands high and weighed about fourteen hundred pounds and he was well muscled and heavily boned for his breed. When they brought him back from the Distrito Federal in the same trailer in the third week of May and John Grady and Sr Rocha walked out to the barn to look at him John Grady simply pushed open the door to the stall and entered and walked up to the horse and leaned against it and began to rub it and talk to it softly in spanish. The hacendado offered no advice about the horse at all. John Grady walked all around it talking to it. He lifted up one front hoof and examined it.

Have you ridden him? he said.

But of course.

I'd like to ride him. Con su permiso.

The hacendado nodded. Yes, he said. Of course.

He came out of the stall and shut the door and they stood looking at the stallion.

Le gusta? said the hacendado.

John Grady nodded. That's a hell of a horse, he said.

In the days to follow the hacendado would come up to the corral where they'd shaped the manada and he and John Grady would walk among the mares and John Grady would argue their points and the hacendado would muse and walk away a fixed distance and stand looking back and nod and muse again and walk off with his eyes to the ground to a fresh vantage point and then look up to see the mare anew, willing to see a new mare should one present itself. Where he could find no gifts of either stance or conformation to warrant his young breeder's confidence John Grady would likely defer to his judgment. Yet every mare could be pled for on the basis of what they came to call la única cosa and that one thing—which could absolve them of any but the grossest defect—was an interest in cattle. For he'd broken the more promising mares to ride and he'd take them upcountry through the ciénaga pasture where the cows and calves stood in the lush grass along the edge of the marshlands and he would show them the cows and let them move among them. And in the manada were mares who took a great interest in what they saw and some would look back at the cows as they were ridden from the pasture. He claimed that cowsense could be bred for. The hacendado was less sure. But there were two things they agreed upon wholly and that were never spoken and that was that God had put horses on earth to work cattle and that other than cattle there was no wealth proper to a man.

They stabled the stallion away from the mares in a barn up at the gerente's and as the mares came into season he and Antonio bred them. They bred mares almost daily for three weeks and sometimes twice daily and Antonio regarded the stallion with great reverence and great love and he called him caballo padre and like John Grady he would talk to the horse and often make promises to him and he never lied to the horse. The horse would hear him coming and set to walking about in the chaff on its hindlegs and he'd stand talking to the horse and describing to him the mares in his low voice. He never bred the horse at the same hour two days running and he conspired with John Grady in telling the hacendado that the horse needed to be ridden to keep it manageable. Because John Grady loved to ride the horse. In truth he loved to be seen riding it. In truth he loved for her to see him riding it.

He'd go to the kitchen in the dark for his coffee and saddle the horse at daybreak with only the little desert doves waking in the orchard and the air still fresh and cool and he and the stallion would come sideways out of the stable with the animal prancing and pounding the ground and arching its neck. They'd ride out along the ciénaga road and along the verge of the marshes while the sun rose riding up flights of ducks out of the shallows or geese or mergansers that would beat away over the water scattering the haze and rising up would turn to birds of gold in a sun not yet visible from the bolsón floor.

He'd ride sometimes clear to the upper end of the laguna before the horse would even stop trembling and he spoke constantly to it in spanish in phrases almost biblical repeating again and again the strictures of a yet untabled law. Soy comandante de las yeguas, he would say, yo y yo sólo. Sin la caridad de estas manos no tengas nada. Ni comida ni agua ni hijos. Soy yo que traigo las yeguas de las montañas, las yeguas jóvenes, las yeguas salvajes y ardientes. While inside the vaulting of the ribs between his knees the darkly meated heart pumped of who's will and the blood pulsed and the bowels shifted in their massive blue convolutions of who's will and the stout thighbones and knee and cannon and the tendons like flaxen hawsers that drew and flexed and drew and flexed at their articulations and of who's will all sheathed and muffled in the flesh and the hooves that stove wells in the morning groundmist and the head turning side to side and the great slavering keyboard of his teeth and the hot globes of his eyes where the world burned.

There were times in those early mornings in the kitchen when he returned to the house for his breakfast with María stirring about and stoking with wood the great nickelmounted cookstove or rolling out dough on the marble countertop that he would hear her singing somewhere in the house or smell the faintest breath of hyacinth as if she'd passed in the outer hall. On mornings when Carlos was to butcher he'd come up the walkway through a great convocation of cats all sitting about on the tiles under the ramada each in its ordered place and he'd pick one up and stroke it standing there at the patio gate through which he'd once seen her gathering limes and he'd stand for a while holding the cat and then let it slip to the tiles again whereupon it would return at once to the spot from which it had been taken and he would enter the kitchen and take off his hat. And sometimes she would ride in the mornings also and he knew she was in the diningroom across the hall by herself and Carlos would take her breakfast tray to her with coffee and fruit and once riding in the low hills to the north he'd seen her below on the ciénaga road two miles distant and he had seen her riding in the parkland above the marshes and once he came upon her leading the horse through the shallows of the lakeshore among the tules with her skirts caught up above her knees while redwing blackbirds circled and cried, pausing and bending and gathering white waterlilies with the black horse standing in the lake behind her patient as a dog.

He'd not spoken to her since the night of the dance at La Vega. She went with her father to Mexico and he returned alone. There was no one he could ask about her. By now he'd taken to riding the stallion bareback, kicking off his boots and swinging up while Antonio still stood holding the trembling mare by the twitch, the mare standing with her legs spread and her head down and the breath rifling in and out of her. Coming out of the barn with his bare heels under the horse's barrel and the horse lathered and dripping and half crazed and pounding up the ciénaga road riding with just a rope hackamore and the sweat of the horse and the smell of the mare on him and the veins pulsing under the wet hide and him leaning low along the horse's neck talking to him softly and obscenely. It was in this condition that all unexpectedly one evening he came upon her returning on the black Arabian down the ciénaga road.

He reined in the horse and it stopped and stood trembling and stepped about in the road slinging its head in a froth from side to side. She sat her horse. He took off his hat and passed his shirtsleeve across his forehead and waved her forward and put his hat back on and reined the horse off the road and through the sedge and turned so that he could watch her pass. She put the horse forward and came on and as she came abreast of him he touched the brim of his hat with his forefinger and nodded and he thought she would go past but she did not. She stopped and turned her wide face to him. Skeins of light off the water played upon the black hide of the horse. He sat the sweating stallion like a highwayman under her gaze. She was waiting for him to speak and afterwards he would try to remember what it was he'd said. He only knew it made her smile and that had not been his intent. She turned and looked off across the lake where the late sun glinted and she looked back at him and at the horse.

I want to ride him, she said.

What?

I want to ride him.

She regarded him levelly from under the black hatbrim.

He looked out across the sedge tilting in the wind off the lake as if there might be some help for him in that quarter. He looked at her.

When? he said.

When?

When did you want to ride him?

Now. I want to ride him now.

He looked down at the horse as if surprised to see it there.

He dont have a saddle on.

Yes, she said. I know.

He pressed the horse between his heels and at the same time pulled on the reins of the hackamore to make the horse appear uncertain and difficult but the horse only stood.

I dont know if the patrón would want you to ride him. Your father.

She smiled at him a pitying smile and there was no pity in it. She stepped to the ground and lifted the reins over the black horse's head and turned and stood looking at him with the reins behind her back.

Get down, she said.

Are you sure about this?

Yes. Hurry.

He slid to the ground. The insides of his trouserlegs were hot and wet.

What do you aim to do with your horse?

I want you to take him to the barn for me.

Somebody will see me at the house.

Take him to Armando's.

You're fixin to get me in trouble.

You are in trouble.

She turned and looped the reins over the saddlehorn and came forward and took the hackamore reins from him and put them up and turned and put one hand on his shoulder. He could feel his heart pumping. He bent and made a stirrup of his laced fingers and she put her boot into his hands and he lifted her and she swung up onto the stallion's back and looked down at him and then booted the horse forward and went loping out up the track along the edge of the lake and was lost to view.

He rode back slowly on the Arabian. The sun was a long time descending. He thought she might overtake him that they could change the horses back again but she did not and in the red twilight he led the black horse past Armando's house afoot and took it to the stable behind the house and removed the bridle and loosed the cinches and left it standing in the bay saddled and tied with a rope halter to the hitchingrail. There was no light on at the house and he thought perhaps there was no one home but as he walked back out down the drive past the house the light came on in the kitchen. He walked more quickly. He heard the door open behind him but he didnt turn to look back to see who it was and whoever it was they did not speak or call to him.

The last time that he saw her before she returned to Mexico she was coming down out of the mountains riding very stately and erect out of a rainsquall building to the north and the dark clouds towering above her. She rode with her hat pulled down in the front and fastened under her chin with a drawtie and as she rode her black hair twisted and blew about her shoulders and the lightning fell silently through the black clouds behind her and she rode all seeming unaware down through the low hills while the first spits of rain blew on the wind and onto the upper pasturelands and past the pale and reedy lakes riding erect and stately until the rain caught her up and shrouded her figure away in that wild summer landscape: real horse, real rider, real land and sky and yet a dream withal.

THE DUEÑA ALFONSA was both grandaunt and godmother to the girl and her life at the hacienda invested it with oldworld ties and with antiquity and tradition. Save for the old leatherbound volumes the books in the library were her books and the piano was her piano. The ancient stereopticon in the parlor and the matched pair of Greener guns in the italian wardrobe in Don Héctor's room had been her brother's and it was her brother with whom she stood in the photos taken in front of cathedrals in the capitals of Europe, she and her sister-in-law in white summer clothes, her brother in vested suit and tie and panama hat. His dark moustache. Dark spanish eyes. The stance of a grandee. The most antique of the several oilportraits in the parlor with its dark patina crazed like an old porcelain glazing was of her great-grandfather and dated from Toledo in seventeen ninety-seven. The most recent was she herself full length in formal gown on the occasion of her quinceañera at Rosario in eighteen ninety-two.

John Grady had never seen her. Perhaps a figure glimpsed passing along the hallway. He did not know that she was aware of his existence until a week after the girl returned to Mexico he was invited to come to the house in the evening to play chess. When he showed up at the kitchen dressed in the new shirt and canvas pants María was still washing the supper dishes. She turned and studied him where he stood with his hat in his hands. Bueno, she said. Te espera.

He thanked her and crossed the kitchen and went up the hall and stood in the diningroom door. She rose from the table where she was sitting. She inclined her head very slightly. Good evening, she said. Please come in. I am señorita Alfonsa.

She was dressed in a dark gray skirt and a white pleated

blouse and her gray hair was gathered up behind and she looked like the schoolteacher she in fact had been. She spoke with an english accent. She held out one hand and he almost stepped forward to take it before he realized that she was gesturing toward the chair at her right.

Evenin, mam, he said. I'm John Grady Cole.

Please, she said. Be seated. I am happy that you have come.

Thank you mam.

He pulled back the chair and sat and put his hat in the chair beside him and looked at the board. She set her thumbs against the edge and pushed it slightly towards him. The board was pieced from blocks of circassian walnut and birdseye maple with a border of inlaid pearl and the chessmen were of carved ivory and black horn.

My nephew will not play, she said. I trounce him. Is it trounce?

Yes mam. I believe it is.

Like him she was lefthanded or she played chess with her left hand. The last two fingers were missing and yet he did not notice it until the game was well advanced. Finally when he took her queen she conceded and smiled her compliments and gestured at the board with a certain impatience. They were well into the second game and he had taken both knights and a bishop when she made two moves in succession which gave him pause. He studied the board. It occurred to him that she might be curious to know if he would throw the game and he realized that he had in fact already considered it and he knew she'd thought of it before he had. He sat back and looked at the board. She watched him. He leaned forward and moved his bishop and mated her in four moves.

That was foolish of me, she said. The queen's knight. That was a blunder. You play very well.

Yes mam. You play well yourself.

She pushed back the sleeve of her blouse to look at a small silver wristwatch. John Grady sat. It was two hours past his bedtime.

One more? she said.

Yes mam.

She used an opening he'd not seen before. In the end he lost his queen and conceded. She smiled and looked up at him. Carlos had entered with a tea tray and he set it on the table and she pushed aside the board and pulled the tray forward and set out the cups and saucers. There were slices of cake on a plate and a plate of crackers and several kinds of cheese and a small bowl of brown sauce with a silver spoon in it.

Do you take cream? she said.

No mam.

She nodded. She poured the tea.

I could not use that opening again with such effect, she said. I'd never seen it before.

Yes. It was invented by the Irish champion Pollock. He called it the King's Own opening. I was afraid you might know it.

I'd like to see it again some time.

Yes. Of course.

She pushed the tray forward between them. Please, she said. Help yourself.

I better not. I'll have crazy dreams eatin this late.

She smiled. She unfolded a small linen napkin from off the tray.

I've always had strange dreams. But I'm afraid they are quite independent of my dining habits.

Yes mam.

They have a long life, dreams. I have dreams now which I had as a young girl. They have an odd durability for something not quite real.

Do you think they mean anything?

She looked surprised. Oh yes, she said. Dont you?

Well. I dont know. They're in your head.

She smiled again. I suppose I dont consider that to be the condemnation you do. Where did you learn to play chess?

My father taught me.

He must be a very good player.

He was about the best I ever saw.

Could you not win against him?

Sometimes. He was in the war and after he come back I got to where I could beat him but I dont think his heart was in it. He dont play at all now.

That's a pity.

Yes mam. It is.

She poured their cups again.

I lost my fingers in a shooting accident, she said. Shooting live pigeons. The right barrel burst. I was seventeen. Alejandra's age. There is nothing to be embarrassed about. People are curious. It's only natural. I'm going to guess that the scar on your cheek was put there by a horse.

Yes mam. It was my own fault.

She watched him, not unkindly. She smiled. Scars have the strange power to remind us that our past is real. The events that cause them can never be forgotten, can they?

No mam.

Alejandra will be in Mexico with her mother for two weeks. Then she will be here for the summer.

He swallowed.

Whatever my appearance may suggest, I am not a particularly oldfashioned woman. Here we live in a small world. A close world. Alejandra and I disagree strongly. Quite strongly in fact. She is much like me at that age and I seem at times to be struggling with my own past self. I was unhappy as a child for reasons that are no longer important. But the thing in which we are united, my niece and I . . .

She broke off. She set the cup and saucer to one side. The polished wood of the table held a round shape of breath where they'd stood that diminished from the edges in and vanished. She looked up.

I had no one to advise me, you see. Perhaps I would not have listened anyway. I grew up in a world of men. I thought this would have prepared me to live in a world of men but it did not. I was also rebellious and so I recognize it in others. Yet I think that I had no wish to break things. Or perhaps only those things that wished to break me. The names of the entities that have power to constrain us change with time. Convention and authority are replaced by infirmity. But my attitude toward them has not changed. Has not changed.

You see that I cannot help but be sympathetic to Alejandra. Even at her worst. But I wont have her unhappy. I wont have her spoken ill of. Or gossiped about. I know what that is. She thinks that she can toss her head and dismiss everything. In an ideal world the gossip of the idle would be of no consequence. But I have seen the consequences in the real world and they can be very grave indeed. They can be consequences of a gravity not excluding bloodshed. Not excluding death. I saw this in my own family. What Alejandra dismisses as a matter of mere appearance or outmoded custom . . .

She made a whisking motion with the imperfect hand that was both a dismissal and a summation. She composed her hands again and looked at him.

Even though you are younger than she it is not proper for you to be seen riding in the campo together without supervision. Since this was carried to my ears I considered whether to speak to Alejandra about it and I have decided not to.

She leaned back. He could hear the clock ticking in the hall. There was no sound from the kitchen. She sat watching him.

What do you want me to do? he said.

I want you to be considerate of a young girl's reputation.

I never meant not to be.

She smiled. I believe you, she said. But you must understand. This is another country. Here a woman's reputation is all she has.

Yes mam.

There is no forgiveness, you see.

Mam?

There is no forgiveness. For women. A man may lose his honor and regain it again. But a woman cannot. She cannot.

They sat. She watched him. He tapped the crown of his seated hat with the tips of his four fingers and looked up.

I guess I'd have to say that that dont seem right.

Right? she said. Oh. Yes. Well.

She turned one hand in the air as if reminded of something she'd misplaced. No, she said. No. It's not a matter of right. You must understand. It is a matter of who must say. In this matter I get to say. I am the one who gets to say.

The clock ticked in the hall. She sat watching him. He picked up his hat.

Well. I guess I ought to say that you didnt have to invite me over just to tell me that.

You're quite right, she said. It was because of it that I almost didnt invite you.

ON THE MESA they watched a storm that had made up to the north. At sundown a troubled light. The dark jade shapes of the lagunillas below them lay in the floor of the desert savannah like piercings through to another sky. The laminar bands of color to the west bleeding out under the hammered clouds. A sudden violetcolored hooding of the earth.

They sat tailorwise on ground that shuddered under the thunder and they fed the fire out of the ruins of an old fence. Birds were coming down out of the half darkness upcountry and shearing away off the edge of the mesa and to the north the lightning stood along the rimlands like burning mandrake.

What else did she say? said Rawlins.

That was about it.

You think she was speakin for Rocha?

I dont think she speaks for anybody but her.

She thinks you got eyes for the daughter.

I do have eyes for the daughter.

You got eyes for the spread?

John Grady studied the fire. I dont know, he said. I aint thought about it.

Sure you aint, said Rawlins.

He looked at Rawlins and he looked into the fire again.

When is she comin back?

About a week.

I guess I dont see what evidence you got that she's all that interested in you.

John Grady nodded. I just do. I can talk to her.

The first drops of rain hissed in the fire. He looked at Rawlins.

You aint sorry you come down here are you?

Not yet.

He nodded. Rawlins rose.

You want your fish or you aim to just set there in the rain?

I'll get it.

I got it.

They sat hooded under the slickers. They spoke out of the hoods as if addressing the night.

I know the old man likes you, said Rawlins. But that dont mean he'll set still for you courtin his daughter.

Yeah, I know.

I dont see you holdin no aces.

Yeah.

What I see is you fixin to get us fired and run off the place.

They watched the fire. The wire that had burned out of the fenceposts lay in garbled shapes about the ground and coils of it stood in the fire and coils of it pulsed red hot deep in the coals. The horses had come in out of the darkness and stood at the edge of the firelight in the falling rain dark and sleek with their red eyes burning in the night.

You still aint told me what answer you give her, said Rawlins.

I told her I'd do whatever she asked.

What did she ask?

I aint sure.

They sat watching the fire.

Did you give your word? said Rawlins.

I dont know. I dont know if I did or not.

Well either you did or you didnt.

That's what I'd of thought. But I dont know.

FIVE NIGHTS later asleep in his bunk in the barn there was a tap at the door. He sat up. Someone was standing outside the door. He could see a light through the boardjoinings.

Momento, he said.

He rose and pulled on his trousers in the dark and opened the door. She was standing in the barn bay holding a flashlight in one hand with the light pointed at the ground.

What is it? he whispered.

It's me.

She held the light up as if to verify the truth of this. He couldnt think what to say.

What time is it?

I dont know. Eleven or something.

He looked across the narrow corridor to the groom's door.

We're going to wake Estéban, he said.

Then invite me in.

He stepped back and she came in past him all rustling of clothes and the rich parade of her hair and perfume. He pulled the door to and ran shut the wooden latch with the heel of his hand and turned and looked at her.

I better not turn the light on, he said.

It's all right. The generator's off anyway. What did she say to you?

She must of told you what she said.

Of course she told me. What did she say?

You want to set down?

She turned and sat sideways on the bed and tucked one foot beneath her. She laid the burning flashlight on the bed and then she pushed it under the blanket where it suffused the room with a soft glow.

She didnt want me to be seen with you. Out on the campo.

Armando told her that you rode my horse in.

I know.

I wont be treated in such a manner, she said.

In that light she looked strange and theatrical. She passed one hand across the blanket as if she'd brush something away. She looked up at him and her face was pale and austere in the uplight and her eyes lost in their darkly shadowed hollows save only for the glint of them and he could see her throat move in the light and he saw in her face and in her figure something he'd not seen before and the name of that thing was sorrow.

I thought you were my friend, she said.

Tell me what to do, he said. I'll do anything you say.

The nightdamp laid the dust going up the ciénaga road and they rode the horses side by side at a walk, sitting the animals bareback and riding with hackamores. Leading the horses by hand out through the gate into the road and mounting up and riding the horses side by side up the ciénaga road with the moon in the west and some dogs barking over toward the shearing-sheds and the greyhounds answering back from their pens and him closing the gate and turning and holding his cupped hands for her to step into and lifting her onto the black horse's naked back and then untying the stallion from the gate and stepping once onto the gateslat and mounting up all in one motion and turning the horse and them riding side by side up the ciénaga road with the moon in the west like a moon of white linen hung from wires and some dogs barking.

They'd be gone sometimes till near daybreak and he'd put the stallion up and go to the house for his breakfast and an hour later meet Antonio back at the stable and walk up past the gerente's house to the trap where the mares stood waiting.

They'd ride at night up along the western mesa two hours from the ranch and sometimes he'd build a fire and they could see the gaslights at the hacienda gates far below them floating in a pool of black and sometimes the lights seemed to move as if the world down there turned on some other center and they saw stars fall to earth by the hundreds and she told him stories of her father's family and of Mexico. Going back they'd walk the horses into the lake and the horses would stand and drink with the water at their chests and the stars in the lake bobbed and tilted where they drank and if it rained in the mountains the air would be close and the night more warm and one night he left her and rode down along the edge of the lake through the sedge and willow and slid from the horse's back and pulled off his boots and his clothes and walked out into the lake where the moon slid away before him and ducks gabbled out there in the dark. The water was black and warm and he turned in the lake and spread his arms in the water and the water was so dark and so silky and he watched across the still black surface to where she stood on the shore with the horse and he watched where she stepped from her pooled clothing so pale, so pale, like a chrysalis emerging, and walked into the water.

She paused midway to look back. Standing there trembling in the water and not from the cold for there was none. Do not speak to her. Do not call. When she reached him he held out his hand and she took it. She was so pale in the lake she seemed to be burning. Like foxfire in a darkened wood. That burned cold. Like the moon that burned cold. Her black hair floating on the water about her, falling and floating on the water. She put her other arm about his shoulder and looked toward the moon in the west do not speak to her do not call and then she turned her face up to him. Sweeter for the larceny of time and flesh, sweeter for the betrayal. Nesting cranes that stood singlefooted among the cane on the south shore had pulled their slender beaks from their wingpits to watch. Me quieres? she said. Yes, he said. He said her name. God yes, he said.

HE CAME UP from the barn washed and combed and a clean shirt on and he and Rawlins sat on crates under the ramada of the bunkhouse and smoked while they waited for supper. There was talking and laughing in the bunkhouse and then it ceased. Two of the vaqueros came to the door and stood. Rawlins turned and looked north along the road. Five Mexican rangers were coming down the road riding singlefile. They were dressed in khaki uniforms and they rode good horses and they wore pistols in beltholsters and carried carbines in their saddlescabbards. Rawlins stood. The other vaqueros had come to the door and stood looking out. As the riders passed on the road the leader glanced across at the bunkhouse at the men under the ramada, at the men standing in the door. Then they went on from sight past the gerente's house, five riders riding singlefile down out of the north through the twilight toward the tile-roofed ranchhouse below them.

When he came back down through the dark to the barn the five horses were standing under the pecan trees at the far side of the house. They hadnt been unsaddled and in the morning they were gone. The following night she came to his bed and she came every night for nine nights running, pushing the door shut and latching it and turning in the slatted light at God knew what hour and stepping out of her clothes and sliding cool and naked against him in the narrow bunk all softness and perfume and the lushness of her black hair falling over him and no caution to her at all. Saying I dont care I dont care. Drawing blood with her teeth where he held the heel of his hand against her mouth that she not cry out. Sleeping against his chest where he could not sleep at all and rising when the east was already gray with dawn and going to the kitchen to get her breakfast as if she were only up early.

Then she was gone back to the city. The following evening when he came in he passed Estéban in the barn bay and spoke to the old man and the old man spoke back but did not look at him. He washed up and went to the house and ate his dinner in the kitchen and after he'd eaten he and the hacendado sat at the diningroom table and logged the stud book and the hacendado questioned him and made notes on the mares and then leaned back and sat smoking his cigar and tapping his pencil against the edge of the table. He looked up.

Good, he said. How are you progressing with the Guzmán?

Well, I'm not ready for volume two.

The hacendado smiled. Guzmán is excellent. You dont read french?

No sir.

The bloody French are quite excellent on the subject of horses. Do you play billiards?

Sir?

Do you play billiards?

Yessir. Some. Pool anyways.

Pool. Yes. Would you like to play?

Yessir.

Good.

The hacendado folded shut the books and pushed back his chair and rose and he followed him out down the hall and through the salon and through the library to the paneled double doors at the far end of the room. The hacendado opened these doors and they entered a darkened room that smelled of must and old wood.

He pulled a tasseled chain and lit an ornate tin chandelier suspended from the ceiling. Beneath it an antique table of some dark wood with lions carved into the legs. The table was covered with a drop of yellow oilcloth and the chandelier had been lowered from the twentyfoot ceiling by a length of common tracechain. At the far end of the room was a very old carved and painted wooden altar above which hung a lifesize carved and painted wooden Christ. The hacendado turned.

I play seldom, he said. I hope you are not an expert?

No sir.

I asked Carlos if he could make the table more level. The last time we played it was quite crooked. We will see what has been done. Just take the corner there. I will show you.

They stood on either side of the table and folded the cloth toward the middle and folded it again and then lifted it away and took it past the end of the table and walked toward each other and the hacendado took the cloth and carried it over and laid it on some chairs.

This was the chapel as you see. You are not superstitious?

No sir. I dont think so.

It is supposed to be made unsacred. The priest comes and says some words. Alfonsa knows about these matters. But of course the table has been here for years now and the chapel has yet to be whatever the word is. To have the priest come and make it be no longer a chapel. Personally I question whether such a thing can be done at all. What is sacred is sacred. The powers of the priest are more limited than people suppose. Of course there has been no Mass said here for many years.

How many years?

The hacendado was sorting through the cues where they stood in and out of a mahogany rack in the corner. He turned.

I received my First Communion in this chapel. I suppose that may have been the last Mass said here. I would say about nineteen eleven.

He turned back to the cues. I would not let the priest come to do that thing, he said. To dissolve the sanctity of the chapel. Why should I do that? I like to feel that God is here. In my house.

He racked the balls and handed the cueball to John Grady. It was ivory and yellow with age and the grain of the ivory was visible in it. He broke the balls and they played straight pool and the hacendado beat him easily, walking about the table and chalking his cue with a deft rotary motion and announcing the shots in spanish. He played slowly and studied the shots and the lay of the table and as he studied and as he played he spoke of the revolution and of the history of Mexico and he spoke of the dueña Alfonsa and of Francisco Madero.

He was born in Parras. In this state. Our families at one time were quite close. Alfonsita may have been engaged to be married to Francisco's brother. I'm not sure. In any case my grandfather would never have permitted the marriage. The political views of the family were quite radical. Alfonsita was not a child.

She should have been left to make her own choice and she was not and whatever were the circumstances she seems to have been very unforgiving of her father and it was a great sorrow to him and one that he was buried with. El cuatro.

The hacendado bent and sighted and banked the fourball the length of the table and stood and chalked his cue.

In the end it was all of no consequence of course. The family was ruined. Both brothers assassinated.

He studied the table.

Like Madero she was educated in Europe. Like him she also learned these ideas, these . . .

He moved his hand in a gesture the boy had seen the aunt make also.

She has always had these ideas. Catorce.

He bent and shot and stood and chalked his cue. He shook his head. One country is not another country. Mexico is not Europe. But it is a complicated business. Madero's grandfather was my padrino. My godfather. Don Evaristo. For this and other reasons my grandfather remained loyal to him. Which was not such a difficult thing. He was a wonderful man. Very kind. Loyal to the regime of Díaz. Even that. When Francisco published his book Don Evaristo refused to believe that he had written it. And yet the book contained nothing so terrible. Perhaps it was only that a wealthy young hacendado had written it. Siete.

He bent and shot the sevenball into the sidepocket. He walked around the table.

They went to France for their education. He and Gustavo. And others. All these young people. They all returned full of ideas. Full of ideas, and yet there seemed to be no agreement among them. How do you account for that? Their parents sent them for these ideas, no? And they went there and received them. Yet when they returned and opened their valises, so to speak, no two contained the same thing.

He shook his head gravely. As if the lay of the table were a trouble to him.

They were in agreement on matters of fact. The names of people. Or buildings. The dates of certain events. But ideas . . . People of my generation are more cautious. I think we dont believe that people can be improved in their character by reason. That seems a very french idea.

He chalked, he moved. He bent and shot and then stood surveying the new lay of the table.

Beware gentle knight. There is no greater monster than reason.

He looked at John Grady and smiled and looked at the table.

That of course is the spanish idea. You see. The idea of Quixote. But even Cervantes could not envision such a country as Mexico. Alfonsita tells me I am only being selfish in not wanting to send Alejandra. Perhaps she is right. Perhaps she is right. Diez.

Send her where?

The hacendado had bent to shoot. He raised up again and looked at his guest. To France. To send her to France.

He chalked his cue again. He studied the table.

Why do I bother myself? Eh? She will go. Who am I? A father. A father is nothing.

He bent to shoot and missed his shot and stepped back from the table.

There, he said. You see? You see how this is bad for one's billiard game? This thinking? The French have come into my house to mutilate my billiard game. No evil is beyond them.

HE SAT on his bunk in the dark with his pillow in his two arms and he leaned his face into it and drank in her scent and tried to refashion in his mind her self and voice. He whispered half aloud the words she'd said. Tell me what to do. I'll do anything you say. The selfsame words he'd said to her. She'd wept against his naked chest while he held her but there was nothing to tell her and there was nothing to do and in the morning she was gone.

The following Sunday Antonio invited him to his brother's house for dinner and afterwards they sat in the shade of the ramada off the kitchen and rolled a cigarette and smoked and discussed the horses. Then they discussed other things. John Grady told him of playing billiards with the hacendado and Antonio—sitting in an old Mennonite chair the caning of which had been replaced with canvas, his hat on one knee and his hands together—received this news with the gravity proper to it, looking down at the burning cigarette and nodding his head. John Grady looked off through the trees toward the house, the white walls and the red clay rooftiles.

Digame, he said. Cuál es lo peor: Que soy pobre o que soy americano?

The vaquero shook his head. Una llave de oro abre cualquier puerta, he said.

He looked at the boy. He tipped the ash from the end of the cigarette and he said that the boy wished to know his thought. Wished perhaps his advice. But that no one could advise him.

Tienes razón, said John Grady. He looked at the vaquero. He said that when she returned he intended to speak to her with the greatest seriousness. He said that he intended to know her heart.

The vaquero looked at him. He looked toward the house. He seemed puzzled and he said that she was here. That she was here now.

Cómo?

Sí. Ella está aquí. Desde ayer.

HE LAY AWAKE all night until the dawn. Listening to the silence in the bay. The shifting of the bedded horses. Their breathing. In the morning he walked up to the bunkhouse to take his breakfast. Rawlins stood in the door of the kitchen and studied him.

You look like you been rode hard and put up wet, he said.

They sat at the table and ate. Rawlins leaned back and fished his tobacco out of his shirtpocket.

I keep waitin for you to unload your wagon, he said. I got to go to work here in a few minutes.

I just come up to see you.

What about.

It dont have to be about somethin does it?

No. Dont have to. He popped a match on the underside of the table and lit his cigarette and shook out the match and put it in his plate.

I hope you know what you're doin, he said.

John Grady drained the last of his coffee and put the cup on his plate along with the silver. He got his hat from the bench beside him and put it on and stood up to take his dishes to the sink.

You said you didnt have no hard feelins about me goin down there.

I dont have no hard feelins about you going down there.

John Grady nodded. All right, he said.

Rawlins watched him go to the sink and watched him go to the door. He thought he might turn and say something else but he didnt.

He worked with the mares all day and in the evening he heard the airplane start up. He came out of the barn and watched. The plane came out of the trees and rose into the late sunlight and banked and turned and leveled out headed southwest. He couldnt see who was in the plane but he watched it out of sight anyway.

Two days later he and Rawlins were in the mountains again. They rode hard hazing the wild manadas out of the high valleys and they camped at their old site on the south slope of the Anteojos where they'd camped with Luis and they ate beans and barbecued goatmeat wrapped in tortillas and drank black coffee.

We aint got many more trips up here, have we? said Rawlins.

John Grady shook his head. No, he said. Probably not.

Rawlins sipped his coffee and watched the fire. Suddenly

three greyhounds trotted into the light one behind the other and circled the fire, pale and skeletal shapes with the hide stretched taut over their ribs and their eyes red in the firelight. Rawlins half rose, spilling his coffee.

What in the hell, he said.

John Grady stood and looked out into the darkness. The dogs vanished as suddenly as they had come.

They stood waiting. No one came.

What the hell, said Rawlins.

He walked out a little ways from the fire and stood listening. He looked back at John Grady.

You want to holler?

No.

Them dogs aint up here by themselves, he said.

I know.

You think he's huntin us?

If he wants us he can find us.

Rawlins walked back to the fire. He poured fresh coffee and stood listening.

He's probably up here with a bunch of his buddies.

John Grady didnt answer.

Dont you reckon? said Rawlins.

They rode up to the catchpen in the morning expecting to come upon the hacendado and his friends but they did not come upon him. In the days that followed they saw no sign of him. Three days later they set off down the mountain herding before them eleven young mares and they reached the hacienda at dark and put the mares up and went to the bunkhouse and ate. Some of the vaqueros were still at the table drinking coffee and smoking cigarettes but one by one they drifted away.

The following morning at gray daybreak two men entered his cubicle with drawn pistols and put a flashlight in his eyes and ordered him to get up.

He sat up. He swung his legs over the edge of the bunk. The man holding the light was just a shape behind it but he could see the pistol he held. It was a Colt automatic service pistol. He shaded his eyes. There were men with rifles standing in the bay.

Quién es? he said.

The man swung the light at his feet and ordered him to get his boots and clothes. He stood and got his trousers and pulled them on and sat and pulled on his boots and reached and got his shirt.

Vámonos, said the man.

He stood and buttoned his shirt.

Dónde están sus armas? the man said.

No tengo armas.

He spoke to the man behind him and two men came forward and began to look through his things. They dumped out the wooden coffeebox on the floor and kicked through his clothes and his shaving things and they turned the mattress over in the floor. They were dressed in greasy and blackened khaki uniforms and they smelled of sweat and woodsmoke.

Dónde está su caballo?

En el segundo puesto.

Vámonos, vámonos.

They led him out down the bay to the saddleroom and he got his saddle and his blankets and by then Redbo was standing in the barn bay, stepping nervously. They came back past Estéban's cuarto but there was no sign that the old man was even awake. They held the light while he saddled his horse and then they walked out into the dawn where the other horses were standing. One of the guards was carrying Rawlins' rifle and Rawlins was sitting slumped in the saddle on his horse with his hands cuffed before him and the reins on the ground.

They jabbed him forward with a rifle.

What's this about, pardner? he said.

Rawlins didnt answer. He leaned and spat and looked away.

No hable, said the leader. Vámonos.

He mounted up and they cuffed his wrists and handed him the reins and then all mounted up and they turned their horses and rode two by two out of the lot through the standing gate. When they passed the bunkhouse the lights were on and the vaqueros were standing in the door or squatting along the ramada. They watched the riders pass, the Americans behind the leader and his lieutenant, the others six in number riding in pairs behind in their caps and uniforms with their carbines resting across the pommels of their saddles, all riding out along the ciénaga road and upcountry toward the north.

III

THEY RODE all day, up through the low hills and into the mountains and along the mesa to the north well beyond the horse range and into the country they'd first crossed into some four months before. They nooned at a spring and squatted about the cold and blackened sticks of some former fire and ate cold beans and tortillas out of a newspaper. He thought the tortillas could have come from the hacienda kitchen. The newspaper was from Monclova. He ate slowly with his manacled hands and drank water from a tin cup that could only be partly filled for the water running out through the rivet holding the handle. The brass showed through the nickelplating where it was worn from the inside of the cuffs and his wrists had already turned a pale and poisonous green. He ate and he watched Rawlins who squatted a little ways off but Rawlins would not meet his eyes. They slept briefly on the ground under the cottonwoods and then rose and drank more water and filled the canteens and waterbottles and rode on.

The country they traversed was advanced in season and the acacia was in bloom and there had been rain in the mountains and the grass along the selvedge of the draws was green and blowsy in the long twilight where they rode. Except for remarks concerning the countryside the guards said little among themselves and to the Americans they said nothing at all. They rode through the long red sunset and they rode on in the dark. The guards had long since scabbarded their rifles and they rode easily, half slouched in the saddle. About ten oclock they halted and made camp and built a fire. The prisoners sat in the sand among old rusted tins and bits of charcoal with their hands still manacled before them and the guards set out an old blue granite-ware coffeepot and a stewpot of the same material and they drank coffee and ate a dish containing some kind of pale and fibrous tuber, some kind of meat, some kind of fowl. All of it stringy, all of it sour.

They spent the night with their hands chained through the stirrups of their saddles, trying to keep warm under their single blankets. They were on the trail again before the sun was up an hour and glad to be so.

This was their life for three days. On the afternoon of the third they rode into the town of Encantada of recent memory.

They sat side by side on a bench of iron slats in the little alameda. A pair of the guards stood a little ways off with their rifles and a dozen children of different ages stood in the dust of the street watching them. Two of the children were girls about twelve years of age and when the prisoners looked at them they turned shyly and twisted at their skirts. John Grady called to them to ask if they could get them cigarettes.

The guards glared at him. He made smoking motions at the girls and they turned and ran off down the street. The other children stood as before.

Ladies' man, said Rawlins.

You dont want a cigarette?

Rawlins spat slowly between his boots and looked up again. They aint goin to bring you no damn cigarette, he said.

I'll bet you.

What the hell you goin to bet with?

I'll bet you a cigarette.

How you goin to do that?

I'll bet you a cigarette she brings em. If she brings em I keep yours.

What are you goin to give me if she dont bring em?

If she dont bring em then you get mine.

Rawlins stared out across the alameda.

I aint above whippin your ass, you know.

Dont you think if we're goin to get out of this jackpot we

might better start thinkin about how to get out of it together?

You mean like we got in it?

You dont get to go back and pick some time when the trouble started and then lay everthing off on your friend.

Rawlins didnt answer.

Dont sull up on me. Let's get it aired.

All right. When they arrested you what did you say?

I didnt say nothin. What would of been the use?

That's right. What would of been the use.

What does that mean?

It means you never asked em to go wake the patrón, did you?

No.

I did.

What did they say?

Rawlins leaned and spat and wiped his mouth.

They said he was awake. They said he'd been awake for a long time. Then they laughed.

You think he sold us down the river?

Dont you?

I dont know. If he did it was because of some lie.

Or some truth.

John Grady sat looking down at his hands.

Would it satisfy you, he said, if I was to just go on and admit to bein a fourteen carat gold plated son of a bitch?

I never said that.

They sat. After a while John Grady looked up.

I cant back up and start over. But I dont see the point in slobberin over it. And I cant see where it would make me feel better to be able to point a finger at somebody else.

It dont make me feel better. I tried to reason with you, that's all. Tried any number of times.

I know you did. But some things aint reasonable. Be that as it may I'm the same man you crossed that river with. How I was is how I am and all I know to do is stick. I never even promised you you wouldnt die down here. Never asked your word on it either. I dont believe in signing on just till it quits suitin you.

You either stick or you quit and I wouldnt quit you I dont care what you done. And that's about all I got to say.

I never quit you, Rawlins said.

All right.

After a while the two girls came back. The taller of them held up her hand with two cigarettes in it.

John Grady looked at the guards. They motioned the girls over and looked at the cigarettes and nodded and the girls approached the bench and handed the cigarettes to the prisoners together with several wooden matches.

Muy amable, said John Grady. Muchas gracias.

They lit the cigarettes off one match and John Grady put the other matches in his pocket and looked at the girls. They smiled shyly.

Son americanos ustedes? they said.

Sí.

Son ladrones?

Sí. Ladrones muy famosos. Bandoleros.

They sucked in their breath. Qué precioso, they said. But the guards called to them and waved them away.

They sat leaning forward on their elbows, smoking the cigarettes. John Grady looked at Rawlins' boots.

Where's them new boots at? he said.

Back at the bunkhouse.

He nodded. They smoked. After a while the others returned and called to the guards. The guards gestured at the prisoners and they rose and nodded to the children and walked out to the street.

They rode out through the north end of the town and they halted before an adobe building with a corrugated tin roof and an empty mud bellcot above it. Scales of old painted plaster still clung to the mud brick walls. They dismounted and entered a large room that might once have been a schoolroom. There was a rail along the front wall and a frame that could once have held a blackboard. The floors were of narrow pine boards and the grain was etched by years of sand trod into them and the windows along both walls had missing panes of glass replaced with squares of tin all cut from the same large sign to form a broken mozaic among the windowlights. At a gray metal desk in one corner sat a stout man likewise in khaki uniform who wore about his neck a scarf of yellow silk. He regarded the prisoners without expression. He gestured slightly with his head toward the rear of the building and one of the guards took down a ring of keys from the wall and the prisoners were led out through a dusty weed yard to a small stone building with a heavy wooden door shod in iron.

There was a square judas-hole cut into the door at eye level and fastened across it and welded to the iron framing was a mesh of lightgauge rebar. One of the guards unfastened the old brass padlock and opened the door. He took a separate ring of keys from his belt.

Las esposas, he said.

Rawlins held up his handcuffs. The guard undid them and he entered and John Grady followed. The door groaned and creaked and thudded shut behind them.

There was no light in the room save what fell through the grate in the door and they stood holding their blankets waiting for their eyes to grade the darkness. The floor of the cell was concrete and the air smelled of excrement. After a while someone to the rear of the room spoke.

Cuidado con el bote.

Dont step in the bucket, said John Grady.

Where is it?

I dont know. Just dont step in it.

I caint see a damn thing.

Another voice spoke out of the darkness. It said: Is that you all?

John Grady could see part of Rawlins' face broken into squares in the light from the grid. Turning slowly. The pain in his eyes. Ah God, he said.

Blevins? said John Grady.

Yeah. It's me.

He made his way carefully to the rear. An outstretched leg withdrew along the floor like a serpent recoiling underfoot. He squatted and looked at Blevins. Blevins moved and he could see his teeth in the partial light. As if he were smiling.

What a man wont see when he aint got a gun, said Blevins.

How long have you been here?

I dont know. A long time.

Rawlins made his way toward the back wall and stood looking down at him. You told em to hunt us, didnt you? he said.

Never done no such a thing, said Blevins.

John Grady looked up at Rawlins.

They knew there were three of us, he said.

Yeah, said Blevins.

Bullshit, said Rawlins. They wouldnt of hunted us once they got the horse back. He's done somethin.

It was my goddamn horse, said Blevins.

They could see him now. Scrawny and ragged and filthy.

It was my horse and my saddle and my gun.

They squatted. No one spoke.

What have you done? said John Grady.

Aint done nothin that nobody else wouldnt of.

What have you done.

You know what he's done, said Rawlins.

Did you come back here?

Damn right I come back here.

You dumb shit. What did you do? Tell me the rest of it.

Aint nothin to tell.

Oh hell no, said Rawlins. Aint a damn thing to tell.

John Grady turned. He looked past Rawlins. An old man sat quietly against the wall watching them.

De qué crimen queda acusado el joven? he said.

The man blinked. Asesinato, he said.

El ha matado un hombre?

The man blinked again. He held up three fingers.

What did he say? said Rawlins.

John Grady didnt answer.

What did he say? I know what the son of a bitch said.

He said he's killed three men.

That's a damn lie, said Blevins.

Rawlins sat slowly on the concrete.

We're dead, he said. We're dead men. I knew it'd come to this. From the time I first seen him.

That aint goin to help us, said John Grady.

Aint but one of em died, said Blevins.

Rawlins raised his head and looked at him. Then he got up and stepped to the other side of the room and sat down again.

Cuidado con el bote, said the old man.

John Grady turned to Blevins.

I aint done nothin to him, said Blevins.

Tell me what happened, said John Grady.

He'd worked for a German family in the town of Palau eighty miles to the east and at the end of two months he'd taken the money he'd earned and ridden back across the selfsame desert and staked out the horse at the selfsame spring and dressed in the common clothes of the country he'd walked into town and sat in front of the tienda for two days until he saw the same man go by with the Bisley's worn guttapercha grips sticking out of his belt.

What did you do?

You aint got a cigarette have you?

No. What did you do?

Didnt think you did.

What did you do?

Lord what wouldnt I give for a chew of tobacco.

What did you do?

I walked up behind him and snatched it out of his belt. That's what I done.

And shot him.

He come at me.

Come at you.

Yeah.

So you shot him.

What choice did I have?

What choice, said John Grady.

I didnt want to shoot the dumb son of a bitch. That was never no part of my intention.

What did you do then?

Time I got back to the spring where my horse was at they was on me. That boy I shot off his horse thowed down on me with a shotgun.

What happened then?

I didnt have no more shells. I'd shot em all up. My own damn fault. All I had was what was in the gun.

You shot one of the rurales?

Yeah.

Dead?

Yeah.

They sat quietly in the dark.

I could of bought shells in Muñoz, said Blevins. Fore I even come here. I had the money too.

John Grady looked at him. You got any idea the kind of mess you're in?

Blevins didnt answer.

What did they say they mean to do with you?

Send me to the penitentiary I reckon.

They aint goin to send you to the penitentiary.

Why aint they?

You aint goin to be that lucky, said Rawlins.

I aint old enough to hang.

They'll lie about your age for you.

They dont have capital punishment in this country, said John Grady. Dont listen to him.

You knew they was huntin us, didnt you? said Rawlins.

Yeah, I knew it. What was I supposed to do, send you a telegram?

John Grady waited for Rawlins to answer but he didnt. The shadow of the iron grid over the judas-hole lay skewed upon the far wall like a waiting chalkgame which the space in that dark and stinking cubicle had somehow rendered out of true. He folded his blanket and sat on it and leaned against the wall.

Do they ever let you out? Do you get to walk around?

I dont know.

What do you mean you dont know?

I caint walk.

You cant walk?

That's what I said.

How come you caint walk, said Rawlins.

Cause they busted my feet all to hell is how come.

They sat. No one spoke. Soon it was dark. The old man on the other side of the room had begun to snore. They could hear sounds from the distant village. Dogs. A mother calling. Ranchero music with its falsetto cries almost like an agony played out of a cheap radio somewhere in the nameless night.

THAT NIGHT he dreamt of horses in a field on a high plain where the spring rains had brought up the grass and the wildflowers out of the ground and the flowers ran all blue and yellow far as the eye could see and in the dream he was among the horses running and in the dream he himself could run with the horses and they coursed the young mares and fillies over the plain where their rich bay and their rich chestnut colors shone in the sun and the young colts ran with their dams and trampled down the flowers in a haze of pollen that hung in the sun like powdered gold and they ran he and the horses out along the high mesas where the ground resounded under their running hooves and they flowed and changed and ran and their manes and tails blew off of them like spume and there was nothing else at all in that high world and they moved all of them in a resonance that was like a music among them and they were none of them afraid horse nor colt nor mare and they ran in that resonance which is the world itself and which cannot be spoken but only praised.

In the morning two guards came and opened the door and handcuffed Rawlins and led him away. John Grady stood and asked where they were taking him but they didnt answer. Rawlins didnt even look back.

The captain was sitting at his desk drinking coffee and reading a three day old newspaper from Monterrey. He looked up. Pasaporte, he said.

I dont have no passport, said Rawlins.

The captain looked at him. He raised his eyebrows in mock surprise. Dont have no passport, he said. You have identification?

Rawlins reached around to his left rear pocket with his manacled hands. He could reach the pocket but he couldnt reach into it. The captain nodded and one of the guards stepped forward and took out the billfold and handed it across to the captain. The captain leaned back in the chair. Quita las esposas, he said.

The guard swung his keys forward and took hold of Rawlins' wrists and unlocked the handcuffs and stepped back and put them in his belt. Rawlins stood rubbing his wrists. The captain turned the sweatblackened leather in his hand. He looked at both sides of it and he looked up at Rawlins. Then he opened it and took out the cards and he took out the photograph of Betty Ward and he took out the american money and then the mexican peso bills which alone were unmutilated. He spread these things out on the desk and leaned back in his chair and folded his hands together and tapped his chin with his forefingers and looked at Rawlins again. Outside Rawlins could hear a goat. He could hear children. The captain made a little rotary motion with one finger. Turn around, he said.

He did so.

Put down your pants.

Do what?

Put down your pants.

What the hell for?

The captain must have made another gesture because the guard stepped forward and took a leather sap from his rear pocket and struck Rawlins across the back of the head with it. The room Rawlins was in lit up all white and his knees buckled and he reached about him in the air.

He was lying with his face against the splintry wooden floor. He didnt remember falling. The floor smelled of dust and grain. He pushed himself up. They waited. They seemed to have nothing else to do.

He got to his feet and faced the captain. He felt sick to his stomach.

You must co-po-rate, said the captain. Then you dont have no troubles. Turn around. Put down your pants.

He turned around and unbuckled his belt and pushed his trousers down around his knees and then the cheap cotton undershorts he'd bought in the commissary at La Vega.

Lift your shirt, said the captain.

He lifted the shirt.

Turn around, said the captain.

He turned.

Get dressed.

He let the shirt fall and reached and hauled up his trousers and buttoned them and buckled back the belt.

The captain was sitting holding the drivers license from his billfold.

What is your date of birth, he said.

September twenty-sixth nineteen and thirty-two.

What is your address.

Route Four Knickerbocker Texas. United States of America.

How much is your height.

Five foot eleven.

How much is your weight.

A hundred and sixty pounds.

The captain tapped the license on the desk. He looked at Rawlins.

You have a good memory. Where is this man?

What man?

He held up the license. This man. Rawlins.

Rawlins swallowed. He looked at the guard and he looked at the captain again. I'm Rawlins, he said.

The captain smiled sadly. He shook his head.

Rawlins stood with his hands dangling.

Why aint I? he said.

Why you come here? said the captain.

Come where?

Here. To this country.

We come down here to work. Somos vaqueros.

Speak english please. You come to buy cattle?

No sir.

No. You have no permit, correct?

We just come down here to work.

At La Purísima.

Anywhere. That's just where we found work.

How much they pay you?

We was gettin two hundred pesos a month.

In Texas what do they pay for this work.

I dont know. Hundred a month.

Hundred dollars.

Yessir.

Eight hundred pesos.

Yessir. I reckon.

The captain smiled again.

Why you must leave Texas?

We just left. We didnt have to.

What is your true name.

Lacey Rawlins.

He pushed the forearm of his sleeve against his forehead and wished at once he hadnt.

Blevins is your brother.

No. We got nothin to do with him.

What is the number of horses you steal.

We never stole no horses.

These horses have no marca.

They come from the United States.

You have a factura for these horses?

No. We rode down here from San Angelo Texas. We dont have no papers on them. They're just our horses.

Where do you cross the border.

Just out of Langtry Texas.

What is the number of men you kill.

I never killed nobody. I never stole nothin in my life. That's the truth.

Why you have guns for.

To shoot game.

Ghem?

Game. To hunt. Cazador.

Now you are hunters. Where is Rawlins.

Rawlins was close to tears. You're lookin at him, damn it.

What is the true name of the assassin Blevins.

I dont know.

How long since you know him.

I dont know him. I dont know nothin about him.

The captain pushed back the chair and stood. He pulled down the hem of his coat to correct the wrinkles and he looked at Rawlins. You are very foolish, he said. Why do you want to have these troubles?

They let Rawlins go just inside the door and he slid to the floor and sat for a moment and then bent slowly forward and to one side and lay holding himself. The guard crooked his finger at John Grady who sat squinting up at them in the sudden light. He rose. He looked down at Rawlins.

You sons of bitches, he said.

Tell em whatever they want to hear, bud, whispered Rawlins. It dont make a damn.

Vámonos, said the guard.

What did you tell them?

Told em we was horsethieves and murderers. You will too.

But by then the guard had come forward and seized his arm and shoved him out the door and the other guard shut the door and pushed the boltshackle home in the padlock.

When they entered the office the captain sat as before. His hair newly slicked. John Grady stood before him. In the room aside from the desk and the chair that the captain sat in there were three folding metal chairs against the far wall that had an uncomfortable emptiness about them. As if people had got up and left. As if people expected were not coming. An old seed-company calendar from Monterrey was nailed to the wall above them and in the corner stood an empty wire birdcage hung from a floorpedestal like some baroque lampstand.

On the captain's desk was a glass oil-lamp with a blackened chimney. An ashtray. A pencil that had been sharpened with a knife. Las esposas, he said.

The guard stepped forward and unlocked the handcuffs. The captain was looking out the window. He'd taken the pencil from the desk and was tapping his lower teeth with it. He turned and tapped the desk twice with the pencil and laid it down. Like a man calling a meeting to order.

Your friend has told us everything, he said.

He looked up.

You will find it is best to tell everything right away. That way you dont have no troubles.

You didnt have no call to beat up on that boy, said John Grady. We dont know nothin about Blevins. He asked to ride with us, that's all. We dont know nothin about the horse. The horse got away from him in a thunderstorm and showed up here and that's when the trouble started. We didnt have nothin to do with it. We been workin for señor Rocha goin on three months down at La Purísima. You went down there and told him a bunch of lies. Lacey Rawlins is as good a boy as ever come out of Tom Green County.

He is the criminal Smith.

His name aint Smith its Rawlins. And he aint a criminal. I've known him all my life. We were raised together. We went to the same school.

The captain sat back. He unbuttoned his shirtpocket and pushed his cigarettes up from the bottom in their package and took one out without removing the pack and buttoned the shirt again. The shirt had been tailored in military fashion and fit tightly and the cigarettes fit tightly in the pocket. He leaned in his chair and took a lighter from his coat and lit the cigarette and put the lighter on the desk beside the pencil and pulled the ashtray to him with one finger and leaned back in the chair and sat with his arm upright and the burning cigarette a few inches from his ear in a posture that seemed alien to him. As if perhaps he'd admired it somewhere in others.

What is your age, he said.

Sixteen. I'll be seventeen in six weeks.

What is the age of the assassin Blevins.

I dont know. I dont know nothin about him. He says he's sixteen. I'd guess fourteen is more like it. Thirteen even.

He dont have no feathers.

He what?

He dont have no feathers.

I wouldnt know about that. It dont interest me.

The captain's face darkened. He puffed on the cigarette. Then he put his hand on the desk palm upward and snapped his fingers.

Deme su billetera.

John Grady took his billfold from his hip pocket and stepped forward and laid it on the desk and stepped back. The captain looked at him. He leaned forward and took the billfold and sat back and opened it and began to take out the money, the cards. The photos. He spread everything out and looked up.

Where is your license of operator.

I dont have one.

You have destroy it.

I dont have one. I never did have one.

The assassin Blevins has no documents.

Probably not.

Why dont he have no documents.

He lost his clothes.

He lose his clothes?

Yes.

Why he come here to steal horses?

It was his horse.

The captain leaned back, smoking.

The horse is not his horse.

Well, you have it your own ignorant way.

Cómo?

As far as I know that horse is his horse. He had it with him in Texas and I know he brought it into Mexico because I seen him ride it across the river.

The captain sat drumming his fingers on the arm of the chair. I dont believe you, he said.

John Grady didnt answer.

These are not the facts.

He half swiveled in his chair to look out the window.

Not the facts, he said. He turned and looked across his shoulder at the prisoner.

You have the opportunity to tell the truth here. Here. In three days you will go to Saltillo and then you will no have this opportunity. It will be gone. Then the truth will be in other hands. You see. We can make the truth here. Or we can lose it. But when you leave here it will be too late. Too late for truth. Then you will be in the hands of other parties. Who can say what the truth will be then? At that time? Then you will blame yourself. You will see.

There aint but one truth, said John Grady. The truth is what happened. It aint what come out of somebody's mouth.

You like this little town? said the captain.

It's all right.

It is very quiet here.

Yes.

The peoples in this town are quiet peoples. Everybody here is quiet all the time.

He leaned forward and stubbed out the cigarette in the ashtray.

Then comes the assassin Blevins to steal horses and kill everybody. Why is this? He was a quiet boy and never do no harm and then he come here and do these things something like that?

He leaned back and shook his head in that same sad way.

No, he said. He wagged one finger. No.

He watched John Grady.

What is the truth is this: He was no a quiet boy. He was this other kind of boy all the time. All the time.

When the guards brought John Grady back they took Blevins away with them. He could walk but not well. When the padlock had clicked shut and rattled and swung to rest John Grady squatted facing Rawlins.

How you doin? he said.

I'm okay. How are you?

I'm all right.

What happened?

Nothin.

What'd you tell him?

I told him you were full of shit.

You didnt get to go to the shower room?

No.

You were gone a long time.

Yeah.

He keeps a white coat back there on a hook. He takes it down and puts it on and ties it around his waist with a string.

John Grady nodded. He looked at the old man. The old man was watching them even if he didnt speak english.

Blevins is sick.

Yeah, I know. I think we're goin to Saltillo.

What's in Saltillo?

I dont know.

Rawlins shifted against the wall. He closed his eyes.

Are you all right? said John Grady.

Yeah, I'm all right.

I think he wants to make some kind of a deal with us.

The captain?

Captain. Whatever he is.

What kind of a deal.

To keep quiet. That kind of a deal.

Like we had some kind of a choice. Keep quiet about what?

About Blevins.

Keep quiet about what about Blevins?

John Grady looked at the little square of light in the door and at the skew of it on the wall above the old man's head where he sat. He looked at Rawlins.

I think they aim to kill him. I think they aim to kill Blevins.

Rawlins sat for a long time. He sat with his head turned away against the wall. When he looked at John Grady again his eyes were wet.

Maybe they wont, he said.

I think they will.

Ah damn, said Rawlins. Just goddamn it all to hell.

When they brought Blevins back he sat in the corner and didnt speak. John Grady talked with the old man. His name was Orlando. He didnt know what crime he was accused of. He'd been told he could go when he signed the papers but he couldnt read the papers and no one would read them to him. He didnt know how long he'd been here. Since sometime in the winter. While they were talking the guards came again and the old man shut up.

They unlocked the door and entered and set two buckets in the floor together with a stack of enameled tin plates. One of them looked into the waterpail and the other took the slop pail from the corner and they went out again. They had about them a perfunctory air, like men accustomed to caring for livestock. When they were gone the prisoners squatted about the buckets and John Grady handed out the plates. Of which there were five. As if some unknown other were expected. There were no utensils and they used the tortillas to spoon the beans from the bucket.

Blevins, said John Grady. You aim to eat?

I aint hungry.

Better get you some of this.

You all go on.

John Grady scooped beans into one of the spare dishes and folded the tortilla along the edge of the dish and got up and carried it to Blevins and came back. Blevins sat holding the dish in his lap.

After a while he said: What'd you tell em about me?

Rawlins stopped chewing and looked at John Grady. John Grady looked at Blevins.

Told em the truth.

Yeah, said Blevins.

You think it would make any difference what we told them? said Rawlins.

You could of tried to help me out.

Rawlins looked at John Grady.

Could of put in a good word for me, said Blevins.

Good word, said Rawlins.

Wouldnt of cost you nothin.

Shut the hell up, said Rawlins. Just shut up. You say anything more I'll come over there and stomp your skinny ass. You hear me? If you say one more goddamn word.

Leave him alone, said John Grady.

Dumb little son of a bitch. You think that man in there dont know what you are? He knew what you were fore he ever set eyes on you. Before you were born. Damn you to hell. Just damn you to hell.

He was almost in tears. John Grady put a hand on his shoulder. Let it go, Lacey, he said. Just let it go.

In the afternoon the guards came and left the slop bucket and took away the plates and pails.

How do you reckon the horses are makin it? said Rawlins.

John Grady shook his head.

Horses, the old man said. Caballos.

Sí. Caballos.

They sat in the hot silence and listened to the sounds in the village. The passing of some horses along the road. John Grady asked the old man if they had mistreated him but the old man waved one hand and passed it off. He said they didnt bother him much. He said there was no sustenance in it for them. An old man's dry moans. He said that pain for the old was no longer a surprise.

Three days later they were led blinking from their cell into the early sunlight and through the yard and the schoolhouse and out into the street. Parked there was a ton-and-a-half flatbed Ford truck. They stood in the street dirty and unshaven holding their blankets in their arms. After a while one of the guards motioned to them to climb up on the truck. Another guard came out of the building and they were handcuffed with the same plateworn cuffs and then chained together with a towchain that lay coiled in the spare tire in the forward bed of the truck. The captain came out and stood in the sunlight rocking on his heels and drinking a cup of coffee. He wore a pipeclayed leather belt and holster, the 45 automatic slung at full cock butt-forward at his left side. He spoke to the guards and they waved their arms and a man standing on the front bumper of the truck raised up out of the engine compartment and gestured and spoke and then bent under the hood again.

What did he say? said Blevins.

No one answered. There were bundles and crates piled forward on the truckbed together with some fivegallon army gascans. People of the town kept arriving with parcels and handing slips of paper to the driver who stuffed them into his shirtpocket without comment.

Yonder stands your gals, said Rawlins.

I see em, said John Grady.

They were standing close together, the one clinging to the arm of the other, both of them crying.

What the hell sense does that make? said Rawlins.

John Grady shook his head.

The girls stood watching while the truck was loaded and while the guards sat smoking with their rifles propped against their shoulders and they were still standing there an hour later when the truck finally started and the hood dropped shut and the truck with the prisoners in their chains jostling slightly pulled away down the narrow dirt street and faded from sight in a rolling wake of dust and motorsmoke.

There were three guards on the truckbed with the prisoners, young boys from the country in illfitting and unpressed uniforms. They must have been ordered not to speak to the prisoners because they took care to avoid their eyes. They nodded or raised one hand gravely to people they knew standing in the doorways as they rolled out down the dusty street. The captain sat in the cab with the driver. Some dogs came out to chase the truck and the driver cut the wheel sharply to try to run them down and the guards on the truckbed grabbed wildly for handholds and the driver looked back at them through the rear window of the cab laughing and they all laughed and punched one another and then sat gravely with their rifles.

They turned down a narrow street and stopped in front of a house that was painted bright blue. The captain leaned across the cab and blew the horn. After a while the door opened and a man came out. He was rather elegantly dressed after the manner of a charro and he walked around the truck and the captain got out and the man got into the cab and the captain climbed in after him and shut the door and they pulled away.

They drove down the street past the last house and the last of the corrals and mud pens and crossed a shallow ford where the slow water shone like oil in its colors and mended itself behind them before the run-off from the trucktires had even finished draining back. The truck labored up out of the ford over the scarred rock of the roadbed and then leveled out and set off across the desert in the flat midmorning light.

The prisoners watched the dust boil from under the truck and hang over the road and drift slowly off across the desert. They slammed about on the rough oak planks of the truckbed and tried to keep their blankets folded under them. Where the road forked they turned out onto the track that would take them to Cuatro Ciénagas and on to Saltillo four hundred kilometers to the south.

Blevins had unfolded his blanket and was stretched out on it with his arms under his head. He lay staring up at the pure blue desert sky where there was no cloud, no bird. When he spoke, his voice shuddered from the hammering of the truckbed against his back.

Boys, he said, this is goin to be a long old trip.

They looked at him, they looked at each other. They didnt say if they thought it would be or not.

The old man said it'd take all day to get there, said Blevins. I asked him. Said all day.

Before noon they struck the main road coming down out of Boquillas on the border and they took the road downcountry. Through the pueblos of San Guillermo, San Miguel, Tanque el Revés. The few vehicles they encountered on that hot and guttered track passed in a storm of dust and flying rock and the riders on the truckbed turned away with their faces in their elbow sleeves. They stopped in Ocampo and offloaded some crates of produce and some mail and drove on toward El Oso. In the early afternoon they pulled in at a small cafe by the roadside and the guards climbed down and went in with their guns. The prisoners sat chained on the truckbed. In the dead mud yard some children who'd been playing stopped to watch them and a thin white dog who seemed to have been awaiting just such an arrival came over and urinated for a long time against the rear tire of the truck and went back.

When the guards came out they were laughing and rolling cigarettes. One of them carried three bottles of orange soda-water and he passed them up to the prisoners and stood waiting for the bottles while they drank. When the captain appeared in the doorway they climbed back onto the truck. The guard who'd taken the bottles back came out and then the man in the charro outfit and then the driver. When they were all in their places the captain stepped from the shade of the doorway and crossed the gravel apron and climbed into the cab and they went on.

At Cuatro Ciénagas they struck the paved road and turned south toward Torreón. One of the guards stood up and holding on to the shoulder of his companion looked back at the roadsign. He sat again and they glanced at the prisoners and then just sat looking out over the countryside as the truck gathered speed. An hour later they left the road altogether, the truck laboring over a dirt track across rolling fields, a great and fallow baldíos such as was common to that country where feral cattle the color of candlewax come up out of the arroyos to feed at night like alien principals. Summer thunderheads were building to the north and Blevins was studying the horizon and watching the thin wires of lightning and watching the dust to see how the wind blew. They crossed a broad gravel riverbed dry and white in the sun and they climbed into a meadow where the grass was tall as the tires and passed under the truck with a seething sound and they entered a grove of ebony trees and drove out a nesting pair of hawks and pulled up in the yard of an abandoned estancia, a quadrangle of mud buildings and the remains of some sheep-pens.

No one in the truckbed moved. The captain opened the door and stepped out. Vámonos, he said.

They climbed down with their guns. Blevins looked about at the ruined buildings.

What's here? he said.

One of the guards leaned his rifle against the truck and sorted through the ring of keys and reached and unlocked the chain and threw the loose ends up onto the truckbed and picked up the rifle again and gestured for the prisoners to get down. The captain had sent one of the guards to scout the perimeter and they stood waiting for him to come back. The charro stood leaning against the front fender of the truck with one thumb in his carved leather belt smoking a cigarette.

What do we do here? said Blevins.

I dont know, said John Grady.

The driver hadnt gotten out of the truck. He was slumped back in the seat with his hat over his eyes and looked to be sleeping.

I got to take a leak, said Rawlins.

They walked out through the grass, Blevins hobbling after them. No one looked at them. The guard came back and reported to the captain and the captain took the guard's rifle from him and handed it to the charro and the charro hefted it in his hands as if it were a game gun. The prisoners straggled back to the truck. Blevins sat down a little apart and the charro looked at him and then took his cigarette from his mouth and dropped it in the grass and stepped on it. Blevins got up and moved to the rear of the truck where John Grady and Rawlins were standing.

What are they goin to do? he said.

The guard with no rifle came to the rear of the truck.

Vámonos, he said.

Rawlins raised up from where he was leaning on the bed of the truck.

Sólo el chico, said the guard. Vámonos.

Rawlins looked at John Grady.

What are they goin to do? said Blevins.

They aint goin to do nothin, said Rawlins.

He looked at John Grady. John Grady said nothing at all. The guard reached and took Blevins by the arm. Vámonos, he said.

Wait a minute, said Blevins.

Están esperando, said the guard.

Blevins twisted out of his grip and sat on the ground. The guard's face clouded. He looked toward the front of the truck where the captain stood. Blevins had wrenched off one boot and was reaching down inside it. He pulled up the black and sweaty innersole and threw it away and reached in again. The guard bent and got hold of his thin arm. He pulled Blevins up. Blevins was flailing about trying to hand something to John Grady.

Here, he hissed.

John Grady looked at him. What do I want with that? he said.

Take it, said Blevins.

He thrust into his hand a wad of dirty and crumpled peso notes and the guard jerked him around by his arm and pushed him forward. The boot had fallen to the ground.

Wait, said Blevins. I need to get my boot.

But the guard shoved him on past the truck and he limped away, looking back once mute and terrified and then going on with the captain and the charro across the clearing toward the trees. The captain had put one arm around the boy, or he put his hand in the small of his back. Like some kindly advisor. The other man walked behind them carrying the rifle and Blevins disappeared into the ebony trees hobbling on one boot much as they had seen him that morning coming up the arroyo after the rain in that unknown country long ago.

Rawlins looked at John Grady. His mouth was tight. John Grady watched the small ragged figure vanish limping among the trees with his keepers. There seemed insufficient substance to him to be the object of men's wrath. There seemed nothing about him sufficient to fuel any enterprise at all.

Dont you say nothin, said Rawlins.

All right.

Dont you say a damn word.

John Grady turned and looked at him. He looked at the guards and he looked at the place where they were, the strange land, the strange sky.

All right, he said. I wont.

At some time the driver had got out and gone off somewhere to inspect the buildings. The others stood, the two prisoners, the three guards in their rumpled suits. The one guard with no rifle squatting by the tire. They waited a long time. Rawlins leaned and put his fists on the truckbed and laid his forehead down and closed his eyes tightly. After a while he raised up again. He looked at John Grady.

They caint just walk him out there and shoot him, he said. Hell fire. Just walk him out there and shoot him.

John Grady looked at him. As he did so the pistol shot came from beyond the ebony trees. Not loud. Just a flat sort of pop. Then another.

When they came back out of the trees the captain was carrying the handcuffs. Vámonos, he called.

The guards moved. One of them stood on the rear axlehub and reached across the boards of the truckbed for the chain. The driver came from the ruins of the quinta.

We're okay, whispered Rawlins. We're okay.

John Grady didnt answer. He almost reached to pull down the front of his hatbrim but then he remembered that they had no hats anymore and he turned and climbed up on the bed of the truck and sat waiting to be chained. Blevins' boot was still lying in the grass. One of the guards bent and picked it up and pitched it into the weeds.

When they wound back up out of the glade it was already evening and the sun lay long in the grass and across the shallow swales where the land dipped in pockets of darkness. Small birds come to feed in the evening cool of the open country flushed and flared away over the grasstops and the hawks in silhouette against the sunset waited in the upper limbs of a dead tree for them to pass.

They rode into Saltillo at ten oclock at night, the populace out for their paseos, the cafes full. They parked on the square opposite the cathedral and the captain got out and crossed the street. There were old men sitting on benches under the yellow lamplight having their shoes polished and there were little signs warning people off the tended gardens. Vendors were selling paletas of frozen fruitjuices and young girls with powdered faces went hand in hand by pairs and peered across their shoulders with dark uncertain eyes. John Grady and Rawlins sat with their blankets pulled about them. No one paid them any mind. After a while the captain came back and climbed into the truck and they went on again.

They drove through the streets and made stops at little dimlit doorways and small houses and tiendas until nearly all the parcels in the bed of the truck had been dispersed and a few new ones taken aboard. When they pulled up before the massive doors of the old prison on Castelar it was past midnight.

They were led into a stonefloored room that smelled of disinfectant. The guard uncuffed their wrists and left them and they squatted and leaned against the wall with their blankets about their shoulders like mendicants. They squatted there for a long time. When the door opened again the captain came in and stood looking at them in the dead flat glare of the single bulb in the ceiling overhead. He was not wearing his pistol. He gestured with his chin and the guard who'd opened the door withdrew and closed the door behind him.

The captain stood regarding them with his arms crossed and his thumb beneath his chin. The prisoners looked up at him, they looked at his feet, they looked away. He stood watching them for a long time. They all seemed to be waiting for something. Like passengers in a halted train. Yet the captain inhabited another space and it was a space of his own election and outside the common world of men. A space privileged to men of the irreclaimable act which while it contained all lesser worlds within it contained no access to them. For the terms of election were of a piece with its office and once chosen that world could not be quit.

He paced. He stood. He said that the man they called the charro had suffered from a failure of nerve out there among the ebony trees beyond the ruins of the estancia and this a man whose brother was dead at the hand of the assassin Blevins and this a man who had paid money that certain arrangements be made which the captain had been at some pains himself to make.

This man came to me. I dont go to him. He came to me. Speaking of justice. Speaking of the honor of his family. Do you think men truly want these things? I dont think many men want these things.

Even so I was surprise. I was surprise. We have no death here for the criminals. Other arrangements must be made. I tell you this because you will be making arrangements you self.

John Grady looked up.

You are not the first Americans to be here, said the captain. In this place. I have friends in this place and you will be making these arrangements with these peoples. I dont want you to make no mistakes.

We dont have any money, said John Grady. We aint fixin to make any arrangements.

Excuse me but you will be making some arrangements. You dont know nothing.

What did you do with our horses.

We are not talking about horses now. Those horses must wait. The rightful owners must be found of those horses.

Rawlins stared bleakly at John Grady. Just shut the hell up, he said.

He can talk, said the captain. It is better when everybody is understand. You cannot stay here. In this place. You stay here you going to die. Then come other problems. Papers is lost. Peoples cannot be found. Some peoples come here to look for some man but he is no here. No one can find these papers. Something like that. You see. No one wants these troubles. Who can say that some body was here? We dont have this body. Some crazy person, he can say that God is here. But everybody knows that God is no here.

The captain reached out with one hand and rapped with his knuckles agains the door.

You didnt have to kill him, said John Grady.

Cómo?

You could of just brought him back. You could of just brought him on back to the truck. You didnt have to kill him.

A keyring rattled outside. The door opened. The captain held up one hand to an unseen figure in the partial dark of the corridor.

Momento, he said.

He turned and stood studying them.

I will tell you a story, he said. Because I like you. I was young man like you. You see. And this time I tell you I was always with these older boys because I want to learn every thing. So on this night at the fiesta of San Pedro in the town of Linares in Nuevo León I was with these boys and they have some mescal and everything—you know what is mescal?—and there was this woman and all these boys is go out to this woman and they is have this woman. And I am the last one. And I go out to the place where is this woman and she is refuse me because she say I am too young or something like that.

What does a man do? You see. I can no go back because they will all see that I dont go with this woman. Because the truth is always plain. You see. A man cannot go out to do some thing and then he go back. Why he go back? Because he change his mind? A man does not change his mind.

The captain made a fist and held it up.

Maybe they tell her to refuse to me. So they can laugh. They give her some money or something like that. But I dont let whores make trouble for me. When I come back there is no laughing. No one is laughing. You see. That has always been my way in this world. I am the one when I go someplace then there is no laughing. When I go there then they stop laughing.

They were led up four flights of stone stairs and through a steel door out onto an iron catwalk. The guard smiled back at them in the light from the bulb over the door. Beyond lay the night sky of the desert mountains. Below them the prison yard.

Se llama la periquera, he said.

They followed him down the catwalk. A sense of some brooding and malignant life slumbering in the darkened cages they passed. Here and there along the tiers of catwalks on the far side of the quadrangle a dull light shaped out the grating of the cells where votive candles burned the night long before some santo. The bell in the cathedral tower three blocks away sounded once with a deep, an oriental solemnity.

They were locked into a cell in the topmost corner of the prison. The ironbarred door clanged shut and the latch rattled home and they listened as the guard went back down the catwalk and they listened as the iron door shut and then all was silence.

They slept in iron bunks chained to the walls on thin trocheros or mattress pads that were greasy, vile, infested. In the morning they climbed down the four flights of steel ladders into the yard and stood among the prisoners for the morning lista. The lista was called by tiers yet it still took over an hour and their names were not called.

I guess we aint here, said Rawlins.

Their breakfast was a thin pozole and nothing more and afterward they were simply turned out into the yard to fend for themselves. They spent the whole of the first day fighting and when they were finally shut up in their cell at night they were bloody and exhausted and Rawlins' nose was broken and badly swollen. The prison was no more than a small walled village and within it occurred a constant seethe of barter and exchange in everything from radios and blankets down to matches and buttons and shoenails and within this bartering ran a constant struggle for status and position. Underpinning all of it like the fiscal standard in commercial societies lay a bedrock of depravity and violence where in an egalitarian absolute every man was judged by a single standard and that was his readiness to kill.

They slept and in the morning it all began again. They fought back to back and picked each other up and fought again. At noon Rawlins could not chew. They're goin to kill us, he said.

John Grady mashed beans in a tin can with water till he'd made a gruel out of it and pushed it at Rawlins.

You listen to me, he said. Dont you let em think they aint goin to have to. You hear me? I intend to make em kill me. I wont take nothin less. They either got to kill us or let us be. There aint no middle ground.

There aint a place on me that dont hurt.

I know it. I know it and I dont care.

Rawlins sucked at the gruel. He looked at John Grady from over the rim of the can. You look like a goddamn racoon, he said.

John Grady grinned crookedly. What the hell you think you look like?

Shit if I know.

You ought to wish you looked as good as a coon.

I caint laugh. I think my jaw's broke.

There aint nothin wrong with you.

Shit, said Rawlins.

John Grady grinned. You see that big old boy standin yonder that's been watchin us?

I see the son of a bitch.

See him lookin over here?

I see him.

What do you think I'm fixin to do?

I got no idea in this world.

I'm goin to get up from here and walk over there and bust him in the mouth.

The hell you are.

You watch me.

What for?

Just to save him the trip.

By the end of the third day it seemed to be pretty much over. There were both half naked and John Grady had been blind-sided with a sock full of gravel that took out two teeth in his lower jaw and his left eye was closed completely. The fourth day was Sunday and they bought clothes with Blevins' money and they bought a bar of soap and took showers and they bought a can of tomato soup and heated it in the can over a candlestub and wrapped the sleeve of Rawlins' old shirt around it for a handle and passed it back and forth between them while the sun set over the high western wall of the prison.

You know, we might just make it, said Rawlins.

Dont start gettin comfortable. Let's just take it a day at a time.

How much money you think it would take to get out of here?

I dont know. I'd say a lot.

I would too.

We aint heard from the captain's buddies in here. I guess they're waitin to see if there's goin to be anything left to bail out.

He held out the can toward Rawlins.

Finish it, said Rawlins.

Take it. There aint but a sup.

He took the can and drained it and poured a little water in and swirled it about and drank that and sat looking into the empty can.

If they think we're rich how come they aint looked after us no better? he said.

I dont know. I know they dont run this place. All they run is what comes in and what goes out.

If that, said Rawlins.

The floodlights came on from the upper walls. Figures that had been moving in the yard froze, then they moved again.

The horn's fixin to blow.

We got a couple of minutes.

I never knowed there was such a place as this.

I guess there's probably every kind of place you can think of.

Rawlins nodded. I wouldnt of thought of this one, he said.

It was raining somewhere out in the desert. They could smell the wet creosote on the wind. Lights came on in a makeshift cinderblock house built into one corner of the prison wall where a prisoner of means lived like an exiled satrap complete with cook and bodyguard. There was a screen door to the house and a figure crossed behind it and crossed back. On the roof a clothesline where the prisoner's clothes luffed gently in the night breeze like flags of state. Rawlins nodded toward the lights.

You ever see him?

Yeah. One time. He was standin in the door one evenin smokin him a cigar.

You picked up on any of the lingo in here?

Some.

What's a pucha?

A cigarette butt.

Then what's a tecolata?

Same thing.

How many damn names have they got for a cigarette butt?

I dont know. You know what a papazote is?

No, what?

A big shot.

That's what they call the dude that lives yonder.

Yeah.

And we're a couple of gabachos.

Bolillos.

Pendejos.

Anybody can be a pendejo, said John Grady. That just means asshole.

Yeah? Well, we're the biggest ones in here.

I wont dispute it.

They sat.

What are you thinkin about, said Rawlins.

Thinkin about how much it's goin to hurt to get up from here.

Rawlins nodded. They watched the prisoners moving under the glare of the lights.

All over a goddamned horse, said Rawlins.

John Grady leaned and spat between his boots and leaned back. Horse had nothin to do with it, he said.

That night they lay in their cell on the iron racks like acolytes and listened to the silence and a rattling snore somewhere in the block and a dog barking faintly in the distance and the silence and each other breathing in the silence both still awake.

We think we're a couple of pretty tough cowboys, said Rawlins.

Yeah. Maybe.

They could kill us any time.

Yeah. I know.

Two days later the papazote sent for them. A tall thin man crossed the quadrangle in the evening to where they sat and bent and asked them to come with him and then rose and strode off again. He didnt even look back to see if they'd rise to follow.

What do you want to do? said Rawlins.

John Grady rose stiffly and dusted the seat of his trousers with one hand.

Get your ass up from there, he said.

The man's name was Pérez. His house was a single room in the center of which stood a tin foldingtable and four chairs. Against one wall was a small iron bed and in one corner a cupboard and a shelf with some dishes and a threeburner gasring. Pérez was standing looking out his small window at the yard. When he turned he made an airy gesture with two fingers and the man who'd come to fetch them stepped back out and closed the door.

My name is Emilio Pérez, he said. Please. Sit down.

They pulled out chairs at the table and sat. The floor of the room was made of boards but they were not nailed to anything. The blocks of the walls were not mortared and the unpeeled roofpoles were only dropped loosely into the topmost course and the sheets of roofingtin overhead were held down by blocks stacked along their edges. A few men could have disassembled and stacked the structure in half an hour. Yet there was an electric light and a gasburning heater. A carpet. Pictures from calendars pinned to the walls.

You young boys, he said. You enjoy very much to fight, yes?

Rawlins started to speak but John Grady cut him off. Yes, he said. We like it a lot.

Pérez smiled. He was a man about forty with graying hair and moustache, lithe and trim. He pulled out the third chair and stepped over the back of it with a studied casualness and sat and leaned forward with his elbows on the table. The table had been painted green with a brush and the logo of a brewery was partly visible through the paint. He folded his hands.

All this fighting, he said. How long have you been here?

About a week.

How long do you plan to stay?

We never planned to come here in the first place, Rawlins said. I dont believe our plans has got much to do with it.

Pérez smiled. The Americans dont stay so long with us, he said. Sometimes they come here for some months. Two or three. Then they leave. Life here is not so good for the Americans. They dont like it so much.

Can you get us out of here?

Pérez spaced his hands apart and made a shrugging gesture. Yes, he said. I can do this, of course.

Why dont you get yourself out, said Rawlins.

He leaned back. He smiled again. The gesture he made of throwing his hands suddenly away from him like birds dismissed sorted oddly with his general air of containment. As if he thought it perhaps an american gesture which they would understand.

I have political enemies. What else? Let me be clear with you. I do not live here so very good. I must have money to make my own arrangements and this is a very expensive business. A very expensive business.

You're diggin a dry hole, said John Grady. We dont have no money.

Pérez regarded them gravely.

If you dont have no money how can you be release from your confinement?

You tell us.

But there is nothing to tell. Without money you can do nothing.

Then I dont guess we'll be goin anywheres.

Pérez studied them. He leaned forward and folded his hands again. He seemed to be giving thought how to put things.

This is a serious business, he said. You dont understand the life here. You think this struggle is for these things. Some shoelaces or some cigarettes or something like that. The lucha. This is a naive view. You know what is naive? A naive view. The real facts are always otherwise. You cannot stay in this place and be independent peoples. You dont know what is the situation here. You dont speak the language.

He speaks it, said Rawlins.

Pérez shook his head. No, he said. You dont speak it. Maybe in a year here you might understand. But you dont have no year. You dont have no time. If you dont show faith to me I cannot help you. You understand me? I cannot offer to you my help.

John Grady looked at Rawlins. You ready, bud?

Yeah. I'm ready.

They pushed back their chairs and rose.

Pérez looked up at them. Sit down please, he said.

There's nothin to sit about.

He drummed his fingers on the table. You are very foolish, he said. Very foolish.

John Grady stood with his hand on the door. He turned and looked at Pérez. His face misshapen and his jaw bowed out and his eye still swollen closed and blue as a plum.

Why dont you tell us what's out there? he said. You talk about showin faith. If we dont know then why dont you tell us?

Pérez had not risen from the table. He leaned back and looked at them.

I cannot tell you, he said. That is the truth. I can say certain things about those who come under my protection. But the others?

He made a little gesture of dismissal with the back of his hand.

The others are simply outside. They live in a world of possibility that has no end. Perhaps God can say what is to become of them. But I cannot.

The next morning crossing the yard Rawlins was set upon by a man with a knife. The man he'd never seen before and the knife was no homemade trucha ground out of a trenchspoon but an italian switchblade with black horn handles and nickle bolsters and he held it at waist level and passed it three times across Rawlins' shirt while Rawlins leaped three times backward with his shoulders hunched and his arms outflung like a man refereeing his own bloodletting. At the third pass he turned and ran. He ran with one hand across his stomach and his shirt was wet and sticky.

When John Grady got to him he was sitting with his back to the wall holding his arms crossed over his stomach and rocking back and forth as if he were cold. John Grady knelt and tried to pull his arms away.

Let me see, damn it.

That son of a bitch. That son of a bitch.

Let me see.

Rawlins leaned back. Aw shit, he said.

John Grady lifted the bloodsoaked shirt.

It aint that bad, he said. It aint that bad.

He cupped his hand and ran it across Rawlins' stomach to chase the blood. The lowest cut was the deepest and it had severed the outer fascia but it had not gone through into the stomach wall. Rawlins looked down at the cuts. It aint good, he said. Son of a bitch.

Can you walk?

Yeah, I can walk.

Come on.

Aw shit, said Rawlins. Son of a bitch.

Come on, bud. You cant set here.

He helped Rawlins to his feet.

Come on, he said. I got you.

They crossed the quadrangle to the gateshack. The guard looked out through the sallyport. He looked at John Grady and he looked at Rawlins. Then he opened the gate and John Grady passed Rawlins into the hands of his captors.

They sat him in a chair and sent for the alcaide. Blood dripped slowly onto the stone floor beneath him. He sat holding his stomach with both hands. After a while someone handed him a towel.

In the days that followed John Grady moved about the compound as little as possible. He watched everywhere for the cuchillero who would manifest himself from among the anonymous eyes that watched back. Nothing occurred. He had a few friends among the inmates. An older man from the state of Yucatán who was outside of the factions but was treated with respect. A dark indian from Sierra León. Two brothers named Bautista who had killed a policeman in Monterrey and set fire to the body and were arrested with the older brother wearing the policeman's shoes. All agreed that Pérez was a man whose power could only be guessed at. Some said he was not confined to the prison at all but went abroad at night. That he kept a wife and family in the town. A mistress.

He tried to get some word from the guards concerning Rawlins but they claimed to know nothing. On the morning of the third day after the stabbing he crossed the yard and tapped at Pérez's door. The drone of noise in the yard behind him almost ceased altogether. He could feel the eyes on him and when Pérez's tall chamberlain opened the door he only glanced at him and then looked beyond and raked the compound with his eyes.

Quisiera hablar con el señor Pérez, said John Grady.

Con respecto de que?

Con respecto de mi cuate.

He shut the door. John Grady waited. After a while the door opened again. Pásale, said the chamberlain.

John Grady stepped into the room. Pérez's man shut the door and then stood against it. Pérez sat at his table.

How is the condition of your friend? he said.

That's what I come to ask you.

Pérez smiled.

Sit down. Please.

Is he alive?

Sit down. I insist.

He stepped to the table and pulled back a chair and sat.

Perhaps you like some coffee.

No thank you.

Pérez leaned back.

Tell me what I can do for you, he said.

You can tell me how my friend is.

But if I answer this question then you will go away.

What would you want me to stay for?

Pérez smiled. My goodness, he said. To tell me stories of your life of crime. Of course.

John Grady studied him.

Like all men of means, said Pérez, my only desire is to be entertained.

Me toma el pelo.

Yes. In english you say the leg, I believe.

Yes. Are you a man of means?

No. It is a joke. I enjoy to practice my english. It passes the time. Where did you learn castellano?

At home.

In Texas.

Yes.

You learn it from the servants.

We didnt have no servants. We had people worked on the place.

You have been in some prison before.

No.

You are the oveja negra, no? The black sheep?

You dont know nothin about me.

Perhaps not. Tell me, why do you believe that you can be release from your confinement in some abnormal way?

I told you you're diggin a dry hole. You dont know what I believe.

I know the United States. I have been there many times. You

are like the jews. There is always a rich relative. What prison were you in?

You know I aint been in no prison. Where is Rawlins?

You think I am responsible for the incident to your friend. But that is not the case.

You think I came here to do business. All I want is to know what's happened to him.

Pérez nodded thoughtfully. Even in a place like this where we are concerned with fundamental things the mind of the anglo is closed in this rare way. At one time I thought it was only his life of privilege. But it is not that. It is his mind.

He sat back easily. He tapped his temple. It is not that he is stupid. It is that his picture of the world is incomplete. In this rare way. He looks only where he wishes to see. You understand me?

I understand you.

Good, said Pérez. I can normally tell how intelligent a man is by how stupid he thinks I am.

I dont think you're stupid. I just dont like you.

Ah, said Pérez. Very good. Very good.

John Grady looked at Pérez's man standing against the door. He stood with his eyes caged, looking at nothing.

He doesnt understand what we are saying, said Pérez. Feel free to express yourself.

I've done expressed myself.

Yes.

I got to go.

Do you think you can go if I dont want you to go?

Yes.

Pérez smiled. Are you a cuchillero?

John Grady sat back.

A prison is like a—how do you call it? A salón de belleza.

A beauty parlor.

A beauty parlor. It is a big place for gossip. Everybody knows the story of everybody. Because crime is very interesting. Everybody knows that.

We never committed any crimes.

Perhaps not yet.

What does that mean?

Pérez shrugged. They are still looking. Your case is not decided. Did you think your case was decided?

They wont find anything.

My goodness, said Pérez. My goodness. You think there are no crimes without owners? It is not a matter of finding. It is only a matter of choosing. Like picking the proper suit in a store.

They dont seem to be in any hurry.

Even in Mexico they cannot keep you indefinitely. That is why you must act. Once you are charged it will be too late. They will issue what is called the previas. Then there are many difficulties.

He took his cigarettes from his shirtpocket and offered them across the table. John Grady didnt move.

Please, said Pérez. It is all right. It is not the same as breaking bread. It places one under no obligation.

He leaned forward and took a cigarette and put it in his mouth. Pérez took a lighter from his pocket and snapped it open and lit it and held it across the table.

Where did you learn to fight? he said.

John Grady took a deep pull on the cigarette and leaned back.

What do you want to know? he said.

Only what the world wants to know.

What does the world want to know.

The world wants to know if you have cojones. If you are brave.

He lit his own cigarette and laid the lighter on top of the pack of cigarettes on the table and blew a thin stream of smoke.

Then it can decide your price, he said.

Some people dont have a price.

That is true.

What about those people?

Those people die.

I aint afraid to die.

That is good. It will help you to die. It will not help you to live.

Is Rawlins dead?

No. He is not dead.

John Grady pushed back the chair.

Pérez smiled easily. You see? he said. You do just as I say.

I dont think so.

You have to make up your mind. You dont have so much time. We never have so much time as we think.

Time's the one thing I've had enough of since I come here.

I hope you will give some thought to your situation. Americans have ideas sometimes that are not so practical. They think that there are good things and bad things. They are very superstitious, you know.

You dont think there's good and bad things?

Things no. I think it is a superstition. It is the superstition of a godless people.

You think Americans are godless?

Oh yes. Dont you?

No.

I see them attack their own property. I saw a man one time destroy his car. With a big martillo. What do you call it?

Hammer.

Because it would not start. Would a Mexican do that?

I dont know.

A Mexican would not do that. The Mexican does not believe that a car can be good or evil. If there is evil in the car he knows that to destroy the car is to accomplish nothing. Because he knows where good and evil have their home. The anglo thinks in his rare way that the Mexican is superstitious. But who is the one? We know there are qualities to a thing. This car is green. Or it has a certain motor inside. But it cannot be tainted, you see. Or a man. Even a man. There can be in a man some evil. But we dont think it is his own evil. Where did he get it? How did he come to claim it? No. Evil is a true thing in Mexico. It goes about on its own legs. Maybe some day it will come to visit you. Maybe it already has.

Maybe.

Pérez smiled. You are free to go, he said. I can see you dont believe what I tell you. It is the same with money. Americans have this problem always I believe. They talk about tainted money. But money doesnt have this special quality. And the Mexican would never think to make things special or to put them in a special place where money is no use. Why do this? If money is good money is good. He doesnt have bad money. He doesnt have this problem. This abnormal thought.

John Grady leaned and stubbed out the cigarette in the tin ashtray on the table. Cigarettes in that world were money themselves and the one he left broken and smoldering in front of his host had hardly been smoked at all. I'll tell you what, he said.

Tell me.

I'll see you around.

He rose and looked at Pérez's man standing against the door. Pérez's man looked at Pérez.

I thought you wanted to know what would happen out there? said Pérez.

John Grady turned. Would that change it? he said.

Pérez smiled. You do me too much credit. There are three hundred men in this institution. No one can know what is possible.

Somebody runs the show.

Pérez shrugged. Perhaps, he said. But this type of world, you see, this confinement. It gives a false impression. As if things are in control. If these men could be controlled they would not be here. You see the problem.

Yes.

You can go. I will be interested myself to see what becomes to you.

He made a small gesture with his hand. His man stepped from before the door and held it open.

Joven, said Pérez.

John Grady turned. Yes, he said.

Take care with whom you break bread.

All right. I will.

Then he turned and walked out into the yard.

He still had forty-five pesos left from the money Blevins had given him and he tried to buy a knife with it but no one would sell him one. He couldnt be sure if there were none for sale or only none for sale to him. He moved across the courtyard at a studied saunter. He found the Bautistas under the shade of the south wall and he stood until they looked up and gestured to him to come forward.

He squatted in front of them.

Quiero comprar una trucha, he said.

They nodded. The one named Faustino spoke.

Cúanto dinero tienes?

Cuarenta y cinco pesos.

They sat for a long time. The dark indian face ruminating. Reflective. As if the complexities of this piece of business dragged after it every sort of consequence. Faustino shaped his mouth to speak. Bueno, he said. Dámelo.

John Grady looked at them. The lights in their black eyes. If there was guile there it was of no sort he could reckon with and he sat in the dirt and pulled off his left boot and reached down into it and took out the small damp sheaf of bills. They watched him. He pulled the boot back on and sat for a moment with the money palmed between his index and middle finger and then with a deft cardflip shot the folded bills under Faustino's knee. Faustino didnt move.

Bueno, he said. La tendré esta tarde.

He nodded and rose and walked back across the yard.

The smell of diesel smoke drifted across the compound and he could hear the buses in the street outside the gate and he realized that it was Sunday. He sat alone with his back to the wall. He heard a child crying. He saw the indian from Sierra León coming across the yard and he spoke to him.

The indian came over.

Siéntate, he said.

The indian sat. He took from inside his shirt a small paper bag limp with sweat and passed it to him. Inside was a handful of punche and a sheaf of cornhusk papers.

Gracias, he said.

He took a paper and folded it and dabbed the rough stringy tobacco in and rolled it shut and licked it. He handed the tobacco back and the indian rolled a cigarette and put the bag back inside his shirt and produced an esclarajo made from a half-inch waterpipe coupling and struck a light and cupped it in his hands and blew up the fire and held it for John Grady and then lit his own cigarette.

John Grady thanked him. No tienes visitantes? he said.

The indian shook his head. He didnt ask John Grady if he had visitors. John Grady thought he might have something to tell him. Some news that had moved through the prison but bypassed him in his exile. But the indian seemed to have no news at all and they sat leaning against the wall smoking until the cigarettes had burned away to nothing and the indian let the ashes fall between his feet and then rose and moved on across the yard.

He didnt go to eat at noon. He sat and watched the yard and tried to read the air. He thought men crossing were looking at him. Then he thought they were at pains not to. He said half aloud to himself that all this thinking could get a man killed. Then he said that talking to yourself could also get you killed. A little later he jerked awake and put one hand up. He was horrified to have fallen asleep there.

He looked at the width of the shadow of the wall before him. When the yard was half in the shade it would be four oclock. After a while he got up and walked down to where the Bautistas were sitting.

Faustino looked up at him. He gestured for him to come forward. He told him to step slightly to the left. Then he told him he was standing on it.

He almost looked down but he didnt. Faustino nodded. Siéntate, he said.

He sat.

Hay un cordón. He looked down. A small piece of string lay under his boot. When he pulled it up under his hand a knife emerged out of the gravel and he palmed it and slid it inside the waistband of his trousers. Then he got up and walked away.

It was better than what he'd expected. A switchblade with the handles missing, made in Mexico, the brass showing through the plating on the bolsters. He untied the piece of twine from around it and wiped it on his shirt and blew down into the blade channel and tapped it against the heel of his boot and blew again. He pushed the button and it clicked open. He wet a patch of hair on the back of his wrist and tried the edge. He was standing on one foot with his leg crossed over his knee honing the blade against the sole of his boot when he heard someone coming and he folded the knife and slid it into his pocket and turned and went out, passing two men who smirked at him on their way to the vile latrine.

A half hour later the horn sounded across the yard for the evening meal. He waited until the last man had entered the hall and then walked in and got his tray and moved down the line. Because it was Sunday and many of the prisoners had eaten food brought by their wives or family the hall was half empty and he turned and stood with his tray, the beans and tortillas and the anonymous stew, and picked a table in the corner where a boy not much older than he sat alone smoking and drinking water from a cup.

He stood at the end of the table and set his tray down. Con permiso, he said.

The boy looked at him and blew two thin streams of smoke from his nose and nodded and reached for his cup. On the inside of his right forearm was a blue jaguar struggling in the coils of an anaconda. In the web of his left thumb the pachuco cross and the five marks. Nothing out of the ordinary. But as he sat he suddenly knew why this man was eating alone. It was too late to rise again. He picked up the spoon with his left hand and began to eat. He heard the latch click shut on the door across the hall even above the muted scrape and click of spoons on the metal trays. He looked toward the front of the hall. There was no one behind the serving line. The two guards were gone. He continued to eat. His heart was pounding and his mouth was dry and the food was ashes. He took the knife from his pocket and put it in the waist of his trousers.

The boy stubbed out the cigarette and set his cup in the tray. Outside somewhere in the streets beyond the prison walls a dog barked. A tamalera cried out her wares. John Grady realized he could not have heard these things unless every sound in the hall had ceased. He opened the knife quietly against his leg and slid it open longwise under the buckle of his belt. The boy stood and stepped over the bench and took up his tray and turned and started down along the far side of the table. John Grady held the spoon in his left hand and gripped the tray. The boy came opposite him. He passed. John Grady watched him with a lowered gaze. When the boy reached the end of the table he suddenly turned and sliced the tray at his head. John Grady saw it all unfold slowly before him. The tray coming edgewise toward his eyes. The tin cup slightly tilted with the spoon in it slightly upended standing almost motionless in the air and the boy's greasy black hair flung across his wedgeshaped face. He flung his tray up and the corner of the boy's tray printed a deep dent in the bottom of it. He rolled away backward over the bench and scrabbled to his feet. He thought the tray would clatter to the table but the boy had not let go of it and he chopped at him with it again, coming along the edge of the bench. He fell back fending him away and the trays clanged and he saw the knife for the first time pass under the trays like a cold steel newt seeking out the warmth within him. He leaped away sliding in the spilled food on the concrete floor. He pulled the knife from his belt and swung the tray backhanded and caught the cuchillero in the forehead with it. The cuchillero seemed surprised. He was trying to block John Grady's view with his tray. John Grady stepped back. He was against the wall. He stepped to the side and gripped his tray and hacked at the cuchillero's tray, trying to hit his fingers. The cuchillero moved between him and the table. He kicked back the bench behind him. The trays rattled and clanged in the otherwise silence of the hall and the cuchillero's forehead had begun to bleed and the blood was running down alongside his left eye. He feinted with the tray again. John Grady could smell him. He feinted and his knife passed across the front of John Grady's shirt. John Grady dropped the tray to his midsection and moved along the wall looking into those black eyes. The cuchillero spoke no word. His movements were precise and without rancor. John Grady knew that he was hired. He swung the tray at his head and the cuchillero ducked and feinted and came forward. John Grady gripped the tray and moved along the wall. He ran his tongue into the corner of his mouth and tasted blood. He knew his face had been cut but he didnt know how bad. He knew the cuchillero had been hired because he was a man of reputation and it occurred to him that he was going to die in this place. He looked deep into those dark eyes and there were deeps there to look into. A whole malign history burning cold and remote and black. He moved along the wall, slicing back at the cuchillero with the tray. He was cut again across the outside of his upper arm. He was cut across his lower chest. He turned and slashed twice at the cuchillero with his knife. The man sucked himself up away from the blade with the boneless grace of a dervish. The men sitting at the table they were approaching had begun to rise one by one silently from the benches like birds leaving a wire. John Grady turned again and hacked at the cuchillero with his tray and the cuchillero squatted and he saw him there thin and bowlegged under his outflung arm for one frozen moment like some dark and reedy homunculous bent upon inhabiting him. The knife passed across his chest and passed back and the figure moved with incredible speed and again stood before him crouching silently, faintly weaving, watching his eyes. They were watching so that they could see if death were coming. Eyes that had seen it before and knew the colors it traveled under and what it looked like when it got there.

The tray clattered on the tiles. He realized he'd dropped it. He put his hand to his shirt. It came away sticky with blood and he wiped it on the side of his trousers. The cuchillero held the tray to his eyes to blind from him his movements. He looked to be adjuring him to read something writ there but there was nothing to see save the dents and dings occasioned by the ten thousand meals eaten off it. John Grady backed away. He sat slowly on the floor. His legs were bent crookedly under him and he slumped against the wall with his arms at either side of him. The cuchillero lowered the tray. He set it quietly on the table. He leaned and took hold of John Grady by the hair and forced his head back to cut his throat. As he did so John Grady brought his knife up from the floor and sank it into the cuchillero's heart. He sank it into his heart and snapped the handle sideways and broke the blade off in him.

The cuchillero's knife clattered on the floor. From the red boutonniere blossoming on the left pocket of his blue workshirt there spurted a thin fan of bright arterial blood. He dropped to his knees and pitched forward dead into the arms of his enemy. Some of the men in the hall had already stood to leave. Like theatre patrons anxious to avoid the crush. John Grady dropped the knifehandle and pushed at the oiled head lolling against his chest. He rolled to one side and scrabbled about until he found the cuchillero's knife. He pushed the dead man away and got hold of the table and struggled up. His clothes sagged with the weight of the blood. He backed away down the tables and turned and staggered to the door and unlatched it and walked wobbling out into the deep blue twilight.

The light from the hall lay in a paling corridor across the yard. Where the men came to the door to watch him it shifted and darkened in the dusk. No one followed him out. He walked with great care, holding his hand to his abdomen. The floodlights along the upper walls would come on at any moment. He walked very carefully. Blood sloshed in his boots. He looked at the knife in his hand and flung it away. The first horn would sound and the lights would come up along the walls. He felt lightheaded and curiously without pain. His hands were sticky with blood and blood was oozing through his fingers where he held himself. The lights would be coming on and the horn would be sounding.

He was halfway to the first steel ladder when a tall man overtook him and spoke to him. He turned, crouching. In the dying light perhaps they would not see he had no knife. Not see how he stood so bloody in his clothes.

Ven conmigo, said the man. Está bien.

No me moleste.

The dark tiers of the prison walls ran forever down the deep cyanic sky. A dog had begun to bark.

El padrote quiere ayudarle.

Mande?

The man stood before him. Ven conmigo, he said.

It was Pérez's man. He held out his hand. John Grady stepped back. His boots left wet tracks of blood in the dry floor of the yard. The lights would come on. Horn would sound. He turned to go, his knees stammering under him. He fell and got up again. The mayordomo reached to help him and he twisted out of his grip and fell again. The world swam. Kneeling he pushed against the ground to rise. Blood dripped between his outstretched hands. The dark bank of the wall rode up. The deep cyanic sky. He was lying on his side. Pérez's man bent over him. He stooped and gathered him up in his arms and lifted him and carried him across the yard into Pérez's house and kicked the door shut behind him as the lights came on and the horn sounded.

HE WOKE in a stone room in total darkness and a smell of disinfectant. He put his hand out to see what it would touch and felt pain all over him like something that had been crouching there in the silence waiting for him to stir. He put his hand down. He turned his head. A thin rod lay luminescing in the blackness. He listened but there was no sound. Every breath he took was like a razor. After a while he put his hand out and touched the cold block wall.

Hola, he said. His voice was weak and reedy, his face stiff and twisted. He tried again. Hola. There was someone there. He could feel them.

Quién está? he said, but no one spoke back.

There was someone there and they had been there. There was no one there. There was someone there and they had been there and they had not left but there was no one there.

He looked at the floating rod of light. It was light from under a door. He listened. He held his breath and listened because the room was small it seemed to be small and if the room was small he could hear them breathing in the dark if they were breathing but he heard nothing. He half wondered if he were not dead and in his despair he felt well up in him a surge of sorrow like a child beginning to cry but it brought with it such pain that he stopped it cold and began at once his new life and the living of it breath to breath.

He knew he was going to get up and try the door and he took a long time getting ready. First he moved onto his stomach. He pushed himself over all at once to get it done with and he was just amazed at the pain. He lay breathing. He reached down to put his hand on the floor. It swung in empty space. He eased his leg over the edge and pushed himself up and his foot touched the floor and he lay resting on his elbows.

When he reached the door it was locked. He stood, the floor cool under his feet. He was trussed in some sort of wrapping and he'd begun to bleed again. He could feel it. He stood resting with his face against the cool of the metal door. He felt the bandage on his face against the door and he touched it and he was thirsty out of all reason and he rested for a long time before starting back across the floor.

When the door did open it was to blinding light and there stood in it no ministress in white but a demandadero in stained and wrinkled khakis bearing a metal messtray with a double spoonful of pozole spilled over it and a glass of orange soda-water. He was not much older than John Grady and he backed into the room with the tray and turned, his eyes looking everywhere but at the bed. Other than a steel bucket in the floor there was nothing in the room but the bed and nowhere to put the tray but on it.

He approached and stood. He looked at once uncomfortable and menacing. He gestured with the tray. John Grady eased himself onto his side and pushed himself up. Sweat stood on his forehead. He was wearing some sort of rough cotton gown and he'd bled through it and the blood had dried.

Dame el refresco, he said. Nada más.

Nada más?

No.

The demandadero handed him the glass of orangewater and he took it and sat holding it. He looked at the little stone block room. Overhead was a single lightbulb in a wire cage.

La luz, por favor, he said.

The demandadero nodded and went to the door and turned and pulled it shut after him. A click of the latch in the darkness. Then the light came on.

He listened to the steps down the corridor. Then the silence. He raised the glass and slowly drank the soda. It was tepid, only faintly effervescent, delicious.

He lay there three days. He slept and woke and slept again. Someone turned off the light and he woke in the dark. He called out but no one answered. He thought of his father in Goshee. He knew that terrible things had been done to him there and he had always believed that he did not want to know about it but he did want to know. He lay in the dark thinking of all the things he did not know about his father and he realized that the father he knew was all the father he would ever know. He would not think about Alejandra because he didnt know what was coming or how bad it would be and he thought she was something he'd better save. So he thought about horses and they were always the right thing to think about. Later someone turned the light back on again and it did not go off again after that. He slept and when he woke he'd dreamt of the dead standing about in their bones and the dark sockets of their eyes that were indeed without speculation bottomed in the void wherein lay a terrible intelligence common to all but of which none would speak. When he woke he knew that men had died in that room.

When the door opened next it was to admit a man in a blue suit carrying a leather bag. The man smiled at him and asked after his health.

Mejor que nunca, he said.

The man smiled again. He set the bag on the bed and opened it and took out a pair of surgical scissors and pushed the bag to the foot of the bed and pulled back the bloodstained sheet.

Quién és usted? said John Grady.

The man looked surprised. I am the doctor, he said.

The scissors had a spade end that was cold against his skin and the doctor slid them under the bloodstained gauze cummerbund and began to cut it away. He pulled the dressing from under him and they looked down at the stitches.

Bien, bien, said the doctor. He pushed at the sutures with two fingers. Bueno, he said.

He cleaned the sutured wounds with an antiseptic and taped gauze pads over them and helped him to sit up. He took a large roll of gauze out of the bag and reached around John Grady's waist and began to wrap it.

Put you hands on my shoulders, he said.

What?

Put you hands on my shoulders. It is all right.

He put his hands on the doctor's shoulders and the doctor wrapped the dressing. Bueno, he said. Bueno.

He rose and closed the bag and stood looking down at his patient.

I will send for you soap and towels, he said. So you can wash yourself.

All right.

You are a fasthealer.

A what?

A fasthealer. He nodded and smiled and turned and went out. John Grady didnt hear him latch the door but there was no place to go anyway.

His next visitor was a man he'd never seen before. He wore a uniform that looked to be military. He did not introduce himself. The guard who brought him shut the door and stood outside it. The man stood at his bed and took off his hat as though in deference to some wounded hero. Then he took a comb from the breastpocket of his tunic and passed it once along each side of his oiled head and put the hat back on again.

How soon you can walk around, he said.

Where do you want me to walk to?

To your house.

I can walk right now.

The man pursed his lips, studying him.

Show me you walk.

He pushed back the sheets and rolled onto his side and stepped down to the floor. He walked up and back. His feet left cold wet tracks on the polished stones that sucked up and vanished like the tale of the world itself. The sweat stood quivering on his forehead.

You are fortunate boys, he said.

I dont feel so fortunate.

Fortunate boys, he said again, and nodded and left.

He slept and woke. He knew night from day only by the meals. He ate little. Finally they brought him half a roast chicken with rice and two halves of a tinned pear and this he ate slowly, savoring each bite and proposing and rejecting various scenarios that might have occurred in the outer world or be occurring. Or were yet to come. He still thought that he might be taken out into the campo and shot.

He practiced walking up and down. He polished the underside of the messtray with the sleeve of his shift and standing in the center of the room under the lightbulb he studied the face that peered dimly out of the warped steel like some maimed and raging djinn enconjured there. He peeled away the bandage from his face and inspected the stitches there and felt them with his fingers.

When next he woke the demandadero had opened the door and stood with a pile of clothes and with his boots. He let them fall in the floor. Sus prendas, he said, and shut the door.

He stripped out of the shift and washed himself with soap and rag and dried himself with the towel and dressed and pulled on the boots. Someone had washed the blood out of the boots and they were still wet and he tried to take them off again but he could not and he lay on the bunk in his clothes and boots waiting for God knew what.

Two guards came. They stood at the open door and waited for him. He got up and walked out.

They went down a corridor and across a small patio and entered another part of the building. They walked down another corridor and the guards tapped at a door and then opened it and one of them motioned for him to enter.

At a desk sat the commandante who'd been to his cell to see if he could walk.

You be seated, said the commandante.

He sat.

The commandante opened his desk drawer and took out an envelope and handed it across the desk.

This is you, he said.

John Grady took the envelope.

Where's Rawlins? he said.

Excuse me?

Dónde está mi compadre.

You friend.

Yes.

He wait outside.

Where are we going?

You going away. You going away to you house.

When.

Excuse me?

Cuándo.

You going now. I dont want to see you no more.

The commandante waved his hand. John Grady put one hand on the back of the chair and rose and turned and walked out the door and he and the guards went down the hallway and out through the office to the sallygate where Rawlins stood waiting in a costume much like his own. Five minutes later they were standing in the street outside the tall ironshod wooden doors of the portal.

There was a bus standing in the street and they climbed laboriously aboard. Women in the seats with their empty hampers and baskets spoke to them softly as they made their way down the aisle.

I thought you'd died, said Rawlins.

I thought you had.

What happened?

I'll tell you. Let's just sit here. Let's not talk. Let's just sit here real quiet.

Are you all right?

Yeah. I'm all right.

Rawlins turned and looked out the window. All was gray and still. A few drops of rain had begun to fall in the street. They dropped on the roof of the bus solitary as a bell. Down the street he could see the arched buttresses of the cathedral dome and the minaret of the belltower beyond.

All my life I had the feelin that trouble was close at hand. Not that I was about to get into it. Just that it was always there.

Let's just sit here real quiet, said John Grady.

They sat watching the rain in the street. The women sat quietly. Outside it was darkening and there was no sun nor any paler place to the sky where sun might be. Two more women climbed aboard and took their seats and then the driver swung up and closed the door and looked to the rear in the mirror and put the bus in gear and they pulled away. Some of the women wiped at the glass with their hands and peered back at the prison standing in the gray rain of Mexico. So like some site of siege in an older time, in an older country, where the enemies were all from without.

It was only a few blocks to the centro and when they eased themselves down from the bus the gaslamps were already on in the plaza. They crossed slowly to the portales on the north side of the square and stood looking out at the rain. Four men in maroon band uniforms stood along the wall with their instruments. John Grady looked at Rawlins. Rawlins looked lost standing there hatless and afoot in his shrunken clothes.

Let's get somethin to eat.

We dont have no money.

I got money.

Where'd you get any money at? Rawlins said.

I got a whole envelope full.

They walked into a cafe and sat in a booth. A waiter came over and put menus in front of them and went away. Rawlins looked out the window.

Get a steak, said John Grady.

All right.

We'll eat and get a hotel room and get cleaned up and get some sleep.

All right.

He ordered steaks and fried potatoes and coffee for both of them and the waiter nodded and took the menus. John Grady rose and made his way slowly to the counter and bought two packs of cigarettes and a penny box of matches each. People at their tables watched him cross the room.

Rawlins lit a cigarette and looked at him.

Why aint we dead? he said.

She paid us out.

The señora?

The aunt. Yes.

Why?

I dont know.

Is that where you got the money?

Yes.

It's got to do with the girl, dont it?

I expect it does.

Rawlins smoked. He looked out the window. Outside it was already dark. The streets were wet from the rain and the lights from the cafe and from the lamps in the plaza lay bleeding in the black pools of water.

There aint no other explanation, is there?

No.

Rawlins nodded. I could of run off from where they had me. It was just a hospital ward.

Why didnt you?

I dont know. You think I was dumb not to of?

I dont know. Yeah. Maybe.

What would you of done?

I wouldnt of left you.

Yeah. I know you wouldnt.

That dont mean it aint dumb.

Rawlins almost smiled. Then he looked away.

The waiter brought the coffee.

There was another old boy in there, said Rawlins. All cut up. Probably wasnt a bad boy. Set out on Saturday night with a few dollars in his pocket. Pesos. Goddamned pathetic.

What happened to him?

He died. When they carried him out of there I thought how peculiar it would of seemed to him if he could of seen it. It did to me and it wasnt even me. Dying aint in people's plans, is it?

No.

He nodded. They put Mexican blood in me, he said.

He looked up. John Grady was lighting a cigarette. He shook out the match and put it in the ashtray and looked at Rawlins.

So.

So what does that mean? said Rawlins.

Mean about what?

Well does it mean I'm part Mexican?

John Grady drew on the cigarette and leaned back and blew the smoke into the air. Part Mexican? he said.

Yeah.

How much did they put?

They said it was over a litre.

How much over a litre?

I dont know.

Well a litre would make you almost a halfbreed.

Rawlins looked at him. It dont, does it? he said.

No. Hell, it dont mean nothin. Blood's blood. It dont know where it come from.

The waiter brought the steaks. They ate. He watched Rawlins. Rawlins looked up.

What? he said.

Nothin.

You ought to be happier about bein out of that place.

I was thinkin the same thing about you.

Rawlins nodded. Yeah, he said.

What do you want to do?

Go home.

All right.

They ate.

You're goin back down there, aint you? said Rawlins.

Yeah. I guess I am.

On account of the girl?

Yeah.

What about the horses?

The girl and the horses.

Rawlins nodded. You think she's lookin for you to come back?

I dont know.

I'd say the old lady might be surprised to see you.

No she wont. She's a smart woman.

What about Rocha?

He'll have to do whatever he has to do.

Rawlins crossed his silver in the platter beside the bones and took out his cigarettes.

Dont go down there, he said.

I done made up my mind.

Rawlins lit the cigarette and shook out the match. He looked up.

There's only one kind of deal I can see that she could of made with the old woman.

I know. But she's goin to have to tell me herself.

If she does will you come back?

I'll come back.

All right.

I still want the horses.

Rawlins shook his head and looked away.

I aint askin you to go with me, said John Grady.

I know you aint.

You'll be all right.

Yeah. I know.

He tapped the ash from his cigarette and pushed at his eyes with the heel of his hand and looked out the window. Outside it was raining again. There was no traffic in the streets.

Kid over yonder tryin to sell newspapers, he said. Aint a soul in sight and him standin there with his papers up under his shirt just a hollerin.

He wiped his eyes with the back of his hand.

Ah shit, he said.

What?

Nothin. Just shit.

What is it?

I keep thinkin about old Blevins.

John Grady didnt answer. Rawlins turned and looked at him. His eyes were wet and he looked old and sad.

I caint believe they just walked him out there and done him that way.

Yeah.

I keep thinkin about how scared he was.

You'll feel better when you get home.

Rawlins shook his head and looked out the window again. I dont think so, he said.

John Grady smoked. He watched him. After a while he said: I aint Blevins.

Yeah, said Rawlins. I know you aint. But I wonder how much better off you are than him.

John Grady stubbed out his cigarette. Let's go, he said.

They bought toothbrushes and a bar of soap and a safety-razor at a farmacia and they found a room in a hotel two blocks down Aldama. The key was just a common doorkey tied to a wooden fob with the number of the room burned into the wood with a hot wire. They walked out across the tiled courtyard where the rain was falling lightly and found the room and opened the door and turned on the light. A man sat up in the bed and looked at them. They backed out and turned off the light and shut the door and went back to the desk where the man gave them another key.

The room was bright green and there was a shower in one corner with an oilcloth curtain on a ring. John Grady turned on the shower and after a while there was hot water in the pipes. He turned it off again.

Go ahead, he said.

You go ahead.

I got to come out of this tape.

He sat on the bed and peeled away the dressings while Rawlins showered. Rawlins turned off the water and pushed back the curtain and stood drying himself with one of the threadbare towels.

We're a couple of good'ns, aint we? he said.

Yeah.

How you goin to get them stitches out?

I guess I'll have to find a doctor.

It hurts worse takin em out than puttin em in.

Yeah.

Did you know that?

Yeah. I knew that.

Rawlins wrapped the towel around himself and sat on the bed opposite. The envelope with the money was lying on the table.

How much is in there?

John Grady looked up. I dont know, he said. Considerable less than what there was supposed to be, I'll bet. Go ahead and count it.

He took the envelope and counted the bills out on the bed.

Nine hundred and seventy pesos, he said.

John Grady nodded.

How much is that?

About a hundred and twenty dollars.

Rawlins tapped the sheaf of bills together on the glass of the tabletop and put them back in the envelope.

Split it in two piles, said John Grady.

I dont need no money.

Yes you do.

I'm goin home.

Dont make no difference. Half of it's yours.

Rawlins stood and hung the towel over the iron bedstead and pulled back the covers. I think you're goin to need ever dime of it, he said.

When he came out of the shower he thought Rawlins was asleep but he wasnt. He crossed the room and turned off the light and came back and eased himself into the bed. He lay in the dark listening to the sounds in the street, the dripping of rain in the courtyard.

You ever pray? said Rawlins.

Yeah. Sometimes. I guess I got kindly out of the habit.

Rawlins was quiet for a long time. Then he said: What's the worst thing you ever done?

I dont know. I guess if I done anything real bad I'd rather not tell it. Why?

I dont know. I was in the hospital cut I got to thinkin: I wouldnt be here if I wasnt supposed to be here. You ever think like that?

Yeah. Sometimes.

They lay in the dark listening. Someone crossed the patio. A door opened and closed again.

You aint never done nothin bad, said John Grady.

Me and Lamont one time drove a pickup truckload of feed to Sterling City and sold it to some Mexicans and kept the money.

That aint the worst thing I ever heard of.

I done some other stuff too.

If you're goin to talk I'm goin to smoke a cigarette.

I'll shut up.

They lay quietly in the dark.

You know about what happened, dont you? said John Grady.

You mean in the messhall?

Yeah.

Yeah.

John Grady reached and got his cigarettes off the table and lit one and blew out the match.

I never thought I'd do that.

You didnt have no choice.

I still never thought it.

He'd of done it to you.

He drew on the cigarette and blew the smoke unseen into the darkness. You dont need to try and make it right. It is what it is.

Rawlins didnt answer. After a while he said: Where'd you get the knife?

Off the Bautistas. I bought it with the last forty-five pesos we had.

Blevins' money.

Yeah. Blevins' money.

Rawlins was lying on his side in the springshot iron bedstead watching him in the dark. The cigarette glowed a deep red where John Grady drew on it and his face with the sutures in his cheek emerged from the darkness like some dull red theatric mask indifferently repaired and faded back again.

I knew when I bought the knife what I'd bought it for.

I dont see where you were wrong.

The cigarette glowed, it faded. I know, he said. But you didnt do it.

In the morning it was raining again and they stood outside the same cafe with toothpicks in their teeth and looked at the rain in the plaza. Rawlins studied his nose in the glass.

You know what I hate?

What?

Showin up at the house lookin like this.

John Grady looked at him and looked away. I dont blame you, he said.

You dont look so hot yourself.

John Grady grinned. Come on, he said.

They bought new clothes and hats in a Victoria Street haberdashery and wore them out into the street and in the slow falling rain walked down to the bus station and bought Rawlins a ticket for Nuevo Laredo. They sat in the bus station cafe in the stiff new clothes with the new hats turned upside down on the chairs at either side and they drank coffee until the bus was announced over the speaker.

That's you, said John Grady.

They rose and put on their hats and walked out to the gates.

Well, said Rawlins. I reckon I'll see you one of these days.

You take care.

Yeah. You take care.

He turned and handed his ticket to the driver and the driver punched it and handed it back and he climbed stiffly aboard. John Grady stood watching while he passed along the aisle. He thought he'd take a seat at the window but he didnt. He sat on the other side of the bus and John Grady stood for a while and then turned and walked back out through the station to the street and walked slowly back through the rain to the hotel.

He exhausted in the days following the roster of surgeons in that small upland desert metropolis without finding one to do what he asked. He spent his days walking up and down in the narrow streets until he knew every corner and callejón. At the end of a week he had the stitches removed from his face, sitting in a common metal chair, the surgeon humming to himself as he snipped with his scissors and pulled with his clamp. The surgeon said that the scar would improve in its appearance. He said for him not to look at it because it would get better with time. Then he put a bandage over it and charged him fifty pesos and told him to come back in five days and he would remove the stitches from his belly.

A week later he left Saltillo on the back of a flatbed truck heading north. The day was cool and overcast. There was a large diesel engine chained to the bed of the truck. He sat in the truckbed as they jostled out through the streets, trying to brace himself, his hands at either side on the rough boards. After a while he pulled his hat down hard over his eyes and stood and placed his hands outstretched on the roof of the cab and rode in that manner. As if he were some personage bearing news for the countryside. As if he were some newfound evangelical being conveyed down out of the mountains and north across the flat bleak landscape toward Monclova.

IV

AT A CROSSROADS STATION somewhere on the other side of Paredón they picked up five farmworkers who climbed up on the bed of the truck and nodded and spoke to him with great circumspection and courtesy. It was almost dark and it was raining lightly and they were wet and their faces were wet in the yellow light from the station. They huddled forward of the chained engine and he offered them his cigarettes and they thanked him each and took one and they cupped their hands over the small flame against the falling rain and thanked him again.

De dónde viene? they said.

De Tejas.

Tejas, they said. Y dónde va?

He drew on his cigarette. He looked at their faces. One of them older than the rest nodded at his cheap new clothes.

Él va a ver a su novia, he said.

They looked at him earnestly and he nodded and said that it was true.

Ah, they said. Qué bueno. And after and for a long time to come he'd have reason to evoke the recollection of those smiles and to reflect upon the good will which provoked them for it had power to protect and to confer honor and to strengthen resolve and it had power to heal men and to bring them to safety long after all other resources were exhausted.

When the truck finally pulled out and they saw him still standing they offered their bundles for him to sit on and he did so and he nodded and dozed to the hum of the tires on the blacktop and the rain stopped and the night cleared and the moon that was already risen raced among the high wires by the highway side like a single silver music note burning in the constant and lavish dark and the passing fields were rich from the rain with the smell of earth and grain and peppers and the sometime smell of horses. It was midnight when they reached Monclova and he shook hands with each of the workers and walked around the truck and thanked the driver and nodded to the other two men in the cab and then watched the small red taillight recede down the street and out toward the highway leaving him alone in the darkened town.

The night was warm and he slept on a bench in the alameda and woke with the sun already up and the day's commerce begun. Schoolchildren in blue uniforms were passing along the walkway. He rose and crossed the street. Women were washing the sidewalks in front of the shops and vendors were setting up their wares on small stands or tables and surveying the day.

He ate a breakfast of coffee and pan dulce at a cafe counter in a sidestreet off the square and he entered a farmacia and bought a bar of soap and put it in the pocket of his jacket along with his razor and toothbrush and then set out along the road west.

He got a ride to Frontera and another to San Buenaventura. At noon he bathed in an irrigation ditch and he shaved and washed and slept lying on his jacket in the sun while his clothes dried. Downstream was a small wooden cofferdam and when he woke there were naked children splashing in the pool there and he rose and wrapped his jacket about his waist and walked out along the bank where he could sit and watch them. Two girls passed down the bankside path bearing between them a cloth-covered tub and carrying covered pails in their free hand. They were taking dinner to workers in the field and they smiled shyly at him sitting there half naked and so pale of skin with the angry red suture marks laddered across his chest and stomach. Quietly smoking. Watching the children bathe in the silty ditch-water.

He walked all afternoon out the dry hot road toward Cuatro Ciénagas. No one he met passed without speaking. He walked along past fields where men and women were hoeing the earth and those at work by the roadside would stop and nod to him and say how good the day was and he agreed with all they said. In the evening he took his supper with workers in their camp, five or six families seated together at a table made of cut poles bound with hemp twine. The table was pitched under a canvas fly and the evening sun resolved within the space beneath a deep orange light where the seams and stitching passed in shadow over their faces and their clothes as they moved. The girls set out the dishes on little pallets made from the ends of crates that nothing overbalance on the uncertain surface of the table and an old man at the farthest end of the table prayed for them all. He asked that God remember those who had died and he asked that the living gathered together here remember that the corn grows by the will of God and beyond that will there is neither corn nor growing nor light nor air nor rain nor anything at all save only darkness. Then they ate.

They'd have made a bed for him but he thanked them and walked out in the dark along the road until he came to a grove of trees and there he slept. In the morning there were sheep in the road. Two trucks carrying fieldhands were coming along behind the sheep and he walked out to the road and asked the driver for a ride. The driver nodded him aboard and he dropped back along the bed of the moving truck and tried to pull himself up. He could not and when the workers saw his condition they rose instantly and pulled him aboard. By a series of such rides and much walking he made his way west through the low mountains beyond Nadadores and down into the barrial and took the clay road out of La Madrid and in the late afternoon entered once more the town of La Vega.

He bought a Coca-Cola in the store and stood leaning against the counter while he drank it. Then he drank another. The girl at the counter watched him uncertainly. He was studying a calendar on the wall. He did not know the date within a week and when he asked her she didnt know either. He set the second bottle on the counter alongside the first one and walked back out into the mud street and set off afoot up the road toward La Purísima.

He'd been gone seven weeks and the countryside was changed, the summer past. He saw almost no one on the road and he reached the hacienda just after dark.

When he knocked at the gerente's door he could see the family at dinner through the doorway. The woman came to the door and when she saw him she went back to get Armando. He came to the door and stood picking his teeth. No one invited him in. When Antonio came out they sat under the ramada and smoked.

Quién está en la casa? said John Grady.

La dama.

Y el señor Rocha?

En Mexico.

John Grady nodded.

Se fue él y la hija a Mexico. Por avión. He made an airplane motion with one hand.

Cuándo regresa?

Quién sabe?

They smoked.

Tus cosas quedan aquí.

Sí?

Sí. Tu pistola. Todas tus cosas. Y las de tu compadre.

Gracias.

De nada.

They sat. Antonio looked at him.

Yo no sé nada, joven.

Entiendo.

En serio.

Está bien. Puedo dormir en la cuadra?

Sí. Si no me lo digas.

Cómo están las yeguas?

Antonio smiled. Las yeguas, he said.

He brought him his things. The pistol had been unloaded and the shells were in the mochila along with his shaving things, his father's old Marble huntingknife. He thanked Antonio and walked down to the barn in the dark. The mattress on his bed had been rolled up and there was no pillow and no bedding. He unrolled the tick and sat and kicked off his boots and stretched out. Some of the horses that were in the stalls had come up when he entered the barn and he could hear them snuffling and stirring and he loved to hear them and he loved to smell them and then he was asleep.

At daylight the old groom pushed open the door and stood looking in at him. Then he shut the door again. When he had gone John Grady got up and took his soap and his razor and walked out to the tap at the end of the barn.

When he walked up to the house there were cats coming from the stable and orchard and cats coming along the high wall or waiting their turn to pass under the worn wood of the gate. Carlos had slaughtered a sheep and along the dappled floor of the portal more cats sat basking in the earliest light falling through the hydrangeas. Carlos in his apron looked out from the doorway of the keep at the end of the portal. John Grady wished him a good morning and he nodded gravely and withdrew.

María did not seem surprised to see him. She gave him his breakfast and he watched her and he listened as she spoke by rote. The señorita would not be up for another hour. A car was coming for her at ten. She would be gone all day visiting at the quinta Margarita. She would return before dark. She did not like to travel the roads at night. Perhaps she could see him before he left.

John Grady sat drinking his coffee. He asked her for a cigarette and she brought her pack of El Toros from the window above the sink and put them on the table for him. She neither asked where he'd been nor how things had been with him but when he rose to go she put her hand on his shoulder and poured more coffee into his cup.

Puedes esperar aquí, she said. Se levantará pronto.

He waited. Carlos came in and put his knives in the sink and went out again. At seven oclock she went out with the breakfast tray and when she returned she told him that he was invited to come to the house at ten that evening, that the señorita would see him then. He rose to go.

Quisiera un caballo, he said.

Caballo.

Sí. Por el día, no más.

Momentito, she said.

When she returned she nodded. Tienes tu caballo. Espérate un momento. Siéntate.

He waited while she fixed him a lunch and wrapped it in a paper and tied it with string and handed it to him.

Gracias, he said.

De nada.

She took the cigarettes and the matches from the table and handed them to him. He tried to read in her countenance any disposition of the mistress so recently visited that might reflect upon his case. In all that he saw he hoped to be wrong. She pushed the cigarettes at him. Ándale pues, she said.

There were new mares in some of the stalls and as he passed through the barn he stopped to look them over. In the saddle-room he pulled on the light and got a blanket and the bridle he'd always used and he pulled down what looked to be the best of the half dozen saddles from the rack and looked it over and blew the dust from it and checked the straps and slung it over his shoulder by the horn and walked out and up to the corral.

The stallion when it saw him coming began to trot. He stood at the gate and watched it. It passed with its head canted and its eyes rolling and its nostrils siphoning the morning air and then it recognized him and turned and came to him and he pushed open the gate and the horse whinnied and tossed its head and snorted and pushed its long sleek nose against his chest.

When he went past the bunkhouse Morales was sitting out under the ramada peeling onions. He waved idly with his knife and called out. John Grady called back his thanks to the old man before he realized that the old man had not said that he was glad to see him but that the horse was. He waved again and touched up the horse and they went stamping and skittering as if the horse could find no gait within its repertoire to suit the day until he rode him through the gate and out of view of house and barn and cook and slapped the polished flank trembling under him and they went on at a hard flat gallop up the ciénaga road.

He rode among the horses on the mesa and he walked them up out of the swales and cedar brakes where they'd gone to hide and he trotted the stallion along the grassy rims for the wind to cool him. He rode up buzzards out of a draw where they'd been feeding on a dead colt and he sat the horse and looked down at the poor form stretched in the tainted grass eyeless and naked.

Noon he sat with his boots dangling over the rimrock and ate the cold chicken and bread she'd fixed for him while the staked horse grazed. The country rolled away to the west through broken light and shadow and the distant summer storms a hundred miles downcountry to where the cordilleras rose and sank in the haze in a frail last shimmering restraint alike of the earth and the eye beholding it. He smoked a cigarette and then pushed in the crown of his hat with his fist and put a rock in it and lay back in the grass and put the weighted hat over his face. He thought what sort of dream might bring him luck. He saw her riding with her back so straight and the black hat set level on her head and her hair loose and the way she turned with her shoulders and the way she smiled and her eyes. He thought of Blevins. He thought of his face and his eyes when he pressed his last effects upon him. He'd dreamt of him one night in Saltillo and Blevins came to sit beside him and they talked of what it was like to be dead and Blevins said it was like nothing at all and he believed him. He thought perhaps if he dreamt of him enough he'd go away forever and be dead among his kind and the grass scissored in the wind at his ear and he fell asleep and dreamt of nothing at all.

As he rode down through the parkland in the evening the cattle kept moving out of the trees before him where they'd gone to shade up in the day. He rode through a grove of apple trees gone wild and brambly and he picked an apple as he rode and bit into it and it was hard and green and bitter. He walked the horse through the grass looking for apples on the ground but the cattle had eaten them all. He rode past the ruins of an old cabin. The lintel was gone from the door and he walked the horse inside. The vigas were partly down and hunters or herdsmen had built fires in the floor. An old calfhide was nailed to one wall and there was no glass to the windows for the frames and sash were long since burned for firewood. There was a strange air to the place. As of some site where life had not succeeded. The horse liked nothing about it and he dabbed the reins against its neck and touched it with the heel of his boot and they turned carefully in the room and went out and rode down through the orchard and out past the marshlands toward the road. Doves called in the winey light. He tacked and quartered the horse to keep it from treading constantly in its own shadow for it seemed uneasy doing so.

He washed at the spigot in the corral and put on his other shirt and wiped the dust from his boots and walked up to the bunkhouse. It was already dark. The vaqueros had finished their meal and were sitting out under the ramada smoking.

Buenas noches, he said.

Eres tú, Juan?

Claro.

There was a moment of silence. Then someone said: Estás bienvenido aquí.

Gracias, he said.

He sat and smoked with them and told them all that had happened. They were concerned about Rawlins, more a friend to them than he. They were saddened that he was not coming back but they said that a man leaves much when he leaves his own country. They said that it was no accident of circumstance that a man be born in a certain country and not some other and they said that the weathers and seasons that form a land form also the inner fortunes of men in their generations and are passed on to their children and are not so easily come by otherwise.

They spoke of the cattle and the horses and the young wild mares in their season and of a wedding in La Vega and a death at Víbora. No one spoke of the patrón or of the dueña. No one spoke of the girl. In the end he wished them a good night and walked back down to the barn and lay on the cot but he had no way to tell the time and he rose and walked up to the house and knocked at the kitchen door.

He waited and knocked again. When María opened the door to let him in he knew that Carlos had just left the room. She looked at the clock on the wall over the sink.

Ya comiste? she said.

No.

Siéntate. Hay tiempo.

He sat at the table and she made a plate for him of roast mutton with adobada sauce and put it to warm in the oven and in a few minutes brought it to him with a cup of coffee. She finished washing the dishes at the sink and a little before ten she dried her hands on her apron and went out. When she came back she stood in the door. He rose.

Está en la sala, she said.

Gracias.

He went out down the hall to the parlor. She was standing almost formally and she was dressed with an elegance chilling to him. She came across the room and sat and nodded at the chair opposite.

Sit down please.

He walked slowly across the patterned carpet and sat. Behind her on the wall hung a large tapestry that portrayed a meeting in some vanished landscape between two horsemen on a road. Above the double doors leading into the library the mounted head of a fighting bull with one ear missing.

Héctor said that you would not come here. I assured him he was wrong.

When is he coming back?

He will not be back for some time. In any event he will not see you.

I think I'm owed an explanation.

I think the accounts have been settled quite in your favor. You have been a great disappointment to my nephew and a considerable expense to me.

No offense, mam, but I've been some inconvenienced myself.

The officers were here once before, you know. My nephew sent them away until he was able to have an investigation performed. He was quite confident that the facts were otherwise. Quite confident.

Why didnt he say something to me.

He'd given his word to the commandante. Otherwise you would have been taken away at once. He wished to have his own investigation performed. I think you can understand that the commandante would be reluctant to notify people prior to arresting them.

I should of been let to tell my side of it.

You had already lied to him twice. Why should he not assume you would do so a third time?

I never lied to him.

The affair of the stolen horse was known here even before you arrived. The thieves were known to be Americans. When he questioned you about this you denied everything. Some months later your friend returned to the town of Encantada and committed murder. The victim an officer of the state. No one can dispute these facts.

When is he comin back?

He wont see you.

You think I'm a criminal.

I'm prepared to believe that certain circumstances must have conspired against you. But what is done cannot be undone.

Why did you buy me out of prison?

I think you know why.

Because of Alejandra.

Yes.

And what did she have to give in return?

I think you know that also.

That she wont see me again.

Yes.

He leaned back in the chair and stared past her at the wall. At the tapestry. At a blue ornamental vase on a sideboard of figured walnut.

I can scarcely count on my two hands the number of women in this family who have suffered disastrous love affairs with men of disreputable character. Of course the times enabled some of these men to style themselves revolutionaries. My sister Matilde was widowed twice by the age of twenty-one, both husbands shot. That sort of thing. Bigamists. One does not like to entertain the notion of tainted blood. A family curse. But no, she will not see you.

You took advantage of her.

I was pleased to be in a bargaining position at all.

Dont ask me to thank you.

I shant.

You didnt have the right. You should of left me there.

You would have died.

Then I'd of died.

They sat in silence. The hall clock ticked.

We're willing that you should have a horse. I'll trust Antonio to supervise the selection. Have you any money?

He looked at her. I'd of thought maybe the disappointments in your own life might of made you more sympathetic to other people.

You would have thought wrongly.

I guess so.

It is not my experience that life's difficulties make people more charitable.

I guess it depends on the people.

You think you know something of my life. An old woman whose past perhaps has left her bitter. Jealous of the happiness of others. It is an ordinary story. But it is not mine. I put forward your cause even in the teeth of the most outrageous tantrums on the part of Alejandra's mother—whom mercifully you have never met. Does that surprise you?

Yes.

Yes. Were she a more civil person perhaps I'd have been less of an advocate. I am not a society person. The societies to which I have been exposed seemed to me largely machines for the suppression of women. Society is very important in Mexico. Where women do not even have the vote. In Mexico they are mad for society and for politics and very bad at both. My family are considered gachupines here, but the madness of the Spaniard is not so different from the madness of the creole. The political tragedy in Spain was rehearsed in full dress twenty years earlier on Mexican soil. For those with eyes to see. Nothing was the same and yet everything. In the Spaniard's heart is a great yearning for freedom, but only his own. A great love of truth and honor in all its forms, but not in its substance. And a deep conviction that nothing can be proven except that it be made to bleed. Virgins, bulls, men. Ultimately God himself. When I look at my grandniece I see a child. And yet I know very well who and what I was at her age. In a different life I could have been a soldadera. Perhaps she too. And I will never know what her life is. If there is a pattern there it will not shape itself to anything these eyes can recognize. Because the question for me was always whether that shape we see in our lives was there from the beginning or whether these random events are only called a pattern after the fact. Because otherwise we are nothing. Do you believe in fate?

Yes mam. I guess I do.

My father had a great sense of the connectedness of things. I'm not sure I share it. He claimed that the responsibility for a decision could never be abandoned to a blind agency but could only be relegated to human decisions more and more remote from their consequences. The example he gave was of a tossed coin that was at one time a slug in a mint and of the coiner who took that slug from the tray and placed it in the die in one of two ways and from whose act all else followed, cara y cruz. No matter through whatever turnings nor how many of them. Till our turn comes at last and our turn passes.

She smiled. Thinly. Briefly.

It's a foolish argument. But that anonymous small person at his workbench has remained with me. I think if it were fate that ruled our houses it could perhaps be flattered or reasoned with. But the coiner cannot. Peering with his poor eyes through dingy glasses at the blind tablets of metal before him. Making his selection. Perhaps hesitating a moment. While the fates of what unknown worlds to come hang in the balance. My father must have seen in this parable the accessibility of the origins of things, but I see nothing of the kind. For me the world has always been more of a puppet show. But when one looks behind the curtain and traces the strings upward he finds they terminate in the hands of yet other puppets, themselves with their own strings which trace upward in turn, and so on. In my own life I saw these strings whose origins were endless enact the deaths of great men in violence and madness. Enact the ruin of a nation. I will tell you how Mexico was. How it was and how it will be again. You will see that those things which disposed me in your favor were the very things which led me to decide against you in the end.

When I was a girl the poverty in this country was very terrible. What you see today cannot even suggest it. And I was very affected by this. In the towns there were tiendas which rented clothes to the peasants when they would come to market. Because they had no clothes of their own and they would rent them for the day and return home at night in their blankets and rags. They had nothing. Every centavo they could scrape together went for funerals. The average family owned nothing machine-made except for a kitchen knife. Nothing. Not a pin or a plate or a pot or a button. Nothing. Ever. In the towns you'd see them trying to sell things which had no value. A bolt fallen from a truck picked up in the road or some wornout part of a machine that no one could even know the use of. Such things as that. Pathetic things. They believed that someone must be looking for these things and would know how to value these things if only that person could be found. It was a faith that no disappointment seemed capable of shaking. What else had they? For what other thing would they abandon it? The industrial world was to them a thing unimaginable and those who inhabited it wholly alien to them. And yet they were not stupid. Never stupid. You could see it in the children. Their intelligence was frightening. And they had a freedom which we envied. There were so few restraints upon them. So few expectations. Then at the age of eleven or twelve they would cease being children. They lost their childhood overnight and they had no youth. They became very serious. As if some terrible truth had been visited upon them. Some terrible vision. At a certain point in their lives they were sobered in an instant and I was puzzled by this but of course I could not know what it was they saw. What it was they knew.

By the time I was sixteen I had read many books and I had become a freethinker. In all cases I refused to believe in a God who could permit such injustice as I saw in a world of his own making. I was very idealistic. Very outspoken. My parents were horrified. Then in the summer of my seventeenth year my life changed forever.

In the family of Francisco Madero there were thirteen children and I had many friends among them. Rafaela was my own age within three days and we were very close. Much more so than with the daughters of Carranza. Teníamos compadrazgo con su familia. You understand? There is no translation. The family had given me my quinceañera at Rosario. In that same year Don Evaristo took a group of us to California. All young girls from the haciendas. From Parras and Torreón. He was quite old even then and I marvel at his courage. But he was a wonderful man. He had served a term as governor of the state. He was very wealthy and he was very fond of me and not at all put off by my philosophizing. I loved going to Rosario. In those days there was more social life about the haciendas. Very elaborate parties were given with orchestras and champagne and often there were European visitors and these affairs would continue until dawn. To my surprise I found myself quite popular and very likely I'd have been cured of my overwrought sensibilities except for two things. The first of these was the return of the two oldest boys, Francisco and Gustavo.

They had been in school in France for five years. Before that they had studied in the United States. In California and in Baltimore. When I was again introduced to them it was to old friends, almost family. Yet my recollection of them was a child's recollection and I must have been to them something wholly unknown.

Francisco as the eldest son enjoyed a special place in the house. There was a table under the portal where he held court with his friends. In the fall of that year I was invited to the house many times and it was in that house that I first heard the full expression of those things closest to my heart. I began to see how the world must become if I were to live in it.

Francisco began to set up schools for the poor children of the district. He dispensed medicines. Later he would feed hundreds of people from his own kitchen. It is not easy to convey the excitement of those times to people today. People were greatly attracted to Francisco. They took pleasure in his company. At that time there was no talk of his entering politics. He was simply trying to implement the ideas he had discovered. To make them work in everyday life. People from Mexico began to come to see him. In every undertaking he was seconded by Gustavo.

I'm not sure you can understand what I am telling you. I was seventeen and this country to me was like a rare vase being carried about by a child. There was an electricity in the air. Everything seemed possible. I thought that there were thousands like us. Like Francisco. Like Gustavo. There were not. Finally in the end it seemed there were none.

Gustavo wore an artificial eye as a result of an accident when he was a young boy. This did not lessen his attractiveness to me. I think perhaps the contrary. Certainly there was no company I preferred to his. He gave me books to read. We talked for hours. He was very practical. Much more so than Francisco. He did not share Francisco's taste for the occult. Always he talked of serious things. Then in the autumn of that year I went with my father and uncle to a hacienda in San Luis Potosí and there I suffered the accident to my hand of which I have spoken.

To a boy this would have been an event of consequence. To a girl it was a devastation. I would not be seen in public. I even imagined I saw a change in my father towards me. That he could not help but view me as something disfigured. I thought it would now be assumed that I could not make a good marriage and perhaps it was so assumed. There was no longer even a finger on which to place the ring. I was treated with great delicacy. Perhaps like a person returned home from an institution. I wished with all my heart that I'd been born among the poor where such things are so much more readily accepted. In this condition I awaited old age and death.

Some months passed. Then one day just before Christmas Gustavo came to call on me. I was terrified. I told my sister to beg him to go away. He would not. When my father returned quite late that night he was rather taken aback to find him seated in the parlor by himself with his hat in his lap. He came to my room to talk to me. I put my hands over my ears. I dont remember what happened. Only that Gustavo continued to sit. He passed the night in the parlor like a mozo. Here. In this house.

The next day my father was very angry with me. I will not entertain you with the scene that followed. I'm sure my howls of rage and anguish reached Gustavo's ears. But of course I could not oppose my father's will and in the end I appeared. Rather elegantly dressed if I remember. I'd learned to affect a handkerchief in my left hand in such a way as to cover my deformity. Gustavo rose and smiled at me. We walked in the garden. In those days rather better tended. He told me of his plans. Of his work. He gave me news of Francisco and of

Rafaela. Of our friends. He treated me no differently than before. He told me how he had lost his eye and of the cruelty of the children at his school and he told me things he had never told anyone, not even Francisco. Because he said that I would understand.

He talked of those things we had spoken of so often at Rosario. So often and so far into the night. He said that those who have endured some misfortune will always be set apart but that it is just that misfortune which is their gift and which is their strength and that they must make their way back into the common enterprise of man for without they do so it cannot go forward and they themselves will wither in bitterness. He said these things to me with great earnestness and great gentleness and in the light from the portal I could see that he was crying and I knew that it was my soul he wept for. I had never been esteemed in this way. To have a man place himself in such a position. I did not know what to say. That night I thought long and not without despair about what must become of me. I wanted very much to be a person of value and I had to ask myself how this could be possible if there were not something like a soul or like a spirit that is in the life of a person and which could endure any misfortune or disfigurement and yet be no less for it. If one were to be a person of value that value could not be a condition subject to the hazards of fortune. It had to be a quality that could not change. No matter what. Long before morning I knew that what I was seeking to discover was a thing I'd always known. That all courage was a form of constancy. That it was always himself that the coward abandoned first. After this all other betrayals came easily.

I knew that courage came with less struggle for some than for others but I believed that anyone who desired it could have it. That the desire was the thing itself. The thing itself. I could think of nothing else of which that was true.

So much depends on luck. It was only in later years that I understood what determination it must have taken for Gustavo to speak to me as he did. To come to my father's house in that way. Undeterred by any thought of rejection or ridicule. Above all I understood that his gift to me was not even in the words. The news he brought he could not speak. But it was from that day that I began to love the man who had brought me that news and though he is dead now close on to forty years those feelings have not changed.

She took a handkerchief from her sleeve and with it touched the underlid of each eye. She looked up.

Well, you see. Anyway you are quite patient. The rest of the story is not so difficult to imagine since the facts are known. In the months that followed my revolutionary spirit was rekindled and the political aspects of Francisco Madero's activities became more manifest. As he came to be taken more seriously enemies arose and his name soon reached the ear of the dictator Díaz. Francisco was forced to sell the property he had acquired at Australia in order to finance his undertakings. Before long he was arrested. Later still he fled to the United States. His determination never wavered, yet in those years few could have foreseen that he would become president of Mexico. When he and Gustavo returned they returned with guns. The revolution had begun.

In the meantime I was sent to Europe and in Europe I remained. My father was outspoken in his views concerning the responsibilities of the landed class. But revolution was another matter altogether. He would not bring me home unless I promised to disassociate myself from the Maderos and this I would not do. Gustavo and I were never engaged. His letters to me became less frequent. Then they stopped. Finally I was told that he had married. I did not blame him then or now. There were months in the revolution when the entire campaign was financed out of his pocket. Every bullet. Every crust of bread. When Díaz was at last made to flee and a free election was held Francisco became the first president of this republic ever to be placed in office by popular vote. And the last.

I will tell you about Mexico. I will tell you what happened to these brave and good and honorable men. By that time I was teaching in London. My sister came to join me and she stayed with me until the summer. She begged me to return with her but I would not. I was very proud. Very stubborn. I could not forgive my father either for his political blindness or for his treatment of me.

Francisco Madero was surrounded by plotters and schemers from his first day in office. His trust in the basic goodness of humankind became his undoing. At one point Gustavo brought General Huerta to him at gunpoint and denounced him as a traitor but Francisco would not hear of it and reinstated him. Huerta. An assassin. An animal. This was in February of nineteen thirteen. There was an armed uprising. Huerta of course was the secret accomplice. When he felt his position secure he capitulated to the rebels and led them against the government. Gustavo was arrested. Then Francisco and Pino Suárez. Gustavo was turned over to the mob in the courtyard of the ciudadela. They crowded about him with torches and lanterns. They abused and tormented him, calling him Ojo Parado. When he asked to be spared for the sake of his wife and children they called him a coward. Him, a coward. They pushed him and struck him. They burned him. When he begged them again to cease one of them came forward with a pick and pried out his good eye and he staggered away moaning in his darkness and spoke no more. Someone came forward with a revolver and put it to his head and fired but the crowd jostled his arm and the shot tore away his jaw. He collapsed at the feet of the statue of Morelos. Finally a volley of rifle shots was fired into him. He was pronounced dead. A drunk in the crowd pushed forward and shot him again anyway. They kicked his dead body and spat upon it. One of them pried out his artificial eye and it was passed among the crowd as a curiosity.

They sat in silence, the clock ticked. After a while she looked up at him.

So. This was the community of which he spoke. This beautiful boy. Who had given everything.

What happened to Francisco?

He and Pino Suárez were driven out behind the penitentiary and shot. It was no test of the cynicism of their murderers to claim that they were shot in attempting to escape. Francisco's mother had sent a telegram to President Taft asking him to intercede to save her son's life. Sara delivered it herself to the ambassador at the American Embassy. Most probably it was never sent. The family went into exile. They went to Cuba. To the United States. To France. There had always been a rumor that they were of jewish extraction. Possibly it's true. They were all very intelligent. Certainly theirs seemed to me at least to be a jewish destiny. A latterday diaspora. Martyrdom. Persecution. Exile. Sara today lives at Colonia Roma. She has her grandchildren. We see one another seldom yet we share an unspoken sisterhood. That night in the garden here at my father's house Gustavo said to me that those who have suffered great pain of injury or loss are joined to one another with bonds of a special authority and so it has proved to be. The closest bonds we will ever know are bonds of grief. The deepest community one of sorrow. I did not return from Europe until my father died. I regret now that I did not know him better. I think in many ways he also was ill suited to the life he chose. Or which chose him. Perhaps we all were. He used to read books on horticulture. In this desert. He'd already begun the cultivation of cotton here and he would have been pleased to see the success it has made. In later years I came to see how alike were he and Gustavo. Who was never meant to be a soldier. I think they did not understand Mexico. Like my father he hated bloodshed and violence. But perhaps he did not hate it enough. Francisco was the most deluded of all. He was never suited to be president of Mexico. He was hardly even suited to be Mexican. In the end we all come to be cured of our sentiments. Those whom life does not cure death will. The world is quite ruthless in selecting between the dream and the reality, even where we will not. Between the wish and the thing the world lies waiting. I've thought a great deal about my life and about my country. I think there is little that can be truly known. My family has been fortunate. Others were less so. As they are often quick to point out.

When I was in school I studied biology. I learned that in making their experiments scientists will take some group— bacteria, mice, people—and subject that group to certain conditions. They compare the results with a second group which has not been disturbed. This second group is called the control group. It is the control group which enables the scientist to gauge the effect of his experiment. To judge the significance of what has occurred. In history there are no control groups. There is no one to tell us what might have been. We weep over the might have been, but there is no might have been. There never was. It is supposed to be true that those who do not know history are condemned to repeat it. I dont believe knowing can save us. What is constant in history is greed and foolishness and a love of blood and this is a thing that even God—who knows all that can be known—seems powerless to change.

My father is buried less than two hundred meters from where we now sit. I walk out there often and I talk to him. I talk to him as I could never do in life. He made me an exile in my own country. It was not his intention to do so. When I was born in this house it was already filled with books in five languages and since I knew that as a woman the world would be largely denied me I seized upon this other world. I was reading by the time I was five and no one ever took a book from my hands. Ever. Then my father sent me to two of the best schools in Europe. For all his strictness and authority he proved to be a libertine of the most dangerous sort. You spoke of my disappointments. If such they are they have only made me reckless. My grandniece is the only future I contemplate and where she is concerned I can only put all my chips forward. It may be that the life I desire for her no longer even exists, yet I know what she does not. That there is nothing to lose. In January I will be seventy-three years old. I have known a great many people in that time and few of them led lives that were satisfactory to them. I would like for my grandniece to have the opportunity to make a very different marriage from the one which her society is bent upon demanding of her. I wont accept a conventional marriage for her. Again, I know what she cannot. That there is nothing to lose. I dont know what sort of world she will live in and I have no fixed opinions concerning how she should live in it. I only know that if she does not come to value what is true above what is useful it will make little difference whether she lives at all. And by true I do not mean what is righteous but merely what is so. You think I have rejected your suit because you are young or without education or from another country but that is not the case. I was never remiss in poisoning Alejandra's mind against the conceits of the sorts of suitors available to her and we have both long been willing to entertain the notion of rescue arriving in whatever garb it chose. But I also spoke to you of a certain extravagance in the female blood of this family. Something willful. Improvident. Knowing this in her I should have been more wary where you were concerned. I should have seen you more clearly. Now I do.

You wont let me make my case.

I know your case. Your case is that certain things happened over which you had no control.

It's true.

I'm sure it is. But it's no case. I've no sympathy with people to whom things happen. It may be that their luck is bad, but is that to count in their favor?

I intend to see her.

Am I supposed to be surprised? I'll even give you my permission. Although that seems to be a thing you have never required. She will not break her word to me. You will see.

Yes mam. We will.

She rose and swept her skirt behind her to let it fall and she held out her hand. He rose and took it in his, very briefly, so fineboned and cool.

I'm sorry I shant see you again. I've been at some pains to tell you about myself because among other reasons I think we should know who our enemies are. I've known people to spend their lives nursing a hatred of phantoms and they were not happy people.

I dont hate you.

You shall.

We'll see.

Yes. We'll see what fate has in store for us, wont we?

I thought you didnt believe in fate.

She waved her hand. It's not so much that I dont believe in it. I dont subscribe to its nomination. If fate is the law then is fate also subject to that law? At some point we cannot escape naming responsibility. It's in our nature. Sometimes I think we are all like that myopic coiner at his press, taking the blind slugs one by one from the tray, all of us bent so jealously at our work, determined that not even chaos be outside of our own making.

IN THE MORNING he walked up to the bunkhouse and ate breakfast with the vaqueros and said goodbye to them. Then he walked down to the gerente's and he and Antonio went out to the barn and saddled mounts and rode up through the trap looking at the greenbroke horses. He knew the one he wanted. When it saw them it snorted and turned and went trotting. It was Rawlins' grullo and they got a rope on it and brought it down to the corral and by noon he had the animal in a half manageable condition and he walked it around and left it to cool. The horse had not been ridden in weeks and it had no cinchmarks on it and it barely knew how to eat grain. He walked down to the house and said goodbye to María and she gave him the lunch she had packed for him and handed him a rosecolored envelope with the La Purísima emblem embossed in the upper left corner. When he got outside he opened it and took out the money and folded it and put it into his pocket without counting it and folded the envelope and put it in his shirtpocket. Then he walked out through the pecan trees in front of the house where

Antonio stood waiting with the horses and they stood for a moment in a wordless abrazo and then he mounted up into the saddle and turned the horse into the road.

He rode through La Vega without dismounting, the horse blowing and rolling its eyes at all it saw. When a truck started up in the street and began to come toward them the animal moaned in despair and tried to turn and he sawed it down almost onto its haunches and patted it and talked constantly to it until the vehicle was past and then they went on again. Once outside the town he left the road altogether and set off across the immense and ancient lakebed of the bolsón. He crossed a dry gypsum playa where the salt crust stove under the horse's hooves like trodden isinglass and he rode up through white gypsum hills grown with stunted datil and through a pale bajada crowded with flowers of gypsum like a cavefloor uncovered to the light. In the shimmering distance trees and jacales stood along the slender bights of greenland pale and serried and half fugitive in the clear morning air. The horse had a good natural gait and as he rode he talked to it and told it things about the world that were true in his experience and he told it things he thought could be true to see how they would sound if they were said. He told the horse why he liked it and why he'd chosen it to be his horse and he said that he would allow no harm to come to it.

By noon he was riding a farmland road where the acequias carried the water down along the foot-trodden selvedges of the fields and he stood the horse to water and walked it up and back in the shade of a cottonwood grove to cool it. He shared his lunch with children who came to sit beside him. Some of them had never eaten leavened bread and they looked to an older boy among them for guidance in the matter. They sat in a row along the edge of the path, five of them, and the sandwich halves of cured ham from the hacienda were passed to left and to right and they ate with great solemnity and when the sandwiches were gone he divided with his knife the freshbaked tarts of apple and guava.

Dónde vive? said the oldest boy.

He mused on the question. They waited. I once lived at a great hacienda, he told them, but now I have no place to live.

The children's faces studied him with great concern. Puede vivir con nosotros, they said, and he thanked them and he told them that he had a novia who was in another town and that he was riding to her to ask her to be his wife.

Es bonita, su novia? they asked, and he told them that she was very beautiful and that she had blue eyes which they could scarcely believe but he told them also that her father was a rich hacendado while he himself was very poor and they heard this in silence and were greatly cast down at his prospects. The older of the girls said that if his novia truly loved him she would marry him no matter what but the boy was not so encouraging and he said that even in families of the rich a girl could not go against the wishes of her father. The girl said that the grandmother must be consulted because she was very important in these matters and that he must take her presents and try to win her to his side for without her help little could be expected. She said that all the world knew this to be true.

John Grady nodded at the wisdom of this but he said that he had already given offense where the grandmother was concerned and could not depend upon her assistance and at this several of the children ceased to eat and stared at the earth before them.

Es un problema, said the boy.

De acuerdo.

One of the younger girls leaned forward. Qué ofensa le dio a la abuelita? she said.

Es una historia larga, he said.

Hay tiempo, they said.

He smiled and looked at them and as there was indeed time he told them all that had happened. He told them how they had come from another country, two young horsemen riding their horses, and that they had met with a third who had no money nor food to eat nor scarcely clothes to cover himself and that he had come to ride with them and share with them in all they had. This horseman was very young and he rode a wonderful horse but among his fears was the fear that God would kill him with lightning and because of this fear he lost his horse in the desert. He then told them what had happened concerning the horse and how they had taken the horse from the village of Encantada and he told how the boy had gone back to the village of Encantada and there had killed a man and that the police had come to the hacienda and arrested him and his friend and that the grandmother had paid their fine and then forbidden the novia to see him anymore.

When he was done they sat in silence and finally the girl said that what he must do is bring the boy to the grandmother so that he would tell her that he was the one at fault and John Grady said that this was not possible because the boy was dead. When the children heard this they blessed themselves and kissed their fingers. The older boy said that the situation was a difficult one but that he must find an intercessor to speak on his behalf because if the grandmother could be made to see that he was not to blame then she would change her mind. The older girl said that he was forgetting about the problem that the family was rich and he was poor. The boy said that as he had a horse he could not be so very poor and they looked at John Grady for a decision on this question and he told them that in spite of appearances he was indeed very poor and that the horse had been given to him by the grandmother herself. At this some of them drew in their breath and shook their heads. The girl said that he needed to find some wise man with whom he could discuss his difficulties or perhaps a curandera and the younger girl said that he should pray to God.

It was late night and dark when he rode into Torreón. He haltered the horse and tied it in front of a hotel and went in and asked about a livery stable but the clerk knew nothing of such things. He looked out the front window at the horse and he looked at John Grady.

Puede dejarlo atrás, he said.

Atrás?

Sí. Afuera. He gestured toward the rear.

John Grady looked toward the rear of the building.

Por dónde? he said.

The clerk shrugged. He passed the flat of his hand past the desk toward the hallway. Por aquí.

There was an old man sitting in a sofa in the lobby who'd been watching out the window and he turned to John Grady and told him that it was all right and that far worse things than horses had passed through that hotel lobby and John Grady looked at the clerk and then went out and untied the horse and led it in. The clerk had preceded him down the hallway and he opened the rear doors and stood while John Grady led the horse out into the yard. He'd bought a small sack of grain in Tlahualilo and he watered the horse in a washtrough and broke open the grainsack and poured the grain out into the upturned lid of a trashcan and he unsaddled the horse and wet the empty sack and rubbed the horse down with it and then carried the saddle in and got his key and went up to bed.

When he woke it was noon. He'd slept almost twelve hours. He rose and went to the window and looked out. The window gave onto the little yard behind the hotel and the horse was patiently walking the enclosure with three children astride it and another leading it and yet another hanging on to its tail.

He stood in line most of the morning at the telephone exchange waiting for his turn at one of the four cabinets and when he finally got his call through she could not be reached. He signed up again at the counter and the girl behind the glass read his face and told him that he would have better luck in the afternoon and he did. A woman answered the phone and sent someone to get her. He waited. When she came to the phone she said that she knew it would be him.

I have to see you, he said.

I cant.

You have to. I'm coming down there.

No. You cant.

I'm leaving in the morning. I'm in Torreón.

Did you talk to my aunt?

Yes.

She was quiet. Then she said: I cant see you.

Yes you can.

I wont be here. I go to La Purísima in two days.

I'll meet you at the train.

You cant. Antonio is coming to meet me.

He closed his eyes and held the phone very tightly and he told her that he loved her and that she'd had no right to make the promise that she'd made even if they killed him and that he would not leave without seeing her even if it was the last time he would see her ever and she was quiet for a long time and then she said that she would leave a day early. That she would say her aunt was ill and she would leave tomorrow morning and meet him in Zacatecas. Then she hung up.

He boarded the horse at a stable out beyond the barrios south of the railtracks and told the patrón to be wary of the horse as he was at best half broke and the man nodded and called to the boy but John Grady could tell he had his own ideas about horses and would come to his own conclusions. He lugged the saddle into the saddleroom and hung it up and the boy locked the door behind him and he walked back out to the office.

He offered to pay in advance but the proprietor dismissed him with a small wave of the hand. He walked out into the sun and down the street where he caught the bus back to town.

He bought a small awol bag in a store and he bought two new shirts and a new pair of boots and he walked down to the train station and bought his ticket and went to a cafe and ate. He walked around to break in the boots and then went back to the hotel. He rolled the pistol and knife and his old clothes up in the bedroll and had the clerk put the bedroll in the storage room and he told the clerk to wake him at six in the morning and then went up to bed. It was hardly even dark.

It was cool and gray when he left the hotel in the morning and by the time he got settled into the coach there were spits of rain breaking on the glass. A young boy and his sister sat in the seat opposite and after the train pulled out the boy asked him where he was from and where he was going. They didnt seem surprised to hear he was from Texas. When the porter came through calling breakfast he invited them to eat with him but the boy looked embarrassed and would not. He was embarrassed himself. He sat in the diner and ate a big plate of huevos rancheros and drank coffee and watched the gray fields pass beyond the wet glass and in his new boots and shirt he began to feel better than he'd felt in a long time and the weight on his heart had begun to lift and he repeated what his father had once told him, that scared money cant win and a worried man cant love. The train passed through a dreadful plain grown solely with cholla and entered a vast forest of china palm. He opened the pack of cigarettes he'd bought at the station kiosk and lit one and laid the pack on the tablecloth and blew smoke at the glass and at the country passing in the rain.

The train pulled into Zacatecas in the late afternoon. He walked out of the station and up the street through the high portales of the old stone aqueduct and down into the town. The rain had followed them down from the north and the narrow stone streets were wet and the shops were closed. He walked up Hidalgo past the cathedral to the Plaza de Armas and checked into the Reina Cristina Hotel. It was an old colonial hotel and it was quiet and cool and the stones of the lobby floor were dark and polished and there was a macaw in a cage watching the people go in and out. In the diningroom adjoining the lobby there were people still at lunch. He got his key and went up, a porter carrying his small bag. The room was large and high ceilinged and there was a chenille cover on the bed and a cutglass decanter of water on the table. The porter swept open the window drapes and went into the bathroom to see that all was in order. John Grady leaned on the window balustrade. In the courtyard below an old man knelt among pots of red and white geraniums, singing softly a single verse from an old corrido as he tended the flowers.

He tipped the porter and put his hat on the bureau and shut the door. He stretched out on the bed and looked up at the carved vigas of the ceiling. Then he got up and got his hat and went down to the diningroom to get a sandwich.

He walked through the narrow twisting streets of the town with its ancient buildings and small sequestered plazas. The people seemed dressed with a certain elegance. It had stopped raining and the air was fresh. Shops had begun to open. He sat on a bench in the plaza and had his boots shined and he looked in the shopwindows trying to find something for her. He finally bought a very plain silver necklace and paid the woman what she asked and the woman tied it in a paper with a ribbon and he put it in the pocket of his shirt and went back to the hotel.

The train from San Luis Potosí and Mexico was due in at eight oclock. He was at the station at seven-thirty. It was almost nine when it arrived. He waited on the platform among others and watched the passengers step down. When she appeared on the steps he almost didnt recognize her. She was wearing a blue dress with a skirt almost to her ankles and a blue hat with a wide brim and she did not look like a schoolgirl either to him or to the other men on the platform. She carried a small leather suitcase and the porter took it from her as she stepped down and then handed it back to her and touched his cap. When she turned and looked at him where he was standing he realized she had seen him from the window of the coach. As she walked toward him her beauty seemed to him a thing altogether improbable. A presence unaccountable in this place or in any place at all. She came toward him and she smiled at him sadly and she touched her fingers to the scar on his cheek and leaned and kissed it and he kissed her and took the suitcase from her.

You are so thin, she said. He looked into those blue eyes like a man seeking some vision of the increate future of the universe. He'd hardly breath to speak at all and he told her that she was very beautiful and she smiled and in her eyes was the sadness he'd first seen the night she came to his room and he knew that while he was contained in that sadness he was not the whole of it.

Are you all right? she said.

Yes. I'm all right.

And Lacey?

He's all right. He's gone home.

They walked out through the small terminal and she took his arm.

I'll get a cab, he said.

Let's walk.

All right.

The streets were filled with people and in the Plaza de Armas there were carpenters nailing up the scaffolding for a crepe-covered podium before the Governor's Palace where in two days' time orators would speak on the occasion of Independence Day. He took her hand and they crossed the street to the hotel. He tried to read her heart in her handclasp but he knew nothing.

They ate dinner in the hotel diningroom. He'd never been in a public place with her and he was not prepared for the open glances from older men at nearby tables nor for the grace with which she accepted them. He'd bought a pack of american cigarettes at the desk and when the waiter brought the coffee he lit one and placed it in the ashtray and said that he had to tell her what had happened.

He told her about Blevins and about the prisión Castelar and he told her about what happened to Rawlins and finally he told her about the cuchillero who had fallen dead in his arms with his knife broken off in his heart. He told her everything. Then they sat in silence. When she looked up she was crying.

Tell me, he said.

I cant.

Tell me.

How do I know who you are? Do I know what sort of man you are? What sort my father is? Do you drink whiskey? Do you go with whores? Does he? What are men?

I told you things I've never told anybody. I told you all there was to tell.

What good is it? What good?

I dont know. I guess I just believe in it.

They sat for a long time. Finally she looked up at him. I told him that we were lovers, she said.

The chill that went through him was so cold. The room so quiet. She'd hardly more than whispered yet he felt the silence all around him and he could scarcely look. When he spoke his voice was lost.

Why?

Because she threatened to tell him. My aunt. She told me I must stop seeing you or she would tell him.

She wouldnt have.

No. I dont know. I couldnt stand for her to have that power. I told him myself.

Why?

I dont know. I dont know.

Is it true? You told him?

Yes. It's true.

He leaned back. He put both hands to his face. He looked at her again.

How did she find out?

I dont know. Different things. Estéban perhaps. She heard me leave the house. Heard me return.

You didnt deny it.

No.

What did your father say?

Nothing. He said nothing.

Why didnt you tell me?

You were on the mesa. I would have. But when you returned you were arrested.

He had me arrested.

Yes.

How could you tell him?

I dont know. I was so foolish. It was her arrogance. I told her I would not be blackmailed. She made me crazy.

Do you hate her?

No. I dont hate her. But she tells me I must be my own person and with every breath she tries to make me her person. I dont hate her. She cant help it. But I broke my father's heart. I broke his heart.

He said nothing at all?

No.

What did he do?

He got up from the table. He went to his room.

You told him at the table?

Yes.

In front of her?

Yes. He went to his room and the next morning he left before daylight. He saddled a horse and left. He took the dogs. He went up into the mountains alone. I think he was going to kill you.

She was crying. People were looking toward their table. She lowered her eyes and sat sobbing silently, just her shoulders moving and the tears running down her face.

Dont cry. Alejandra. Dont cry.

She shook her head. I destroyed everything. I only wanted to die.

Dont cry. I'll make it right.

You cant, she said. She raised her eyes and looked at him. He'd never seen despair before. He thought he had, but he had not.

He came to the mesa. Why didnt he kill me?

I dont know. I think he was afraid that I would take my life.

Would you?

I dont know.

I will make it right. You have to let me.

She shook her head. You dont understand.

What dont I understand?

I didnt know that he would stop loving me. I didnt know he could. Now I know.

She took a handkerchief from her purse. I'm sorry, she said. People are looking at us.

IT RAINED in the night and the curtains kept lifting into the room and he could hear the splash of the rain in the courtyard and he held her pale and naked against him and she cried and she told him that she loved him and he asked her to marry him. He told him that he could make a living and that they could go to live in his country and make their life there and no harm would come to them. She did not sleep and when he woke in the dawn she was standing at the window wearing his shirt.

Viene la madrugada, she said.

Yes.

She came to the bed and sat. I saw you in a dream. I saw you dead in a dream.

Last night?

No. Long ago. Before any of this. Hice una manda.

A promise.

Yes.

For my life.

Yes. They carried you through the streets of a city I'd never seen. It was dawn. The children were praying. Lloraba tu madre. Con más razón tu puta.

He put his hand to her mouth. Dont say that. You cant say that.

She took his hand and held it in hers and touched the veins.

They went out in the dawn in the city and walked in the streets. They spoke to the streetsweepers and to women opening the small shops, washing the steps. They ate in a cafe and walked in the little paseos and callejones where old vendresses of sweets, melcochas and charamuscas, were setting out their wares on the cobbles and he bought strawberries for her from a boy who weighed them in a small brass balance and twisted up a paper alcatraz to pour them into. They walked in the old Jardín Independencia where high above them stood a white stone angel with one broken wing. From her stone wrists dangled the broken chains of the manacles she wore. He counted in his heart the hours until the train would come again from the south which when it pulled out for Torreón would either take her or would not take her and he told her that if she would trust her life into his care he would never fail her or abandon her and that he would love her until he died and she said that she believed him.

In the forenoon as they were returning to the hotel she took his hand and led him across the street.

Come, she said. I will show you something.

She led him down past the cathedral wall and through the vaulted arcade into the street beyond.

What is it? he said.

A place.

They walked up the narrow twisting street. Past a tannery. A tinsmith shop. They entered a small plaza and here she turned.

My grandfather died here, she said. My mother's father.

Where?

Here. In this place. Plazuela de Guadalajarita.

In the revolution.

Yes. In nineteen-fourteen. The twenty-third of June. He was with the Zaragoza Brigade under Raúl Madero. He was twenty-four years old. They came down from north of the city. Cerro de Loreto. Tierra Negra. Beyond here at that time all was campo. He died in this strange place. Esquina de la Calle del Deseo y el Callejón del Pensador Mexicano. There was no mother to cry. As in the corridos. Nor little bird that flew. Just the blood on the stones. I wanted to show you. We can go.

Quién fue el Pensador Mexicano?

Un poeta. Joaquín Fernández de Lizardi. He had a life of great difficulty and died young. As for the Street of Desire it is like the Calle de Noche Triste. They are but names for Mexico. We can go now.

When they got to the room the maid was cleaning and she left and they closed the curtains and made love and slept in each other's arms. When they woke it was evening. She came from the shower wrapped in a towel and she sat on the bed and took his hand and looked down at him. I cannot do what you ask, she said. I love you. But I cannot.

He saw very clearly how all his life led only to this moment and all after led nowhere at all. He felt something cold and soulless enter him like another being and he imagined that it smiled malignly and he had no reason to believe that it would ever leave. When she came out of the bathroom again she was dressed and he made her sit on the bed and he held her hands both of them and talked to her but she only shook her head and she turned away her tearstained face and told him that it was time to go and that she could not miss the train.

They walked through the streets and she held his hand and he carried her bag. They walked through the alameda above the old stone bullring and came down the steps past the carved stone bandstand. A dry wind had come up from the south and in the eucalyptus trees the grackles teetered and screamed. The sun was down and a blue twilight filled the park and the yellow gaslamps came on along the aqueduct walls and down the walkways among the trees.

They stood on the platform and she put her face against his shoulder and he spoke to her but she did not answer. The train came huffing in from the south and stood steaming and shuddering with the coach windows curving away down the track like great dominoes smoldering in the dark and he could not but compare this arrival to that one twenty-four hours ago and she touched the silver chain at her throat and turned away and bent to pick up the suitcase and then leaned and kissed him one last time her face all wet and then she was gone. He watched her go as if he himself were in some dream. All along the platform families and lovers were greeting one another. He saw a man with a little girl in his arms and he whirled her around and she was laughing and when she saw his face she stopped laughing.

He did not see how he could stand there until the train pulled out but stand he did and when it was gone he turned and walked back out into the street.

He paid the bill at the hotel and got his things and left. He went to a bar in a sidestreet where the raucous hybrid beerhall music of the north was blaring from an open door and he got very drunk and got in a fight and woke in the gray dawn on an iron bed in a green room with paper curtains at a window beyond which he could hear roosters calling.

He studied his face in a clouded glass. His jaw was bruised and swollen. If he moved his head in the mirror to a certain place he could restore some symmetry to the two sides of his face and the pain was tolerable if he kept his mouth shut. His shirt was torn and bloody and his bag was gone. He remembered things from the night of whose reality he was uncertain. He remembered a man in silhouette at the end of a street who stood much as Rawlins had stood when last he saw him, half turned in farewell, a coat slung loosely over one shoulder. Who'd come to ruin no man's house. No man's daughter. He saw a light over a doorway in the corrugated iron wall of a warehouse where no one came and no one went. He saw a vacant field in a city in the rain and in the field a wooden crate and he saw a dog emerge from the crate into the slack and sallow lamplight like a carnival dog forlorn and pick its way brokenly across the rubble of the lot to vanish without fanfare among the darkened buildings.

When he walked out the door he did not know where he was. A fine rain was falling. He tried to take his bearings from La Bufa standing above the city to the west but he was easily lost in the winding streets and he asked a woman for the way to the centro and she pointed out the street and then watched him as he went. When he reached Hidalgo a pack of dogs was coming up the street at a high trot and as they crossed in front of him one of their number slipped and scrabbled on the wet stones and went down. The others turned in a snarling mass of teeth and fur but the fallen dog struggled up before he could be set upon and all went on as before. He walked out to the edge of the town along the highway north and put out his thumb. He had almost no money and he'd a long way to go.

He rode all day in an old LaSalle phaeton with the top down driven by a man in a white suit. He said that his was the only car of its type in all of Mexico. He said that he had traveled all over the world when he was young and that he had studied opera in Milan and in Buenos Aires and as they rolled through the countryside he sang arias and gestured with great vigor.

By this and other conveyance he reached Torreón around noon of the following day and went to the hotel and got his bedroll. Then he went to fetch his horse. He'd not shaved nor bathed and he had no other clothes to wear and the hostler when he saw him nodded his head in sympathy and seemed unsurprised at his condition. He rode the horse out into the noon traffic and the horse was fractious and scared and it skittered about in the street and kicked a great dish into the side of a bus to the delight of the passengers who leaned out and called challenges from the safety of the windows.

There was an armería in the calle Degollado and he dismounted in front of it and tied the horse to a lampstandard and went in and bought a box of 45 Long Colt shells. He stopped at a tienda on the outskirts of town and bought some tortillas and some tins of beans and salsa and some cheese and he rolled them up in his blanket and tied the bedroll on behind the saddle again and refilled the canteen and mounted up and turned the horse north. The rain had ripened all the country around and the roadside grass was luminous and green from the run-off and flowers were in bloom across the open country. He slept that night in a field far from any town. He built no fire. He lay listening to the horse crop the grass at his stakerope and he listened to the wind in the emptiness and watched stars trace the arc of the hemisphere and die in the darkness at the edge of the world and as he lay there the agony in his heart was like a stake. He imagined the pain of the world to be like some formless parasitic being seeking out the warmth of human souls wherein to incubate and he thought he knew what made one liable to its visitations. What he had not known was that it was mindless and so had no way to know the limits of those souls and what he feared was that there might be no limits.

By afternoon of the day following he was deep in the bolsón and a day later he was entering the range country and the broken land that enabled the desert mountains to the north. The horse was not in condition for the riding he called upon it to do and he was forced to rest it often. He rode at night that its hooves might benefit from the damp or from what damp there was and as he rode he saw small villages distant on the plain that glowed a faint yellow in that incoordinate dark and he knew that the life there was unimaginable to him. Five days later he rode at night into a small crossroads pueblo nameless to him and he sat the horse in the crossroads and by the light of a full moon read the names of towns burned into crateslats with a hot iron and nailed to a post. San Jerónimo. Los Pintos. La Rosita. At the bottom a board with the arrow pointed the other way that said La Encantada. He sat a long time. He leaned and spat. He looked toward the darkness in west. The hell with it, he said. I aint leavin my horse down here.

He rode all night and in the first gray light with the horse badly drawn down he walked it out upon a rise beneath which he could make out the shape of the town, the yellow windows in the old mud walls where the first lamps were lit, the narrow spires of smoke standing vertically into the windless dawn so still the village seemed to hang by threads from the darkness. He dismounted and unrolled his plunder and opened the box of shells and put half of them in his pocket and checked the pistol that it was loaded all six cylinders and closed the cylinder gate and put the pistol into his belt and rolled his gear back up and retied the roll behind the saddle and mounted the horse again and rode into the town.

There was no one in the streets. He tied the horse in front of the store and walked down to the old school and stood on the porch and looked in. He tried the door. He walked around to the rear and broke out the glass and reached in and unlocked the doorlatch and walked in with the pistol in his hand. He crossed the room and looked out the window at the street. Then he turned and walked back to the captain's desk. He opened the top drawer and took out the handcuffs and laid them on top of the desk. Then he sat down and put his feet up.

An hour later the maid arrived and opened the door with her key. She was startled to see him sitting there and she stood uncertainly.

Pásale, pásale, he said. Está bien.

Gracias, she said.

She'd have crossed the room and gone on to the rear but that he stopped her and made her take a seat in one of the metal folding chairs against the wall. She sat very quietly. She didnt ask him anything at all. They waited.

He saw the captain cross the street. He heard his boots on the boards. He came in with his coffee in one hand and the ring of keys in the other and the mail under his arm and he stood looking at John Grady and at the pistol he was holding with the butt resting on the desktop.

Cierra la puerta, said John Grady.

The captain's eyes darted toward the door. John Grady stood. He cocked the pistol. The click of the sear and the click of the cylinderhand falling into place were sharp and clear in the morning silence. The maid put her hands over her ears and closed her eyes. The captain shut the door slowly with his elbow.

What do you want? he said.

I come to get my horse.

You horse?

Yes.

I dont have you horse.

You better know where he's at.

The captain looked at the maid. She still had her hands over her ears but she had looked up.

Come over here and put that stuff down, said John Grady.

He walked to the desk and put down his coffee and the mail and stood holding the keys.

Put down the keys.

He put the keys on the desk.

Turn around.

You make bad troubles for you self.

I got troubles you never even heard of. Turn around.

He turned around. John Grady leaned forward and unsnapped the flap of the holster he wore and took out the pistol and uncocked it and put it in his belt.

Turn around, he said.

He turned around. He hadnt been told to put his hands up but he'd put them up anyway. John Grady picked up the handcuffs from the desk and stuck them in his belt.

Where do you want to put the criada? he said.

Mande?

Never mind. Let's go.

He picked up the keys and came around from behind the desk and pushed the captain forward. He gestured at the woman with his chin.

Vámonos, he said.

The back door was still open and they walked out and down the path to the jail. John Grady unlocked the padlock and opened the door. Blinking in the pale triangular light sat the old man as before.

Ya estás, viejo?

Sí, cómo no.

Ven aquí.

He was a long time rising. He shuffled forward with one hand on the wall and John Grady told him he was free to go. He motioned for the cleaning woman to enter and he apologized for inconveniencing her and she said not to give it a thought and he closed and locked the door.

When he turned the old man was still standing there. John Grady told him to go home. The old man looked at the captain.

No lo mire a él, said John Grady. Te lo digo yo. Ándale.

The old man seized his hand and was about to kiss it when John Grady snatched it away.

Get the hell out of here, he said. Dont be lookin at him. Go on.

The old man hobbled off toward the gate and unlatched it and stepped out into the street and turned and shut the gate again and was gone.

When he and the captain went up the street John Grady was riding the horse with the pistols stuck in his belt and his jacket over them. His hands were handcuffed before him and the captain was leading the horse. They turned down the street to the blue house where the charro lived and the captain knocked at his door. A woman came to the door and looked at the captain and went back down the zaguán and after a while the charro came to the door and nodded and stood picking his teeth. He looked at John Grady and he looked at the captain. Then he looked at John Grady again.

Tenemos un problema, said the captain.

He sucked on the toothpick. He hadnt seen the pistol in John Grady's belt and he was having trouble understanding the captain's demeanor.

Ven aquí, said John Grady. Cierra la puerta.

When the charro looked up into the pistolbarrel John Grady could see the gears meshing in his head and everything turning and falling into place. He reached behind him and pulled the door shut. He looked up at the rider. The sun was in his eyes and he stepped slightly to one side and looked up again.

Quiero mi caballo, said John Grady.

He looked at the captain. The captain shrugged. He looked up at the rider again and his eyes started to cut away to the right and then he looked down. John Grady looked off across the ocotillo fence where from horseback he could see some mud sheds and the rusted tin roof of a larger building. He swung down from the horse, the handcuffs dangling from one wrist.

Vámonos, he said.

Rawlins' horse was in a mud barn in the lot behind the house. He spoke to it and it lifted its head at his voice and nickered at him. He told the charro to get a bridle and he stood holding the pistol while the charro bridled the horse and then he took the reins from him. He asked him where the other horses were. The charro swallowed and looked at the captain. John Grady reached and got the captain by the collar and put the pistol to the captain's head and he told the charro that if he looked at the captain again he would shoot him. He stood looking down. John Grady told him that he had no more patience and no more time and that the captain was a dead man anyway but that he could still save himself. He told them that Blevins was his brother and he'd taken a bloodoath not to return to his father without the captain's head and he said that if he failed there were more brothers each waiting his turn. The charro lost control of his eyes and looked at the captain anyway and then he closed his eyes and turned away and clutched the top of his thin head with one hand. But John Grady was watching the captain and he saw doubt cloud his face for the first time. The captain started to speak to the charro but he pulled him around by the collar with the pistol against his head and told him that if he spoke again he would shoot him where he stood.

Tú, he said. Dónde están los otros caballos.

The charro stood looking out down the barn bay. He looked like an extra in a stageplay reciting his only lines.

En la hacienda de Don Rafael, he said.

They rode out through the town with the captain and the charro doubled on Rawlins' horse bareback and John Grady riding behind them with his hands manacled as before. He carried a spare bridle slung over one shoulder. They rode dead through the center of town. Old women out sweeping the mud street in the early morning air stood and watched them go.

It was some ten kilometers to the hacienda so spoken and they reached it midmorning and rode through the open gate and on past the house toward the stables at the rear attended by dogs who pranced and barked and ran before the horses.

At the corral John Grady halted and removed the cuffs and put them in his pocket and drew the pistol from his belt. Then he dismounted and opened the gate and waved them through.

He led the grullo through and closed the gate and ordered them off the horse and gestured toward the stable with the pistol.

The building was new and built of adobe brick and had a high tin roof. The doors at the far end were closed and the stalls were shuttered and there was little light in the bay. He pushed the captain and the charro ahead of him at gunpoint. He could hear horses snuffing in the stalls and he could hear pigeons cooing somewhere in the loft overhead.

Redbo, he called.

The horse nickered at him from the far end of the stable.

He motioned them forward. Vámonos, he said.

As he turned a man stepped into the doorway behind them and stood in silhouette.

Quién está? he said.

John Grady moved behind the charro and put the gunbarrel in his ribs. Respóndele, he said.

Luis, said the charro.

Luis?

Sí.

Quién más?

Raúl. El capitán.

The man stood uncertainly. John Grady stepped behind the captain. Tenemos un preso, he said.

Tenemos un preso, called the captain.

Un ladrón, whispered John Grady.

Un ladrón.

Tenemos que ver un caballo.

Tenemos que ver un caballo, said the captain.

Cúal caballo?

El caballo americano.

The man stood. Then he stepped out of the doorway light. No one spoke.

Qúe pasó, hombre? called the man.

No one answered. John Grady watched the sunlit ground beyond the stable door. He could see the shadow of the man where he stood to the side of the door. Then the shadow withdrew. He listened. He pushed the two men toward the rear of the stable. Vámonos, he said.

He called his horse again and located the stall and opened the door and turned the horse out. The horse pushed his nose and forehead against John Grady's chest and John Grady spoke to him and he whinnied and turned and went trotting toward the sunlight in the door without bridle or halter. As they were coming back up the bay two other horses put their heads out over the stall doors. The second one was the big bay horse of Blevins'.

He stopped and looked at the animal. He still had the spare bridle looped over his shoulder and he called the charro by name and shrugged the bridle off his shoulder and handed it to him and told him to bridle the horse and bring it out. He knew that the man who'd come to the stable door had seen the two horses standing in the corral, one saddled and bridled and the other bridled and bareback, and he reckoned he'd gone to the house for a rifle and that he would probably be back before the charro could even get the bridle on Blevins' horse and in all of this he was correct. When the man called from outside the stable again he called for the captain. The captain looked at John Grady. The charro stood with the bridle in one hand and the horse's nose in the crook of his arm.

Ándale, said John Grady.

Raúl, called the man.

The charro pushed the headstall over the horse's ears and stood in the stall door holding the reins.

Vámonos, said John Grady.

There were ropes and rope halters and other bits of tack hanging from the hitchrail in the hall and he took a coil of rope and handed it to the charro and told him to tie one end to the bridle throatlatch of Blevins' horse. He knew he didnt have to check anything that the man did because the charro could not have brought himself to do it wrong. His own horse stood in the doorway looking back. Then it turned and looked at the man standing outside against the wall of the stable.

Quién está contigo? the man called.

John Grady took the handcuffs from his pocket and told the captain to turn around and put his hands behind him. The captain hesitated and looked toward the door. John Grady raised the pistol and cocked it.

Bien, bien, the captain said. John Grady snapped the cuffs onto his wrists and pushed him forward and motioned to the charro to bring the horse. Rawlins' horse had appeared in the stable door and stood nuzzling Redbo. He raised his head and he and Redbo looked at them as they came up the bay leading the other horse.

At the edge of the shadowline where the light fell into the stable John Grady took the lead rope from the charro.

Espera aquí, he said.

Sí.

He pushed the captain forward.

Quiero mis caballos, he called. Nada más.

No one answered.

He dropped the lead rope and slapped the horse on the rump and it went trotting out of the stable holding its head to one side so as not to step on the trailing rope. Outside it turned and nudged Rawlins' horse with its forehead and then stood looking at the man crouching against the wall. The man must have made a hazing motion at it because it jerked its head and blinked but it did not move. John Grady picked up the end of the rope the horse was trailing and passed it between the captain's handcuffed arms and stepped forward and halfhitched it to the stanchion the stable door was hung from. Then he stepped out through the door and put the barrel of the revolver between the eyes of the man crouched there.

The man had been holding the rifle at his waist and he dropped it in the dirt and held his hands up. Almost instantly John Grady's legs were slammed from under him and he went down. He never even heard the crack of the rifle but Blevins' horse did and it reared onto its hind legs above him and sprang and hit the end of the rope and was snatched sideways and fell with a great whump in the dust. A flock of pigeons burst flapping out of the gable end of the loft overhead into the morning sun. The other two horses went trotting and the grullo started to run along the fence. He held onto the pistol and tried to rise. He knew he'd been shot and he was trying to see where the man was hidden. The other man reached to retrieve the rifle lying on the ground but John Grady turned and threw down on him with the pistol and then reached and got hold of the rifle and rolled over and covered the head of the horse that was down and struggling so that it would not rise. Then he raised up cautiously to look.

No tire el caballo, called the man behind him. He saw the man who'd shot him standing in the bed of a truck a hundred feet away across the lot with the barrel of the rifle resting on top of the cab. He pointed the pistol at him and the man crouched down and watched him through the rear window of the cab and out through the windshield. He cocked and leveled the pistol and shot a hole in the windshield and cocked the pistol again and spun and pointed it at the man kneeling behind him. The horse moaned under him. He could feel it breathing slow and steady in the pit of his stomach. The man held out his hands. No me mate, he said. John Grady looked toward the truck. He could see the man's boots below the axle carrier where he stood at the rear of the vehicle and he spread himself over the horse and cocked the pistol and fired at them. The man stepped behind the rear wheel and he fired again and hit a tire. The man ran from behind the truck across the open ground toward a shed. The tire was whistling with a single long steady note in the morning silence and the truck had begun to settle at one corner.

Redbo and Junior stood trembling in the shadow of the stable wall with their legs slightly spread and their eyes rolling. John Grady lay covering the horse and held the pistol on the man behind him and called to the charro. The charro didnt answer and he called to him again and told him to bring a saddle and bridle for the other horse and to bring a rope or he would kill the patrón. Then they all waited. In a few minutes the charro came to the door. He called out his own name before him like a talisman against harm.

Pásale, called John Grady. Nadie le va a molestar.

He talked to Redbo while the charro saddled and bridled him. Blevins' horse was breathing with slow regularity and his stomach was warm and his shirt damp from the horse's breath. He found he was breathing in rhythm with the horse as if some part of the horse were within him breathing and then he descended into some deeper collusion for which he had not even a name. He looked down at his leg. His trousers were dark with blood and there was blood on the ground. He felt numb and strange but he felt no pain. The charro brought Redbo to him saddled and he eased himself up from the horse and looked down at it. Its eye rolled up at him, at the endless and eternal blue beyond. He stood the rifle on the ground and tried to get up. When he put his weight on the gunshot leg a white pain went up his right side and he sucked in all the air he could get. Blevins' horse lurched and scrambled to its feet and snatched the rope taut and there was a cry from the barn and the captain tottered forth bent double with his arms up behind him along the quivering length of rope like something smoked out of a hole. He'd lost his hat and his lank black hair hung down and his face was a gray color and he called out to them to help him. The horse hitting the end of the rope at the first gunfire had snatched him up and had already dislocated his shoulder and he was in great pain. John Grady stood and unfastened the rope from the throatlatch of the bay horse and tied on the rope the charro had brought and handed the rope end off to the charro and told him to dally it to Redbo's saddlehorn and bring him the other two horses. He looked at the captain. He was sitting on the ground bent over slightly sideways with his hands cuffed behind him. The second man was still kneeling a few feet away with his hands up. When John Grady looked down at him he shook his head.

Está loco, he said.

Tiene razón, said John Grady.

He told him to call the carabinero out from the shed and he called to him twice but the man would not come out. He knew he would not ride out of the compound without the man trying to stop him and he knew he had to do something about Blevins' thundercrazed horse. The charro stood holding the horses and he took the rope and handed him back the reins and told him to go get the captain and to mount him on the grullo and he leaned against the side of Blevins' horse and got his breath and looked down at his leg. When he looked at the charro he was standing over the captain holding the horse behind him but the captain wasnt going anywhere. He raised the pistol and was about to shoot into the ground in front of the captain when he remembered about Blevins' horse. He looked at the kneeling man again and then using the rifle for a crutch he swung under the horse's neck and picked up Redbo's bridlereins from the ground and jammed the pistol into his belt and put his foot in the stirrup and stood and swung his bloodied leg over into the saddle. He swung it harder than he needed because he knew that if he failed the first time he wouldnt be able to do it again and he almost cried out with the pain. He unhitched the rope from the sad- dlehorn and backed the horse to where the captain was sitting. He had the rifle under his arm and he was watching the shed where the rifleman was holed up. He almost backed over the captain with the horse and he didnt care if he had. He told the charro to unhitch the rope from the stabledoor stanchion and bring it to him. He'd already figured out that there was bad blood between the two men. When the charro brought the rope end he told him to tie it to the captain's handcuffs and he did so and stepped back.

Gracias, said John Grady. He had coiled the rope and now he dallied it midrope to the horn and put the horse forward. When the captain saw his situation he stood up.

Momento, he called.

John Grady rode forward, watching the shed. The captain when he saw the slack rope running out along the ground called out to him and began to run, his hands behind him. Momento, he called.

When they rode out through the gate the captain was riding Redbo and he was doubled on behind him with his arm around the captain's waist. They led the Blevins horse on the rope and drove the other two horses before them. He was determined to get the four horses out of the stable yard if he died in the road and beyond that he had not thought much. His leg was numb and bleeding and felt heavy as a sack of meal and his boot was filling up with blood. When he passed through the gate the charro was standing there holding his hat and he reached down and took it from him and put it on and nodded.

Adiós, he said.

The charro nodded and stepped back. He put the horse forward and they went down the drive, him holding on to the captain and turned partly sideways with the rifle at his waist, watching back toward the corral. The charro was still at the gate but there was no sign of the other two men. The captain in the saddle before him smelled rank and sweaty. He'd partly unbuttoned the front of his tunic and had put his hand inside to sling the arm. When they passed the house there was no one about but by the time they reached the road there were half a dozen women and young girls from the kitchen all peering past the corner of the house.

In the road he got Junior and the grullo horse looseherded in front of him and with the Blevins horse on the leadrope behind they set out back toward Encantada at a trot. He didnt know if the grullo horse would try and quit them or not and he wished he had the spare saddle on Junior instead but there was nothing to be done about it. The captain complained about his shoulder and tried to take the reins and then he said he needed a doctor and then he said he needed to urinate. John Grady was watching the road behind. Go ahead, he said. You couldnt smell much worse.

It was a good ten minutes before the riders appeared, four of them at a hard gallop, leaning forward, holding their rifles out to one side. John Grady let go the reins and swiveled and cocked the rifle and fired. Blevins' horse stood twisting like a circus horse and the captain must have sawed back on Redbo's reins because he stopped dead in the middle of the road and John Grady fell against him and almost pushed him forward out of the saddle. Behind him the riders were pulling up their mounts and milling in the road and he levered a fresh round into the rifle and fired again and by now Redbo had turned in the road to face the pull of the rope and the Blevins horse was wholly out of control and he swung around and whacked the captain's arm with the barrel of the rifle to make him drop the reins and he took the reins up and hauled Redbo around and whacked him with the rifle and looked back again. The riders had quit the road but he saw the last horse disappear into the brush and he knew which side they'd taken. He leaned down and got hold of the rope and drew the walleyed horse to him and coiled the rope and snubbed the horse up short and whacked Redbo again and trotting side by side they overtook the two horses in the road before them and herded them off into the brush and out onto the rolling country west of the town. The captain half turned to him with some new complaint but he only hugged his loathesome charge more fondly, the captain tottering woodenly in the saddle before him with his pain like a storedummy carried off for a prank.

They rode down into a broad flat arroyo and he put the horses into a lope, his leg throbbing horribly and the captain crying out to be left. The arroyo bore east by the sun and they followed it for a good distance until it began to narrow and grow rocky and the loose horses before him to step cautiously and look toward the slopes above them. He hazed them on and they clambered up through traprock fallen from the rim country above and they led up onto the northfacing slope and along a barren gravel ridge where he gripped the captain anew and looked back. The riders were fanned over the open country a mile below him and he counted not four but six of them before they dropped from sight into a draw. He loosed the rope from the saddlehorn in front of the captain and dallied it again with more slack.

You must owe them sons of bitches money, he said.

He put the horse forward again and caught up to the other horses standing looking back a hundred feet out along the ridge. There was no place to go up the draw and no place to hide in the open country beyond. He needed fifteen minutes and he didnt have them. He slid down and caught the Purísima horse, hobbling after it on one leg and the horse shifting and eyeing him nervously. He unhitched the bridlereins from about the saddlehorn and stood into the stirrup and pulled himself painfully onto the horse and turned and looked at the captain.

I want you to follow me, he said. And I know what you're thinkin. But if you think I cant ride you down you better think some more. And if I have to come get you I'm goin to whip you like a dog. Me entiende?

The captain didnt answer. He managed a sardonic smile and John Grady nodded. You just keep smilin. When I die you die.

He turned the horse and rode back down into the arroyo. The captain followed. At the rockslide he dismounted and tied the horse and took out a cigarette and lit it and hobbled up around the tumbled rocks and boulders carrying the rifle. In the sheltered lee of the slide he stopped and took the captain's pistol out of his belt and laid it on the ground and he took out his knife and cut a long narrow strip from his shirt and twisted it into a string. Then he cut the string in two and tied the trigger back on the pistol. He wrapped it tightly so as to depress the grip safety and he broke off a dead limb and tied the other string to it and tied the free end to the hammer of the pistol. He put a goodsized rock on top of the stick to hold it and he stretched the pistol out until the string cocked the hammer and then laid the pistol down and rolled a rock over it and when he slowly released it it held. He took a good draw on the cigarette to get it burning and then laid it carefully across the string and stepped back and picked up the rifle and turned and hobbled back out to where the horses stood.

He took the waterbottles and he slid the bridle down off the grullo's head and caught it and he stroked the grullo under the jaw. I hate to leave you old pardner, he said. You been a goodn.

He handed the waterbottles up to the captain and slung the bridle over his shoulder and reached a hand up and the captain looked down at him and then reached down with his good hand and he struggled up onto the horse behind the captain and reached around and took the reins and turned the horse back up the ridge again.

He caught up the loose horses and drove them down off the ridge and out across the open country. The ground was volcanic gravel and not easy to track a horse over but not impossible either. He pushed the horses hard. There was a low rocky mesa two miles across the floodplain and he could see trees and the promise of broken country. Not half way across he heard the dead flat pop of the pistol he'd been listening for.

Captain, he said. You just fired a shot for the common man.

The trees he'd seen from the distance were the breaks of a dry rivercourse and he pushed the horses through the brush and entered a stand of cottonwoods and turned the horse and sat watching back across the plain they'd traversed. There were no riders in sight. He looked at the sun in the south and he judged it a good four hours till dark. The horse was hot and lathered and he looked back across the open country one more time and then pushed on to where the other two horses were standing upriver in a grove of willows drinking from a riverbed pothole. He rode alongside them and slid to the ground and caught Junior and took the bridle from his shoulder and bridled him with it and with the rifle motioned the captain down off the horse. He unbuckled the girthstraps and pulled the saddle and the blanket down onto the ground and picked up the blanket and threw it over Junior and leaned against him to get his breath. His leg was beginning to hurt horribly. He stood the rifle against the actual horse and picked up the saddle and managed to get it on and he pulled the girthstrap and rested and he and the horse blew and then he pulled the strap again and cinched it.

He picked up the rifle and turned to the captain.

You want a drink of water you better get you one, he said.

The captain walked up past the horses holding his arm and he knelt and drank and laved water over the back of his neck with his good hand. When he rose he looked very serious.

Why you no leave me here? he said.

I aint leavin you here. You're a hostage.

Mande?

Let's go.

The captain stood uncertainly.

Why you come back? he said.

I come back for my horse. Let's go.

The captain nodded at the wound in his leg, still bleeding. The whole trouserleg dark with blood.

You going to die, he said.

We'll let God decide about that. Let's go.

Are you no afraid of God?

I got no reason to be afraid of God. I've even got a bone or two to pick with Him.

You should be afraid of God, the captain said. You are not the officer of the law. You dont have no authority.

John Grady stood leaning on the rifle. He turned and spat dryly and eyed the captain.

Get on that horse, he said. You ride ahead of me. You drift out of my sight and I'll shoot you.

Nightfall found them in the foothills of the Sierra Encantada. They followed a dry watercourse up under a dark rincón in the rocks and picked their way over a flood barricade of boulders tumbled in the floor of the wash and emerged upon a stone tinaja in the center of which lay a shallow basin of water, perfectly round, perfectly black, where the night stars were lensed in perfect stillness. The loose horses walked uncertainly down the shallow rock incline of the basin and blew at the water and drank.

They dismounted and walked around to the far side of the tinaja and lay on their bellies on the rocks where the day's heat was still rising and sucked at the water cool and soft and black as velvet and they laved water over their faces and the backs of their necks and watched the horses drink and then drank again.

He left the captain at the tank and hobbled with the rifle up the arroyo and gathered dead floodwash brush and hobbled back and made a fire at the upper end of the basin. He fanned the blaze with his hat and piled on more wood. The horses in the firelight reflected off the water were rimed with drying sweat and shifted pale and ghostly and blinked their red eyes. He looked at the captain. The captain was lying on his side on the smooth rock incline of the basin like something that had not quite made it to water.

He limped around to the horses and got the rope and sat with his knife and cut hobbles from it for all the horses and looped them about their forefeet. Then he levered all the shells out of the rifle and put them in his pocket and took one of the water bottles and went back to the fire.

He fanned the fire and he took the pistol out of his belt and pulled the cylinder pin and put the loaded cylinder and the pin in his pocket along with the rifle shells. Then he took out his knife and with the point of it unscrewed the screw from the grips and put the grips and the screw into his other pocket. He fanned the coals in the heart of the fire with his hat and with a stick he raked them into a pile and then he bent and stuck the barrel of the pistol into the coals.

The captain had sat up to look at him.

They will find you, he said. In this place.

We aint stayin in this place.

I cant ride no more.

You'll be surprised at what you can do.

He took off his shirt and soaked it in the tinaja and came back to the fire and he fanned the fire again with his hat and then he pulled off his boots and unbuckled his belt and let down his trousers.

The rifle bullet had entered his thigh high up on the outside and the exit wound was in a rotation at the rear such that by turning his leg he could see both wounds clearly. He took up the wet shirt and very carefully wiped away the blood until the wounds were clear and stark as two holes in a mask. The area around the wounds was discolored and looked blue in the firelight and the skin around that was yellow. He leaned and ran a stick through the gripframes of the pistol and swung it up and away from the fire into his shadow and looked at it and then put it back. The captain was sitting holding his arm in his lap and watching him.

It's fixin to get kindly noisy in here, he said. Watch out you dont get run over by a horse.

The captain didnt answer. He watched him while he fanned the fire. When next he dragged the pistol from the coals the end of the barrel glowed at a dull red heat and he laid it on the rocks and picked it up quickly by the grips in the wet shirt and jammed the redhot barrel ash and all down into the hole in his leg.

The captain either did not know what he was going to do or knowing did not believe. He tried to rise to his feet and fell backwards and almost slid into the tinaja. John Grady had begun to shout even before the gunmetal hissed in the meat. His shout clapped shut the calls of lesser creatures everywhere about them in the night and the horses all stood swimming up into the darkness beyond the fire and squatting in terror on their great thighs screaming and pawing the stars and he drew breath and howled again and jammed the gunbarrel into the second wound and held it the longer in deference to the cooling of the metal and then he fell over on his side and dropped the revolver on the rocks where it clattered and turned and slid down the basin and vanished hissing into the pool.

He'd seized the fleshy part of his thumb in his teeth, shaking in agony. With the other hand he reached for the waterbottle standing unstoppered on the rocks and poured water over his leg and heard the flesh hiss like something on a spit and he gasped and let the bottle fall and he raised up and called out his horse's name to him softly where he scrabbled and fell on the rocks in his hobbles among the others that he might ease the fright in the horse's heart.

When he turned and reached for the water bottle where it lay draining on the rocks the captain kicked it away with his boot. He looked up. He was standing over him with the rifle. He held it with the stock under his armpit and he gestured upward with it.

Get up, he said.

He pushed himself up on the rocks and looked across the tank toward the horses. He could only see two of them and he thought the third one must have run out down the arroyo and he couldnt tell which one was missing but guessed it was the Blevins horse. He got hold of his belt and managed to get his breeches back on.

Where is the keys? said the captain.

He pushed himself up and rose and turned and took the rifle away from the captain. The hammer dropped with a dull metallic snap.

Get back over there and set down, he said.

The captain hesitated. The man's dark eyes were turned toward the fire and he could see the calculation in them and he was in such a rage of pain he thought he might have killed him had the gun been loaded. He grabbed the chain between the handcuffs and yanked the man past him and the captain gave out a low cry and went tottering off bent over and holding his arm.

He got the shells out and sat and reloaded the rifle. He reloaded it one shell at a time sweating and wheezing and trying to concentrate. He hadnt known how stupid pain could make you and he thought it should be the other way around or what was the good of it. When he'd got the rifle loaded he picked up the wet rag of a shirt and used it to carry a brand from the fire down to the edge of the tank where he stood holding it out over the water. The water was dead clear in the stone pool and he could see the pistol and he waded out and bent and picked it up and stuck it in his belt. He walked out in the tank till the water was to his thigh which was as deep as it got and he stood there soaking the blood out of his trousers and the fire out of his wounds and talking to his horse. The horse limped down to the edge of the water and stood and he stood in the dark tinaja with the rifle over his shoulder holding the brand above him until it burned out and then he stood holding the crooked orange ember of it, still talking to the horse.

They left the fire burning in the tank and rode out down the draw and picked up the Blevins horse and pushed on. The night was overcast to the south the way they'd come and there was rain in the air. He rode Redbo bareback in the fore of their little caravan and he held up from time to time to listen but there was nothing to hear. The fire in the tank behind them was invisible save for the play of it on the rocks of the rincón and as they rode it receded to a faint glow pocketed in the otherwise dark of the desert night and then vanished altogether.

They rode up out of the wash and went on along the south-facing slope of the ridge, the country dark and silent and without boundary and the tall aloes passing blackly along the ridge one by one. He reckoned it to be some time past midnight. He looked back at the captain from time to time but the captain rode slumped in the saddle on Rawlins' horse and seemed much reduced by his adventures. They rode on. He'd knotted his wet rag of a shirt through his belt and he rode naked to the waist and he was very cold and he told the horse that it was going to be a long night and it was. Sometime in the night he fell asleep. The clatter of the rifle dropping on the rocky ground woke him and he pulled up and turned and rode back. He sat looking down at the rifle. The captain sat Rawlins' horse watching him. He wasnt sure he could get back on the horse and he thought about leaving the rifle there. In the end he slid down and picked up the rifle and then led the horse up along Junior's offside and told the captain to shuck his foot out of the stirrup and he used the stirrup to mount up onto his own horse and they rode on again.

Dawn found him sitting alone on the gravel face of the slope with the rifle leaning against his shoulder and the waterbottle at his feet watching the shape of the desert country form itself out of the gray light. Mesa and plain, the dark shape of the mountains to the east beyond which the sun was rising.

He picked up the waterbottle and twisted out the stopper and drank and sat holding the bottle. Then he drank again. The first bars of sunlight broke past the rock buttes of the mountains to the east and fell fifty miles across the plain. Nothing moved. On the facing slope of the valley a mile away seven deer stood watching him.

He sat for a long time. When he climbed back up the ridge to the cedars where he'd left the horses the captain was sitting on the ground and he looked badly used up.

Let's go, he said.

The captain looked up. I can go no farther, he said.

Let's go, he said. Podemos descansar un poco mas adelante. Vámonos.

They rode down off the ridge and up a long narrow valley looking for water but there was no water. They climbed out and crossed into the valley to the east and the sun was well up and felt good on his back and he tied the shirt around his waist so it would dry. By the time they crested out above the valley it was midmorning and the horses were in badly failing plight and it occurred to him that the captain might die.

The water they found was at a stone stocktank and they dismounted and drank from the standpipe and watered the horses and sat in the bands of shade from the dead and twisted oaks at the tank and watched the open country below them. A few cattle stood perhaps a mile away. They were looking to the east, not grazing. He turned to see what they were watching but there was nothing there. He looked at the captain, a gray and shrunken figure. The heel was missing from one boot. There were streaks of black and streaks of ash on his trouserlegs from the fire and his buckled belt hung in a loop from his neck where he'd been using it to sling his arm.

I aint goin to kill you, he said. I'm not like you.

The captain didnt answer.

He pulled himself up and took out the keys from his pocket and using the rifle to steady himself he hobbled over and bent and took hold of the captain's wrists and unmanacled them. The captain looked down at his wrists. They were discolored and raw from the cuffs and he sat rubbing them gently. John Grady stood over him.

Take off your shirt, he said. I'm goin to pull that shoulder.

Mande? said the captain.

Quítese su camisa.

The captain shook his head and held his arm against him like a child.

Dont sull up cn me. I aint askin, I'm tellin.

Cómo?

No tiene otra salida.

He got the captain's shirt off and spread it out and made him lie on his back. The shoulder was badly discolored and his whole upper arm was a deep blue. He looked up. The beaded sweat glistened on his forehead. John Grady sat and put his booted foot in the captain's armpit and gripped the captain's arm by the wrist and upper elbow and rotated it slightly. The captain looked at him like a man falling from a cliff.

Dont worry, he said. My family's been practicin medicine on Mexicans a hundred years.

If the captain had made up his mind not to cry out he did not succeed. The horses started and milled and tried to hide behind one another. He reached up and grabbed his arm as if he'd reclaim it but John Grady had felt the coupling pop into place and he gripped the shoulder and rotated the arm again while the captain tossed his head and gasped. Then he let him go and picked up the rifle and rose.

Está compuesto? wheezed the captain.

Yeah. You're all set.

He held his arm and lay blinking.

Put on your shirt and let's go, said John Grady. We aint settin out here in the open till your friends show up.

Ascending into the low hills they passed a small estancia and they dismounted and went afoot through the ruins of a cornfield and found some melons and sat in the stony washedout furrows and ate them. He hobbled down the rows and gathered melons and carried them out through the field to where the horses stood and broke them open on the ground at their feet for them to feed on and he stood leaning on the rifle and looked toward the house. Some turkeys stepped about in the yard and there was a pole corral beyond the house in which stood several horses. He went back and got the captain and they mounted up and rode on. When he looked back from the ridge above the estancia he could see that it was more extensive. There was a cluster of buildings above the house and he could see the quadrangles laid out by the fences and the adobe walls and irrigation ditches. A number of rangy and slatribbed cattle stood about in the scrub. He heard a rooster crow in the noon heat. He heard a steady distant hammering of metal as of someone at a forge.

They plodded on at a poor pace up through the hills. He'd unloaded the rifle to save carrying it and it was tied along the saddleskirt of the captain's horse and he had reassembled the fireblackened revolver and loaded it and put it in his belt. He rode Blevins' horse and the animal had an easy gait and his leg had not stopped hurting but it was the only thing keeping him awake.

In the early evening from the eastern rim of the mesa he sat and studied the country while the horses rested. A hawk and a hawk's shadow that skated like a paper bird crossed the slopes below. He studied the terrain beyond and after a while he saw riders riding. They were perhaps five miles away. He watched them and they dropped from sight into a cut or into a shadow. Then they appeared again.

He mounted up and they rode on. The captain slept tottering in the saddle with his arm slung through his belt. It was cool in the higher country and when the sun set it was going to be cold. He pushed on and before dark they found a deep ravine in the north slope of the ridge they'd crossed and they descended and found standing water among the rocks and the horses clambered and scrabbled their way down and stood drinking.

He unsaddled Junior and cuffed the captain's bracelets through the wooden stirrups and told him he was free to go as far as he thought he could carry the saddle. Then he built a fire in the rocks and kicked out a place in the ground for his hip and lay down and stretched out his aching leg and put the pistol in his belt and closed his eyes.

In his sleep he could hear the horses stepping among the rocks and he could hear them drink from the shallow pools in the dark where the rocks lay smooth and rectilinear as the stones of ancient ruins and the water from their muzzles dripped and rang like water dripping in a well and in his sleep he dreamt of horses and the horses in his dream moved gravely among the tilted stones like horses come upon an antique site where some ordering of the world had failed and if anything had been written on the stones the weathers had taken it away again and the horses were wary and moved with great circumspection carrying in their blood as they did the recollection of this and other places where horses once had been and would be again. Finally what he saw in his dream was that the order in the horse's heart was more durable for it was written in a place where no rain could erase it.

When he woke there were three men standing over him. They wore serapes over their shoulders and one of them was holding the empty rifle and all of them wore pistols. The fire was burning from brush they'd piled on it but he was very cold and he had no way to know how long he'd been sleeping. He sat up. The man with the rifle snapped his fingers and held out his hand.

Deme las llaves, he said.

He reached into his pocket and took out the keys and handed them up. He and one of the other men walked over to where the captain sat chained to the saddle at the far side of the fire. The third man stood by him. They freed the captain and the one carrying the rifle came back.

Cuáles de los caballos son suyos? he said.

Todos son míos.

The man studied his eyes in the firelight. He walked back to the others and they talked. When they came past with the captain the captain's hands were cuffed behind him. The man carrying the rifle levered the action open and when he saw that the gun was empty stood it against a rock. He looked at John Grady.

Donde está su serape? he said.

No tengo.

The man loosed the blanket from his own shoulders and swung it in a slow veronica and handed it to him. Then he turned and they passed on out of the firelight to where their horses were standing in the dark with other companions, other horses.

Quiénes son ustedes? he called.

The man who'd given him his serape turned at the outer edge of the light and touched the brim of his hat. Hombres del país, he said. Then all went on.

Men of the country. He sat listening as they rode up out of the ravine and then they were gone. He never saw them again. In the morning he saddled Redbo and driving the other two horses before him he rode up from the ravine and turned north along the mesa.

He rode all day and the day clouded before him and a cool wind was coming downcountry. He'd reloaded the rifle and he carried it across the bow of the saddle and rode with the serape over his shoulders and looseherded the riderless horses before him. By evening all the north country was black and the wind was cold and he picked his way along the rim country through the sparse swales of grass and broken volcanic rock and he sat above a highland bajada in the cold blue dusk with the rifle across his knee while the staked horses grazed behind him and at the last hour light enough by which to see the iron sights of the rifle five deer entered the bajada and pricked their ears and stood and then bent to graze.

He picked out the smallest doe among them and shot her. Blevins' horse rose howling where he'd tied it and the deer in the bajada leapt away and vanished in the dusk and the little doe lay kicking.

When he reached her she lay in her blood in the grass and he knelt with the rifle and put his hand on her neck and she looked at him and her eyes were warm and wet and there was no fear in them and then she died. He sat watching her for a long time. He thought about the captain and he wondered if he were alive and he thought about Blevins. He thought about Alejandra and he remembered her the first time he ever saw her passing along the ciénaga road in the evening with the horse still wet from her riding it in the lake and he remembered the birds and the cattle standing in the grass and the horses on the mesa. The sky was dark and a cold wind ran through the bajada and in the dying light a cold blue cast had turned the doe's eyes to but one thing more of things she lay among in that darkening landscape. Grass and blood. Blood and stone. Stone and the dark medallions that the first flat drops of rain caused upon them. He remembered Alejandra and the sadness he'd first seen in the slope of her shoulders which he'd presumed to understand and of which he knew nothing and he felt a loneliness he'd not known since he was a child and he felt wholly alien to the world although he loved it still. He thought that in the beauty of the world were hid a secret. He thought the world's heart beat at some terrible cost and that the world's pain and its beauty moved in a relationship of diverging equity and that in this headlong deficit the blood of multitudes might ultimately be exacted for the vision of a single flower.

In the morning the sky was clear and it was very cold and there was snow on the mountains to the north. When he woke he realized that he knew his father was dead. He raked up the coals and blew the fire to life and roasted strips cut from the deer's haunch and cowled in his blanket he sat eating and watching the country to the south out of which he'd ridden.

They moved on. By noon the horses were in snow and there was snow in the pass and the horses trod and broke thin plates of ice in the trail where the snowmelt ran out over the wet black ground dark as ink and they toiled up through the patches of snow glazing over in the sun and rode through a dark corridor of fir trees and descended along the northern slope through pockets of sunlight, pockets of shadow, where the air smelled of rosin and wet stone and no birds sang.

In the evening descending he saw lights in the distance and he pushed on toward them and did not stop and in the dead of night in deep exhaustion both he and the horses they reached the town of Los Picos.

A single mud street rutted from the recent rains. A squalid alameda where there stood a rotting brushwood gazebo and a few old iron benches. The trees in the alameda had been freshly whitewashed and the upper trunks were lost in the dark above the light of the few lamps yet burning so that they looked like plaster stagetrees new from the mold. The horses stepped with great weariness among the dried rails of mud in the street and dogs barked at them from behind the wooden gates and doors they passed.

It was cold when he woke in the morning and it was raining again. He'd bivouacked on the north side of the town and he rose wet and cold and stinking and saddled the horse and rode back into the town wrapped in the serape and driving the two horses before him.

In the alameda a few small tin foldingtables had been set out and young girls were stringing paper ribbon overhead. They were wet from the rain and they were laughing and they were throwing the spools of crepe over the wires and catching them again and the dye was coming off the paper so that their hands were red and green and blue. He tied the horses in front of the tienda he'd passed the night before and went in and bought a sack of oats for the horses and he borrowed a galvanized bucket with which to water them and he stood in the alameda leaning on the rifle and watching them drink. He thought he'd be an object of some curiosity but the people he saw only nodded gravely to him and passed on. He carried the bucket back into the store and went down the street to where there was a small cafe and he entered and sat at one of the three small wooden tables. The floor of the cafe was packed mud newly swept and he was the only customer. He stood the rifle against the wall and ordered huevos revueltos and a cup of chocolate and he sat and waited for it to come and then he ate very slowly. The food was rich to his taste and the chocolate was made with canela and he drank it and ordered another and folded a tortilla and ate and watched the horses standing in the square across the street and watched the girls. They'd hung the gazebo with crepe and it looked like a festooned brush-pile. The proprietor showed him great courtesy and brought him fresh tortillas hot from the comal and told him that there was to be a wedding and that it would be a pity if it rained. He inquired where he might be from and showed surprise he'd come so far. He stood at the window of the empty cafe and watched the activities in the square and he said that it was good that God kept the truths of life from the young as they were starting out or else they'd have no heart to start at all.

By midmorning the rain had stopped. Water dripped from the trees in the alameda and the crepe hung in soggy strings. He stood with the horses and watched the wedding party emerge from the church. The groom wore a dull black suit too large for him and he looked not uneasy but half desperate, as if unused to clothes at all. The bride was embarrassed and clung to him and they stood on the steps for their photograph to be taken and in their antique formalwear posed there in front of the church they already had the look of old photos. In the sepia monochrome of a rainy day in that lost village they'd grown old instantly.

In the alameda an old woman in a black rebozo was going about tilting the metal tables and chairs to let the water run off. She and others began to set out food from pails and baskets and a group of three musicians in soiled silver suits stood by with their instruments. The groom took the bride's hand to help her negotiate the water standing in front of the church steps. In the water they were gray figures reflected against a gray sky. A small boy ran out and stamped in the puddle and sprayed a sheet of the muddy gray water over them and ran away with his companions. The bride clutched her husband. He scowled and looked after the boys but there was nothing to be done and she looked down at her dress and she looked at him and then she laughed. Then the husband laughed and others in the party also and they crossed the road laughing and looking from one to the other and entered the alameda among the tables and the musicians began to play.

With the last of his money he bought coffee and tortillas and some tinned fruit and beans. The tins had been on the shelves so long they'd tarnished and the labels faded. When he passed out along the road the wedding party was seated at the tables eating and the musicians had stopped playing and were squatting together drinking from tin cups. A man sitting alone on one of the benches who seemed no part of the wedding looked up at the sound of the slow hooves in the road and raised one hand to the pale rider passing with blanket and rifle and he raised a hand back and then rode on.

He rode out past the last low mudbuilt houses and took the road north, a mud track that wound up through the barren gravel hills and branched and broke and finally terminated in the tailings of an abandoned mine among the rusted shapes of pipe and pumpstanchions and old jacktimbers. He crossed on through the high country and in the evening descended the north slope and rode out onto the foreplain where the creosote deep olive from the rains stood in solemn colonies as it had stood a thousand years and more in that tenantless waste, older than any living thing that was.

He rode on, the two horses following, riding doves up out of the pools of standing water and the sun descending out of the dark discolored overcast to the west where its redness ran down the narrow band of sky above the mountains like blood falling through water and the desert fresh from the rain turning gold in the evening light and then deepening to dark, a slow inkening over of the bajada and the rising hills and the stark stone length of the cordilleras darkening far to the south in Mexico. The floodplain he crossed was walled about with fallen traprock and in the twilight the little desert foxes had come out to sit along the walls silent and regal as icons watching the night come and the doves called from the acacia and then night fell dark as Egypt and there was just the stillness and the silence and the sound of the horses breathing and the sound of their hooves clopping in the dark. He pointed his horse at the polestar and rode on and they rode the round moon up out of the east and coyotes yammered and answered back all across the plain to the south from which they'd come.

He crossed the river just west of Langtry Texas in a softly falling rain. The wind in the north, the day cold. The cattle along the breaks of the river standing gray and still. He followed a cattletrail down into the willows and across the carrizal to where the gray water lay braided over the gravels.

He studied the cold gray rips in the current and dismounted and loosed the girthstraps and undressed and stogged his boots in the legs of his trousers as he'd done before in that long ago and he put his shirt and jacket and the pistol after and doubled the belt in the loops to draw shut the waist. Then he slung the trousers over his shoulder and mounted up naked with the rifle aloft and driving the loose horses before him he pushed Redbo into the river.

He rode up onto Texas soil pale and shivering and he sat the horse briefly and looked out over the plain to the north where cattle were already beginning to appear slouching slowly out of that pale landscape and bawling softly at the horses and he thought about his father who was dead in that country and he sat the horse naked in the falling rain and wept.

When he rode into Langtry it was early in the afternoon and

it was still raining. The first thing he saw was a pickup truck with the hood up and two men trying to start it. One of them raised up and looked at him. He must have appeared to them some apparition out of the vanished past because he jostled the other with his elbow and they both looked.

Howdy, said John Grady. I wonder if you all could tell me what day this is?

They looked at each other.

It's Thursday, the first one said.

I mean the date.

The man looked at him. He looked at the horses standing behind him. The date? he said.

Yessir.

It's Thanksgiving day, the other man said.

He looked at them. He looked out down the street.

Is that cafe yonder open?

Yeah, its open.

He lifted his hand off the pommel and was about to touch up the horse and then he stopped.

Dont neither of you all want to buy a rifle do you? he said.

They looked at each other.

Earl might buy it off of you, the first man said. He'll generally try and help a feller out.

He the man that runs the cafe?

Yep.

He touched the brim of his hat. Much obliged, he said. Then he put the horse forward and rode on down the street trailing the loose horses behind him. They watched him go. Neither spoke for there was nothing to say. The one holding the socketwrench put the wrench on the fender and they both stood watching until he turned the corner at the cafe and there was nothing more to see.

He rode the border country for weeks seeking the owner of the horse. In Ozona just before Christmas three men swore out papers and the county constable impounded the animal. The hearing was held in the judge's chambers in the old stone court-house and the clerk read the charges and the names and the judge turned and looked down at John Grady.

Son, he said, are you represented by counsel?

No sir I aint, said John Grady. I dont need a lawyer. I just need to tell you about this horse.

The judge nodded. All right, he said. Go ahead.

Yessir. If you dont care I'd like to tell it from the beginning. From the first time ever I seen the horse.

Well if you'd like to tell it we'd like to hear it so just go ahead.

It took him almost half an hour. When he was done he asked if he could have a glass of water. No one spoke. The judge turned to the clerk.

Emil, get the boy a glass of water.

He looked at his notepad and he turned to John Grady.

Son, I'm fixin to ask you three questions and if you can answer em the horse is yours.

Yessir. I'll try.

Well you'll either know em or you wont. The trouble with a liar is he cant remember what he said.

I aint a liar.

I know you aint. This is just for the record. I dont believe anybody could make up the story you just now got done tellin us.

He put his glasses back on and he asked John Grady the number of hectares in the Nuestra Señora de la Purísima Concepción spread. Then he asked the name of the husband of the hacendado's cook. Lastly he laid down his notes and he asked John Grady if he had on clean shorts.

A subdued laughter went around the courtroom but the judge wasnt laughing nor the bailiff.

Yessir. I do.

Well there aint no women present so if you wouldnt find it to be too much of a embarrassment I'd like for you to show the court them bulletholes in your leg. If you dont want to I'll ask you somethin else.

Yessir, said John Grady. He unbuckled his belt and dropped his trousers to his knees and turned his right leg sideways to the judge.

That's fine son. Thank you. Get your water there.

He pulled up his trousers and buttoned them and buckled his belt and reached and got the glass of water from the table where the clerk had set it and drank.

Them are some nasty lookin holes, said the judge. You didnt have no medical attention?

No sir. There wasnt none to be had.

I guess not. You were lucky not to of got gangrene.

Yessir. I burnt em out pretty good.

Burnt em out?

Yessir.

What did you burn em out with?

A pistolbarrel. I burnt em out with a hot pistolbarrel.

There was absolute silence in the courtroom. The judge leaned back.

The constable is instructed to return the property in question to Mr Cole. Mr Smith, you see that the boy gets his horse. Son, you're free to go and the court thanks you for your testimony. I've sat on the bench in this county since it was a county and in that time I've heard a lot of things that give me grave doubts about the human race but this aint one of em. The three plaintiffs in this case I'd like to see here in my chambers after dinner. That means one oclock.

The lawyer for the plaintiffs stood up. Your honor, this is pretty clearly a case of mistook identity.

The judge closed his notebook and rose. Yes it is, he said. Bad mistook. This hearing is dismissed.

That night he knocked at the judge's door while there were still lights on downstairs in the house. A Mexican girl came to the door and asked him what he wanted and he said he wanted to see the judge. He said it in spanish and she repeated it back to him in english with a certain coldness and told him to wait.

The judge when he appeared at the door was still dressed but he had on an old flannel bathrobe. If he was surprised to find the boy on his porch he didnt show it. He pushed open the screen door.

Come in son, he said. Come in.

I didnt want to bother you.

It's all right.

John Grady gripped his hat.

I aint comin out there, said the judge. So if you want to see me you better come on in.

Yessir.

He entered a long hallway. A balustered staircase rose on his right to the upper floor. The house smelled of cooking and furniture polish. The judge was wearing leather slippers and he went silently down the carpeted hallway and entered an open door on the left. The room was filled with books and there was a fire burning in the fireplace.

We're in here, said the judge. Dixie, this is John Cole.

A grayhaired woman rose as he entered and smiled at him. Then she turned to the judge.

I'm goin up, Charles, she said.

All right, Mama.

He turned to John Grady. Set down, son.

John Grady sat and put his hat in his lap.

They sat.

Well go ahead, said the judge. There aint no time like the present.

Yessir. I guess what I wanted to say first of all was that it kindly bothered me in the court what you said. It was like I was in the right about everthing and I dont feel that way.

What way do you feel?

He sat looking at his hat. He sat for a long time. Finally he looked up. I dont feel justified, he said.

The judge nodded. You didnt misrepresent nothin to me about the horse did you?

No sir. It wasnt that.

What was it?

Well sir. The girl I reckon.

All right.

I worked for that man and I respected him and he never had no complaints about the work I done for him and he was awful good to me. And that man come up on the high range where I was workin and I believe he intended to kill me. And I was the one that brought it about. Nobody but me.

You didnt get the girl in a family way did you?

No sir. I was in love with her.

The judge nodded gravely. Well, he said. You could be in love with her and still knock her up.

Yessir.

The judge watched him. Son, he said, you strike me as somebody that maybe tends to be a little hard on theirselves. I think from what you told me you done real well to get out of there with a whole hide. Maybe the best thing to do might be just to go on and put it behind you. My daddy used to tell me not to chew on somethin that was eatin you.

Yessir.

There's somethin else, aint there?

Yessir.

What is it?

When I was in the penitentiary down there I killed a boy.

The judge sat back in his chair. Well, he said. I'm sorry to hear that.

It keeps botherin me.

You must have had some provocation.

I did. But it dont help. He tried to kill me with a knife. I just happened to get the best of him.

Why does it bother you?

I dont know. I dont know nothin about him. I never even knew his name. He could of been a pretty good old boy. I dont know. I dont know that he's supposed to be dead.

He looked up. His eyes were wet in the firelight. The judge sat watching him.

You know he wasnt a pretty good old boy. Dont you?

Yessir. I guess.

You wouldnt want to be a judge, would you?

No sir. I sure wouldnt.

I didnt either.

Sir?

I didnt want to be a judge. I was a young lawyer practicing in San Antonio and I come back out here when my daddy was sick and I went to work for the county prosecutor. I sure didnt want to be a judge. I think I felt a lot like you do. I still do.

What made you change your mind?

I dont know as I did change it. I just saw a lot of injustice in the court system and I saw people my own age in positions of authority that I had grown up with and knew for a calcified fact didnt have one damn lick of sense. I think I just didnt have any choice. Just didnt have any choice. I sent a boy from this county to the electric chair in Huntsville in nineteen thirty-two. I think about that. I dont think he was a pretty good old boy. But I think about it. Would I do it again? Yes I would.

I almost done it again.

Done what, killed somebody?

Yessir.

The Mexican captain?

Yessir. Captain. Whatever he was. He was what they call a madrina. Not even a real peace officer.

But you didnt.

No sir. I didnt.

They sat. The fire had burned to coals. Outside the wind was blowing and he was going to have to go out in it pretty soon.

I hadnt made up my mind about it though. I told myself that I had. But I hadnt. I dont know what would of happened if they hadnt of come and got him. I expect he's dead anyways.

He looked up from the fire at the judge.

I wasnt even mad at him. Or I didnt feel like I was. That boy he shot, I didnt hardly even know him. I felt bad about it. But he wasnt nothin to me.

Why do you think you wanted to kill him?

I dont know.

Well, said the judge. I guess that's somethin between you and the good Lord. Wouldnt you say?

Yessir. I didnt mean that I expected a answer. Maybe there aint no answer. It just bothered me that you might think I was somethin special. I aint.

Well that aint a bad way to be bothered.

He picked up his hat and held it in both hands. He looked like he was about to get up but he didnt get up.

The reason I wanted to kill him was because I stood there and let him walk that boy out in the trees and shoot him and I never said nothin.

Would it have done any good?

No sir. But that dont make it right.

The judge leaned from his chair and took the poker standing on the hearth and jostled the coals and stood the poker back and folded his hands and looked at the boy.

What would you have done if I'd found against you today?

I dont know.

Well, that's a fair answer I guess.

It wasnt their horse. It would of bothered me.

Yes, said the judge. I expect it would.

I need to find out who the horse belongs to. It's gotten to be like a millstone around my neck.

There's nothin wrong with you son. I think you'll get it sorted out.

Yessir. I guess I will. If I live.

He stood.

I thank you for your time. And for invitin me into your home and all.

The judge stood up. You come back and visit any time, he said.

Yessir. I appreciate it.

It was cold out but the judge stood on the porch in his robe and slippers while he untied the horse and got the other two horses sorted out and then mounted up. He turned the horse and looked at him standing in the doorlight and he raised his hand and the judge raised a hand back and he rode out down the street from pool to pool of lamplight until he had vanished in the dark.

ON THE SUNDAY MORNING following he was sitting in a cafe in Bracketville Texas drinking coffee. There was no one else in the cafe except the counterman and he was sitting on the last stool at the end of the counter smoking a cigarette and reading the paper. There was a radio playing behind the counter and after a while a voice said that it was the Jimmy Blevins Gospel Hour.

John Grady looked up. Where's that radio station comin from? he said.

That's Del Rio, said the counterman.

He got to Del Rio about four-thirty in the afternoon and by the time he found the Blevins house it was getting on toward dark. The reverend lived in a white frame house with a gravel drive and John Grady dismounted at the mailbox and led the horses up the drive to the back of the house and knocked at the kitchen door. A small blonde woman looked out. She opened the door.

Yes? she said. Can I help you?

Yes mam. Is the reverend Blevins at home?

What did you want to see him about?

Well. I guess I wanted to see him about a horse.

A horse?

Yes mam.

She looked past him at the standing animals. Which one is it? she said.

The bay. That biggest one.

He'll bless it, but he wont lay hands on.

Mam?

He wont lay hands on. Not on animals.

Who's out there, darlin? called a man from the kitchen.

A boy here with a horse, she called.

The reverend walked out on the porch. My my, he said. Look at them horses.

I'm sorry to bother you sir, but that aint your horse is it?

My horse? I never owned a horse in my life.

Did you want him to bless the horse or not? said the woman.

Did you know a boy about fourteen years old named Jimmy Blevins?

We had a mule one time when I was growin up. Big mule. Mean rascal too. Boy named Jimmy Blevins? You mean just plain Jimmy Blevins?

Yessir.

No. No. Not that I recollect. There's any number of Jimmy Blevinses out there in the world but its Jimmy Blevins Smith and Jimmy Blevins Jones. There aint a week passes we dont get one or two letters tellin us about a new Jimmy Blevins this or Jimmy Blevins that. Aint that right darlin?

That's right reverend.

We get em from overseas you know. Jimmy Blevins Chang. That was one we had here recent. Little old yeller baby. They send photos you know. Snapshots. What was your name?

Cole. John Grady Cole.

The reverend extended his hand and they shook, the reverend thoughtful. Cole, he said. We may of had a Cole. I'd hate to say we hadnt. Have you had your supper?

No sir.

Darlin maybe Mr Cole would like to take supper with us. You like chicken and dumplins Mr Cole?

Yessir I do. I been partial to em all my life.

Well you're fixin to get more partial cause my wife makes the best you ever ate.

They ate in the kitchen. She said: We just eat in the kitchen now that there's just the two of us.

He didnt ask who was missing. The reverend waited for her to be seated and then he bowed his head and blessed the food and the table and the people sitting at it. He went on at some length and blessed everything all the way up to the country and then he blessed some other countries as well and he spoke about war and famine and the missions and other problems in the world with particular reference to Russia and the jews and cannibalism and he asked it all in Christ's name amen and raised up and reached for the cornbread.

People always want to know how I got started, he said. Well, it was no mystery to me. Whenever I first heard a radio I knew what it was for and it wasnt no questions about it neither. My mother's brother built a crystal set. Bought it through the mail. It come in a box and you put it together. We lived in south Georgia and we'd heard about the radio of course. But we never had actually seen one play with our own eyes. It's a world of difference. Well. I knew what it was for. Because there couldnt be no more excuses, you see. A man might harden his heart to where he could no longer hear the word of God, but you turn the radio up real loud? Well, hardness of heart wont do it no more. He's got to be deaf as a post besides. There's a purpose for everthing in this world, you see. Sometimes it might be hard to see what it is. But the radio? Well my my. You cant make it no plainer than that. The radio was in my plans from the start. It's what brought me to the ministry.

He loaded his plate as he talked and then he stopped talking and ate. He was not a large man but he ate two huge platefuls and then a large helping of peach cobbler and he drank several large glasses of buttermilk.

When he was done he wiped his mouth and pushed back his chair. Well, he said. You all excuse me. I got to go to work. The Lord dont take no holidays.

He rose and disappeared into the house. The woman dished out for John Grady a second helping of the cobbler and he thanked her and she sat back down and watched him eat it.

He was the first one to have you put your hands on the radio you know, she said.

Mam?

He started that. Puttin your hands on the radio. He'd pray

over the radio and heal everbody that was settin there with their hands on the radio.

Yes mam.

Fore that he'd have people send in things and he'd pray over em but there was a lot of problems connected with that. People expect a lot of a minister of God. He cured a lot of people and of course everbody heard about it over the radio and I dont like to say this but it got bad. I thought it did.

He ate. She watched him.

They sent dead people, she said.

Mam?

They sent dead people. Crated em up and shipped em railway express. It got out of hand. You cant do nothin with a dead person. Only Jesus could do that.

Yes mam.

Did you want some more buttermilk?

Yes please mam. This is awful good.

Well I'm glad you're enjoyin it.

She poured his glass and sat again.

He works so hard for his ministry. People have no idea. Did you know his voice reaches all over the world?

Is that right?

We've got letters from China. It's hard to imagine. Them little old people settin around their radios over there. Listenin to Jimmy.

I wouldnt think they'd know what he was sayin.

Letters from France. Letters from Spain. The whole world. His voice is like a instrument, you see. When he has the layin on of the hands? They could be in Timbuctoo. They could be on the south pole. It dont make no difference. His voice is there. There's not anyplace you can go he aint there. In the air. All the time. You just turn on your radio.

Of course they tried to close the station down, but it's over in Mexico. That's why Dr Brinkley come here. To found that radio station. Did you know that they can hear it on Mars?

No mam.

Well they can. When I think about them up there hearin the words of Jesus for the very first time it just makes me want to cry. It does. And Jimmy Blevins done it. He was the one.

From inside the house there sounded a long rattling snore. She smiled. Poor darlin, she said. He's just wore out. People have no idea.

He never found the owner of the horse. Along toward the end of February he drifted north again, trailing the horses in the bar ditches along the edge of the blacktop roads, the big semi's blowing them up against the fences. The first week of March he was back in San Angelo and he cut across the country so familiar to him and reached the Rawlins pasture fence just a little past dark on the first warm night of the year and no wind and everything dead still and clear on the west Texas plains. He rode up to the barn and dismounted and walked up to the house. There was a light on in Rawlins' room and he put two fingers to his teeth and whistled.

Rawlins came to the window and looked out. In a few minutes he came from the kitchen and around the side of the house.

Bud is that you?

Yeah.

Sum buck, he said. Sum buck.

He walked around him to get him in the light and he looked at him as if he were something rare.

I figured you might want your old horse back, said John Grady.

I caint believe it. You got Junior with you?

He's standin down yonder at the barn.

Sum buck, said Rawlins. I caint believe it. Sum buck.

They rode out on the prairie and sat on the ground and let the animals drift with the reins down and he told Rawlins all that had happened. They sat very quietly. The dead moon hung in the west and the long flat shapes of the nightclouds passed before it like a phantom fleet.

Have you been to see your mama? said Rawlins.

No.

You knew your daddy died.

Yeah. I guess I knew that.

She tried to get word to you in Mexico.

Yeah.

Luisa's mother is real sick.

Abuela?

Yeah.

How are they makin it?

I guess all right. I seen Arturo over in town. Thatcher Cole got him a job at the school. Cleanin up and stuff like that.

Is she goin to make it?

I dont know. She's pretty old.

Yeah.

What are you goin to do?

Head out.

Where to?

I dont know.

You could get on out on the rigs. Pays awful good.

Yeah. I know.

You could stay here at the house.

I think I'm goin to move on.

This is still good country.

Yeah. I know it is. But it aint my country.

He rose and turned and looked off toward the north where the lights of the city hung over the desert. Then he walked out and picked up the reins and mounted his horse and rode up and caught the Blevins horse by its halter.

Catch your horse, he said. Or else he'll follow me.

Rawlins walked out and caught the horse and stood holding it.

Where is your country? he said.

I dont know, said John Grady. I dont know where it is. I dont know what happens to country.

Rawlins didnt answer.

I'll see you old pardner, said John Grady.

All right. I'll see you.

He stood holding his horse while the rider turned and rode out and dropped slowly down the skyline. He squatted on his heels so as to watch him a little while longer but after a while he was gone.

THE DAY of the burial out at Knickerbocker it was cool and windy. He'd turned the horses into the pasture on the far side of the road and he sat for a long time watching down the road to the north where the weather was building and the sky was gray and after a while the funeral cortege appeared. An old Packard hearse with a varied assortment of dusty cars and trucks behind. They pulled up along the road in front of the little Mexican cemetery and people got out into the road and the pallbearers in their suits of faded black stood at the rear of the hearse and they carried Abuela's casket up through the gate into the cemetery. He stood across the road holding his hat. No one looked at him. They carried her up into the cemetery followed by a priest and a boy in a white gown ringing a bell and they buried her and they prayed and they wept and they wailed and then they came back down out of the cemetery into the road helping each other along and weeping and got into the cars and turned one by one on the narrow blacktop and went back the way they'd come.

The hearse had already gone. There was a pickup truck parked further down the road and he put on his hat and sat there on the slope of the bar ditch and in a little while two men came down the path out of the cemetery with shovels over their shoulders and they walked down the road and put the shovels in the bed of the truck and got in and turned around and drove away.

He stood and crossed the road and walked up into the cemetery past the old stonework crypt and past the little headstones and their small remembrances, the sunfaded paper flowers, a china vase, a broken celluloid Virgin. The names he knew or had known. Villareal, Sosa, Reyes. Jesusita Holguín. Nació.

Falleció. A china crane. A chipped milkglass vase. The rolling parklands beyond, wind in the cedars. Armendares. Ornelos. Tiodosa Tarín, Salomer Jáquez. Epitacio Villareal Cuéllar.

He stood hat in hand over the unmarked earth. This woman who had worked for his family fifty years. She had cared for his mother as a baby and she had worked for his family long before his mother was born and she had known and cared for the wild Grady boys who were his mother's uncles and who had all died so long ago and he stood holding his hat and he called her his abuela and he said goodbye to her in spanish and then turned and put on his hat and turned his wet face to the wind and for a moment he held out his hands as if to steady himself or as if to bless the ground there or perhaps as if to slow the world that was rushing away and seemed to care nothing for the old or the young or rich or poor or dark or pale or he or she. Nothing for their struggles, nothing for their names. Nothing for the living or the dead.

IN FOUR DAYS' riding he crossed the Pecos at Iraan Texas and rode up out of the river breaks where the pumpjacks in the Yates Field ranged against the skyline rose and dipped like mechanical birds. Like great primitive birds welded up out of iron by hearsay in a land perhaps where such birds once had been. At that time there were still indians camped on the western plains and late in the day he passed in his riding a scattered group of their wickiups propped upon that scoured and trembling waste. They were perhaps a quarter mile to the north, just huts made from poles and brush with a few goathides draped across them. The indians stood watching him. He could see that none of them spoke among themselves or commented on his riding there nor did they raise a hand in greeting or call out to him. They had no curiosity about him at all. As if they knew all that they needed to know. They stood and watched him pass and watched him vanish upon that landscape solely because he was passing. Solely because he would vanish.

The desert he rode was red and red the dust he raised, the small dust that powdered the legs of the horse he rode, the horse he led. In the evening a wind came up and reddened all the sky before him. There were few cattle in that country because it was barren country indeed yet he came at evening upon a solitary bull rolling in the dust against the bloodred sunset like an animal in sacrificial torment. The bloodred dust blew down out of the sun. He touched the horse with his heels and rode on. He rode with the sun coppering his face and the red wind blowing out of the west across the evening land and the small desert birds flew chittering among the dry bracken and horse and rider and horse passed on and their long shadows passed in tandem like the shadow of a single being. Passed and paled into the darkening land, the world to come.

Cormac McCarthy
Blood Meridian £5.99

'*Blood Meridian* is a classic American novel of regeneration through violence. McCarthy can only be compared with our greatest writers, with Melville and Faulkner, and this is his masterpiece.'
MICHAEL HERR

'There have been many attempts, on film as well as in books, to subvert the cosy self-satisfaction of the American "wild" west. But McCarthy's achievement, in *Blood Meridian*, is to establish a new mythology which is as potent and vivid as that of the movies, yet one which has absolutely the opposite effect . . . He is a great writer, and *Blood Meridian* is his masterpiece.'
RICHARD BURNS, *THE INDEPENDENT*

'The book reads like a conflation of the *Inferno*, the *Iliad* and *Moby Dick*. I can only declare that *Blood Meridian* is unlike anything I have read in recent years, and seems to me an extraordinary, breath-taking achievement.'
JOHN BANVILLE, *IRISH TIMES*

'McCarthy distances us not only from the historical past, not only from our cowboy-and-Indian images of it, but also revisionist theories that make white men the villains and Indians the victims. All men are unremittingly bloodthirsty here, poised at a peak of violence, the "meridian" from which civilisation will quickly fall.'
NEW YORK TIMES BOOK REVIEW

'In the thirty or so years that I have been reading books about the American West, I have rarely encountered anything as powerful, as unsettling, or as memorable as *Blood Meridian* . . . A nightmare odyssey redolent of the darker imaginations of Hieronymous Bosch, Edgar Allan Poe and the Marquis de Sade.'
FREDERICK NOLAN, *THE STANDARD*

Cormac McCarthy
The Orchard Keeper £5.99

Set in a small, remote community in rural Tennessee in the years between the two world wars, *The Orchard Keeper* is Cormac McCarthy's debut novel. It tells of John Wesley Rattner, a young boy, and Marion Sylder, an outlaw and bootlegger who, unbeknownst to either of them, has killed the boy's father. Together with Rattner's Uncle Ather they enact a compelling drama. Born of the land that surrounds them, the novel is a magnificent evocation of a lost American time.

'The feeling for the land and seasons is so intense as to be part of the story and there are scenes one will never forget . . . A complicated and evocative exposition of the transciency of life.'
HARPER'S

'A master in perfect command of his medium.'
WASHINGTON POST BOOK WORLD

'McCarthy has cut a solitary path into the violent heart of the Old West. There isn't anyone remotely like him in contemporary American literature.'
NEW YORK TIMES

'A true American original.'
NEWSWEEK

Cormac McCarthy
Child of God £5.99

This gripping story tells the tale of Lester Ballard, a solitary and inverted young backwoodsman dispossessed of his ancestral land. Psychologically displaced but endowed with a rich and lurid imagination, he haunts the hill country of East Tennessee. From commonplace brushes with humanity – in homesteads, stores and in the woods – his frustrations mount. His repressed sexuality gradually wells up and spills over, until he is roaming the woods at will, seeking the next victim for his strange lusts. The story moves swiftly to its horrific conclusion.

Cormac McCarthy again succeeds in writing about the most sordid aspects of humanity with humour and compassion. The writing is lyrical in the sympathetic description of Lester and of his pastoral world; but also dark and urgent in describing the terrors within Lester, in the woods, and in the earth itself. Lester's depraved perversities and the chilling horror of the tale are sensitively portrayed by the elemental and erotic style. This is the most accessible of McCarthy's novels.

'His prose, unfailingly beautiful and exact, carries us into a dreamworld of astonishing and violent revelation. It is a frightening, entrancing world, which we must finally recognise as our own.'
TOBIAS WOLFF

'McCarthy charts the terrible decline of Lester Ballard with passion, tenderness, eloquence, and a humour which, at its best, is attuned perfectly to the bitter wryness of the South.'
TIMES LITERARY SUPPLEMENT

'He writes strong, powerful, shocking novels of the American South, doing for Tennessee what Faulkner did for Mississippi.'
FINANCIAL TIMES

'Cormac McCarthy very well may, I believe, be America's greatest writer.'
STANLEY BOOTH

Cormac McCarthy
Outer Dark £5.99

Set in an unnamed part of Appalachia, some time around the turn of the century, *Outer Dark* is a grand, mythic tale of love and loss. The story begins as a woman bears her brother's child, a boy: he leaves the baby in the woods and tells her he died of natural causes. Discovering her brother's lie, she sets forth alone to find her son. Confronted in turn by terrifying strangers, both brother and sister are pulled headlong towards an eerie, apocalyptic resolution. Cormac McCarthy's second novel is a brilliantly poetic evocation of a land and its people.

'A perfectly executed work of the imagination . . . McCarthy has made the fabulous real, the ordinary mysterious'
NEW YORK TIMES

'A profound parable that ultimately speaks to any society in any time'
TIME

Cormac McCarthy
Suttree £5.99

'Sentence for sentence, his work seems to me unsurpassed in American literature'
STANLEY BOOTH

This compelling novel has as its protagonist, Cornelius Suttree, living alone and in exile in a disintegrating houseboat on the wrong side of the Tennessee River close by Knoxville. He stays at the edge of an outcast community inhabited by eccentrics, criminals and the poverty-stricken. Rising above the physical and human squalor around him, his detachment and wry humour enable him to survive dereliction and destitution with dignity.

Cormac McCarthy's astonishingly rich style portrays both the inner and outer states of Suttree's riverbank *demi-monde*; now flowing majestically, then swirling in intricate eddies to raise the comical debris from the riverbed of life, hovering on the brink of despair before finally regaining serenity at the close. The sensitive and compassionate treatment of his anti-hero urges the reader to examine his own reservoir of sympathy towards the socially outcast, and to the human condition itself.

'*Suttree*, which may be McCarthy's *magnum opus*, marks his closest approach to autobiography and is probably the funniest and most unbearably sad of his books.'
STANLEY BOOTH

'Perhaps the closest we have to a genuine heir to the Faulknerian tradition. His novels have a stark, mythic quality that is very much their own.'
THE WASHINGTON POST

'Cormac McCarthy gives us a sense of river life that reads like a doomed *Huckleberry Finn*.'
NEW YORK TIMES BOOK REVIEW

'*Suttree* contains a humour that is Faulknerian in its gentle wryness, and a freakish imaginative flair reminiscent of Flannery O'Connor.'
TIMES LITERARY SUPPLEMENT

Picador books are available from Waterstone's, W H Smith and all good bookshops.

If you would like to receive information on current and forthcoming Picador titles, please send your name and address on a postcard to:

The Marketing Dept
Picador
18–21 Cavaye Place
London SW10 9PG

All Pan books are available at your local bookshop or newsagent, or can be ordered direct from the publisher. Indicate the number of copies required and fill in the form below.

Send to: Pan C. S. Dept
              Macmillan Distribution Ltd
              Houndmills Basingstoke RG21 2XS
or phone: 0256 29242, quoting title, author and Credit Card number.

Please enclose a remittance* to the value of the cover price plus: £1.00 for the first book plus 50p per copy for each additional book ordered.

*Payment may be made in sterling by UK personal cheque, postal order, sterling draft or international money order, made payable to Pan Books Ltd.

Alternatively by Barclaycard/Access/Amex/Diners

Card No. | | | | | | | | | | | | | | | | | | |

Expiry Date | | | | | | |

————————————————————————————————————

Signature:

Applicable only in the UK and BFPO addresses

While every effort is made to keep prices low, it is sometimes necessary to increase prices at short notice. Pan Books reserve the right to show on covers and charge new retail prices which may differ from those advertised in the text or elsewhere.

NAME AND ADDRESS IN BLOCK LETTERS PLEASE:

....

Name _____

Address _____

_____

_____

_____

6/92